BOOTS AT THE HOLLY-TREE INN
AND
OTHER STORIES

BOOTS
AT THE
HOLLY-TREE INN

AND

OTHER STORIES

by

CHARLES DICKENS

VISION

Vision Press Limited
157 Knightsbridge
London, S.W.1

SBN 85478 032 7

Printed in Great Britain
by Clarke, Doble & Brendon Ltd., Plymouth
MCMLXIX

1969

CONTENTS

FOREWORD

Household Words, a weekly periodical which first appeared in March 1850 and ceased publication in 1859, was edited and partly owned by Charles Dickens, who frequently contributed unsigned articles and stories. In April 1859 *Household Words* was succeeded by *All the Year Round*, also edited and partly owned by Dickens but differing from its predecessor in that the major contributions, which included *A Tale of Two Cities* and *Great Expectations*, were signed. The special Christmas Numbers of the two periodicals are the sources of the tales in this volume.

The Holly-Tree Inn formed the 1855 Christmas Number of *Household Words*. *The Boots* was written by Dickens himself, as also were two other tales not included in the present selection. *Doctor Marigold's Prescriptions*, the 1865 Christmas Number of *All the Year Round*, presents a problem familiar to Dickens bibliographers, for, while Chapters I, VI and VIII are entirely Dickens's work, the other chapters are probably examples of his habit of so revising and editing the writings of others that the result is as much his own work as that of the original contributors.

The First Poor Traveller's Tale formed part of *The Seven Poor Travellers*, the 1854 Christmas Number of *Household Words*, and is certainly the work of Dickens. *Mrs. Lirriper's Lodgings* appeared as the Christmas Number of *All the Year Round* in 1863 and was followed at Christmas 1864 by *Mrs. Lirriper's Legacy*. In each of the Lirriper tales the first and last chapters were exclusively the work of Dickens, while the intermediate chapters show signs of the revision and editing which were his habit.

BOOTS AT THE HOLLY-TREE INN

WHERE had he been in his time? Boots repeated, when I asked him the question. Lord, he had been everywhere! And what had he been? Bless you, he had been everything you could mention a'most.

Seen a good deal? Why, of course he had. I should say so, he could assure me, if I only knew about a twentieth part of what had come in *his* way. Why, it would be easier for him, he expected, to tell what he hadn't seen, than what he had. Ah! A deal, it would.

What was the curiousest thing he had seen? Well! He didn't know. He couldn't momently name what was the curiousest thing he had seen—unless it was a Unicorn—and he see *him* once at a Fair. But, supposing a young gentleman not eight year old, was to run away with a fine young woman of seven, might I think *that* a queer start? Certainly! Then, that was a start as he himself had had his blessed eyes on—and he had cleaned the shoes they run away in—and they was so little that he couldn't get his hand into 'em.

Master Harry Walmer's father, you see, he lived at the Elmses, down away by Shooter's Hill there, six or seven mile from Lunnon. He was a gentleman of spirit, and good looking, and held his head up when he walked, and he had what you may call Fire about him. He wrote poetry, and he rode, and he ran, and he cricketed, and he danced, and he acted, and he done it all equally beautiful. He was uncommon proud of Master Harry as was his only child; but didn't spoil him, neither. He was a gentleman as had a will of his own and a eye of his own, and as would be minded. Consequently, though he made quite a companion of the fine bright boy, and was delighted to see him so fond of reading his fairy books, and was never tired of hearing him say my name is Norval, or hearing him sing his songs about

Young May Moons is a beaming love, and When he as adores thee has left but the name, and that :—still he kept the command over the child, and the child *was* a child, and it's to be wished more on 'em was!

How did Boots happen to know all this? Why, through being under-gardener. Of course he couldn't be under-gardener, and be always about, in the summer-time, near the windows on the lawn, a mowing and a sweeping, and a weeding and a pruning, and this and that, without getting acquainted with the ways of the family.—Even supposing Master Harry hadn't come to him one morning early, and said, "Cobbs, how should you spell Norah, if you was asked?" and then begun cutting it in print, all over the fence.

He couldn't say he had taken particular notice of children before that; but really it was pretty to see them two mites a going about the place together, deep in love. And the courage of the boy! Bless your soul, he'd have thrown off his little hat, and tucked up his little sleeves, and gone in at a Lion, he would, if they had happened to meet one, and she had been frightened of him. One day he stops, along with her, where Boots was a hoeing weeds in the gravel, and he says, speaking up, "Cobbs," he says, "I like *you*." "Do you, sir. I'm proud to hear it." "Yes I do, Cobbs. Why do I like you, do you think, Cobbs?" "Don't know, Master Harry, I am sure." "Because Norah likes you, Cobbs." "Indeed, sir? That's very gratifying." "Gratifying, Cobbs? It's better than millions of the brightest diamonds, to be liked by Norah." "Certainly, sir." "You're going away, ain't you, Cobbs?" "Yes, sir." "Would you like another situation, Cobbs?" "Well, sir, I shouldn't object, if it was a good 'un." "Then, Cobbs," says he, "you shall be our Head Gardener when we are married." And he tucks her, in her little sky blue mantle, under his arm, and walks away.

Boots could assure me that it was better than a picter, and equal to a play, to see them babies with their long bright curling hair, their sparkling eyes, and their beautiful light tread, a rambling about the garden, deep in love. Boots was of opinion that the birds believed they was birds, and kept up with 'em, singing to please 'em. Sometimes, they would creep under the Tulip-tree, and would sit there with their arms round one another's necks, and their soft cheeks touching, a reading about the Prince, and the Dragon, and the good and bad enchanters, and the king's fair daughter. Sometimes Boots would hear them planning about having a house in a forest, keeping bees and a cow, and living entirely on milk and honey. Once, he came upon them by the pond, and heard Master Harry say, "Adorable Norah, kiss me, and say you love me to distraction, or I'll jump in head foremost." On the whole, Boots said it had a tendency to make him feel as if he was in love himself—only he didn't exactly know who with.

"Cobbs," says Master Harry, one evening, when Cobbs was watering the flowers; "I am going on a visit, this present Midsummer, to my grandmamma's at York."

"Are you indeed, sir? I hope you'll have a pleasant time. I am going into Yorkshire myself, when I leave here."

"Are you going to your grandmamma's, Cobbs?"

"No, sir. I haven't got such a thing."

"Not as a grandmamma, Cobbs?"

"No, sir."

The boy looked on at the watering of the flowers, for a little while, and then he says, "I shall be very glad indeed to go, Cobbs—Norah's going."

"Ah! You'll be all right then, sir, with your beautiful sweetheart by your side."

"Cobbs," returned the boy, flushing. "I never let anybody joke about it, when I can prevent them."

"It wasn't a joke, sir, I assure you—wasn't so meant."

"I am glad of that, Cobbs, because I like you, you know, and you're going to live with us.—Cobbs!"

"Sir."

"What do you think my grandmamma gives me, when I go down there?"

"I couldn't so much as make a guess, sir."

"A Bank of England five-pound note, Cobbs."

"Whew! That's a spanking sum of money, Master Harry."

"A person could do a good deal with such a sum of money as that. Couldn't a person, Cobbs?"

"I believe you, sir!"

"Cobbs, I'll tell you a secret. At Norah's house, they have been joking her about me, and pretending to laugh at our being engaged. Pretending to make a game of it, Cobbs!"

"Such, sir, is the depravity of human natur."

The boy, looking exactly like his father, stood for a few

minutes with his glowing face towards the sunset, and then departed with "Good-night, Cobbs. I'm going in."

If I was to ask Boots how it happened that he was a going to leave that place just at that present time, well, he couldn't rightly answer me. He did suppose he might have stayed there till now, if he had been anyways inclined. But, you see, he was younger then and he wanted change. That's what he wanted—change. Mr. Walmers, he says to him when he give him notice of his intentions to leave, "Cobbs," he says, "have you anythink to complain of? I make the inquiry, because if I find that any of my people really has anythink to complain of, I wish to make it right if I can." "No, sir," says Cobbs; "thanking you, sir, I find myself as well sitiwated here as I could hope to be anywheres. The truth is, sir, that I'm a going to seek my fortun." "O, indeed, Cobbs?" he says; "I hope you may find it." And Boots could assure me—which he did, touching his hair with his boot-jack—that he hadn't found it yet.

Well, sir! Boots left the Elmses when his time was up, and Master Harry he went down to the old lady's at York, which old lady would have give that child the teeth out of her head (if she had had any), she was so wrapt up in him. What does that Infant do—for Infant you may call him and be within the mark—but cut away from that old lady's with his Norah, on a expedition to go to Gretna Green and be married!

Sir, Boots was at this identical Holly-Tree Inn (having left it several times since to better himself, but always come back through one thing or another), when, one summer afternoon, the coach drives up, and out of the coach gets them two children. The Guard says to our Governor, "I don't quite make out these little passengers, but the young gentleman's words was, that they was to be brought here." The young gentleman gets out; hands his lady out; gives the Guard something for himself; says to our Governor, "We're to stop here to-night, please. Sitting-room and two bed-rooms will be required. Chops and cherry-pudding for two!" and tucks her, in her little sky-blue mantle, under his arm, and walks into the house much bolder than Brass.

Boots leaves me to judge what the amazement of that establishment was, when those two tiny creatures all alone by themselves was marched into the Angel;—much more so, when he, who had seen them without their seeing him, give the Governor his views of the expedition they was upon. "Cobbs," says the

Governor, "if this is so, I must set off myself to York and quiet their friends' minds. In which case you must keep your eye upon 'em, and humour 'em, till I come back. But, before I take these measures, Cobbs, I should wish you to find from themselves whether your opinions is correct." "Sir to you," says Cobbs, "that shall be done directly."

So, Boots goes upstairs to the Angel, and there he finds Master Harry on a e-normous sofa—immense at any time, but looking like the Great Bed of Ware, compared with him—a drying the eyes of Miss Norah with his pocket hankecher. Their little legs was entirely off the ground, of course, and it really is not possible to express how small them children did look.

"It's Cobbs! It's Cobbs!" cries Master Harry, and comes running in to him and catching hold of his hand. Miss Norah comes running to him on t'other side and catching hold of his t'other hand, and they both jump for joy.

"I see you a getting out, sir, says Cobbs. "I thought it was you. I thought I couldn't be mistaken in your heighth and figure. What's the object of your journey, sir?—Matrimonial?"

"We are going to be married, Cobbs, at Gretna Green. We have run away on purpose. Norah has been in rather low spirits, Cobbs; but she'll be happy, now we have found you to be our friend."

"Thank you, sir, and thank *you*, miss, for your good opinion. *Did* you bring any luggage with you, sir?"

If I will believe Boots when he gives me his word and honour upon it, the lady had got a parasol, a smelling bottle, a round and a half of cold buttered toast, eight peppermint drops, and a hair-brush—seemingly, a doll's. The gentleman had got about half-a-dozen yards of string, a knife, three or four sheets of writing-paper folded up surprisingly small, a orange, and a Chaney mug with his name upon it.

"What may be the exact natur of your plans, sir?"

"To go on," replied the boy—which the courage of that boy was something wonderful!—"in the morning, and be married to-morrow."

"Just so, sir. Would it meet your views, sir, if I was to accompany you?"

They both jumped for joy again, and cried out, "O yes, yes, Cobbs! Yes!"

"Well, sir, if you will excuse my having the freedom fur to give

an opinion, what I should recommend would be this. I'm acquainted with a pony, sir, which put in a pheayton that I could
borrow, would take you and Mrs. Harry Walmers Junior (myself
driving, if you approved), to the end of your journey in a very
short space of time. I am not altogether sure, sir, that this pony
will be at liberty till to-morrow, but even if you had to wait over
to-morrow for him, it might be worth your while. As to the small
account here, sir, in case you was to find yourself running at all
short, that don't signify; because I'm a part proprietor of this
inn, and it could stand over."

Boots assures me that when they clapped their hands, and
jumped for joy again, and called him "Good Cobbs!" and "Dear
Cobbs!" and bent across him to kiss one another in the delight
of their confiding hearts, he felt himself the meanest rascal for
deceiving 'em, that ever was born.

"Is there anything you want, just at present, sir?"

"We should like some cakes after dinner," answered Master
Harry, folding his arms, putting out one leg, and looking straight
at him, "and two apples—and jam. With dinner we should like
to have toast and water. But, Norah has always been accustomed
to half a glass of currant wine at dessert. And so have I."

"It shall be ordered at the bar, sir," says Cobbs; and away
he went.

Boots has the feeling as fresh upon him at this minute of
speaking, as he had then, that he would far rather have had it
out in half-a-dozen rounds with the Governor, than have combined with him; and that he wished with all his heart there was
any impossible place where those two babies could make an
impossible marriage, and live impossibly happy ever afterwards.
However, as it couldn't be, he went into the Governor's plans,
and the Governor set off for York in half-an-hour.

The way in which the women of that house—without exception—every one of 'em—married *and* single—took to that boy
when they heard the story, Boots considers surprising. It was as
much as he could do to keep 'em from dashing into the room
and kissing him. They climbed up all sorts of places, at the risk
of their lives to look at him through a pane of glass. They was
seven deep at the key-hole. They was out of their minds about
him and his bold spirit.

In the evening, Boots went into the room to see how the
runaway couple was getting on. The gentleman was on the

window-seat, supporting the lady in his arms. She had tears upon her face, and was lying, very tired and half asleep, with her head upon his shoulder.

"Mrs. Harry Walmers Junior, fatigued, sir?" says Cobbs.

"Yes, she is tired, Cobbs; but, she is not used to be away from home, and she has been in low spirits again. Cobbs, do you think you could bring a biffin, please?"

"I ask your pardon, sir. What was it you?——"

"I think a Norfolk biffin would rouse her, Cobbs. She is very fond of them."

Boots withdrew in search of the required restorative, and when he brought it in, the gentleman handed it to the lady, and fed her with a spoon, and took a little himself. The lady being heavy with sleep, and rather cross, "What should you think, sir," says Cobbs, "of a chamber candlestick?" The gentleman approved; the chambermaid went first, up the great staircase; the lady, in her sky-blue mantle, followed, gallantly escorted by the gentleman; the gentleman embraced her at her door, and retired to his own apartment, where Boots softly locked him up.

Boots couldn't but feel with the increased acuteness what a base deceiver he was, when they consulted him at breakfast (they had ordered sweet milk-and-water, and toast and currant jelly, over-night), about the pony. It really was as much as he could do, he don't mind confessing to me, to look them two young things in the face, and think what a wicked old father of lies he had grown up to be. Howsomever, he went on a lying like a Trojan, about the pony. He told 'em that it did so unfort'nately happen that the pony was half-clipped, you see, and that he couldn't be taken out in that state, for fear it should strike to his inside. But that he'd be finished clipping in the course of the day, and that to-morrow morning at eight o'clock the pheayton would be ready. Boots's view of the whole case is, that Mrs. Harry Walmers Junior was now beginning to give in. She hadn't had her hair curled when she went to bed, and she didn't seem quite up to brushing it herself, and its getting in her eyes put her out. But, nothing put out Master Harry. He sat behind his breakfast-cup, a tearing away at the jelly, as if he had been his own father.

After breakfast, Boots is inclined to consider that they drawed soldiers—at least, he knows that many sich was found in the fire-place, all on horseback. In the course of the morning, Master Harry rung the bell—it was surprising how that there boy did carry on—and said in a sprightly way, "Cobbs, is there any good walks in this neighbourhood?"

"Yes, sir. There's Love Lane."

"Get out with you, Cobbs!"—that was that there boy's expression—"you're joking."

"Begging your pardon, sir, there really is Love Lane. And a pleasant walk it is, and proud shall I be to show it to yourself and Mrs. Harry Walmers Junior."

"Norah, dear," says Master Harry, "this is curious. We really ought to see Love Lane. Put on your bonnet, my sweetest darling, and we will go there with Cobbs."

Boots leave me to judge what a Beast he felt himself to be, when that young pair told him, as they all three jogged along together, that they had made up their minds to give him two thousand guineas a year as head gardener, on accounts of his being so true a friend to 'em. Boots could have wished at the moment that the earth would have opened and swallerd him up; he felt so mean, with their beaming eyes a-looking at him, and believing him. Well, sir, he turned the conversation as well as he could, and he took 'em down Love Lane to the water-meadows, and there Master Harry would have drownded himself in half a moment more, a-getting out a water-lily for her—but nothing daunted that boy. Well, sir, they was tired out. All being so new and strange to 'em, they was as tired as they could be. And they laid down on a bank of daisies, like the children in the wood, leastways meadows, and fell asleep.

Boots don't know—perhaps I do—but never mind, it don't signify either way—why it made a man fit to make a fool of himself, to see them two pretty babies a lying there in the clear still sunny day, not dreaming half so hard when they was asleep, as they done when they was awake. But Lord! When you come to think of yourself, you know, and what a game you have been up to ever since you was in your own cradle, and what a poor sort of chap you are, and how it's always either Yesterday with you, or else To-morrow, and never To-day, that's where it is!

Well, sir, they woke up at last, and then one thing was getting pretty clear: namely, that Mrs. Harry Walmerses Junior's temper was on the move. When Master Harry took her round the waist, she said he "teased her so;" and when he says, "Norah, my young May Moon, your Harry tease you?" she tells him, "Yes; and I want to go home!"

A biled fowl, and baked bread-and-butter pudding, brought Mrs. Walmers up a little; but Boots could have wished, he must privately own to me, to have seen her more sensible of the woice of love, and less abandoning of herself to currants. However, Master Harry he kep up, and his noble heart was as fond as ever. Mrs. Walmers turned very sleepy about dusk, and begun to cry. Therefore, Mrs. Walmers went off to bed as per yesterday; and Master Harry ditto repeated.

About eleven or twelve at night, comes back the Governor in a chaise, along with Mr. Walmers and an elderly lady. Mr. Walmers looks amused and very serious, both at once, and says to our missis, "We are much indebted to you, ma'am, for your kind care of our little children, which we can never sufficiently acknowledge. Pray ma'am, where is my boy?" Our missis says, "Cobbs has the dear child in charge, sir. Cobbs, show Forty!" Then, he says to Cobbs, "Ah Cobbs! I am glad to see *you*. I understood you was here!" And Cobbs says, "Yes sir. Your most obedient, sir."

I may be surprised to hear Boots say it, perhaps; but Boots assures me that his heart beat like a hammer, going up stairs. "I beg your pardon, sir," says he, while unlocking the door; "I hope you are not angry with Master Harry. For, Master Harry is a fine boy, sir, and will do you credit and honour." And Boots signifies to me, that if the fine boy's father had contradicted him in the daring state of mind in which he then was, he thinks he should have "fetched him a crack," and taken the consequences.

But, Mr. Walmers only says, "No, Cobbs. No, my good fellow. Thank you!" And, the door being opened, goes in.

Boots goes in too, holding the light, and he sees Mr. Walmers go up to the bedside, bend gently down, and kiss the little sleeping face. Then, he stands looking at it for a minute, looking wonderfully like it (they do say he ran away with Mrs. Walmers); and then he gently shakes the little shoulder.

"Harry, my dear boy! Harry!"

Master Harry starts up and looks at him. Looks at Cobbs too. Such is the honour of that mite, that he looks at Cobbs, to see whether he has brought him into trouble.

"I am not angry, my child. I only want you to dress yourself and come home."

"Yes, Pa."

Master Harry dresses himself quick. His breast begins to swell when he has nearly finished, and it swells more and more as he stands at last, a-looking at his father : his father standing a-looking at him, the quiet image of him.

"Please may I"—the spirit of that little creatur, and the way he kep his rising tears down!—"Please dear Pa—may I—kiss Norah, before I go?"

"You may, my child."

So he takes Master Harry in his hand, and Boots leads the way with the candle, and they come to that other bedroom : where the elderly lady is seated by the bed, and where poor little Mrs. Harry Walmers Junior is fast asleep. There, the father lifts the child up to the pillow, and he lays his little face down for an instant by the little warm face of poor unconscious little Mrs. Harry Walmers Junior, and gently draws it to him—a sight so touching to the chambermaids who are peeping through the door, that one of them calls out "It's a shame to part 'em!" But this chambermaid was always, as Boots informs me, a soft-hearted one. Not as there was any harm in that girl. Far from it.

Finally, Boots says, that's all about it. Mr. Walmers drove away in the chaise, having hold of Master Harry's hand. The elderly lady and Mrs. Harry Walmers Junior that was never to be (she married a Captain, long afterwards, and died in India), went off next day. In conclusion, Boots puts it to me whether I hold with him in two opinions; firstly, that there are not many couples on their way to be married, who are half as innocent of guile as them two children; secondly, that it would be a jolly good thing for a great many couples on their way to be married, if they could only be stopped in time and brought back separately.

DOCTOR MARIGOLD'S PRESCRIPTIONS

I

I AM a Cheap Jack, and my own father's name was Willum
Marigold. It was in his lifetime supposed by some that his name
was William, but my own father always consistently said, No, it
was Willum. On which point I content myself with looking at
the argument this way :—If a man is not allowed to know his
own name in a free country, how much is he allowed to know
in a land of slavery? As to looking at the argument through the
medium of the Register, Willum Marigold come into the world
before Registers come up much—and went out of it too. They
wouldn't have been greatly in his line neither, if they had chanced
to come up before him.

I was born on the Queen's highway, but it was the King's at
that time. A doctor was fetched to my own mother by my own
father, when it took place on a common; and in consequence of
his being a very kind gentleman, and accepting no fee but a tea-
tray, I was named Doctor, out of gratitude and compliment to
him. There you have me. Doctor Marigold.

I am at present a middle-aged man of a broadish build, in
cords, leggings, and a sleeved waistcoat the strings of which is
always gone behind. Repair them how you will, they go like
fiddle-strings. You have been to the theatre, and you have seen
one of the wiolin-players screw up his wiolin, after listening to
it as if it had been whispering the secret to him that it feared it
was out of order, and then you have heard it snap. That's as
exactly similar to my waistcoat, as a waistcoat and a wiolin can
be like one another.

B

I am partial to a white hat, and I like a shawl round my neck wore loose and easy. Sitting down is my favourite posture. If I have a taste in point of personal jewellery, it is mother-of-pearl buttons. There you have me again, as large as life.

The doctor having accepted a tea-tray, you'll guess that my father was a Cheap Jack before me. You are right. He was. It was a pretty tray. It represented a large lady going along a serpentining up-hill gravel-walk, to attend a little church. Two swans had likewise come astray with the same intentions. When I call her a large lady, I don't mean in point of breadth, for there she fell below my views, but she more than made it up in heighth; her heighth and slimness was—in short THE heighth of both.

I often saw that tray, after I was the innocently smiling cause (or more likely screeching one) of the doctor's standing it up on a table against the wall in his consulting-room. Whenever my own father and mother were in that part of the country, I used to put my head (I have heard my own mother say it was flaxen curls at that time, though you wouldn't know an old hearth-broom from it now, till you come to the handle and found it wasn't me) in at the doctor's door, and the doctor was always glad to see me, and said, "Aha, my brother practitioner! Come in, little M.D. How are your inclinations as to sixpence?"

You can't go on for ever, you'll find, nor yet could my father nor yet my mother. If you don't go off as a whole when you are about due, you're liable to go off in part and two to one your head's the part. Gradually my father went off his, and my mother went off hers. It was in a harmless way, but it put out the family where I boarded them. The old couple, though retired, got to be wholly and solely devoted to the Cheap Jack business, and were always selling the family off. Whenever the cloth was laid for dinner, my father began rattling the plates and dishes, as we do in our line when we put up crockery for a bid, only he had lost the trick of it, and mostly let 'em drop and broke 'em. As the old lady had been used to sit in the cart, and hand the articles out one by one to the old gentleman on the footboard to sell, just in the same way she handed him every item of the family's property, and they disposed of it in their own imaginations from morning to night. At last the old gentleman, lying bedridden in the same room with the old lady, cries out in the old patter, fluent, after having been silent for two days and nights : "Now here, my jolly companions every one—which the Nightingale club in a village was held, At the sign of the Cabbage and Shears, Where the singers no doubt would have greatly excelled, But for want of taste voices and ears—now here, my jolly companions every one, is a working model of a used-up old Cheap Jack, without a tooth in his head, and with a pain in every bone : so like life that it would be just as good if it wasn't better, just as bad if it wasn't worse, and just as new if it wasn't worn out. Bid for the working model of the old Cheap Jack, who has drunk more gunpowder-tea with the ladies in his time than would blow the lid off a washerwoman's copper, and carry it as many thousands of miles higher than the moon as nought nix nought, divided by the national debt, carry nothing to the poor-rates, three under, and two over. Now my hearts of oak and men of straw, what do you say for the lot? Two shillings, a shilling, tenpence, eightpence, sixpence, fourpence. Twopence? Who said twopence? The gentleman in the scarecrow's hat? I am ashamed of the gentleman in the scarecrow's hat. I really am ashamed of him for his want of public spirit. Now I'll tell you what I'll do with you. Come! I'll throw you in a working model of a old woman that was married to the old Cheap Jack so long ago, that upon my word and honour it took place in Noah's Ark, before the Unicorn could get in to forbid the banns by blowing a tune upon his horn. There now! Come! What do you say for both? I'll tell you what I'll do with you. I don't bear you malice for being so backward. Here! If you make me a bid that'll only reflect a little credit on your town, I'll throw you in a warming-pan for nothing, and lend you a toasting-fork for life. Now come; what do you say after that splendid offer? Say two pound, say thirty shillings, say a pound, say ten shillings, say five, say two and six. You don't say even two and six? You say two and three? No. You shan't have the lot for two and three. I'd sooner give it you, if you was good looking enough. Here! Missis! Chuck the old man and woman into the cart, put the horse to, and drive 'em away and bury 'em!" Such were the last words of Willum Marigold, my own father, and they were carried out, by him and by his wife my own mother on one and the same day, as I ought to know, having followed as mourner.

My father had been a lovely one in his time at the Cheap Jack work, as his dying observations went to prove. But I top him. I don't say it because it's myself, but because it has been

universally acknowledged by all that has had the means of comparison. I have worked at it. I have measured myself against
other public speakers, Members of Parliament, Platforms, Pulpits,
Counsel learned in the law—and where I have found 'em good,
I have took a bit of imitation from 'em, and where I have found
'em bad, I have let 'em alone. Now I'll tell you what. I mean
to go down into my grave declaring that of all the callings ill
used in Great Britain, the Cheap Jack calling is the worst used.
Why ain't we a profession? Why ain't we endowed with privileges? Why are we forced to take out a hawkers' licence, when
no such thing is expected of the political hawkers? Where's the
difference betwixt us? Except that we are Cheap Jacks and they
are Dear Jacks, *I* don't see any difference but what's in our
favour.

For look here! Say it's election-time. I am on the footboard
of my cart in the market-place on a Saturday night. I put up
a general miscellaneous lot. I say: "Now here my free and
independent woters, I'm a going to give you such a chance as
you never had in all your born days, nor yet the days preceding.
Now I'll show you what I am a going to do with you. Here's a
pair of razors that'll shave you closer than the Board of Guar-
dians, here's a flat-iron worth its weight in gold, here's a frying-
pan artificially flavoured with essence of beefsteaks to that degree
that you've only got for the rest of your lives to fry bread and
dripping in it and there you are replete with animal food, here's
a genuine chronometer watch in such a solid silver case that
you may knock at the door with it when you come home late
from a social meeting and rouse your wife and family and save
up your knocker for the postman, and here's half a dozen dinner
plates that you may play the cymbals with to charm the baby
when it's fractious. Stop! I'll throw you in another article and
I'll give you that, and it's a rolling-pin, and if the baby can only
get it well into its mouth when its teeth is coming and rub the
gums once with it, they'll come through double, in a fit of laughter
equal to being tickled. Stop again! I'll throw you in another
article, because I don't like the looks of you, for you haven't the
appearance of buyers unless I lose by you, and because I'd
rather lose than not take money to-night, and that's a looking-
glass in which you may see how ugly you look when you don't
bid. What do you say now? Come! Do you say a pound? Not
you, for you haven't got it. Do you say ten shillings? Not you,

for you owe more to the tallyman. Well then, I'll tell you what
I'll do with you. I'll heap 'em all on the footboard of the cart—
there they are! razors, flat-iron, frying-pan, chronometer watch,
dinner plates, rolling-pin, and looking-glass—take 'em all away
for four shillings, and I'll give you sixpence for your trouble!"
This is me, the Cheap Jack. But on the Monday morning, in
the same market-place, comes the Dear Jack on the hustings—
his cart—and what does *he* say? "Now my free and independent
woters, I am a going to give you such a chance" (he begins just
like me) "as you never had in all your born days, and that's the
chance of sending Myself to Parliament. Now I'll tell you what
I am a going to do for you. Here's the interests of this magnificent
town promoted above all the rest of the civilised and uncivilised
earth. Here's your railways carried, and your neighbours' railways
jockeyed. Here's all your sons in the Post-office. Here's Britannia
smiling on you. Here's the eyes of Europe on you. Here's uniwersal
prosperity for you, repletion of animal food, golden cornfields,
gladsome homesteads, and rounds of applause from your own
hearts, all in one lot and that's myself. Will you take me as I
stand? You won't? Well then, I'll tell you what I'll do with
you. Come now! I'll throw you in anything you ask for. There!
Church-rates, abolition of church-rates, more malt tax, no malt
tax, uniwersal education to the highest mark or uniwersal ignorance to the lowest, total abolition of flogging in the army or a
dozen for every private once a month all round, Wrongs of Men
or Rights of Women,—only say which it shall be, take 'em or
leave 'em, and I'm of your opinion altogether, and the lot's
your own on your own terms. There! You won't take it yet?
Well then, I'll tell you what I'll do with you. Come! You *are*
such free and independent woters, and I *am* so proud of you—
you *are* such a noble and enlightened constituency, and I *am* so
ambitious of the honour and dignity of being your member, which
is by far the highest level to which the wings of the human mind
can soar—that I'll tell you what I'll do with you. I'll throw you
in all the public-houses in your magnificent town for nothing.
Will that content you? It won't? You won't take the lot yet?
Well then, before I put the horse in and drive away, and make
the offer to the next most magnificent town that can be discovered, I'll tell you what I'll do. Take the lot, and I'll drop
two thousand pound in the streets of your magnificent town for
them to pick up that can. Not enough? Now look here. This is

the very furthest that I'm a going to. I'll make it two thousand five hundred. And still you won't? Here, missis! Put the horse—no, stop half a moment, I shouldn't like to turn my back upon you neither for a trifle, I'll make it two thousand seven hundred and fifty pound. There! Take the lot on your own terms, and I'll count out two thousand seven hundred and fifty pound on the footboard of the cart, to be dropped in the streets of your magnificent town for them to pick up that can. What do you say? Come now! You won't do better, and you may do worse. You take it? Hooray! Sold again, and got the seat!"

These Dear Jacks soap the people shameful, but we Cheap Jacks don't. We tell 'em the truth about themselves to their faces, and scorn to court 'em. As to wenturesomeness in the way of puffing up the lots, the Dear Jacks beat us hollow. It is considered in the Cheap Jack calling that better patter can be made out of a gun than any article we put up from the cart, except a pair of spectacles. I often hold forth about a gun for a quarter of an hour, and feel as if I need never leave off. But when I tell 'em what the gun can do, and what the gun has brought down, I never go half so far as the Dear Jacks do when they make speeches in praise of *their* guns—their great guns that set 'em on to do it. Besides, I'm in business for myself, I ain't sent down into the market-place to order, as they are. Besides again, my guns don't know what I say in their laudation, and their guns do, and the whole concern of 'em have reason to be sick and ashamed all round. These are some of my arguments for declaring that the Cheap Jack calling is treated ill in Great Britain, and for turning warm when I think of the other Jacks in question setting themselves up to pretend to look down upon it.

I courted my wife from the footboard of the cart. I did indeed. She was a Suffolk young woman, and it was in Ipswich market-place right opposite the corn-chandler's shop. I had noticed her up at a window last Saturday that was, appreciating highly. I had took to her, and I had said to myself, "If not already disposed of, I'll have that lot." Next Saturday that come, I pitched the cart on the same pitch, and I was in very high feather indeed, keeping 'em laughing the whole of the time and getting off the goods briskly. At last I took out of my waistcoat-pocket, a small lot wrapped in soft paper, and I put it this way (looking up at the window where she was). "Now here my blooming English maidens is an article, the last article of the present evening's sale, which I offer to only you the lovely Suffolk Dumplings boiling over with beauty, and I won't take a bid of a thousand pound for, from any man alive. Now what is it? Why, I'll tell you what it is. It's made of fine gold, and it's not broke though there's a hole in the middle of it, and it's stronger than any fetter that ever was forged, though it's smaller than any finger in my set of ten. Why ten? Because when my parents made over my property to me, I tell you true, there was twelve sheets, twelve towels, twelve tablecloths, twelve knives, twelve forks, twelve tablespoons, and twelve teaspoons, but my set of fingers was two short of a dozen and could never since be matched. Now what else is it? Come I'll tell you. It's a hoop of solid gold, wrapped in a silver curl-paper that I myself took off the shining locks of the ever beautiful old lady in Threadneedle-street, London city. I wouldn't tell you so if I hadn't the paper to show, or you mightn't believe it even of me. Now what else is it? It's a man-trap and a handcuff, the parish stocks and a leg-lock, all in gold and all in one. Now what else is it? It's a wedding ring. Now I'll tell you what I'm a-going to do with it. I'm not a-going to offer this lot for money, but I mean to give it to the next of you beauties that laughs, and I'll pay her a visit to-morrow morning at exactly half after nine o'clock as the chimes go, and I'll take her out for a walk to put up the banns." *She* laughed, and got the ring handed up to her. When I called in the morning, she says, "Oh dear! It's never you and you never mean it." "It's ever me," says I, "and I am ever yours, and I ever mean it?" So we got married, after being put up three times—which, by-the-by, is quite in the Cheap Jack way again, and shows once more how the Cheap Jack customs pervade society.

She wasn't a bad wife, but she had a temper. If she could have parted with that one article at a sacrifice, I wouldn't have swopped her away in exchange for any other woman in England. Not that I ever did swop her away, for we lived together till she died, and that was thirteen year. Now my lords and ladies and gentlefolks all, I'll let you into a secret, though you won't believe it. Thirteen year of temper in a Palace would try the worst of you, but thirteen year of temper in a Cart would try the best of you. You are kept so very close to it in a cart, you see. There's thousands of couples among you, getting on like sweet ile upon a whetstone in houses five and six pairs of stairs high, that would go to the Divorce Court in a cart. Whether the jolting makes it worse, I don't undertake to decide, but in a cart it does come home to you and stick to you. Wiolence in a cart is *so* wiolent, and aggrawation in a cart is *so* aggrawating.

We might have had such a pleasant life! A roomy cart, with the large goods hung outside and the bed slung underneath it when on the road, an iron pot and a kettle, a fireplace for the cold weather, a chimney for the smoke, a hanging shelf and a cupboard, a dog, and a horse. What more do you want? You draw off upon a bit of turf in a green lane or by the roadside, you hobble your old horse and turn him grazing, you light your fire upon the ashes of the last visitors, you cook your stew, and you wouldn't call the Emperor of France your father. But have a temper in the cart, flinging language and the hardest goods in stock at you, and where are you then? Put a name to your feelings.

My dog knew as well when she was on the turn as I did. Before she broke out, he would give a howl, and bolt. How he knew it, was a mystery to me, but the sure and certain knowledge of it would wake him up out of his soundest sleep, and he would give a howl, and bolt. At such times I wished I was him.

The worst of it was, we had a daughter born to us, and I love children with all my heart. When she was in her furies, she beat the child. This got to be so shocking as the child got to be four or five year old, that I have many a time gone on with my whip over my shoulder, at the old horse's head, sobbing and crying worse than ever little Sophy did. For how could I prevent it? Such a thing is not to be tried with such a temper—in a cart—without coming to a fight. It's in the natural size and formation of a cart to bring it to a fight. And then the poor child got worse terrified than before, as well as worse hurt generally, and her mother made complaints to the next people we lighted on, and the word went round, "Here's a wretch of a Cheap Jack been a beating his wife."

Little Sophy was such a brave child! She grew to be quite devoted to her poor father, though he could do so little to help her. She had a wonderful quantity of shining dark hair, all curling natural about her. It is quite astonishing to me now, that I didn't go tearing mad when I used to see her run from her mother before the cart, and her mother catch her by this hair, and pull her down by it, and beat her.

Such a brave child I said she was. Ah! with reason.

"Don't you mind next time, father dear," she would whisper to me, with her little face still flushed, and her bright eyes still wet; "if I don't cry out, you may know I am not much hurt. And even if I do cry out, it will only be to get mother to let go and leave off." What I have seen the little spirit bear—for me—without crying out!

Yet in other respects her mother took great care of her. Her clothes were always clean and neat, and her mother was never tired of working at 'em. Such is the inconsistency in things. Our being down in the marsh country in unhealthy weather, I consider the cause of Sophy's taking bad low fever; but however she took it, once she got it she turned away from her mother for evermore, and nothing would persuade her to be touched by her mother's hand. She would shiver and say "No, no, no," when it was offered at, and would hide her face on my shoulder, and hold me tighter round the neck.

The Cheap Jack business had been worse than ever I had known it, what with one thing and what with another (and not least what with railroads, which will cut it all to pieces, I expect at last), and I was run dry of money. For which reason, one night at that period of little Sophy's being so bad, either we must have come to a dead-lock for victuals and drink, or I must have pitched the cart as I did.

I couldn't get the dear child to lie down or leave go of me, and indeed I hadn't the heart to try, so I stepped out on the footboard with her holding round my neck. They all set up a laugh when they see us, and one chuckle-headed Joskin (that I hated for it) made the bidding, "tuppence for her!"

"Now, you country boobies," says I, feeling as if my heart was a heavy weight at the end of a broken sash-line, "I give you notice that I am a going to charm the money out of your pockets, and to give you so much more than your money's worth that you'll only persuade yourselves to draw your Saturday night's wages ever again arterwards, by the hopes of meeting me to lay 'em out with, which you never will, and why not? Because I've made my fortune by selling my goods on a large scale for seventy-five per cent less than I give for 'em, and I am consequently to be elevated to the House of Peers next week, by the title of the Duke of Cheap and Markis Jackaloorul. Now let's know what you want to-night, and you shall have it. But first of all, shall I tell you why I have got this little girl round my neck? You don't want to know? Then you shall. She belongs to the Fairies. She's a fortune-teller. She can tell me all about you in a whisper, and can put me up to whether you're a-going to buy a lot or leave it. Now do you want a saw? No, she says you don't, because you're too clumsy to use one. Else here's a saw which would be a lifelong blessing to a handy man, at four shillings, at three and six, at three, at two and six, at two, at eighteenpence. But none of you shall have it at any price, on account of your well-known awkwardness which would make it manslaughter. The same objection applies to this set of three planes which I won't let you have neither, so don't bid for 'em. Now I am a-going to ask her what you do want. (Then I whispered, "Your head burns so, that I am afraid it hurts you bad, my pet," and she answered, without opening her heavy eyes, "Just a little, father.") Oh! This little fortune-teller says it's a memorandum-book you want. Then why didn't you mention it? Here it is. Look at it. Two hundred superfine hot-pressed wire-wove pages—if you don't believe me, count 'em—ready ruled for your expenses, an everlastingly-pointed pencil to put 'em down with, a double-bladed penknife to scratch 'em out with, a book of printed tables to calculate your income with, and a camp-stool to sit down upon while you give your mind to it! Stop! And an umbrella to keep the moon off when you give your mind to it on a pitch dark night. Now I won't ask you how much for the lot, but how little? How little are you thinking of? Don't be ashamed to mention it, because my fortune-teller knows already. (Then making believe to whisper, I kissed her, and she kissed me.) Why, she says you're thinking of as little as three and threepence! I couldn't have believed it, even of you, unless she told me. Three and three-pence! And a set of printed tables in the lot that'll calculate your income up to forty thousand a year! With an income of forty thousand a year, you grudge three and sixpence. Well then, I'll tell you my opinion. I so despise the threepence, that I'd sooner take three shillings. There. For three shillings, three shillings, three shillings! Gone. Hand 'em over to the lucky man."

As there had been no bid at all, everybody looked about and grinned at everybody, while I touched little Sophy's face and asked her if she felt faint or giddy. "Not very, father. It will soon be over." Then turning from the pretty patient eyes, which were opened now, and seeing nothing but grins across my lighted grease-pot, I went on again in my Cheap Jack style. "Where's the butcher?" (My sorrowful eye had just caught sight of a fat young butcher on the outside of the crowd.) She says the good luck is the butcher's. "Where is he?" Everybody handed on the blushing butcher to the front, and there was a roar, and the butcher felt himself obliged to put his hand in his pocket and take the lot. The party so picked out, in general does feel obliged to take the lot—good four times out of six. Then we had another lot the counterpart of that one, and sold it sixpence cheaper, which is always wery much enjoyed. Then we had the spectacles. It ain't a special profitable lot, but I put 'em on, and I see what the Chancellor of the Exchequer is going to take off the taxes, and I see what the sweetheart of the young woman in the shawl is doing at home, and I see what the Bishops has got for dinner, and a deal more that seldom fails to fetch 'em up in their spirits; and the better their spirits, the better their bids. Then we had the ladies' lot—the teapot, tea-caddy, glass sugar basin, half a dozen spoons, and caudle-cup—and all the time I was making similar excuses to give a look or two and say a word or two to my poor child. It was while the second ladies' lot was holding 'em enchained that I felt her lift herself a little on my shoulder, to look across the dark street. "What troubles you, darling?" "Nothing troubles me, father. I am not at all troubled. But don't I see a pretty churchyard over there?" "Yes, my dear." "Kiss me twice, dear father, and lay me down to rest upon that church-yard grass so soft and green." I staggered back into the cart with her head dropped on my shoulder, and I says to her mother, "Quick. Shut the door! Don't let those laughing people see!" "What's the matter?" she cries. "O, woman, woman," I tells her, "you'll never catch my little Sophy by her hair again, for she has flown away from you!"

Maybe those were harder words than I meant 'em, but from that time forth my wife took to brooding, and would sit in the cart or walk beside it, hours at a stretch, with her arms crossed and her eyes looking on the ground. When her furies took her (which was rather seldomer than before) they took her in a new way, and she banged herself about to that extent that I was forced to hold her. She got none the better for a little drink now and then, and through some years I used to wonder as I plodded along at the old horse's head whether there was many carts upon the road that held so much dreariness as mine, for all my being looked up to as the King of the Cheap Jacks. So

sad our lives went on till one summer evening, when as we were
coming into Exeter out of the further West of England, we saw
a woman beating a child in a cruel manner, who screamed,
"Don't beat me! O mother, mother, mother!" Then my wife
stopped her ears and ran away like a wild thing, and next day
she was found in the river.

Me and my dog were all the company left in the cart now,
and the dog learned to give a short bark when they wouldn't
bid, and to give another and a nod of his head when I asked
him: "Who said half-a-crown? Are you the gentleman, sir, that
offered half-a-crown?" He attained to an immense heighth of
popularity, and I shall always believe taught himself entirely
out of his own head to growl at any person in the crowd that
bid as low as sixpence. But he got to be well on in years, and
one might when I was conwulsing York with the spectacles, he
took a conwulsion on his own account upon the very footboard
by me, and it finished him.

Being naturally of a tender turn, I had dreadful lonely feelings
on me arter this. I conquered 'em at selling times, having a
reputation to keep (not to mention keeping myself), but they
got me down in private and rolled upon me. That's often the
way with us public characters. See us on the footboard, and
you'd give pretty well anything you possess to be us. See us off
the footboard, and you'd add a trifle to be off your bargain.
It was under those circumstances that I come acquainted with
a giant. I might have been too high to fall into conversation with
him, had it not been for my lonely feelings. For the general rule
is, going round the country, to draw the line at dressing up.
When a man can't trust his getting a living to his undisguised
abilities, you consider him below your sort. And this giant when
on view figured as a Roman.

He was a languid young man, which I attribute to the distance
betwixt his extremities. He had a little head and less in it, he
had weak eyes and weak knees, and altogether you couldn't look
at him without feeling that there was greatly too much of him
both for his joints and his mind. But he was an amiable though
timid young man (his mother let him out, and spent the money),
and we come acquainted when he was walking to ease the horse
betwixt two fairs. He was called Rinaldo di Velasco, his name
being Pickleson.

This giant otherwise Pickleson mentioned to me under the

seal of confidence, that beyond his being a burden to himself, his life was made a burden to him, by the cruelty of his master towards a step-daughter who was deaf and dumb. Her mother was dead, and she had no living soul to take her part, and was used most hard. She travelled with his master's caravan only because there was nowhere to leave her, and this giant otherwise Pickleson did go so far as to believe that his master often tried to lose her. He was such a very languid young man, that I don't know how long it didn't take him to get this story out, but it passed through his defective circulation to his top extremity in course of time.

When I heard this account from the giant otherwise Pickleson, and likewise that the poor girl had beautiful long dark hair, and was often pulled down by it and beaten, I couldn't see the giant through what stood in my eyes. Having wiped 'em, I give him sixpence (for he was kept as short as he was long), and he laid it out in two threepennorths of gin-and-water, which so brisked him up, that he sang the Favourite Comic of Shivery Shakey, ain't it cold. A popular effect which his master had tried every other means to get out of him as a Roman, wholly in vain.

His master's name was Mim, a wery hoarse man and I knew him to speak to. I went to that Fair as a mere civilian, leaving the cart outside the town, and I looked about the back of the Vans while the performing was going on, and at last sitting dozing against a muddy cartwheel, I come upon the poor girl who was deaf and dumb. At the first look I might almost have judged that she had escaped from the Wild Beast Show, but at the second I thought better of her, and thought that if she was more cared for and more kindly used she would be like my child. She was just the same age that my own daughter would have been, if her pretty head had not fell down upon my shoulder that unfortunate night.

To cut it short, I spoke confidential to Mim while he was beating the gong outside betwixt two lots of Pickleson's publics, and I put it to him, "She lies heavy on your own hands; what'll you take for her?" Mim was a most ferocious swearer. Suppressing that part of his reply, which was much the longest part, his reply was, "A pair of braces." "Now I'll tell you," says I, "what I'm a going to do with you. I'm a going to fetch you half a dozen pair of the primest braces in the cart, and then to take her away with me." Says Mim (again ferocious), "I'll believe it when I've got the goods, and no sooner." I made all the haste I could, lest he should think twice of it, and the bargain was completed, which Pickleson he was thereby so relieved in his mind that he come out at his little back door, longways like a serpent, and give us Shivery Shakey in a whisper among the wheels at parting.

It was happy days for both of us when Sophy and me began to travel in the cart. I at once give her the name of Sophy, to put her ever towards me in the attitude of my own daughter. We soon made out to begin to understand one another through the goodness of the Heavens, when she knowed that I meant true and kind by her. In a very little time she was wonderful fond of me. You have no idea what it is to have any body wonderful fond of you, unless you have been got down and rolled upon by the lonely feelings that I have mentioned as having once got the better of me.

You'd have laughed—or the rewerse—it's according to your disposition—if you could have seen me trying to teach Sophy. At first I was helped—you'd never guess by what—milestones. I got some large alphabets in a box, all the letters separate on bits of bone, and say we was going to WINDSOR, I give her those letters in that order, and then at every milestone I showed her those same letters in that same order again, and pointed towards the abode of royalty. Another time I give her C A R T, and then chalked the same upon the cart. Another time I give her D O C T O R   M A R I G O L D, and hung a corresponding inscription outside my waistcoat. People that met us might stare a bit and laugh, but what did *I* care if she caught the idea? She caught it after long patience and trouble, and then we did begin to get on swimmingly, I believe you! At first she was a little given to consider me the cart, and the cart the abode of royalty, but that soon wore off.

We had our signs, too, and they was hundreds in number. Sometimes, she would sit looking at me and considering hard how to communicate with me about something fresh—how to ask me what she wanted explained—and then she was (or I thought she was; what does it signify?) so like my child with those years added to her, that I half believed it was herself, trying to tell me where she had been to up in the skies, and what she had seen since that unhappy night when she flied away. She had a pretty face, and now that there was no one to drag at her bright dark hair and it was all in order, there was a something touching in her looks that made the cart most peaceful and most quiet, though not at all melancholly. [N.B. In the Cheap Jack patter, we generally sound it, lemonjolly, and it gets a laugh.]

The way she learnt to understand any look of mine was truly surprising. When I sold of a night, she would sit in the cart unseen by them outside, and would give a eager look into my eyes when I looked in, and would hand me straight the precise article or articles I wanted. And then she would clap her hands and laugh for joy. And as for me, seeing her so bright, and remembering what she was when I first lighted on her, starved and beaten and ragged, leaning asleep against the muddy cart-wheel, it give me such heart that I gained a greater heighth of reputation than ever, and I put Pickleson down (by the name of Mim's Travelling Giant otherwise Pickleson) for a fypunnote in my will.

This happiness went on in the cart till she was sixteen year old. By which time I began to feel not satisfied that I had done my whole duty by her, and to consider that she ought to have better teaching than I could give her. It drew a many tears on both sides when I commenced explaining my views to her, but what's right is right and you can't neither by tears nor laughter do away with its character.

So I took her hand in mine, and I went with her one day to the Deaf and Dumb Establishment in London, and when the gentleman come to speak to us, I says to him : "Now I'll tell you what I'll do with you sir. I am nothing but a Cheap Jack, but of late years I have laid by for a rainy day notwithstanding. This is my only daughter (adopted) and you can't produce a deafer nor a dumber. Teach her the most that can be taught her, in the shortest separation that can be named—state the figure for it—and I am game to put the money down. I won't bate you a single farthing sir but I'll put down the money here and now, and I'll thankfully throw you in a pound to take it. There!" The gentleman smiled, and then, "Well, well," says he, "I must first know what she has learnt already. How do you communicate with her?" Then I showed him, and she wrote in printed writing many names of things and so forth, and we held some sprightly conversation, Sophy and me, about a little story in a book which the gentleman showed her and which she was able to read. "This is most extraordinary," says the gentleman; "is it possible that you have been her only teacher?" "I have been her only teacher, sir," I says, "besides herself." "Then," says the gentleman, and more acceptable words was never spoke to me, "you're a clever fellow, and a good fellow." This he makes known to Sophy, who kisses his hands, claps her own, and laughs and cries upon it.

We saw the gentleman four times in all, and when he took down my name and asked how in the world it ever chanced to be Doctor, it come out that he was own nephew by the sister's side, if you'll believe me, to the very Doctor that I was called after. This made our footing still easier, and he says to me:

"Now Marigold, tell me what more do you want your adopted daughter to know?"

"I want her sir to be cut off from the world as little as can be, considering her deprivations, and therefore to be able to read whatever is wrote, with perfect ease and pleasure."

"My good fellow," urges the gentleman, opening his eyes wide, "why *I* can't do that myself!"

I took his joke and give him a laugh (knowing by experience how flat you fall without it) and I mended my words accordingly.

"What do you mean to do with her afterwards?" asks the gentleman, with a sort of a doubtful eye. "To take her about the country?"

"In the cart sir, but only in the cart. She will live a private life, you understand, in the cart. I should never think of bringing her infirmities before the public. I wouldn't make a show of her, for any money."

The gentleman nodded and seemed to approve.

"Well," says he, "can you part with her for two years?"

"To do her that good—yes, sir."

"There's another question," says the gentleman, looking towards her: "Can she part with you for two years?"

I don't know that it was a harder matter of itself (for the other was hard enough to me), but it was harder to get over. However, she was pacified to it at last, and the separation betwixt us was settled. How it cut up both of us when it took place, and when I left her at the door in the dark of an evening, I don't tell. But I know this:—remembering that night, I shall never pass that same establishment without a heart-ache and a swelling in the throat, and I couldn't put you up the best of lots in sight of it with my usual spirit—no, not even the gun, nor the pair of spectacles—for five hundred pound reward from the

Secretary of State for the Home Department, and throw in the honour of putting my legs under his mahogany arterwards.

Still, the loneliness that followed in the cart was not the old loneliness, because there was a term put to it however long to look forward to, and because I could think, when I was anyways down, that she belonged to me and I belonged to her. Always planning for her coming back, I bought in a few months' time another cart, and what do you think I planned to do with it? I'll tell you. I planned to fit it up with shelves, and books for her reading, and to have a seat in it where I could sit and see her read, and think that I had been her first teacher. Not hurrying over the job, I had the fittings knocked together in contriving ways under my own inspection, and here was her bed in a berth with curtains, and there was her reading-table, and here was her writing-desk, and elsewhere was her books in rows upon rows, picters and no picters, bindings and no bindings, gilt-edged and plain, just as I could pick 'em up for her in lots up and down the country, North and South and West and East, Winds liked best and winds liked least, Here and there and gone astray, Over the hills and far away. And when I had got together pretty well as many books as the cart would neatly hold, a new scheme come into my head which, as it turned out, kept my time and attention a good deal employed and helped me over the two years stile.

Without being of an awaricious temper, I like to be the owner of things. I shouldn't wish, for instance, to go partners with yourself in the Cheap Jack cart. It's not that I mistrust you, but that I'd rather know it was mine. Similarly, very likely you'd rather know it was yours. Well! A kind of a jealousy began to creep into my mind when I reflected that all those books would have been read by other people long before they was read by her. It seemed to take away from her being the owner of 'em like. In this way, the question got into my head:—Couldn't I have a book new-made express for her, which she should be the first to read?

It pleased me, that thought did, and as I never was a man to let a thought sleep (you must wake up all the whole family of thoughts you've got and burn their nightcaps, or you won't do in the Cheap Jack line), I set to work at it. Considering that I was in the habit of changing so much about the country, and that I should have to find out a literary character here to make a deal with, and another literary character there to make a deal with, as opportunities presented, I hit on the plan that this same book should be a general miscellaneous lot—like the razors, flat-iron, chronometer watch, dinner plates, rolling-pin, and looking-glass —and shouldn't be offered as a single indiwidual article like the spectacles or the gun. When I had come to that conclusion, I come to another, which shall likewise be yours.

Often had I regretted that she never had heard me on the footboard, and that she never could hear me. It ain't that *I* am vain, but that *you* don't like to put your own light under a bushel. What's the worth of your reputation, if you can't convey the reason for it to the person you most wish to value it? Now I'll put it to you. Is it worth sixpence, fippence, fourpence, three-pence, twopence, a penny, a halfpenny, a farthing? No, it ain't. Not worth a farthing. Very well then. My conclusion was, that I would begin her book with some account of myself. So that, through reading a specimen or two of me on the footboard, she might form an idea of my merits there. I was aware that I couldn't do myself justice. A man can't write his eye (at least *I* don't know how to), nor yet can a man write his voice, nor the rate of his talk, nor the quickness of his action, nor his general spicy way. But he can write his turns of speech, when he is a public speaker—and indeed I have heard that he very often does, before he speaks 'em.

Well! Having formed that resolution, then come the question of a name. How did I hammer that hot iron into shape? This way. The most difficult explanation I had ever had with her was, how I come to be called Doctor, and yet was no Doctor. After all, I felt that I had failed of getting it correctly into her mind, with my utmost pains. But trusting to her improvement in the two years, I thought that I might trust to her understanding it when she should come to read it as put down by my own hand. Then I thought I would try a joke with her and watch how it took, by which of itself I might fully judge of her understanding it. We had first discovered the mistake we had dropped into, through her having asked me to prescribe for her when she had supposed me to be a Doctor in a medical point of view, so thinks I, "Now, if I give this book the name of my Prescriptions, and if she catches the idea that my only Prescriptions are for her amusement and interest—to make her laugh in a pleasant way, or to make her cry in a pleasant way—it will be a delightful proof to both of us that we have got over our difficulty. It fell out to absolute perfection. For when she saw the book, as I had it got up—the printed and pressed book—lying on her desk in her cart, and saw the title, DOCTOR MARIGOLD'S PRESCRIPTIONS, she looked at me for a moment with astonishment, then fluttered the leaves, then broke out a laughing in the charmingest way, then felt her pulse and shook her head, then turned the pages pretending to read them most attentive, then kissed the book to me, and put it to her bosom with both her hands. I never was better pleased in all my life!

But let me not anticipate. (I take that expression out of a lot of romances I bought for her. I never opened a single one of 'em—and I have opened many—but I found the romancer saying "let me not anticipate." Which being so, I wonder why he did anticipate, or who asked him to it.) Let me not, I say, anticipate. This same book took up all my spare time. It was no play to get the other articles together in the general miscellaneous lot, but when it come to my own article! There! I couldn't have believed the blotting, nor yet the buckling to at it, nor the patience over it. Which again is like the footboard. The public have no idea.

At last it was done, and the two years' time was gone after all the other time before it, and where it's all gone to, who knows? The new cart was finished—yellow outside, relieved with wermillion and brass fittings—the old horse was put in it, a new 'un and a boy being laid on for the Cheap Jack cart—and I cleaned myself up to go and fetch her. Bright cold weather it was, cart-chimneys smoking, carts pitched private on a piece of waste ground over at Wandsworth where you may see 'em from the Sou' Western Railway when not upon the road. (Look out of the right-hand window going down.)

"Marigold," says the gentleman, giving his hand hearty, "I am very glad to see you."

"Yet I have my doubts, sir," says I, "if you can be half as glad to see me, as I am to see you."

"The time has appeared so long; has it, Marigold?"

"I won't say that, sir, considering its real length; but——"

"What a start, my good fellow!"

Ah! I should think it was! Grown such a woman, so pretty, so intelligent, so expressive! I knew then that she must be really like my child, or I could never have known her, standing quiet by the door.

"You are affected," says the gentleman in a kindly manner.

"I feel, sir," says I, "that I am but a rough chap in a sleeved waistcoat."

"*I* feel," says the gentleman, "that it was you who raised her from misery and degradation, and brought her into communication with her kind. But why do we converse alone together, when we can converse so well with her? Address her in your own way."

"I am such a rough chap in a sleeved waistcoat, sir," says I, "and she is such a graceful woman, and she stands so quiet at the door!"

"Try if she moves at the old sign," says the gentleman.

They had got it up together o' purpose to please me! For when I give her the old sign, she rushed to my feet, and dropped upon her knees, holding up her hands to me with pouring tears of love and joy; and when I took her hands and lifted her, she clasped me round the neck and lay there; and I don't know what a fool I didn't make of myself, until we all three settled down into talking without sound, as if there was a something soft and pleasant spread over the whole world for us.

Now I'll tell you what I am a going to do with you. I am a going to offer you the general miscellaneous lot, her own book, never read by anybody else but me, added to and completed by me after her first reading of it, eight-and-forty printed pages, six-and-ninety columns, Whiting's own work, Beaufort House to wit, thrown off by the steam-ingine, best of paper, beautiful green wrapper, folded like clean linen come home from the clear-starcher's, and so exquisitely stitched that, regarded as a piece of needlework alone it's better than the sampler of a seamstress undergoing a Competitive Examination for Starvation before the Civil Service Commissioners—and I offer the lot for what? For eight pound? Not so much. For six pound? Less. For four pound? Why, I hardly expect you to believe me, but that's the sum. Four pound! The stitching alone cost half as much again. Here's forty-eight original pages, ninety-six original columns, for four pound. You want more for the money? Take it. Three whole pages of advertisements of thrilling interest thrown in for nothing. Read 'em and believe 'em. More? My best of wishes for your merry Christmases and your happy New Years, your long lives and your true prosperities. Worth twenty pound good if they are delivered as I send them. Remember! Here's a final prescription added, "To be taken for life," which will tell you how the cart broke down, and where the journey ended. You think Four Pound too much? And still you think so? Come! I'll tell you what then. Say Four Pence, and keep the secret.

II

NOT TO BE TAKEN AT BED-TIME

This is the legend of a house called the Devil's Inn, standing in the heather on the top of the Connemara mountains, in a shallow valley hollowed between five peaks. Tourists sometimes come in sight of it on September evenings; a crazy and weather-stained apparition, with the sun glaring at it angrily between the hills, and striking its shattered window-panes. Guides are known to shun it, however.

The house was built by a stranger, who came no one knew whence, and whom the people nicknamed Coll Dhu (Black Coll), because of his sullen bearing and solitary habits. His dwelling they called the Devil's Inn, because no tired traveller had ever been asked to rest under its roof, nor friend known to cross its threshold. No one bore him company in his retreat but a wizen-faced old man, who shunned the good-morrow of the trudging peasant when he made occasional excursions to the nearest village for provisions for himself and master, and who was as secret as a stone concerning all the antecedents of both.

For the first year of their residence in the country, there had been much speculations as to who they were, and what they did with themselves up there among the clouds and eagles. Some said that Coll Dhu was a scion of the old family from whose hands the surrounding lands had passed; and that, embittered by poverty and pride, he had come to bury himself in solitude, and brood over his misfortunes. Others hinted of crime, and flight from another country; others again whispered of those who were cursed from their birth, and could never smile, nor yet make friends with a fellow-creature till the day of their death. But when two years had passed, the wonder had somewhat died out, and Coll Dhu was little thought of, except when a herd looking for sheep crossed the track of a big dark man walking the mountains gun in hand, to whom he did not dare say "Lord save you!" or when a housewife rocking her cradle of a winter's night, crossed herself as a gust of storm thundered over her cabin-roof, with the exclamation, "Oh, then, it's Coll Dhu that has enough o' the fresh air about his head up there this night, the crature!"

Coll Dhu had lived thus in his solitude for some years, when it became known that Colonel Blake, the new lord of the soil, was coming to visit the country. By climbing one of the peaks encircling his eyrie, Coll could look sheer down a mountain-side, and see in miniature beneath him, a grey old dwelling with ivied chimneys and weather-slated walls, standing amongst straggling trees and grim warlike rocks, that gave it the look of a fortress, gazing out to the Atlantic for ever with the eager eyes of all its windows, as if demanding perpetually, "What tidings from the New World?"

He could see now masons and carpenters crawling about below, like ants in the sun, over-running the old house from base to chimney, daubing here and knocking there, tumbling down walls that looked to Coll, up among the clouds, like a handful of jack-stones, and building up others that looked like the toy fences in a child's Farm. Throughout several months he must have watched the busy ants at their task of breaking and mending again, disfiguring and beautifying; but when all was done he had not the curiosity to stride down and admire the handsome paneling of the new billiard-room, nor yet the fine view which the enlarged bay-window in the drawing-room commanded of the watery highway to Newfoundland.

Deep summer was melting into autumn, and the amber streaks of decay were beginning to creep out and trail over the ripe purple of moor and mountain, when Colonel Blake, his only daughter, and a party of friends, arrived in the country. The grey house below was alive with gaiety, but Coll Dhu no longer found an interest in observing it from his eyrie. When he watched the sun rise or set, he chose to ascend some crag that looked on no human habitation. When he sallied forth on his excursions, gun in hand, he set his face towards the most isolated wastes, dipping into the loneliest valleys, and scaling the nakedest ridges. When he came by chance within call of other excursionists, gun in hand he plunged into the shade of some hollow, and avoided an encounter. Yet it was fated, for all that, that he and Colonel Blake should meet.

Towards the evening of one bright September day, the wind changed, and in half an hour the mountains were wrapped in a thick blinding mist. Coll Dhu was far from his den, but so well had he searched these mountains, and inured himself to their climate, that neither storm, rain, nor fog, had power to disturb him. But while he stalked on his way, a faint and agonised cry from a human voice reached him through the smothering mist. He quickly tracked the sound, and gained the side of a man who was stumbling along in danger of death at every step.

"Follow me!" said Coll Dhu to this man, and, in an hour's time, brought him safely to the lowlands, and up to the walls of the eager-eyed mansion.

"I am Colonel Blake," said the frank soldier, when, having left the fog behind him, they stood in the starlight under the lighted windows. "Pray tell me quickly to whom I owe my life."

As he spoke, he glanced up at his benefactor, a large man with a sombre sun-burned face.

"Colonel Blake," said Coll Dhu, after a strange pause, "your father suggested to my father to stake his estates at the gaming table. They were staked, and the tempter won. Both are dead; but you and I live, and I have sworn to injure you."

The colonel laughed good humouredly at the uneasy face above him.

"And you began to keep your oath to-night by saving my life?" said he. "Come! I am a soldier, and know how to meet an enemy; but I had far rather meet a friend. I shall not be happy till you have eaten my salt. We have merry-making to-night in honour of my daughter's birthday. Come in and join us?"

Coll Dhu looked at the earth doggedly.

"I have told you," he said, "who and what I am, and I will not cross your threshold."

But at this moment (so runs my story) a French window opened among the flower-beds by which they were standing, and a vision appeared which stayed the words on Coll's tongue. A stately girl, clad in white satin, stood framed in the ivied window, with the warm light from within streaming around her richly-moulded figure into the night. Her face was as pale as her gown, her eyes were swimming in tears, but a firm smile sat on her lips as she held out both hands to her father. The light behind her, touched the glistening folds of her dress—the lustrous pearls round her throat—the coronet of blood-red roses which encircled the knotted braids at the back of her head. Satin, pearls, and roses—had Coll Dhu, of the Devil's Inn, never set eyes upon such things before?

Evleen Blake was no nervous tearful miss. A few quick words— "Thank God! you're safe; the rest have been home an hour"— and a tight pressure of her father's fingers between her own jewelled hands, were all that betrayed the uneasiness she had suffered.

"Faith, my love, I owe my life to this brave gentleman!" said the blithe colonel. "Press him to come in and be our guest, Evleen. He wants to retreat to his mountains, and lose himself again in the fog where I found him; or, rather, where he found me! Come, sir" (to Coll), "you must surrender to this fair besieger."

An introduction followed. "Coll Dhu!" murmured Evleen Blake, for she had heard the common tales of him; but with a frank welcome she invited her father's preserver to taste the hospitality of that father's house.

"I beg you to come in, sir," she said; "but for you our gaiety must have been turned into mourning. A shadow will be upon our mirth if our benefactor disdains to join in it."

With a sweet grace, mingled with a certain hauteur from which she was never free, she extended her white hand to the tall looming figure outside the window; to have it grasped and wrung in a way that made the proud girl's eyes flash their amazement, and the same little hand clench itself in displeasure, when it had hid itself like an outraged thing among the shining folds of her gown. Was this Coll Dhu mad, or rude?

The guest no longer refused to enter, but followed the white figure into a little study where a lamp burned; and the gloomy stranger, the bluff colonel, and the young mistress of the house, were fully discovered to each other's eyes. Evleen glanced at the newcomer's dark face, and shuddered with a feeling of indescribable dread and dislike; then, to her father, accounted for the shudder after a popular fashion, saying lightly: "There is some one walking over my grave."

So Coll Dhu was present at Evleen Blake's birthday ball. Here he was, under a roof which ought to have been his own, a stranger, known only by a nickname, shunned and solitary. Here he was, who had lived among the eagles and foxes, lying in wait with a fell purpose, to be revenged on the son of his father's foe for poverty and disgrace, for the broken heart of a dead mother, for the loss of a self-slaughtered father, for the dreary scattering of brothers and sisters. Here he stood, a Samson shorn of his strength; and all because a haughty girl had melting eyes, a winning mouth, and looked radiant in satin and roses.

Peerless where many were lovely, she moved among her friends, trying to be unconscious of the gloomy fire of those strange eyes which followed her unweariedly wherever she went. And when her father begged her to be gracious to the unsocial guest whom he would fain conciliate, she courteously conducted him to see the new picture-gallery adjoining the drawing-rooms; explained under what odd circumstances the colonel had picked up this little painting or that; using every delicate art her pride would allow to achieve her father's purpose, whilst maintaining at the same time her own personal reserve; trying to divert the guest's oppressive attention from herself to the objects for which she claimed his notice. Coll Dhu followed his conductress and listened to her voice, but what she said mattered nothing; nor did she wring many words of comment or reply from his lips, until they paused in a retired corner where the light was dim, before a window from which the curtain was withdrawn. The sashes were open, and nothing was visible but water; the night Atlantic, with the full moon riding high above a bank of clouds, making silvery tracks outward towards the distance of infinite mystery dividing two worlds. Here the following little scene is said to have been enacted.

"This window of my father's own planning, is it not creditable to his taste?" said the young hostess, as she stood, herself glittering like a dream of beauty, looking on the moonlight.

Coll Dhu made no answer; but suddenly, it is said, asked her for a rose from a cluster of flowers that nestled in the lace on her bosom.

For the second time that night Evleen Blake's eyes flashed with no gentle light. But this man was the saviour of her father. She broke off a blossom, and with such good grace, and also with such queen-like dignity as she might assume, presented it to him. Whereupon, not only was the rose seized, but also the hand that gave it, which was hastily covered with kisses.

Then her anger burst upon him.

"Sir," she cried, "if you are a gentleman you must be mad! If you are not mad, then you are not a gentleman!"

"Be merciful," said Coll Dhu; "I love you. My God, I never

loved a woman before! Ah!" he cried, as a look of disgust crept over her face, "you hate me. You shuddered the first time your eyes met mine. I love you, and you hate me!"

"I do," cried Evleen, vehemently, forgetting everything but her indignation. "Your presence is like something evil to me. Love me?—your looks poison me. Pray, sir, talk no more to me in this strain."

"I will trouble you no longer," said Coll Dhu. And, stalking to the window, he placed one powerful hand upon the sash, and vaulted from it out of her sight.

Bare-headed as he was, Coll Dhu strode off to the mountains, but not towards his own home. All the remaining dark hours of that night he is believed to have walked the labyrinths of the hills, until dawn began to scatter the clouds with a high wind. Fasting, and on foot from sunrise the morning before, he was then glad enough to see a cabin right in his way. Walking in, he asked for water to drink, and a corner where he might throw himself to rest.

There was a wake in the house, and the kitchen was full of people, all wearied out with the night's watch; old men were dozing over their pipes in the chimney-corner, and here and there a woman was fast asleep with her head on a neighbour's knee. All who were awake crossed themselves when Coll Dhu's figure darkened the door, because of his evil name; but an old man of the house invited him in, and offering him milk, and promising him a roasted potato by-and-by, conducted him to a small room off the kitchen, one end of which was strewed with heather, and where there were only two women sitting gossiping over a fire.

"A thraveller," said the old man, nodding his head at the women, who nodded back, as if to say "he has the traveller's right." And Coll Dhu flung himself on the heather, in the furthest corner of the narrow room.

The women suspended their talk for a while; but presently, guessing the intruder to be asleep, resumed it in voices above a whisper. There was but a patch of window with the grey dawn behind it, but Coll could see the figures by the firelight over which they bent: an old woman sitting forward with her withered hands extended to the embers, and a girl reclining against the hearth wall, with her healthy face, bright eyes, and crimson draperies, glowing by turns in the flickering blaze.

"I do' know," said the girl, "but it's the quarest marriage iver I h'ard of. Sure it's not three weeks since he tould right an' left that he hated her like poison!"

"Whist, asthoreen!" said the colliagh, bending forward confidentially; "throth an' we all know that o' him. But what could he do, the crature! When she put the burragh-bos on him!"

"The *what*?" asked the girl.

"Then the burragh-bos machree-o? That's the spanchel o' death, avourneen; an' well she has him tethered to her now, bad luck to her!"

The old woman rocked herself and stifled the Irish cry breaking from her wrinkled lips by burying her face in her cloak.

"But what is it?" asked the girl, eagerly. "What's the burragh-bos, anyways, an' where did she get it?"

"Och, och! it's not fit for comin' over to young ears, but cuggir (whisper), acushla! It's a sthrip o' the skin o' a corpse, peeled from the crown o' the head to the heel, without crack or split, or the charrm's broke; an' that, rowled up, an' put on a sthring roun' the neck o' the wan that's cowld by the wan that wants to be loved. An' sure enough it puts the fire in their hearts, hot an' sthrong, afore twinty-four hours is gone."

The girl had started from her lazy attitude, and gazed at her companion with eyes dilated by horror.

"Marciful Saviour!" she cried. "Not a sowl on airth would bring the curse out o' heaven by sich a black doin'!"

"Aisy, Biddeen alanna! an' there's wan that does it, an' isn't the divil. Arrah, asthoreen, did ye niver hear tell o' Pexie na Pishrogie, that lives betune two hills o' Maam Turk?"

"I h'ard o' her," said the girl, breathlessly.

"Well, sorra bit lie, but it's hersel' that does it. She'll do it for money any day. Sure they hunted her from the graveyard o' Salruck, where she had the dead raised; an' glory be to God! they would ha' murthered her, only they missed her thracks, an' couldn't bring it home to her afther."

"Whist, a-wauher" (my mother), said the girl; "here's the thraveller gettin' up to set off on his road again! Och, then, it's the short rest he tuk, the sowl!"

It was enough for Coll, however. He had got up, and now went back to the kitchen, where the old man had caused a dish of potatoes to be roasted, and earnestly pressed his visitor to sit down and eat of them. This Coll did readily; having recruited his strength by a meal, he betook himself to the mountains again, just as the rising sun was flashing among the waterfalls, and sending the night mists drifting down the glens. By sundown the same evening he was striding over the hills of Maam Turk, asking of herds his way to the cabin of one Pexie na Pishrogie.

In a hovel on a brown desolate heath, with scared-looking hills flying off into the distance on every side, he found Pexie : a yellow-faced hag, dressed in a dark-red blanket, with elf-locks of coarse black hair protruding from under an orange kerchief swathed round her wrinkled jaws. She was bending over a pot upon her fire, where herbs were simmering, and she looked up with an evil glance when Coll Dhu darkened her door.

"The burragh-bos is it her honour wants?" she asked, when he had made known his errand. "Ay, ay; but the arighad, the arighad (money) for Pexie. The burragh-bos is ill to get."

"I will pay," said Coll Dhu, laying a sovereign on the bench before her.

The witch sprang upon it, and chuckling, bestowed on her visitor a glance which made even Coll Dhu shudder.

"Her honour is a fine king," she said, "an' her is fit to get the burragh-bos. Ha! ha! her sall get the burragh-bos from Pexie. But the arighad is not enough. More, more!"

She stretched out her claw-like hand, and Coll dropped another sovereign into it. Whereupon she fell into more horrible convulsions of delight.

"Hark ye!" cried Coll. "I have paid you well, but if your infernal charm does not work, I will have you hunted for a witch!"

"Work!" cried Pexie, rolling up her eyes. "If Pexie's charrm not work, then her honour come back here an' carry these bits o' mountain away on her back. Ay, her will work. If the colleen hate her honour like the old diaoul hersel', still an' withal her will love her honour like her own white sowl afore the sun sets or rises. That, (with a furtive leer,) or the colleen dhas go wild mad afore wan hour."

"Hag!" returned Coll Dhu; "the last part is a hellish invention of your own. I heard nothing of madness. If you want more money, speak out, but play none of your hideous tricks on me."

The witch fixed her cunning eyes on him, and took her cue at once from his passion.

"Her honour guess thrue," she simpered; "it is only the little bit more arighad poor Pexie want."

Again the skinny hand was extended. Coll Dhu shrank from touching it, and threw his gold upon the table.

"King, king!" chuckled Pexie. "Her honour is a grand king. Her honour is fit to get the burragh-bos. The colleen dhas sall love her like her own white sowl. Ha, ha!"

"When shall I get it?" asked Coll Dhu, impatiently.

"Her honour sall come back to Pexie in so many days, do-deag (twelve), so many days, fur that the burragh-bos is hard to get. The lonely graveyard is far away, an' the dead man is hard to raise——"

"Silence!" cried Coll Dhu; "not a word more. I will have your hideous charm, but what it is, or where you get it, I will not know."

Then, promising to come back in twelve days, he took his departure. Turning to look back when a little way across the heath, he saw Pexie gazing after him, standing on her black hill in relief against the lurid flames of the dawn, seeming to his dark imagination like a fury with all hell at her back.

At the appointed time Coll Dhu got the promised charm. He sewed it with perfumes into a cover of cloth of gold, and slung it to a fine-wrought chain. Lying in a casket which had once held the jewels of Coll's broken-hearted mother, it looked a glittering bauble enough. Meantime the people of the mountains were cursing over their cabin fires, because there had been another unholy raid upon their graveyard, and were banding themselves to hunt the criminal down.

A fortnight passed. How or where could Coll Dhu find an opportunity to put the charm round the neck of the colonel's proud daughter? More gold was dropped into Pexie's greedy claw, and then she promised to assist him in his dilemma.

Next morning the witch dressed herself in decent garb, smoothed her elf-locks under a snowy cap, smoothed the evil wrinkles out of her face, and with a basket on her arm locked the door of the hovel, and took her way to the lowlands. Pexie seemed to have given up her disreputable calling for that of a simple mushroom-gatherer. The housekeeper at the grey house bought poor Muireade's mushrooms of her every morning. Every morning she left unfailingly a nosegay of wild flowers for Miss

Evleen Blake, "God bless her! She had never seen the darling young lady with her own two longing eyes, but sure hadn't she heard tell of her sweet purty face, miles away!" And at last, one morning, whom should she meet but Miss Evleen herself returning alone from a ramble. Whereupon poor Muireade "made bold" to present her flowers in person.

"Ah," said Evleen, "it is you who leave me the flowers every morning? They are very sweet."

Muireade had sought her only for a look at her beautiful face. And now that she had seen it, as bright as the sun, and as fair as the lily, she would take up her basket and go away contented. Yet she lingered a little longer.

"My lady never walk up big mountain?" said Pexie.

"No," Evleen said, laughing; she feared she could not walk up a mountain.

"Ah yes; my lady ought to go, with more gran' ladies an' gentlemen, ridin' on purty little donkeys, up the big mountain. Oh, gran' things up big mountain for my lady to see!"

Thus she set to work, and kept her listener enchained for an hour, while she related wonderful stories of those upper regions. And as Evleen looked up to the burly crowns of the hills, perhaps she thought there might be sense in this wild old woman's suggestion. It ought to be a grand world up yonder.

Be that as it may, it was not long after this when Coll Dhu got notice that a party from the grey house would explore the mountain next day; that Evleen Blake would be of the number; and that he, Coll, must prepare to house and refresh a crowd of weary people, who in the evening should be brought, hungry and faint, to his door. The simple mushroom gatherer should be discovered laying in her humble stock among the green places between the hills, should volunteer to act as guide to the party, should lead them far out of their way through the mountains and up and down the most toilsome ascents and across dangerous places; to escape safely from which, the servants should be told to throw away the baskets of provisions which they carried.

Coll Dhu was not idle. Such a feast was set forth, as had never been spread so near the clouds before. We are told of wonderful dishes furnished by unwholesome agency, and from a place believed much hotter than is necessary for purposes of cookery. We are told also how Coll Dhu's barren chambers were suddenly hung with curtains of velvet, and with fringes of gold; how the blank white walls glowed with delicate colours and gilding; how gems of pictures sprang into sight between the panels; how the tables blazed with plate and gold, and glittered with the rarest glass; how such wines flowed, as the guests had never tasted; how servants in the richest livery, amongst whom the wizen-faced old man was a mere nonentity, appeared, and stood ready to carry in the wonderful dishes, at whose extraordinary fragrance the eagles came pecking to the windows, and the foxes drew near the walls, snuffing. Sure enough, in all good time, the weary party came within sight of the Devil's Inn, and Coll Dhu sallied forth to invite them across his lonely threshold. Colonel Blake (to whom Evleen, in her delicacy, had said no word of the solitary's strange behaviour to herself) hailed his appearance with delight, and the whole party sat down to Coll's banquet in high good humour. Also, it is said, in much amazement at the magnificence of the mountain recluse.

All went in to Coll's feast, save Evleen Blake, who remained standing on the threshold of the outer door; weary, but unwilling to rest there; hungry, but unwilling to eat there. Her white cambric dress was gathered on her arms, crushed and sullied with the toils of the day; her bright cheek was a little sun-burned; her small dark head, with its braids a little tossed, was bared to the mountain air and the glory of the sinking sun; her hands were loosely tangled in the strings of her hat; and her foot sometimes tapped the threshold stone. So she was seen.

The peasants tell that Coll Dhu and her father came praying her to enter, and that the magnificent servants brought viands to the threshold; but no step would she move inward, no morsel would she taste.

"Poison, poison!" she murmured, and threw the food in handfuls to the foxes, who were snuffing on the hearth.

But it was different when Muireade, the kindly old woman, the simple mushroom-gatherer, with all the wicked wrinkles smoothed out of her face, came to the side of the hungry girl, and coaxingly presented a savoury mess of her own sweet mushrooms, served on a common earthern platter.

"An' darlin', my lady, poor Muireade her cook them hersel', an' no thing o' this house touch them or look at poor Muireade's mushrooms."

Then Evleen took the platter and ate a delicious meal. Scarcely was it finished when a heavy drowsiness fell upon her, and, unable to sustain herself on her feet, she presently sat down upon the door-stone. Leaning her head against the framework of the door, she was soon in a deep sleep, or trance. So she was found.

"Whimsical, obstinate little girl!" said the colonel, putting his hand on the beautiful slumbering head. And taking her in his arms, he carried her into a chamber which had been (say the story-tellers) nothing but a bare and sorry closet in the morning, but which was now fitted up with Oriental splendour. And here on a luxurious couch she was laid, with a crimson coverlet wrapping her feet. And here in the tempered light coming through jewelled glass, where yesterday had been a coarse rough-hung window, her father looked his last upon her lovely face.

The colonel returned to his host and friends, and by-and-by the whole party sallied forth to see the after-glare of a fierce sunset swathing the hills in flames. It was not until they had gone some distance that Coll Dhu remembered to go back and fetch his telescope. He was not long absent. But he was absent long enough to enter that glowing chamber with a stealthy step, to throw a light chain around the neck of the sleeping girl, and to slip among the folds of her dress the hideous glittering burragh-bos.

After he had gone away again, Pexie came stealing to the door, and, opening it a little, sat down on the mat outside, with her cloak wrapped round her. An hour passed, and Evleen Blake still slept, her breathing scarcely stirring the deadly bauble on her breast. After that, she began to murmur and moan, and Pexie pricked up her ears. Presently a sound in the room told that the victim was awake and had risen. Then Pexie put her face to the aperture of the door and looked in, gave a howl of dismay, and fled from the house, to be seen in that country no more.

The light was fading among the hills, and the ramblers were returning towards the Devil's Inn, when a group of ladies who were considerably in advance of the rest, met Evleen Blake advancing towards them on the heath, with her hair disordered as by sleep, and no covering on her head. They noticed something bright, like gold, shifting and glancing with the motion of her figure. There had been some jesting among them about Evleen's fancy for falling asleep on the door-step instead of coming in to dinner, and they advanced laughing, to rally her on the subject. But she stared at them in a strange way, as if she did not know them, and passed on. Her friends were rather offended, and commented on her fantastic humour; only one looked after her, and got laughed at by her companions for expressing uneasiness on the wilful young lady's account.

So they kept their way, and the solitary figure went fluttering on, the white robe blushing, and the fatal burragh-bos glittering in the reflexion from the sky. A hare crossed her path, and she laughed out loudly, and clapping her hands, sprang after it. Then she stopped and asked questions of the stones, striking them with her open palm because they would not answer. (An amazed little herd sitting behind a rock, witnessed these strange proceedings.) By-and-by she began to call after the birds, in a wild shrill way, startling the echoes of the hills as she went along. A party of gentlemen, returning by a dangerous path, heard the unusual sound and stopped to listen.

"What is that?" asked one.

"A young eagle," said Coll Dhu, whose face had become livid; "they often give such cries."

"It was uncommonly like a woman's voice!" was the reply; and immediately another wild note rang towards them from the rocks above : a bare saw-like ridge, shelving away to some distance ahead, and projecting one hungry tooth over an abyss. A few more moments and they saw Evleen Blake's light figure fluttering out towards this dizzy point.

"My Evleen!" cried the colonel, recognising his daughter, "she is mad to venture on such a spot!"

"Mad!" repeated Coll Dhu. And then dashed off to the rescue with all the might and swiftness of his powerful limbs.

When he drew near her, Evleen had almost reached the verge of the terrible rock. Very cautiously he approached her, his object being to seize her in his strong arms before she was aware of his presence, and carry her many yards away from the spot of danger. But in a fatal moment Evleen turned her head and saw him. One wild ringing cry of hate and horror, which startled the very eagles and scattered a flight of curlews above her head, broke from her lips. A step backward brought her within a foot of death.

One desperate though wary stride, and she was struggling in Coll's embrace. One glance in her eyes, and he saw that he was striving with a mad woman. Back, back, she dragged him, and he had nothing to grasp by. The rock was slippery and his shod feet would not cling to it. Back, back! A hoarse panting, a dire swinging to and fro; and then the rock was standing naked

D

against the sky, no one was there, and Coll Dhu and Evleen Blake lay shattered far below.

III

TO BE TAKEN AT THE DINNER-TABLE

Does anyone know who gives the names to our streets? Does any one know who invents the mottoes which are inserted in the cracker-papers, along with the sugar-plums?—I don't envy him his intellectual faculties, by-the-by, and I suspect him to be the individual who translates the books of the foreign operas. Does any one know who introduces the new dishes, Kromeski's, and such-like? Does any one know who is responsible for new words, such as shunt and thud, shimmer, ping (denoting the crack of the rifle), and many others? Does any one know who has obliged us to talk for ever about "fraternising" and "cropping up"? Does any one know the Sage to whom perfumers apply when they have invented a shaving-soap, or hair-wash, and who furnishes the trade with such names for their wares as Rypophagon, Euxesis, Depilatory, Bostrakeison? Does any one know who makes the riddles?

To the last question—only—I answer, Yes; *I* know.

In a certain year, which, I don't mind mentioning may be looked upon as included in the present century, I was a little boy —a sharp little boy, though I say it, and a skinny little boy. The two qualities not unfrequently go together. I will not mention what my age was at the time, but I was at school not far from London, and I was of an age when it is customary, or *was* customary, to wear a jacket and frill.

In riddles, I had at that early age a profound and solemn joy. To the study of those problems, I was beyond measure addicted, and in the collecting of them I was diligent in the extreme. It was the custom at the time for certain periodicals to give the question of a conundrum in one number, and the answer in the next. There was an interval of seven days and nights between the propounding of the question, and the furnishing of the reply. What a time was that for me! I sought the solution of the enigma, off and on (generally on), during the leisure hours of the week (no wonder I was skinny!), and sometimes, I am proud to remember, I became acquainted with the answer before the number containing it reached me from the official source. There was another kind of puzzle which used to appear when my sharp and skinny boyhood was at its sharpest and skinniest, by which I was much more perplexed than by conundrums or riddles conveyed in mere words. I speak of what may be called symbolical riddles—rebus is, I believe, their true designation—little squalid woodcuts representing all sorts of impossible objects huddled together in incongruous disorder; letters of the alphabet, at times, and even occasionally fragments of words, being introduced here and there, to add to the general confusion. Thus you would have : a Cupid mending a pen, a gridiron, the letter x, a bar of music, p. u. g. and a fife—you would have these presented to you on a certain Saturday, with the announcement that on the following Saturday there would be issued an explanation of the mysterious and terrific jumble. That explanation would come, but with it new difficulties worse than the former. A birdcage, a setting sun (not like), the word "snip," a cradle, and some quadruped to which it would have puzzled Buffon himself to give a name. With these problems I was not successful, never having solved but one in my life, as will presently appear. Neither was I good at poetical riddles, in parts—slightly forced—as "My first is a boa-constrictor, My second's a Roman lictor, My third is a Dean and Chipter, And my whole goes always on tip-ter." These were too much for me.

I remember on one occasion accidentally meeting with a publication in which there was a rebus better executed than those to which I had been accustomed, and which mystified me greatly. First of all there was the letter A; then came a figure of a clearly virtuous man in a long gown, with a scrip, and a staff, and a cockle-shell on his hat; then followed a representation of an extremely old person with flowing white hair and beard; the figure 2 was the next symbol, and beyond this was a gentleman on crutches, looking at a five-barred gate. Oh, how that rebus haunted me! It was at a sea-side library that I met with it during the holidays, and before the next number came out I was back at school. The publication in which this remarkable picture had appeared was an expensive one, and quite beyond my means, so there was no way of getting at the explanation. Determined to conquer, and fearing that one of the symbols might escape my memory, I wrote them down in order. In doing so, an inter-

pretation flashed upon me. A—Pilgrim—Age—To—Cripple—
Gate. Ah! was it the right one? Had I triumphed, or had I
failed? My anxiety on the subject attained such a pitch at last,
that I determined to write to the editor of the periodical in which
the rebus had appeared, and implore him to take compassion
upon me and relieve my mind. To that communication I received
no answer. Perhaps there was one in the notices to correspondents
—but then I must have purchased the periodical to get it.

I mention these particulars because they had something—not
a little—to do with a certain small incident which, small though
it was, had influence on my after life. The incident in question
was the composition of a riddle by the present writer. It was
composed with difficulty, on a slate; portions of it were frequently
rubbed out, the wording of it gave me a world of trouble, but the
work was achieved at last. "Why," it was thus that I worded it
in its final and corrected form, "Why does a young gentleman
who has partaken freely of the pudding, which at this establishment precedes the meat, resemble a meteor?—Because he's efful-
gent—a full gent!"

Hopeful, surely! Nothing unnaturally premature in the composition. Founded on a strictly boyish grievance. Possessing a
certain archæological interest in its reference to the now obsolete
practice of administering pudding before meat at educational
establishments, with the view of damping the appetite (and constitution) of the pupils.

Though inscribed upon perishable and greasy slate, in ephe-
meral slate-pencil, my riddle lived. It was repeated. It became
popular. It was all over the school, and at last it came to the
ears of the master. That unimaginative person had no taste for
the fine arts. I was sent for, interrogated as to whether this work
of art was the product of my brain, and, having given an answer
in the affirmative, received a distinct, and even painful, punch
on the head, accompanied by specific directions to inscribe
straightway the words "Dangerous Satirising," two thousand
times, on the very slate on which my riddle had been originally
composed.

Notwithstanding this act of despotism on the part of the unap-
preciative Beast who invariably treated me as if I were not
profitable (when I knew the contrary), my reverence for the great
geniuses who have excelled in the department of which I am
speaking, grew with my growth, and strengthened with &c. Think

of the pleasure, the rapture, which Riddles afford to persons of wholesomely constituted mind! Think of the innocent sense of triumph felt by the man who propounds a riddle to a company, to every member of which it is a novelty. He alone is the proprietor of the answer. His is a glorious position. He keeps everybody waiting. He wears a calm and placid smile. He has the rest at his mercy. He is happy—innocently happy.

But who makes the Riddles?

I DO.

Am I going to let out a great mystery? Am I going to initiate the uininitiated? Am I going to let the world know *how it is done*?

Yes. I am.

It is done in the main by the Dictionary; but the consultation of that work of reference, with a view to the construction of riddles, is a process so bewildering—it puts such a strain upon the faculties—that at first you cannot work at it for more than a quarter of an hour at once. The process is terrific. First of all you get yourself thoroughly awake and on the alert—it is good to run the fingers through the hair roughly at this crisis—then you take your Dictionary, and, selecting a particular letter, you go down the column, stopping at every word that looks in the slightest degree promising, drawing back from it as artists draw back from a picture to see it the better, twisting it, and turning it, and if it yield nothing, passing it on to the next. With the substantives you occupy yourself in an especial manner, as more may be done with them than with any of the other parts of speech; while as to the words with two meanings, you must be in a bad state indeed, or have particular ill luck, if you fail to get something out of them.

Suppose that you are going in for a day's riddling—your dinner depending on the success of your efforts. I take your Dictionary, and open it at hap-hazard. You open, say, among the Fs, and you go to work.

You make several stoppages as you go down the column. You pause naturally at the word Felt. It is a past participle of the verb to feel, and it is a substance used in making hats. You press it hard. Why is a hatter—No—Why may a hatter invariably be looked upon as a considerate person? Because he has always *felt* for—No. That won't do. You go on. "Fen"—a chance here for a well-timed thing about the Fenian Brotherhood. This is worth a struggle, and you make a desperate one. A Fen is a marsh. In a marsh there is mud. Why was it always to be expected that the Irish rebels must ultimately stick in the mud? Because theirs was a *Fen*-ian movement.—Intolerable! Yet you are loth to abandon the subject. A Fen is a Morass. More-ass. Why is an Irish rebel more ass than knave? No, again it won't do!

Disconsolate, but dogged, you go on till you arrive at "Fertile." Fer-tile. Tile—Tile, a Hat. Why is a Hat made of Beaver, like land that always yields fine crops? Because it may be called **Fertile (Fur-tile)**. That will do. Not first-class, but it will do. Riddling is very like fishing. Sometimes you get a small trout, sometimes a large one. This is a small trout, but it shall go into the basket, nevertheless. And now you are fairly warming to your work. You come to "Forgery." You again make a point. Forgery. For-gery—For Jerry. A complicated riddle of a high order. Intricate, and of the Coleridge kind. Why—No, If—If a gentleman, having a favourite son of tender years, named Jeremiah, were in the course of dessert to put a pear in his pocket, stating, as he did so, that the fruit was intended for his beloved boy, why, in making such an explanation, would he mention a certain act of felony once punishable by death?—because he would say that it was Forgery—For Jerry. Into the basket.

It never rains but it pours. Another complex one, of the same type. Fungus! If a well-bred lady should, in sport, poke her cousin *Augustus* in the ribs with her lilac and white parasol, and hurt him, what vegetable product would she mention in facetiously apologising? Fungus. Fun Gus! In with it.

The Fs being exhausted, you take a short rest. Then, screwing your faculties up afresh, and seizing the Dictionary again, you open it once more. Cs this time lie before you, a page of Cs. You pause, hopeful, at corn. The word has two meanings, it ought to answer. It shall be made to answer. This is a case of a peculiar kind. You determine to construct a riddle by rule. There is no genius needed here. The word has two meanings; both shall be used; it is a mechanical process. Why is a reaper at his work, like a chiropodist?—Because he's a corn-cutter. Made by rule, complete, impregnable; but yet not interesting. The Cs are not propitious, and you apply to the Bs. In your loitering mood you drop down upon the word "Bring," and with idiocy at hand sit gazing at it. Suddenly you revive—Bring, Brought, Brought up. Brought up will do. Why is the coal-scuttle which Mary has conveyed from the kitchen to the second floor, like an infant put out to dry-nurse?—Because it's brought up by hand. You try once more, and this time it is the letter H on which your hopes depend. The columns under H, duly perused, bring you in due time to Horse. Why is a horse attached to the vehicle of a miser, like a war-steamer of the present day?—Because he's driven by a screw. Another? Hoarse. Why is a family, the members of which have always been subject to sore-throats, like "The Derby?"—Because it's a hoarse-race (Horse-race).

It is by no means always the case, however, that the Dictionary affords so large a yield as this. It is hard work—exhausting work—and, worst of all, *there is no end to it.* You get, after a certain time, incapable of shaking off the shop even in your moments of relaxation. Nay, worse. You feel as if you *ought* to be always at it, lest you should miss a good chance, that would never return. It is this that makes epigrammatic literature wearing. If you go to the play, if you take up a newspaper, if you ensconce yourself in a corner with a blessed work of fiction, you find yourself still pursued and haunted by your profession. The dialogue to which you listen when you go to the theatre, the words of the book you are reading, may suggest something, and it behoves you to be on the look-out. Horrible and distracting calling! You may get rid of your superfluous flesh more quickly by going through a course of riddling, than by running up-hill in blankets for a week together, or going through a systematic course of Turkish baths.

Moreover, the cultivator of epigrammatic literature has much to undergo in the disposal of his wares, when they are once ready for the market. There is a public sale for them, and, between ourselves, there is a private ditto. The public demand for the article, which it has been so long my lot to supply, is not large, nor, I am constrained to say, is it entirely cordial. The periodicals in which your rebus or your conundrum appears hebdomadally, are not numerous; nor are the proprietors of such journals respectfully eager for this peculiar kind of literature. The conundrum of the rebus will knock about the office for a long time, and, perhaps, only get inserted at last because it fits a vacant space. When we *are* inserted, we always—always mind—occupy an ignoble place. We come in at the bottom of a column, or occupy the very last lines of the periodical in which we appear—in company with that inevitable game at chess in which white is to check-mate in four moves. One of the best riddles—*the* best, I think, that I ever made—was knocking about at the office of a certain journal six weeks before it got before the public. It ran thus : Why is a little man who is always telling long stories about nothing, like a certain new kind of rifle? Answer : Because he's a small-bore.

This work was the means of bringing me acquainted with the fact that there was a Private as well as a Public sale for the productions of the epigrammatic artist. A gentleman, who did not give his name—neither will I give it, though I know it well—called at the office of the periodical in which this particular riddle appeared, on the day succeeding its publication, and asked for the name and address of its author. The sub-editor of the journal, a fast friend of mine, to whom I owe many a good turn, furnished him with both, and, on a certain day, a middle-aged gentleman of rather plethoric appearance, with a sly twinkle in his eye, and with humorous lines about his mouth—both eye and mouth were utter impostors, for my friend had not a particle of humour in his composition—came gasping up my stairs, and introducing himself as an admirer of genius—"and therefore," he added, with a courteous wave of the hand, "your very humble servant"—wished to know whether it would suit my purpose to supply him, from time to time, with certain specimens of epigrammatic literature, now a riddle, now an epigram, now a short story that could be briefly and effectively told, all of which should be guaranteed to be entirely new and original, which should be made over wholly and solely to him, and to which no other human being should have access on any consideration whatever. My gentleman added that he was prepared to pay very handsomely for what he had, and, indeed, mentioned terms which caused me to open my eyes to the fullest extent of which those organs are capable.

I soon found out what my friend Mr. Price Scrooper was at. I call him by this name (which is fictitious, but something like his own), for the sake of convenience. He was a diner-out, who held a somewhat precarious reputation, which, by hook or crook, he had acquired as a sayer of good things, a man sure to have the last new story at the end of his tongue. Mr. Scrooper liked dining-out above all things, and the horror of that day when there should come a decline in the number of his invitations was always before his eyes. Thus it came about that relations were established between us—between me, the epigrammatic artist, and Price Scrooper, the diner-out.

I fitted him with a good thing or two even on the very day of his paying me a first visit. I gave him a story which I remembered to have heard my father tell when I was an infant—a perfectly safe story, which had been buried for years in oblivion. I supplied him with a riddle or two which I happened to have by me, and which were so very bad that no company could ever suspect them of a professional origin. I set him up in epigram for some time, and he set me up to the necessaries of life for some time, and so we parted mutually satisfied.

The commercial dealings thus satisfactorily established were renewed steadily and at frequent intervals. Of course, as in all earthly relations, there were not wanting some unpleasant elements to qualify the generally comfortable arrangements. Mr. Scrooper would sometimes complain that some of the witticisms with which I had supplied him, had failed in creating an effect—had hardly proved remunerative, in short. What could I reply? I could not tell him that this was his fault. I told him a story given by Isaac Walton, of a clergyman who, hearing a sermon preached by one of his cloth with immense effect, asked for the loan of it. On returning the sermon, however, after having tried it on his own congregation, he complained that it had proved a total failure, and that his audience had responded in no degree to his eloquence. The answer of the original proprietor of the sermon was crushing: "I lent you," he said, "indeed, my fiddle, but not my fiddle-stick;" meaning, as Isaac explains, rather unnecessarily, "the manner and intelligence with which the sermon was to be delivered."

My friend did not seem to feel the application of this anecdote. I believe he was occupied, while I spoke, in committing the story to his memory for future use—thus getting it gratuitously out of me—which was mean.

In fact, Mr. Scrooper, besides his original irreparable deficiency, was getting old and stupid, and would often forget or misapply the point of a story, or the answer to a conundrum. With these last I supplied him freely, working really hard to prepare for his use such articles as were adapted to his peculiar exigencies. As a diner-out, riddles of a convivial sort—alluding to matters connected with the pleasures of the table—are generally in request, and with a supply of these I fitted Mr. Scrooper, much to his satisfaction. Here are some specimens, for which I charged him rather heavily :

Why is wine—observe how easily this is brought in after dinner —why is wine, made up for the British market, like a deserter from the army?

Because it's always brandied (branded) before it's sent off.

Why is a ship, which has to encounter rough weather before it reaches its destination, like a certain wine which is usually adulterated with logwood and other similar matters?

Because it goes through a vast deal before it comes into port.

What portion of the trimming of a lady's dress resembles East India sherry of the first quality?

That which goes round the Cape.

One of his greatest difficulties, my patron told me—for he was as frank with me as a man is with his doctor or his lawyer— was in remembering which were the houses where he had related a certain story, or propounded a certain conundrum; who were the people to whom such and such a riddle would be fresh; who were the people to whom it was already but too familiar. Mr. Scrooper had also a habit of sometimes asking the answer to a riddle instead of the question, which was occasionally productive of confusion; or, giving the question properly, he would, when his audience became desperate and gave it up, supply them with the answer to an altogether different conundrum.

One day, my patron came to me in a state of high indignation. A riddle—bran-new, and for which I had demanded a high price, thinking well of it myself—had failed, and Mr. Scrooper came to me in a rage to expostulate.

"It fell as flat as ditch-water," he said. "Indeed, one very disagreeable person said there was nothing in it, and he thought there must be some mistake. A very nasty thing to say, considering that the riddle was given as my own. How could I be mistaken in my own riddle?"

"May I ask," said I, politely, "how you worded the question?"

"Certainly. I worded it thus : Why are we justified in believing that the pilgrims to Mecca, undertake the journey with mercenary motives?"

"Quite right," said I; "and the answer?"

"The answer," replied my patron, "was as you gave it me : Because they go for the sake of Mahomet."

"I am not surprised," I said coldly, for I felt that I had been unjustly blamed, "that your audience was mystified. The answer, as I gave it to you, ran thus : Because they go for the sake of the profit (Prophet) !"

Mr. Scrooper subsequently apologised.

I draw near to the end of my narrative. The termination is painful, so is that of King Lear. The worst feature in it is, that it involves the acknowledgment of a certain deplorable piece of weakness on my own part.

I was really in receipt of a very pretty little income from Mr. Scrooper, when one morning I was again surprised by a visit from a total stranger—again, as on a former occasion, a middle-aged gentleman—again an individual with a twinkling eye and a humorous mouth—again a diner-out, with two surnames—Mr. Kerby Postlethwaite I will call him, which is sailing as near the wind as I consider safe.

Mr. Kerby Postlethwaite came on the errand which had already brought Mr. Scrooper to the top of my stairs. He, too, had seen one of my productions in a certain journal (for I still kept up my relation with the public press), and he too having a similar reputation to maintain, and finding his brain at times rather sterile, had come to me to make exactly the same proposal which had already been made by Mr. Price Scrooper.

For a time the singularity of the coincidence absolutely took my breath away, and I remained staring speechlessly at my visitor in a manner which might have suggested to him that I was hardly the man to furnish him with anything very brilliant. However, I managed to recover myself in time. I was very guarded and careful in my speech, but finally expressed my readiness to come to terms with my new employer. These were soon settled : Mr. Kerby Postlethwaite having even more liberal views as to this part of the business than those entertained by Mr. Price Scrooper.

The only difficulty was to supply this gentleman quickly enough with what he wanted. He was in a hurry. He was going that very evening to a dinner-party, and it was supremely important that he should distinguish himself. The occasion was a special one. It must be something good. He would not stick at a trifle in the matter of terms, but he did want something super-excellent. A riddle—a perfectly new riddle—he would like best.

My stores were turned over, my desk was ransacked, and still he was not satisfied. Suddenly it flashed into my mind that I had something by me which would exactly do. The very thing;

a riddle alluding to a subject of the day; a subject just at that time in everybody's mouth. One which there would be no difficulty in leading up to. In short, a very neat thing indeed. There was but one doubt in my mind. Had I already sold it to my original employer? That was the question, and for the life of me I could not answer it with certainty. The life of one addicted to such pursuits as mine, is chaotic; and with me more particularly, doing an extensive public *and* private trade, it was especially so. I kept no books, nor any record of my professional transactions. One thing which influenced me strongly to believe the riddle to be still unappropriated, was, that I had certainly received no intelligence as to its success or failure from Mr. Scrooper, whereas that gentleman never failed to keep me informed on that momentous point. I was in doubt, but I ended (so princely were the terms offered by my new patron) in giving myself the benefit of that doubt, and handing over the work of art in question to Mr. Kerby Postlethwaite.

If I were to say that I felt comfortable after having brought this transaction to a close, I should not speak the truth. Horrible misgivings filled my mind, and there were moments when, if it had been possible to undo what was done, I should have taken that retrogressive step. This, however, was out of the question. I didn't even know where my new employer was to be found. I had nothing for it but to wait and try my best to feel sanguine.

The circumstances which distinguished the evening of that eventful day on which I first received a visit from my new patron, were subsequently related to me with great accuracy, and not without rancorous comments, by both of those who sustained leading parts in the evening's performances. Yes, terrible to relate, on the following day both my patrons came to me, overflowing with fury, to tell me what had happened, and to denounce me as the first cause of the mischief. Both were furious, but my more recent acquaintance, Mr. Postlethwaite, was the more vehement in his wrath.

It appeared, according to this gentleman's statement, that having repaired at the proper time to the residence of the gentleman whose guest he was to be that evening, and who, he took occasion to inform me, was a personage of consideration, he found himself in the midst of a highly distinguished company. He had intended to be the last arrival, but a fellow named

Scrooper, or Price, or something of that sort—both names, perhaps—was yet expected. He soon arrived, however, Mr. Postlethwaite said, and the company went down to dinner.

Throughout the meal, the magnificent nature of which I will
not dilate upon, these two gentlemen were continually at logger-
heads. They appear—and in this both the accounts which reached
me tally—to have contradicted each other, interrupted each
other, cut into each other's stories, on every occasion, until that
sort of hatred was engendered between them which Christian
gentlemen sharing a meal together do sometimes feel towards
each other. I suspect that each had heard of the other as a
"diner-out," though they had not met before, and that each was
prepared to hate the other.

Adhering to the Postlethwaitean narrative faithfully, I find that
all this time, and even when most aggravated by the conduct
of my earliest patron, he was able to comfort himself with the
reflection that he had by him in store the weapon wherewith,
when the proper moment should arrive, to inflict the coup de
grace upon his rival. That weapon was my riddle—my riddle
fitted to a topic of the day.

The moment arrived. I shudder as I proceed. The meal was
over, the wines had circulated once, and Mr. Kerby Postlethwaite
began gently, insidiously and with all the dexterity of an old
performer, to lead the conversation in the direction of THE TOPIC.
His place was very near to the seat occupied by my original
patron, Mr. Price Scrooper. What was Mr. Postlethwaite's astonishment to hear that gentleman leading such conversation,
as was within his jurisdiction, *also* in the direction of THE
TOPIC! "Does he see that I want a lead, and is he playing into
my hands?" thought my newest client. "Perhaps he's not such
a bad fellow, after all. I'll do as much for him another time."
This amicable view of the matter was but of brief duration.
Madness was at hand! Two voices were presently heard speaking
simultaneously :

MR. PRICE SCROOPER. The subject suggested
a riddle to me this morning, as I was thinking it
over.
                                   Both speaking
MR. KERBY POSTLETHWAITE. A view of the   at once
thing struck me in the light of a riddle, this
morning, quite suddenly.

The two were silent, each having stopped the other.

"I beg your pardon," said my first patron, with ferocious politeness, "you were saying that you——"

"Had made a riddle," replied my second patron. "Yes. I think that you also alluded to your having done something of the sort?"

"I did."

There was silence all round the table. Some illustrious person broke it at last by saying, "What a strange coincidence!"

"At all events," cried the master of the house, "let us hear one of them. Come, Scrooper, you spoke first."

"Mr. Postlethwaite, I insist upon having your riddle," said the lady of the house, with whom Mr. P. was the favourite.

Under these circumstances both gentlemen paused, and then, each bursting forth suddenly, there was a renewal of duet.

Mr. Price Scrooper. Why does the Atlantic cable, in its present condition— } Both speaking

Mr. Kerby Postlethwaite. Why does the Atlantic cable, in its present condition— } at once.

At this there was a general roar and commotion among those present. "Our riddles appear to be somewhat alike?" remarked Mr. Postlethwaite, in a bitter tone, and looking darkly at my first patron.

"It is the most extraordinary thing," replied that gentleman, "that I ever heard of!"

"Great wits jump," said the illustrious person who had previously spoken of an "extraordinary coincidence."

"At any rate, let us hear one of them," cried the host. "Perhaps they vary after the first few words. Come, Scrooper."

"Yes, let us hear one of them to the end," said the lady of the house, and she looked at Mr. Postlethwaite. This last, however, was sulky. Mr. Price Scrooper took advantage of the circumstance to come out with the conundrum in all its integrity.

"Why," asked this gentleman once more, "is the Atlantic cable, in its present condition, like a schoolmaster?"

"That is my riddle," said Mr. Postlethwaite, as soon as the other had ceased to speak. "I made it myself."

"On the contrary, it is mine, I assure you," replied Mr. Scrooper, very doggedly. "I composed it while shaving this morning."

Here again there was a pause, broken only by interjectional expressions of astonishment on the part of those who were present —led by the illustrious man.

Again the master of the house came to the rescue. "The best way of settling it," he said, "will be to ascertain which of our two friends knows the answer. Whoever knows the answer can claim the riddle. Let each of these gentlemen write down the answer on a piece of paper, fold it up, and give it to me. If the answers are identical, the coincidence will indeed be extraordinary."

"It is impossible that any one but myself *can* know the answer," remarked my first patron, as he wrote on his paper and folded it.

My second patron wrote also, and folded. "The answer," he said, "*can* only be known to me."

The papers were unfolded by the master of the house, and read one after the other.

ANSWER written by Mr. Price Scrooper : "Because it's supported by buoys (boys)."

ANSWER written by Mr. Kerby Postlethwaite : "Because it's supported by buoys (boys)."

There was a scene. There were recriminations. As I have said, on the following morning both gentlemen visited me betimes. They had not much to say after all. Were they not both in my power?

The curious thing is, that from that time dates the decline of my professional eminence. Of course, both my patrons took leave of me for ever. But I have also to relate that my powers of riddling took leave of me also. My mornings with the Dictionary became less and less productive of results, and, only a fortnight ago last Wednesday, I sent to a certain weekly publication a rebus presenting the following combination of objects : A giraffe, a haystack, a boy driving a hoop, the letter X, a crescent, a human mouth, the words "I wish," a dog standing on its hind legs, and a pair of scales. It appeared. It took. It puzzled the public. But for the life of me I cannot form the remotest idea what it meant, and I am ruined.

IV

NOT TO BE TAKEN FOR GRANTED

To-day I, Eunice Fielding, have been looking over the journal which I kept of the first few weeks of my life in the world, after

I left the seclusion of the German Moravian school, where I was educated. I feel a strange pity for myself, the tender ignorant innocent school-girl, freed from the peaceful shelter of the Moravian settlement, and thrust suddenly into the centre of a sorrowful household.

As I turn to this first page, there rises before me, like the memory of a former life, a picture of the noiseless grass-grown streets of the settlement, with the old-fashioned dwellings, and the quiet and serene faces looking out kindly upon the troop of children passing to the church. There is the home of the Single Sisters, with its shining and spotless casements; and close beside it, is the church where they and we worshipped, with its broad central aisle always separating the women from the men. I can see the girls in their picturesque caps, trimmed with scarlet, and the blue ribbons of the matrons, and the pure white head-gear of the widows; the burial-ground, where the separation is still maintained, and where the brethren and the sisters lie in undivided graves; and the kindly simple-hearted pastor, who was always touched with the feeling of our weakness. I see it all, as I turn over the pages of my short journal, with just a faint longing to return to the repose and innocent ignorance which encircled me while I dwelt among them, safely shut in from the sorrows of the world.

Nov. 7. At home once more after an absence of three years; but home is changed. There used to be a feeling of mother's presence everywhere about the house, even if she were in the remotest room; but now, Susannah and Priscilla are wearing her apparel, and as they go in and out, and I catch a glimpse of the soft dove-coloured folds of the dresses, I look up with a start, half in hope of seeing my mother's face again. They are much older than I am, for Priscilla was ten years of age when I was born, and Susannah is three years older than Priscilla. They are very grave and serious, and it is well known, even in Germany, how religious they are. I suppose by the time I am as old as they are, I shall be the same.

I wonder if my father ever felt like a child; he looks as if he had lived for centuries. Last night I could not venture to look too closely into his face; but to-day I can see a very kind and peaceful expression underlying all the wrinkles and lines of care. In his soul there is a calm serene depth which no tempest can touch. That is plain. He is a good man, I know, though his goodness was not talked about at school, as was Susannah's and Priscilla's. When the coach set me down at the door, and he ran out into the street bareheaded, and took me at once into his arms, carrying me like a little child into our home, all my sorrow upon leaving my school-fellows, and the sisters, and our pastor, vanished away in the joy of being with him. God helping me— and surely he will help me to do this—I will be a comfort to my father.

The house is very different to what it was in my mother's time. The rooms look gloomy, for the walls are damp and mildewed, and the carpets are worn threadbare. It seems as if my sister had taken no pride in household matters. To be sure Priscilla is betrothed to one of the brethren, who dwells in Woodbury, about ten miles from here. She told me last night what a beautiful house he had, and how it was furnished with more luxury and costliness than our people often care for, inasmuch as we do not seek worldly show. She also displayed the fine linen she has been preparing for herself, with store of dresses, both in silks and stuffs. They looked so grand, spread out upon the poor furniture of our chamber, that I could not help but cast up in my own mind what the cost would be, and I inquired how my father's business prospered: at which Priscilla coloured, but Susannah uttered a low deep groan, which was answer enough.

This morning I unpacked my trunk, and gave a letter from the church to each of my sisters. It was to make known to them that Brother Schmidt, a missionary in the West Indies, desires that a fitting wife should be chosen for him by casting of lots, and sent out to him. Several of the single sisters in our settlement have given in their names, and such is the repute of Susannah and Priscilla, that they are notified of the application, that they may do likewise. Of course Priscilla, being already betrothed, has no thought of doing so; but Susannah has been deep in meditation all day, and now she is sitting opposite to me, pale and solemn, her brown hair, in which I can detect a silver thread or two, braided closely down her thin cheeks; but as she writes, a faint blush steals over her face, as if she were listening to Brother Schmidt, whom she has never seen, and whose voice she never heard. She has written her name—I can read it, "Susannah Fielding"—in her clear round steady hand, and it will be put into the lot with many others, from among which one will be drawn

E

out, and the name written thereon will be that of Brother
Schmidt's appointed wife.

Nov. 9. Only two days at home; but what a change there is
in me. My brain is all confusion, and it might be a hundred years
since I left school. This morning two strangers came to the house,
demanding to see my father. They were rough hard men, whose
voices sounded into my father's office, where he was busy writing,
while I sat beside the fire, engaged in household sewing. I looked
up at the loud noise of their voices, and saw him turn deadly
pale, and bow his white-haired head upon his hands. But he
went out in an instant, and returning with the strangers, bade
me go to my sisters. I found Susannah in the parlour, looking
scared and bewildered, and Priscilla in hysterics. After much
ado they grew calmer, and when Priscilla was lying quiet on the
sofa, and Susannah had sat down in mother's arm-chair to medi-
tate, I crept back to my father's office, and rapping softly at the
door, heard him say, "Come in." He was alone, and very sad.

"Father," I asked, "what is the matter?" and seeing his dear
kind face, I flew to him.

"Eunice," he whispered very tenderly, "I will tell you all."

So then as I knelt at his knee, with my eyes fastened upon his,
he told me a long history of troubles, every word of which removed my schooldays farther and farther from me, and made
them seem like the close of a finished life. The end of all was
that these men were sent by his creditors to take possession of
everything in our old home, where my mother had lived and
died.

I caught my breath at first, as if I should go into hysterics like
Priscilla, but I thought what good would that do for my father?
So after a minute or two I was able to look up again bravely into
his eyes. He then said he had his books to examine, so I kissed
him, and came away.

In the parlour Priscilla was lying still, with her eyelids closed,
and Susannah was quite lost in meditation. Neither of them
noticed me entering or departing. I went into the kitchen to
consult Jane about my father's dinner. She was rocking herself
upon a chair, and rubbing her eyes red with her rough apron;
and there in the elbow-chair which once belonged to my grandfather—all the Brethren knew George Fielding—sat one of the
strangers, wearing a shaggy brown hat, from under which he was
staring fixedly at a bag of dried herbs hanging to a hook in the

ceiling. He did not bring his eyes down, even when I entered, and stood thunderstruck upon the door-sill; but he rounded up his large mouth, as if he were going to whistle.

"Good morning, sir," I said, as soon as I recovered myself; for my father had said we must regard these men only as the human instruments permitted to bring affliction to us; "will you please to tell me your name?"

The stranger fixed his eyes steadily upon me. After which he smiled a little to himself.

"John Robins is my name," he said, "and England is my nation, Woodbury is my dwelling-place, and Christ is my salvation."

He spake in a sing-song tone, and his eyes went up again to the bag of marjoram, twinkling as if with great satisfaction; and I pondered over his reply, until it became quite a comfort to me.

"I'm very glad to hear it," I said, at last, "because we are religious people, and I was afraid you might be different."

"Oh, I'll be no kind of nuisance, miss," he answered; "you make yourselves comfortable, and only bid Maria, here, to draw me my beer regular, and I'll not hurt your feelings."

"Thank you," I said. "Jane, you hear what Mr. Robins says. Bring some sheets down to air, and make up the bed in the Brothers' chamber. You'll find a bible and hymn-book on the table there, Mr. Robins." I was leaving the kitchen, when this singular man struck his clenched fist upon the dresser, with a noise which startled me greatly.

"Miss," he said, "don't you put yourself about; and if anybody else should ever put you out, about anything, remember John Robins of Woodbury. I'm your man for anything, whether in my line or out of my line; I am, by——"

He was about to add something more, but he paused suddenly, and his face grew a little more red, as he looked up again to the ceiling. So I left the kitchen.

I have since been helping my father with his books, being very thankful that I was always quick at sums.

P.S. I dreamed that the settlement was invaded by an army of men, led by John Robins, who insisted upon becoming our pastor.

November 10. I have been a journey of fifty miles, one half of it by stage-coach. I learned for the first time that my mother's

brother, a worldly rich man, dwells fifteen miles beyond Woodbury. He does not belong to our people, and he was greatly
displeased by my mother's marriage. It also appears that Susannah and Priscilla were not my mother's own daughters. My
father had a little forlorn hope that our worldly kinsman might
be inclined to help us in our great extremity; so I went forth
with his blessings and prayers upon my errand. Brother More,
who came over to see Priscilla yesterday, met me at Woodbury
Station, and saw me safely on the coach for my uncle's village.
He is much older than I fancied; and his face is large, and coarse,
and flabby-looking. I am surprised that Priscilla should betroth
herself to him. However, he was very kind to me, and watched
the coach out of the inn-yard; but almost before he was out
of my sight, he was out of my mind, and I was considering what
I should say to my uncle.

My uncle's house stands quite alone in the midst of meadows
and groves of trees, all of which are leafless now, and waved to
and fro in the damp and heavy air, like funeral plumes. I trembled greatly as I lifted the brass knocker, which had a grinning
face upon it; and I let it fall with one loud single rap, which
set all the dogs barking, and the rooks cawing in the tops of the
trees. The servant conducted me across a low-roofed hall, to a
parlour beyond: low-roofed also, but large and handsome, with
a warm glow of crimson, which was pleasant to my eyes, after
the grey gloom of the November day. It was already afternoon;
and a tall fine-looking old man was lying comfortably upon a
sofa fast asleep; while upon the other side of the hearth sat a
dwarfed old lady, who lifted her fore-finger with a gesture of
silence, and beckoned me to take a seat near the fire. I obeyed,
and presently fell into a meditation.

At length a man's voice broke the silence, asking in a drowsy
tone,

"What young lass is this?"

"I am Eunice Fielding," I replied, rising with reverence to
the aged man, my uncle; and he gazed upon me with his keen
grey eyes, until I was abashed, and a tear or two rolled down my
cheeks in spite of myself, for my heart was very heavy.

"By Jove!" he exclaimed, "as like Sophy as two peas out of
one pod!" and he laughed a short laugh, which, in my ears,
lacked merriment. "Come here, Eunice," he added, "and kiss
me."

Whereupon I walked gravely across the open space between us, and bent my face to his; but he would have me to sit upon his knee, and I, who had been at no time used to be fondled thus, even by my father, sat there uncomfortably.

"Well, my pretty one," said my uncle, "what is your errand and request to me? Upon my soul, I feel ready to promise thee anything."

As he spake, I bethought me of King Herod, and the sinful dancing-girl, and my heart sank within me; but at last I took courage, as did Esther the queen, and I made known my urgent business to him, telling him, even with tears, that my father was threatened with a prison, if he could find none to befriend him.

"Eunice," said my uncle, after a very long silence, "I will make a bargain with you and your father. He stole away my favourite sister from me, and I never saw her face again. I've no children, and I'm a rich man. If your father will give you up to me, keeping no claim upon you—even to never seeing your face again, if I so will it—then I will pay all his debts, and adopt you as my own daughter."

Before he could finish these words, I sprang away from him, feeling more angered than I had ever done in my life.

"It could never be," I cried. "My father could never give me up, and I will never leave him."

"Be in no hurry to decide, Eunice," he said; "your father has two other daughters. I will give you an hour to reflect."

Upon that he and his wife left me alone in the pleasant room. My mind was firmly made up from the beginning. But as I sat before the glowing fire, it seemed as if all the bleak cold days of the coming winter trooped up and gathered round me, chilling the warm atmosphere of the room, and touching me with icy fingers, until I trembled like a coward. So I opened my little lot-book, which our pastor had given unto me, and I looked anxiously at the many slips of paper it contained. Many times I had drawn a lot from it, and found but vague counsel and comfort. But I now drew therefrom again, and the words upon the lot were, "Be of good courage!" Then I was greatly strengthened.

When the hour was ended, my uncle returned, and urged me with many worldly persuasions and allurements, mingled with threatenings, until at length I grew bold to answer him according to his snares.

"It is an evil thing," I said, "to tempt a child to forsake her father. Providence has put it into your power to lessen the sorrows of your fellow-creatures, but you seek to add to them. I would rather dwell with my father in a jail, than with you in a palace."

I turned and left him, finding my way out through the hall into the deepening twilight. It was more than a mile from the village through which the coach passed; and the hedge-banks rose high on each side of the deep lane. Though I walked very swiftly, the night came on before I had proceeded far from my uncle's house, with such thick gloom and fog that I could almost feel the darkness. "Be of good courage, Eunice!" said I; and to drive away the fears which lay in wait for me if I yielded but a little, I lifted up my voice, and began to sing our Evening Hymn.

Suddenly a voice a little way before me, took up the tune, in a clear deep rich tone, like that of the Brother who taught us music in the Settlement. As I stopped instantly, my heart leaping up with fear and a strange gladness, the voice before me ceased singing also.

"Good night," it said. There was such kindness and frankness and sweetness in the voice, that I trusted it at once.

"Wait for me," I said; "I am lost in the night, and I want to find my way to Longville."

"I am going there too," said the voice, to which I drew nearer each moment; and immediately I saw a tall dark figure in the mist beside me.

"Brother," I said, trembling a little, though wherefore I knew not, "are we far from Longville?"

"Only ten minutes' walk," he answered, in a blithe tone, which cheered me not a little. "Take my arm, and we shall soon be there."

As my hand rested on his arm lightly, I felt a sense of great support and protection. As we came near the lighted window of the village inn, we looked into one another's faces. His was pleasant and handsome, like some of the best pictures I have ever seen. I do not know why, but I thought of the Angel Gabriel.

"We are at Longville," he said; "tell me where I can take you to."

"Sir," I answered, for I could not say Brother to him in the light; "I wish first to get to Woodbury."

"To Woodbury," he repeated, "at this time of night, and alone! There is a return coach coming up in a few minutes, by which I travel to Woodbury. Will you accept of my escort there?"

"Sir, I thank you," I answered; and I stood silent beside him, until the coach lamps shone close upon us in the fog. The stranger opened the door, but I hung back with a foolish feeling of shame at my poverty, which it was needful to conquer.

"We are poor people," I stammered. "I must travel outside."

"Not such a winter's night as this," he said. "Jump in."

"No, no," I replied, recovering my senses, "I shall go outside." A decent country woman, with a child, were already seated on the top of the coach, and I quickly followed them. My seat was the outer one, and hung over the wheels. The darkness was so dense that the fitful glimmer of the coach-lamps upon the leafless hedge-rows was the only light to be seen. All else was black, pitchy night. I could think of nothing but my father, and the jail opening to imprison him. Presently I felt a hand laid firmly on my arm, and Gabriel's voice spake to me :

"Your seat is a dangerous one," he said. "A sudden jerk might throw you off."

"I am so miserable," I sobbed, all my courage breaking down; and in the darkness I buried my face in my hands, and wept silently; and even as I wept, the bitterness of my sorrow was assuaged.

"Brother," I said—for in the darkness I could call him so again. "I am only just come home from school, and I have not learned the ways and troubles of the world yet."

"My child," he answered, in a low tone, "I saw you lean your head upon your hands and weep. Can I be of any help to you?"

"No," I replied; "the sorrow belongs to me only, and to my house."

He said no more, but I felt his arm stretched out to form a barrier across the space where I might have fallen; and so through the black night we rode on to Woodbury.

. Brother More was awaiting me at the coach-office. He hurried me away, scarcely giving me time to glance at Gabriel, who stood looking after me. He was eager to hear of my interview with my uncle; when I told him of my failure, he grew thoughtful, saying little until I was in the railway carriage, when he leaned forward and whispered, "Tell Priscilla I will come over in the morning."

Brother More is a rich man; perhaps, for Priscilla's sake, he will free my father.

Nov. 11. I dreamed last night that Gabriel stood beside me, saying, "I come to bring thee glad tidings." But as I listened eagerly, he sighed, and vanished away.

Nov. 15. Brother More is here every day, but he says nothing about helping my father. If help does not come soon, he will be cast into prison. Peradventure, my uncle will relent, and offer us some easier terms. If it were only to live half my time with him, I would consent to dwell in his house, even as Daniel and the three children dwelt unharmed in the court of Babylon. I will write to him to that effect.

Nov. 19. No answer from my uncle. To-day, going to Woodbury with Priscilla, who wished to converse with the pastor of the church there, I spent the hour she was engaged with him in finding my way to the jail, and walking round the outside of its gloomy and massive walls. I felt very mournful and faint-hearted, thinking of my poor father. At last, being very weary, I sat down on the step at the gateway, and looked into my little lot-book again. Once more I drew the verse, "Be of good courage." Just then, Brother More and Priscilla appeared. There was a look upon his face which I disliked, but I remembered that he was to be my sister's husband, and I rose and offered him my hand, which he tucked up under his arm, his fat hand resting upon it. So we three walked to and fro under the prison walls. Suddenly, in a garden sloping away beneath us, I perceived him whom I call Gabriel (not knowing any other name), with a fair sweet-looking young woman at his side. I could not refrain from weeping, for what reason I cannot tell, unless it be my father's affairs. Brother More returned home with us, and sent John Robins away. John Robins desired me to remember him, which I will as long as I live.

Nov. 20. Most miserable day. My poor father is in jail. At dinner-time to-day two most evil-looking men arrested him. God forgive me for wishing they were dead! Yet my father spake very patiently and gently.

"Send for Brother More," he said, after a pause, "and act according to his counsel."

So after a little while they carried him away.

What am I to do?

Nov. 30. Late last night we were still discoursing as to our future plans. Priscilla thinks Brother More will hasten their marriage, and Susannah has an inward assurance that the lot will fall to her to be Brother Schmidt's wife. She spake wisely of the duties of a missionary's life, and of the grace needed to fulfil them. But I could think of nothing but my father trying to sleep within the walls of the jail.

Brother More says he thinks he can see a way to release my father, only we are all to pray that we may have grace to conquer our self-will. I am sure I am willing to do anything, even to selling myself into slavery, as some of our first missionaries did in the slave-times in the West Indies. But in England one cannot sell one's self, though I would be a very faithful servant. I want to get at once a sum large enough to pay our debts. Brother More bids me not spoil my eyes with crying.

Dec. 1. The day on which my father was arrested, I made a last appeal to my uncle. This morning I had a brief note from him, saying he had commissioned his lawyer to visit me, and state the terms on which he was willing to aid me. Even as I read it, his lawyer desired to see me alone. I went to the parlour, trembling with anxiety. It was no other than Gabriel who stood before me, and I took heart, remembering my dream that he appeared to me, saying, "I come to bring thee glad tidings."

"Miss Eunice Fielding," he said, in his pleasant voice, and looking down upon me with a smile which seemed to shed sunshine upon my sad and drooping spirit.

"Yes," I answered, my eyes falling foolishly before his; and I beckoned to him to resume his seat, while I stood leaning against my mother's great arm-chair.

"I have a hard message for you," said Gabriel; "your uncle has dictated this paper, which must be signed by you and your father. He will release Mr. Fielding, and settle one hundred pounds a year upon him, on condition that he will retire to some German Moravian settlement, and that you will accept the former terms."

"I cannot," I cried bitterly. "Oh! sir, ought I to leave my father?"

"I am afraid not," he answered, in a low voice.

"Sir," I said, "you must please say 'no' to my uncle."

"I will," he replied, "and make it sound as gently as I can. You have a friend in me, Miss Eunice."

His voice lingered upon Eunice, as if it were no common

name to him, but something rare and pleasing. I never heard it spoken so pleasantly before. After a little while he rose to take his leave.

"Brother," I said, giving him my hand, "farewell."

"I shall see you again, Miss Eunice," he answered.

He saw me again sooner than he expected, for I travelled by the next train to Woodbury, and, as I left the dark carriage in which I journeyed, I saw him alight from another part of the train, and at the same instant his eyes fell upon me.

"Where are you going to now, Eunice?" he demanded.

It seemed a pleasanter greeting than if he had called me Miss. I told him I knew my way to the jail, for that I had been not long ago to look at the outside of it. I saw the tears stand in his eyes, but, without speaking, he drew my hand through his arm, and I silently, but with a very lightened heart, walked beside him to the great portal of my father's prison.

We entered a square court, with nothing to be seen save the grey winter sky lying, as it were flat, overhead; and there was my father, pacing to and fro, with his arms crossed upon his breast and his head bowed down, as if it would never be raised again. I cried aloud, and ran and fell on his neck, and knew nothing more until I opened my eyes in a small bare room, and felt my father holding me in his arms, and Gabriel kneeling before me, chaffing my hands, and pressing his lips upon them.

Afterwards Gabriel and my father conferred together; but before long Brother More arrived, whereupon Gabriel departed. Brother More said, solemnly :

"That man is a wolf in sheep's clothing, and our Eunice is a tender lamb."

I cannot believe that Gabriel is a wolf.

Dec. 2. I have taken a room in a cottage near the jail, the abode of John Robins and his wife, a decent tidy woman. So I can spend every day with my father.

Dec. 13. My father has been in prison a whole fortnight. Brother More went over to see Priscilla last night, and this morning he is to lay before us his plan for my father's release. I am going to meet him at the jail.

When I entered the room, my father and Brother More looked greatly perturbed, and my poor father leaned back in his chair, as if exhausted after a long conflict.

"Speak to her, brother," he said.

Then Brother More told us of a heavenly vision which had appeared to him, directing him to break off his betrothal to Priscilla, and to take me—*me!*—for his wife. After which he awoke, and these words abode in his mind, "The dream is certain, and the interpretation thereof sure."

"Therefore, Eunice," he said, in an awful voice, "do you and Priscilla see to it, lest you should be found fighting against the Lord."

I was struck dumb as with a great shock, but I heard him add these words :

"I was also instructed in the vision, to set your father free, upon the day that you become my wife."

"But," I said at last, my whole heart recoiling from him, "this would be a shameful wrong to Priscilla. It cannot be a vision from Heaven, but a delusion and snare. Marry Priscilla, and set my father free? Surely, surely, it was a lying vision."

"No," he said, fastening his gaze upon me; I chose Priscilla rashly of my own judgment. Therein I erred; but I have promised her half her dowry as a compensation for my error."

"Father," I cried, "surely I ought to have some direction also. as well as he. Why should only he have a vision?" Then I added that I would go home and see Priscilla, and seek a sign for my own guidance.

December 14. Priscilla was ill in bed when I reached home, and refused to see me. I arose at five o'clock this morning, and stole down into the parlour. As I lighted the lamp, the parlour looked forlorn and deserted, and yet there lingered about it a ghostly feeling, as if perhaps my mother, and the dead children whom I never saw, had been sitting on the hearth in the night, as we sat in the daytime. Maybe she knew of my distress, and had left some tokens for my comfort and counsel. My Bible lay upon the table, but it was closed; her angel fingers had not opened it upon any verse that might have guided me. There was no mode of seeking direction, save by casting of lots.

I cut three little slips of paper of one length, and exactly similar—*three*, though surely I only needed two. Upon the first I wrote, "To be Brother More's wife," and upon the second, "To be a Single Sister." The third lay upon the desk, blank and white, as if waiting for some name to be written upon it, and suddenly all the chilly cold of the winter morning passed into a sultry heat, until I threw open the casement, and let the frosty air breathe upon my face. I said in my own heart I would leave myself a chance, though my conscience smote me for that word "chance." So I laid the three slips of paper between the leaves of my Bible, and sat down opposite to them, afraid of drawing the lot which held the secret of my future life.

There was no mark to guide me in the choice of one slip of paper from another; and I dared not stretch out my hand to draw one of them. For I was bound to abide by the solemn decision. It seemed too horrible to become Brother More's wife; and to me the Sister's Home, where the Single Sisters dwell, having all things in common, seems dreary and monotonous and somewhat desolate. But if I should draw the blank paper! My heart fluttered; again and again I stretched out my hand, and withdrew it; until at last the oil in the lamp being spent, its light grew dimmer, and dimmer, and, fearful of being still longer without guidance, I snatched the middle lot from between the leaves of my Bible. There was only a glimmer of dying light, by which I read the words, "To be Brother More's wife."

That is the last entry in my journal, written three years ago.

When Susannah came down stairs and entered the parlour, she found me sitting before my desk, almost in an idiotic state, with that miserable lot in my hand. There was no need to explain it to her; she looked at the other slip of paper, one blank, and the other inscribed, "To be a Single Sister," and she knew I had been casting lots. I remember her crying over me a little, and kissing me with unaccustomed tenderness; and then she returned to her chamber, and I heard her speaking to Priscilla in grave and sad tones. After that, we were all passive; even Priscilla was stolidly resigned. Brother More came over, and Susannah informed him of the irrevocable lot which I had drawn; but besought him to refrain from seeing me that day; and he left me alone to grow somewhat used to the sense of my wretchedness.

Early the next morning I returned to Woodbury; my only consolation being the thought that my dear father would be set free, and might live with me in wealth and comfort all the rest of his life. During the succeeding days I scarcely left his side, never suffering Brother More to be alone with me; and morning and night John Robins or his wife accompanied me to the gate of the jail, and waited for me to return with them to their cottage.

My father was to be set free, only on my wedding-day, and the marriage was hurried on. Many of Priscilla's store of wedding garments were suitable for me. Every hour brought my doom nearer.

One morning, in the gloom and twilight of a December dawn, I suddenly met Gabriel in my path. He spake rapidly and earnestly, but I scarcely knew what he said, and I answered, falteringly.

"I am going to be married to Brother Joshua More on New Year's-day, and he will then release my father."

"Eunice," he cried, standing before me in the narrow path, "you can never marry him. I knew the fat hypocrite. Good Heaven! I love you a hundred times better than he does. Love! The rascal does not know what it means."

I answered him not a word, for I felt afraid both of myself and him, though I did not believe Gabriel to be a wolf in sheep's clothing.

"Do you know who I am?" he asked.

"No," I whispered.

"I am your uncle's nephew by marriage," he said, "and I have been brought up in his house. Break off this wicked marriage with the fellow More, and I will engage to release your father. I am young, and can work. I will pay your father's debts."

"It is impossible," I replied. "Brother More has had a heavenly vision, and I have drawn the lot. There is no hope. I must marry him upon New Year's-day."

Then Gabriel persuaded me to tell him the whole story of my trouble. He laughed a little, and bade me be of good comfort; and I could not make him understand how impossible it was that I should contend against the dispensation of the lot.

Always when I was with my father I strove to conceal my misery, talking to him of the happy days we should spend together some time. Likewise I sang within the walls of the prison, the simple hymns which we had been wont to sing in the peaceful church at school amid a congregation of serene hearts, and I strengthened my own heart and my father's by the recollected counsels of my dear lost pastor. Thus my father guessed little of my hidden suffering, and looked forward with hope to the day that would throw open his prison doors.

Once I went to the pastor, dwelling in Woodbury, and poured out my heart to him—save that I made no mention of Gabriel—and he told me it was often thus with young girls before their marriage, but that I had a clear leading; he also told me that

Brother More was a devout man, and I should soon love and reverence him as my husband.

At length the last day of the year came; a great day among our people, when we drew our lot for the following year. Everything seemed at an end. All hope fled from me, if there ever had been any hope in my heart. I left my father early in the evening, for I could no longer conceal my wretchedness; yet when I was outside the prison walls I wandered to and fro, hovering about it, as if these days, miserable as they had been, were happy to those which were drawing near. Brother More had not been near us all day, but doubtless he was busy in his arrangements to release my father. I was still lingering under the great walls, when a carriage drove up noiselessly—for the ground was sprinkled with soft snow—and Gabriel sprang out, and almost grasped me in his arms.

"My dear Eunice," he said, "you must come with me at once. Our uncle will save you from this hateful marriage."

I do not know what I should have done had not John Robins called out from the driver's seat, "All right, Miss Eunice; remember John Robins."

Upon that I left myself in Gabriel's hands, and he lifted me into the carriage, wrapping warm coverings about me. It seemed to me no other than a happy dream, as we drove noiselessly along snowy roads, with the pale wan light of the young moon falling upon the white country, and now and then shining upon the face of Gabriel, as he leaned forward from time to time to draw the wrappers closer round me.

We might have been three hours on the way, when we turned into a by-road, which presently I recognised as the deep lane wherein I had first met Gabriel. We were going then to my uncle's house. So with a lightened heart I stepped out of the carriage, and entered his doors for the second time.

Gabriel conducted me into the parlour which I had seen before, and placed me in a chair upon the hearth, removing my shawl and bonnet with a pleasant and courteous care; and he was standing opposite to me, regarding me with a smile upon his handsome face, when the door opened and my uncle entered.

"Come and kiss me, Eunice," he said; and I obeyed him wonderingly.

"Child," he continued, stroking my hair back from my face, "you would not come to me of your own will, so I commissioned this young fellow to kidnap you. We are not going to have you marry Joshua More. I cannot do with him as my nephew. Let him marry Priscilla."

There was such a hearty tone in my uncle's voice, that for a moment I felt comforted, though I knew that he could not set aside my lot. So he seated me beside him, while I still looked with wonderment into his face.

"I am going to draw a lot for you," he said, with an air of merriment; "what would my little rosebud say to her fat suitor, if she knew that her father was a freed man at this moment?"

I dared not look into his face or into Gabriel's. For I remembered that I myself had sought for a token; and that no earthly power could set aside that, or the heavenly vision also, which Brother More had seen.

"Uncle," I said, shuddering, "I have no voice in this matter. I drew the lot fairly, and I must abide by it. You cannot help me."

"We will see," he answered; "it is New Year's-eve, you know, and time to draw again. The lot will neither be to become Brother More's wife, nor a Single Sister, I promise you. We shall draw the blank this time!"

While I yet wondered at these words, I heard a sound of footsteps on the hall, and the door opened, and my beloved father stood upon the threshold, stretching out his arms to me. How he came there I knew not; but I flew to him with a glad cry, and hid my face upon his breast.

"You are welcome, Mr. Fielding," said my uncle; "Phil!"— it did now appear that Gabriel's name was Philip—"bring Mr. More this way."

I started with fright and wonder, and my father also looked troubled, and drew me nearer to his side. Brother More entered with a cowardly and downcast mien, which made him appear a hundred-fold more repulsive in my eyes, as he stood near the door, with his craven face turned towards us.

"Mr. More," said my uncle, "I believe you are to marry my niece, Eunice Fielding, to-morrow?"

"I did not know she was your niece," he answered, in an abject tone. "I would not have presumed——"

"But the heavenly vision, Mr. More?" interrupted my uncle.

He looked round for a moment, with a spiritless glance, and his eyes sank.

"It was a delusion," he muttered.

"It was a lie!" said Gabriel.

"Mr. More," continued my uncle, "if the heavenly vision be true, it will cost you the sum of five thousand five hundred pounds, the amount in which you are indebted to me, with sundry sums due to my nephew here. Yet if it be true, you must abide by it, of course."

"It was not true," he answered; "the vision was concerning Priscilla, to whom I was betrothed. I was ensnared to change the name to that of Eunice."

"Then go and marry Priscilla," said my uncle, good humouredly. "Philip, take him away."

But Priscilla would have no more to do with Brother More, and shortly afterwards she settled among the Single Sisters in the same settlement where I had lived my quiet and peaceful youth. Her store of wedding garments, which had been altered to fit me, came in at last for Susannah, who was chosen to be the wife of Brother Schmidt, according to her inward assurance; and she went out to join him in the West Indies, from whence she writes many happy letters. I was troubled for a time about my lot, but certainly if Brother More's vision was concerning Priscilla, I could not be required to abide by it. Moreover, I never saw him again. My uncle and father, who had never met before, formed a close friendship, and my uncle would hear of nothing but that we should dwell together in his large mansion, where I might be as a daughter unto both of them. People say we have left the Church of the United Brethren; but it is not so. Only, as I had found one evil man within it, so also I have found some good men without it.

Gabriel is not one of the Brethren.

V

TO BE TAKEN IN WATER

Minnie, my blessed little wife, and I, had been just one month married. We had returned only two days from our honeymoon tour at Killarney. I was a junior partner in the firm of Schwarzmoor and Laddock, bankers, Lombard-street (I must conceal real names), and I had four days more of my leave of absence still to enjoy. I was supremely happy in my bright new cottage south-west of London, and was revelling in delicious idleness on that bright October morning, watching the great yellow leaves fall in the sunshine. Minnie sat by me under the hawthorn-tree; otherwise, I should *not* have been supremely happy.

Little Betsy, Minnie's maid, came fluttering down the garden with an ominous-looking letter in her hand.

It was a telegram from Mr. Schwarzmoor. It contained only these words:

"We want you to start to the Continent directly with specie. Neapolitan loan. No delay. Transactions of great importance since you left. Sorry to break up your holiday. Be at office by 6.30. Start from London Bridge by 9.15, and catch Dover night boat."

"Is the boy gone?"

"Boy did not leave it, sir. Elderly gentleman, going to Dawson's, brought it. The office boy was out, and the gentleman happened to be coming past our house."

"Herbert dear, you won't go, you mustn't go," said Minnie, leaning on my shoulder, and bending down her face. "Don't go."

"I must, my dearest. The firm has no one to trust to, but me, in such a case. It is but a week's absence. I must start in ten minutes, and catch the 4.20 on its way up."

"That was a very important telegram," I said sharply to the station-master, "and you ought not to have sent it by any unknown and unauthorised person. Who *was* this old gentleman, pray?"

"Who was it, Harvey?" said the station-master, rather sulkily, to the porter.

"Old gent, sir, very respectable, as comes to the Dawsons', the training-stables. Has horses there."

"Do not let that sort of thing occur again, Mr. Jennings," I said, "or I shall be obliged to report it. I wouldn't have had that telegram mislaid, for a hundred pounds."

Mr. Jennings, the station-master, grumbled something, and then boxed the telegraph boy's ears. Which seemed to do him (Mr. Jennings) good.

"We were getting very anxious," said Mr. Schwarzmoor, as I entered the bank parlour, only three minutes late. "Very anxious, weren't we, Goldrick?"

F

"Very anxious," said the little neat head clerk. "Very anxious."

Mr. Schwarzmoor was a full faced man of about sixty, with thick white eyebrows and a red face—a combination which gave him an expression of choleric old age. He was a shrewd severe man of business: a little impetuous and fond of rule, but polite, kind, and considerate.

"I hope your charming wife is quite well. Sorry, indeed, to break up your holiday; but no help for it, my dear fellow. There is the specie in those two iron boxes, enclosed in leather to look like samples. They are fastened with letter-locks and contain a quarter of a million in gold. The Neapolitan king apprehends a rebellion." (It was three years before Garibaldi's victories.) "You will take the money to Messrs. Pagliavicini and Rossi, No. 172 Toledo, Naples. The names that open the locks are, on the one with the white star on the cover, Masinisa; on the one with the black star, Cotopaxo. Of course you will not forget the talismanic words. Open the boxes at Lyons, to make sure that all is safe. Talk to no one. Make no friends on the road. Your commission is of vast importance."

"I shall pass," said I, "for a commercial traveller."

"Pardon me for my repeated cautions, Blamyre, but I am an older man than you, and know the danger of travelling with specie. If your purpose was known to-night in Paris, your road to Marseilles would be as dangerous as if all the galley-slaves at Toulon had been let loose in special chase of you. I do not doubt your discretion: I only warn you to be careful. Of course, you go armed?"

I opened my coat, and showed a belt under my waistcoat, with a revolver in it. At which war-like spectacle the old clerk drew back in alarm.

"Good!" said Mr. Schwarzmoor. "But one grain of prudence is worth five times the five bullets in those five barrels. You will stop in Paris to-morrow to transact business with Lefebre and Desjeans, and you will go on by the 12.15 (night) to Marseilles, catching the boat on Friday. We will telegraph to you at Marseilles. Are the letters for Paris ready, Mr. Hargrave?"

"Yes, sir, nearly ready. Mr. Wilkins is hard at them."

I reached Dover by midnight, and instantly engaged four porters to carry my specie chests down the stone steps leading from the pier to the Calais boat. The first was taken on board quite safely; but while the second was being carried down, one of the men slipped, and would certainly have fallen into the water, had he not been caught in the arms of a burly old Indian officer, who, laden with various traps, and urging forward his good-natured but rather vulgar wife, was preceding me.

"Steady there, my lad," he said. "Why, what have you got there? Hardware?"

"Don't know, sir; I only know it's heavy enough to break any man's back," was the rough answer, as the man thanked his questioner in his blunt way.

"These steps, sir, are very troublesome for bringing down heavy goods," said an obliging voice behind me. "I presume, sir, from your luggage, that we are of the same profession?"

I looked round as we just then stepped on board. The person who addressed me was a tall thin man, with a long and rather Jewish nose, and a narrow elongated face. He wore a greatcoat too short for him, a flowered waistcoat, tight trousers, a high shirt collar, and a light sprigged stiff neckcloth.

I replied that I *had* the honour to be a commercial traveller, and that I thought we were going to have a rough night of it.

"Decidedly dirty night," he replied; "and I advise you, sir, to secure a berth at once. The boat, I see, is very crowded."

I went straight to my berth, and lay down for an hour; at the end of that time I got up and looked around me. At one of the small tables sat half a dozen of the passengers, including the old Indian and my old-fashioned interrogator. They were drinking bottled porter, and appeared very sociable. I rose and joined them, and we exchanged some remarks not complimentary to night travelling.

"By Jove, sir, it is simply unbearable!" said the jovial Major Baxter (for he soon told us his name); "it is as stifling as Peshawah when the hot Tinsang wind is blowing; suppose we three go on deck and take a little air? My wife suffers in these crossings; she's invisible, I know, till the boat stops. Steward, bring up some more bottled porter."

When we got on deck, I saw, to my extreme surprise, made conspicuous by their black and white stars, four other cases exactly similar to mine, except that they had no painted brand upon them. I could hardly believe my eyes; but there they were; leather covers, letter-locks, and all.

"Those are mine, sir," remarked Mr. Levison (I knew my

fellow-commercial's name from the captain's having addressed him by it). "I am travelling for the house of Mackintosh. Those cases contain waterproof paletots, the best made. Our house has used such cases for forty years. It is sometimes inconvenient, this accidental resemblance of luggage—leads to mistakes. Your goods are much heavier than my goods, as I judge? Gas improvements, railway chairs, cutlery, or something else in iron?"

I was silent, or I made some vague reply.

"Sir," said Levison, "I augur well of your future; trade secrets should be kept inviolate. Don't you think so, sir?"

The major thus appealed to, replied, "Sir, by Jove, you're right! One cannot be too careful in these days. Egad, sir, the world is a mass of deceit."

"There's Calais light!" cried some one at that moment; and there it was, straight ahead, casting sparkles of comfort over the dark water.

I thought no more of my travelling companions. We parted at Paris: I went my way and they went their way. The major was going to pay a visit at Dromont, near Lyons; thence he would go to Marseilles en route for Alexandria. Mr. Levison was bound for Marseilles, like myself and the major, but not by my train—at least he feared not—as he had much to do in Paris.

I had transacted my business in the French capital, and was on my way to the Palais Royal, with M. Lefebre fils, a great friend of mine. It was about six o'clock, and we were crossing the Rue St. Honoré, when there passed us a tall Jewish-looking person, in a huge white mackintosh, whom I recognised as Mr. Levison. He was in a hired open carriage, and his four boxes were by his side. I bowed to him, but he did not seem to notice me.

"Eh bien! That drôle, who is that?" said my friend, with true Parisian superciliousness.

I replied that it was only a fellow-passenger, who had crossed with me the night before.

In the very same street I ran up against the major and his wife, on their way to the railway station.

"Infernal city, this," said the major; "smells so of onion. I should like, if it was mine, to wash it out, house by house; 'tain't wholesome, 'pon my soul 'tain't wholesome. Julia, my dear, this is my pleasant travelling companion of last night. By-the-by, just saw that commercial traveller! Sharp business man that: no sight-seeing about *him*. Bourse and Bank all day,—senior partner some day."

"And how many more?" said my friend Lefebre, when we shook hands and parted with the jolly major. "That is a good boy—he superabounds—he overflows—but he is one of your epicurean lazy officers, I am sure. Your army, it must be re-formed, or India will slip from you like a handful of sand— vous verrez, mon cher."

Midnight came, and I was standing at the terminus, watching the transport of my luggage, when a cab drove up, and an Englishman leaping out asked the driver in excellent French for change for a five-franc piece. It was Levison; but I saw no more of him, for the crowd just then pushed me forward.

I took my seat with only two other persons in the carriage— two masses of travelling cloak and capote—two bears, for all I could see to the contrary.

Once away from the lights of Paris, and in the pitch dark country, I fell asleep and dreamed of my dear little wife, and our dear little home. Then a feeling of anxiety ran across my mind. I dreamed that I had forgotten the words with which to open the letter-locks. I ransacked mythology, history, science, in vain. Then I was in the banking parlour at No. 172 Toledo, Naples, threatened with instant death by a file of soldiers, if I did not reveal the words, or explain where the boxes had been hid; for I had hidden them for some inscrutable no reason. At that moment an earthquake shook the city, a flood of fire rolled past beneath the window, Vesuvius had broken loose and was upon us. I cried in my agony—"Gracious Heaven, reveal to me those words!" when I awoke.

"Dromont! Dromont! Dix minutes d'arrête, messieurs."

Half blinded with the sudden light, I stumbled to the buffet, and asked for a cup of coffee, when three or four noisy young English tourists came hurrying in, surrounding a quiet imperturbable elderly commercial traveller. It was actually Levison again! They led him along in triumph, and called for champagne.

"Yes! yes!" the leader said. "You must have some, old fellow. We have won three games, you know, and you held such cards, too. Come along, look alive, you fellow with the nightcap— Cliquot—gilt top, you duffer. You shall have your revenge before we get to Lyons, old chap."

Levison chattered good humouredly about the last game, and took the wine. In a few minutes the young men had drunk their champagne, and had gone out to smoke. In another moment Levison caught my eye.

"Why, good gracious," he said, "who'd have thought of this! Well, I am glad to see you. Now, my dear sir, you must have some champagne with me. Here, another bottle, monsieur, if you please. I hope, long before we get to Lyons, to join you, my dear sir. I am tired of the noise of those youngsters. Besides, I object to high stakes, on principle."

The moment the waiter brought the champagne, Levison took the bottle.

"No," he said; "I never allow any one to open wine for me." He turned his back from me to remove the wire; removed it; and was filling my glass; when up dashed a burly hearty man to shake hands with me—so awkward in his heartiness that he broke the champagne bottle. Not a drop of the wine was saved. It was the major—hot as usual, and in a tremendous bustle.

"By Jove, sir; dooced sorry. Let me order another bottle. How are you, gentlemen? Lucky, indeed, to meet you both again. Julia's with the luggage. We can be very cozy together. More champagne here. What's the bottle in French? Most shameful thing! Those French friends of Julia's were gone off to Biarritz, pretending to have forgotten that we were coming—after six weeks with us in London, too! Precious shabby, not to put too fine a point upon it. By Jove, sir, there's the bell. We'll all go in the same carriage. They will not bring that champagne."

Levison looked rather annoyed. "I shall not see you," he said, "for a station or two. I must join those boys, and let them give me my revenge. Cleared me out of twenty guineas! I have not been so imprudent since I was first on the road. Good-bye, Major Baxter—good-bye, Mr. Blamyre!"

I wondered how this respectable old fellow, who so keenly relished his game at whist, had got hold of my name; but I remembered in a moment that he must have seen the direction on my luggage.

Flashes of crimson and green lights, a shout from some pointsman, a glimpse of rows of poplars, and lines of suburban houses, and we once more plunged into the yielding darkness.

I found the major very droll and pleasant, but evidently ruled by his fussy, good-natured, managing, masculine wife. He was full of stories of bungalows, compounds, and the hills; in all of which narrations he was perpetually interrupted by Mrs. Baxter.

"By Jove, sir!" he said, "I wish I could sell out, and go into your line of business. I am almost sick of India—it deranges one's liver so infernally."

"Now, John, how can you go on so! You know you never had a day's illness in all your life, except that week when you smoked out a whole box of Captain Mason's cheroots."

"Well, I pulled through it, Julia," said the major, striking himself a tremendous blow on the chest; "but I've been an unlucky devil as to promotion—always bad luck in everything. If I bought a horse, it made a point of going lame next day; never went in a train but it broke down."

"Now don't, John; pray don't go on so," said Mrs. Baxter, "or I shall really be very angry. Such nonsense! You'll get your step in time. Be patient, like me, major; take things more quietly. I hope you put a direction on that hat-box of yours? Where is the sword-case? If it wasn't for me, major, you'd get to Suez with nothing but the coat on your back."

Just then, the train stopped at Charmont, and in tripped Levison, with his white mackintosh over his arm, and his bundle of umbrellas and sticks.

"No more sovereign points for me!" he said, producing a pack of cards. "But if you and the major and Mrs. Baxter would like a rubber—shilling points—I'm for you. Cut for partners."

We assented with pleasure. We cut for partners. I and Mrs. Baxter against the major and Levison. We won nearly every game. Levison played too cautiously, and the major laughed, talked, and always forgot what cards were out.

Still it killed the time; the red and black turned up, changed, and ran into remarkable sequences; and the major's flukes and extraordinary luck in holding (not in playing) cards amused us, we laughed at Levison's punctilious care, and at Mrs. Baxter's avarice for tricks, and were as pleasant a party as the dim lamp of a night-train ever shone on. I could think of little, nevertheless, but my precious boxes.

There we were rushing through France, seeing nothing, heeding nothing, and having as little to do with our means of transit as if we had been four Arabian princes, seated on a flying enchanted carpet.

The game gradually grew more intermittent, the conversation

more incessant. Levison, stiff of neckcloth as ever, and imperturbable and punctilious as ever, became chatty. He grew communicative about his business.

"I have at last," he said, in his precise and measured voice, "after years of attention to the subject, discovered the great secret which the waterproofers have so long coveted; how to let out the heated air of the body, and yet at the same time to exclude the rain. On my return to London, I offer this secret to the Mackintosh firm for ten thousand pounds; if they refuse the offer, I at once open a shop in Paris, call the new fabric Magentosh, in honour of the emperor's great Italian victory, and sit down and quietly realise a cool million—that's my way!"

"That's the real business tone," said the major, admiringly.

"Ah, major," cried his wife, ever ready to improve a subject, "if you had only had a little of Mr. Levison's prudence and energy, then, indeed, you'd have been colonel of your regiment before this."

Mr. Levison then turned the conversation to the subject of locks.

"I always use the letter-lock myself," he said. "My two talismanic words are TURLURETTE and PAPAGAYO—two names I once heard in an old French farce—who could guess them? It would take the adroitest thief seven hours to decipher even one. You find letter-locks safe, sir?" (He turned to me.)

I replied dryly that I did, and asked what time our train was due at Lyons.

"We are due at Lyons at 4.30," said the major; "it is now five to four. I don't know how it is, but I have a sort of presentiment to-night of some break-down. I am always in for it. When I went tiger-hunting, it was always my elephant that the beast pinned. If some of us were ordered up to an unhealthy out-of-the-way fort, it was always my company. It may be superstitious, I own, but I feel we shall have a break-down before we get to Marseilles. How fast we're going! Only see how the carriage rocks!"

I unconsciously grew nervous, but I concealed it. Could the major be a rogue, planning some scheme against me? But no: his red bluff face, and his clear good-natured guileless eyes, refuted the suspicion.

"Nonsense, be quiet, major; that's the way you always make a journey disagreeable," said his wife, arranging herself for sleep.

Then Levison began talking about his early life, and how, in George the Fourth's time, he was travelling for a cravat house in Bond-street. He grew eloquent in favour of the old costume.

"Low Radical fellows," he said, "run down the first gentleman in Europe, as he was justly called. I respect his memory. He was a wit, and the friend of wits; he was lavishly generous, and disdained poor pitiful economy. He dressed well, sir; he looked well, sir; he was a gentleman of perfect manners. Sir, this is a slovenly and shabby age. When I was young, no gentleman ever travelled without at least two dozen cravats, four whalebone stiffeners, and an iron to smooth the tie, and produce a thin equal edge to the muslin. There were no less, sir, than eighteen modes of putting on the cravat; there was the cravate à la Diane, the cravate à l'Anglaise, the cravate au næud Gordien, the cravate——"

The train jolted, moved on, slackened, stopped.

The major thrust his head out of the window, and shouted to a passing guard :

"Where are we?"

"Twenty miles from Lyons—Fort Rouge, monsieur."

"What is the matter? Anything the matter?"

An English voice answered from the next window :

"A wheel broken, they tell us. We shall have to wait two hours, and transfer the luggage."

"Good Heaven !" I could not help exclaiming.

Levison put his head out of window. "It is but too true," he said, drawing it in again; "two hours' delay at least, the man says. Tiresome, very—but such things will happen on the road; take it coolly. We'll have some coffee and another rubber. We must each look to our own luggage; or, if Mr. Blamyre goes in and orders supper, I'll see to it all. But, good gracious, what is that shining out there by the station lamps? Hei, Monsieur !" (to a passing gendarme whom the major had hailed), "what is going on at the station?"

"Monsieur," said the gendarme, saluting, "those are soldiers of the First Chasseurs; they happened to be at the station on their way to Châlons; the station-master has sent them to surround the luggage-van, and see to the transfer of the baggage. No passenger is to go near it, as there are government stores of value in the train."

Levison spat on the ground and muttered execrations to himself :—I supposed at French railways.

"By Jove, sir, did you ever see such clumsy carts?" said Major Baxter, pointing to two country carts, each with four strong horses, that were drawn up under a hedge close to the station; for we had struggled on as far as the first turn-table, some hundred yards from the first houses of the village of Fort Rouge.

Levison and I tried very hard to get near our luggage, but the soldiers sternly refused our approach. It gave me some comfort, however, to see my chests transferred carefully, with many curses on their weight. I saw no sign of government stores, and I told the major so.

"Oh, they're sharp," he replied, "dooced sharp. Maybe the empress's jewels—one little package only, perhaps; but still not difficult to steal in a night confusion."

Just then there was a shrill piercing whistle, as if a signal. The horses in the two carts tore into a gallop, and flew out of sight.

"Savages, sir; mere barbarians still," exclaimed the major; "unable to use railways even now we've given them to them."

"Major!" said his wife, in a voice of awful reproof, "spare the feelings of these foreigners, and remember your position as an officer and a gentleman."

The major rubbed his hands, and laughed uproariously.

"A pack of infernal idiots," cried Levison; "they can do nothing without soldiers; soldiers here, soldiers there, soldiers everywhere."

"Well, these precautions are sometimes useful, sir," said Mrs. B.; "France is a place full of queer characters. The gentleman next you any day at a table d'hôte may be a returned convict. Major, you remember that case at Cairo three years ago?"

"Cairo, Julia my dear, is not in France."

"I know that, major, I hope. But the house was a French hotel, and that's the same thing." Mrs. B. spoke sharply.

"I shall have a nap, gentlemen. For my part, I'm tired," said the major, as we took our places in the Marseilles train, after three hours' tedious delay. "The next thing will be the boat breaking down, I suppose."

"Major, you wicked man, don't fly out against Providence," said his wife.

Levison grew eloquent again about the Prince Regent, his diamond epaulettes, and his inimitable cravats; but Levison's words seemed to lengthen, and gradually became inaudible to me, until I heard only a soothing murmur, and the rattle and jar of the wheels.

Again my dreams were nervous and uneasy. I imagined I was in Cairo, threading narrow dim streets, where the camels jostled me and the black slaves threatened me, and the air was heavy with musk, and veiled faces watched me from latticed casements above. Suddenly a rose fell at my feet. I looked up, and a face like my Minnie's, only with large liquid dark eyes like an antelope's, glanced forth from behind a water-vase and smiled. At that moment, four Mamelukes appeared, riding down the street at full gallop, and came upon me with their sabres flashing. I dreamed I had only one hope, and that was to repeat the talismanic words of my letter-locks. Already I was under the hoofs of the Mamelukes' horses. I cried out with great difficulty, "Cotopaxo! Cotopaxo!" A rough shake awoke me. It was the major, looking bluff but stern.

"Why, you're talking in your sleep!" he said, "why the devil do you talk in your sleep? Bad habit. Here we are at the breakfast-place."

"What was I talking about?" I asked, with ill-concealed alarm.

"Some foreign gibberish," returned the major.

"Greek, I think," said Levison; "but I was just off too."

We reached Marseilles. I rejoiced to see its almond-trees and its white villas. I should feel safer when I was on board ship, and my treasure with me. I was not of a suspicious temperament, but I had thought it remarkable that during that long journey from Lyons to the seaboard, I had never fallen asleep without waking and finding an eye upon me—either the major's or his wife's. Levison had slept during the last four hours incessantly. Latterly, we had all of us grown silent, and even rather sullen. Now we brightened up.

"Hôtel de Londres! Hôtel de l'Univers! Hôtel Impérial!" cried the touts, as we stood round our luggage, agreeing to keep together.

"Hôtel Impérial, of course," said the major; "best house."

A one-eyed saturnine half-caste tout shrunk up to us.

"Hôtel Impérial, sare. I am Hôtel Impérial; all full; not a bed; no—pas de tout—no use, sare!"

"Hang it! the steamer will be the next thing to fail."

"Steamer, sare—accident with boiler; won't start till minuit et vingt minutes—half-past midnight, sare."

"Where shall we go?" said I, turning round and smiling at the three blank faces of my companions. "Our journey seems doomed to be unlucky. Let us redeem it by a parting supper. My telegraphing done, I am free till half-past eleven."

"I will take you," said Levison, "to a small but very decent hotel down by the harbour. The Hôtel des Etrangers."

"Curséd low nasty crib—gambling place!" said the major, lighting a cheroot, as he got into an open fly.

Mr. Levison drew himself up in his punctilious way. "Sir," he said, "the place is in new hands, or I would not have recommended the house, you may rely upon it."

"Sir," said the major, lifting his broad-brimmed white hat, "I offer you my apologies. I was not aware of that."

"My dear sir, never mention the affair again."

"Major, you're a hot-headed simpleton," were Mrs. B.'s last words, as we drove off together.

As we entered a bare-looking salon with a dinner-table in the middle and a dingy billiard-table at one end, the major said to me, "I shall go and wash and dress for the theatre, and then take a stroll while you do your telegraphing. Go up first, Julia, and see the rooms."

"What slaves we poor women are!" said Mrs. B., as she sailed out.

"And I," said Levison, laying down his railway rug, "shall go out and try and do some business before the shops shut. We have agents here in the Canebière."

"Only two double-bedded rooms, sare," said the one-eyed tout, who stood over the luggage.

"That will do," said Levison, promptly, and with natural irritation at our annoyances. "My friend goes by the boat to-night; he does not sleep here. His luggage can be put in my room, and he can take the key, in case he comes in first."

"Then now we are all right," said the major. "So far, so good!"

When I got to the telegraph-office, I found a telegram from London awaiting me. To my surprise and horror, it contained only these words:

"You are in great danger. Do not wait a moment on shore. There is a plot against you. Apply to the prefect for a guard."

It must be the major, and I was in his hands! That rough hearty manner of his was all a trick. Even now, he might be carrying off the chests. I telegraphed back:

"Safe at Marseilles. All right up to this."

Thinking of the utter ruin of our house if I were robbed, and of dear Minnie, I flew back to the hotel, which was situated in a dirty narrow street near the harbour. As I turned down the street, a man darted from a doorway and seized my arm. It was one of the waiters. He said hurriedly, in French: "Quick, quick, monsieur; Major Baxter is anxious to see you, instantly, in the salon. There is no time to lose."

I ran to the hotel, and darted into the salon. There was the major pacing up and down in extraordinary excitement; his wife was looking anxiously out of window. The manner of both was entirely changed. The major ran up and seized me by the hand. "I am a detective officer, and my name is Arnott," he said. "That man Levison is a notorious thief. He is at this moment in his room, opening one of your specie chests. You must help me to nab him. I knew his little game, and have check-mated him. But I wanted to catch him in the act. Julia, finish that brandy-and-water while Mr. Blamyre and myself transact our business. Have you got a revolver, Mr. Blamyre, in case he shows fight? I prefer this." (He pulled out a staff.)

"I have left my revolver in the bedroom," I breathlessly exclaimed.

"That's bad; never mind, he is not likely to hit us in the flurry. He may not even think of it. You must rush at the door at the same moment as I do. These foreign locks are never any good. It's No. 15. Gently!"

We came to the door. We listened a moment. We could hear the sound of money clinking in a bag. Then a low dry laugh, as Levison chuckled over the word he had heard me utter in my sleep. "Cotopaxo—ha! ha!"

The major gave the word, and we both rushed at the door. It shook, splintered, was driven in. Levison, revolver in hand, stood over the open box, ankle deep in gold. He had already filled a huge digger's belt that was round his waist, and a courier's bag that hung at his side. A carpet-bag, half-full, lay at his feet, and, as he let it fall to open the window bolt, it gushed forth a perfect torrent of gold. He did not utter a word. There were ropes at the window, as if he had been lowering, or preparing to lower, bags into the side alley. He gave a whistle, and some vehicle could be heard to drive furiously off.

"Surrender, you gallows-bird! I know you," cried the major. "Surrender! I've got you now, old boy."

Levison's only reply was to pull the trigger of the revolver; fortunately, there was no discharge. I had forgotten to cap it.

"The infernal thing is not capped. One for you, Bobby," he said quietly. Then hurling it at the major with a sudden fury, he threw open the window and leaped out.

I leaped after him—it was a ground floor room—raising a hue and cry. Arnott remained to guard the money.

A moment more and a wild rabble of soldiers, sailors, mongrel idlers, and porters, were pursuing the flying wretch with screams and hoots, as in the dim light (the lamps were just beginning to be kindled) we tore after him, doubling and twisting like a hare, among the obstacles that crowded the quay. Hundreds of blows were aimed at him; hundreds of hands were stretched to seize him; he wrested himself from one; he felled another; he leaped over a third; a Zouave's clutch was all but on him, when suddenly his foot caught in a mooring-ring, and he fell headlong into the harbour. There was a shout as he splashed and disappeared in the dark water, near which the light of only one lamp moved and glittered. I ran down the nearest steps and waited while the gendarmes took a boat and stolidly dragged with hooks for the body.

"They are foxes, these old thieves. I remember this man here at Toulon. I saw him branded. I knew his face again in a moment. He has dived under the shipping, got into some barge and hid. You'll never see him again," said an old grey gendarme who had taken me into the boat.

"Yes we shall, for here he is!" cried a second, stooping down and lifting a body out of the water by the hair.

"Oh, he *was* an artful file," said a man from a boat behind us. It was Arnott. "Just came to see how you were getting on, sir. It's all right with the money; Julia's minding it. I often said that fellow would catch it some day, now he's got it. He all but had you, Mr. Blamyre. He'd have cut your throat when you were asleep, rather than miss the money. But I was on his track. He didn't know me. This was my first cruise for some time against this sort of rogue. Well; his name is off the books; that's one good thing. Come, comrades, bring that body to land. We must strip him of the money he has upon him, which at least did one good thing while in his possession—it sent that scoundrel to the bottom."

Even in death, the long face looked craftily respectable when we turned it to the lamp-light.

Arnott told me all, in his jovial way, on my return to the hotel, where I loaded him and Mrs. B. (another officer) with thanks. On the night I started, he had received orders from the London head office to follow me, and watch Levison. He had not had time to communicate with my partners. The driver of our train had been bribed to make the engine break down at Fort Rouge, where Levison's accomplices were waiting with carts to carry off the luggage in the confusion and darkness, or even during a sham riot and fight. This plan Arnott had frustrated by getting the police to telegraph from Paris, for soldiers to be sent from Lyons, and be kept in readiness, at the station. The champagne he spilt had been drugged. Levison, defeated in his first attempt, had then resolved to try other means. My unlucky disclosure of the mystery of the letter-lock had furnished him with the power of opening that one chest. The break-down of the steamer, which was accidental (as far as could ever be ascertained), gave him a last opportunity.

That night, thanks to Arnott, I left Marseilles with not one single piece of money lost. The journey was prosperous. The loan was effected on very profitable terms. Our house has flourished ever since, and Minnie and I have flourished likewise—and increased.

VI

TO BE TAKEN WITH A GRAIN OF SALT

I have always noticed a prevalent want of courage, even among persons of superior intelligence and culture, as to imparting their own psychological experiences when those have been of a strange sort. Almost all men are afraid that what they could relate in such wise would find no parallel or response in a listener's internal life, and might be suspected or laughed at. A truthful traveller who should have seen some extraordinary creature in the likeness of a sea-serpent, would have no fear of mentioning it; but the same traveller having had some singular presentiment, impulse, vagary of thought, vision (so-called), dream, or other remarkable mental impression, would hesitate considerably before he would own to it. To this reticence I attribute much of the obscurity in which such subjects are involved. We do not habitually communicate our experiences of these subjective things, as we do our experiences of objective creation. The consequence is, that the general stock of experience in this regard appears exceptional, and really is so, in respect of being miserably imperfect.

In what I am going to relate I have no intention of setting up, opposing, or supporting, any theory whatever. I know the history of the Bookseller of Berlin, I have studied the case of the wife of a late Astronomer Royal as related by Sir David Brewster, and I have followed the minutest details of a much more remarkable case of Spectral Illusion occurring within my private circle of friends. It may be necessary to state as to this last that the sufferer (a lady) was in no degree, however distant, related to me. A mistaken assumption on that head, might suggest an explanation of a part of my own case—but only a part—which would be wholly without foundation. It cannot be referred to my inheritance of any developed peculiarity, nor had I ever before any at all similar experience, nor have I ever had any at all similar experience since.

It does not signify how many years ago, or how few, a certain Murder was committed in England, which attracted great attention. We hear more than enough of Murderers as they rise in succession to their atrocious eminence, and I would bury the memory of this particular brute, if I could, as his body was buried, in Newgate Jail. I purposely abstain from giving any direct clue to the criminal's individuality.

When the murder was first discovered, no suspicion fell—or I ought rather to say, for I cannot be too precise in my facts, it was nowhere publicly hinted that any suspicion fell—on the man who was afterwards brought to trial. As no reference was at that time made to him in the newspapers, it is obviously impossible that any description of him can at that time have been given in the newspapers. It is essential that this fact be remembered.

Unfolding at breakfast my morning paper, containing the account of that first discovery, I found it to be deeply interesting, and I read it with close attention. I read it twice, if not three times. The discovery had been made in a bedroom, and, when I laid down the paper, I was aware of a flash—rush—flow—I do not know what to call it—no word I can find is satisfactorily descriptive—in which I seemed to see that bedroom passing through my room, like a picture impossibly painted on a running river. Though almost instantaneous in its passing, it was perfectly clear; so clear that I distinctly, and with a sense of relief, observed the absence of the dead body from the bed.

It was in no romantic place that I had this curious sensation, but in chambers in Piccadilly, very near to the corner of Saint James's-street. It was entirely new to me. I was in my easy-chair at the moment, and the sensation was accompanied with a peculiar shiver which started the chair from its position. (But it is to be noted that the chair ran easily on castors.) I went to one of the windows (there are two in the room, and the room is on the second floor) to refresh my eyes with the moving objects down in Piccadilly. It was a bright autumn morning, and the street was sparkling and cheerful. The wind was high. As I looked out, it brought down from the Park a quantity of fallen leaves, which a gust took, and whirled into a spiral pillar. As the pillar fell and the leaves dispersed, I saw two men on the opposite side of the way, going from West to East. They were one behind the other. The foremost man often looked back over his shoulder. The second man followed him, at a distance of some thirty paces, with his right hand menacingly raised. First, the singularity and steadiness of his threatening gesture in so public a thoroughfare, attracted my attention; and next, the more remarkable circumstance that nobody heeded it. Both men threaded their way among the other passengers, with a smoothness hardly consistent even with the action of walking on a pavement, and no single creature that I could see, gave them place, touched them, or looked after them. In passing before my windows, they both stared up at me. I saw their two faces very distinctly, and I knew that I could recognise them anywhere. Not that I had consciously noticed anything very remarkable in either face, except that the man who went first had an unusually lowering appearance, and that the face of the man who followed him was of the colour of impure wax.

I am a bachelor, and my valet and his wife constitute my whole establishment. My occupation is in a certain Branch Bank, and I wish that my duties as head of a Department were as light

G

as they are popularly supposed to be. They kept me in town that autumn, when I stood in need of change. I was not ill, but I was not well. My reader is to make the most that can be reasonably made of my feeling jaded, having a depressing sense upon me of a monotonous life, and being "slightly dyspeptic." I am assured by my renowned doctor that my real state of health at that time justifies no stronger description, and I quote his own from his written answer to my request for it.

As the circumstances of the Murder, gradually unravelling, took stronger and stronger possession of the public mind, I kept them away from mine, by knowing as little about them as was possible in the midst of the universal excitement. But I knew that a verdict of Wilful Murder had been found against the suspected Murderer, and that he had been committed to Newgate for trial. I also knew that his trial had been postponed over one Sessions of the Central Criminal Court, on the ground of general prejudice and want of time for preparation of the defence. I may further have known, but I believe I did not, when, or about when, the Sessions to which his trial stood postponed would come on.

My sitting-room, bedroom, and dressing-room, are all on one floor. With the last, there is no communication but through the bedroom. True, there is a door in it, once communicating with the staircase; but a part of the fitting of my bath has been— and had then been for some years—fixed across it. At the same period, and as a part of the same arrangement, the door had been nailed up and canvased over.

I was standing in my bedroom late one night, giving some directions to my servant before he went to bed. My face was towards the only available door of communication with the dressing-room, and it was closed. My servant's back was towards that door. While I was speaking to him I saw it open, and a man look in, who very earnestly and mysteriously beckoned to me. That man was the man who had gone second of the two along Piccadilly, and whose face was of the colour of impure wax.

The figure, having beckoned, drew back and closed the door. With no longer pause than was made by my crossing the bedroom, I opened the dressing-room door, and looked in. I had a lighted candle already in my hand. I felt no inward expectation of seeing the figure in the dressing-room, and I did not see it there.

Conscious that my servant stood amazed, I turned round to him, and said : "Derrick, could you believe that in my cool senses I fancied I saw a——" As I there laid my hand upon his breast, with a sudden start he trembled violently, and said, "O Lord yes, sir ! A dead man beckoning !"

Now, I do not believe that this John Derrick, my trusty and attached servant for more than twenty years, had any impression whatever of having seen any such figure, until I touched him. The change in him was so startling when I touched him, that I fully believe he derived his impression in some occult manner from me at that instant.

I bade John Derrick bring some brandy, and I gave him a dram, and was glad to take one myself. Of what had preceded that night's phenomenon, I told him not a single word. Reflecting on it, I was absolutely certain that I had never seen that face before, except on the one occasion in Piccadilly. Comparing its expression when beckoning at the door, with its expression when it had stared up at me as I stood at my window, I came to the conclusion that on the first occasion it had sought to fasten itself upon my memory, and that on the second occasion it had made sure of being immediately remembered.

I was not very comfortable that night, though I felt a certainty, difficult to explain, that the figure would not return. At daylight, I fell into a heavy sleep, from which I was awakened by John Derrick's coming to my bedside with a paper in his hand.

This paper, it appeared, had been the subject of an altercation at the door between its bearer and my servant. It was a summons to me to serve upon a Jury at the forthcoming Sessions of the Central Criminal Court at the Old Bailey. I had never before been summoned on such a Jury, as John Derrick well knew. He believed—I am not certain at this hour whether with reason or otherwise—that that class of Jurors were customarily chosen on a lower qualification than mine, and he had at first refused to accept the summons. The man who sreved it had taken the matter very coolly. He had said that my attendance or non-attendance was nothing to him; there the summons was; and I should deal with it at my own peril; and not at his.

For a day or two I was undecided whether to respond to this call, or take no notice of it. I was not conscious of the slightest mysterious bias, influence, or attraction, one way or other. Of

that I am as strictly sure as of every other statement that I make
here. Ultimately I decided, as a break in the monotony of my
life, that I would go.

The appointed morning was a raw morning in the month of
November. There was a dense brown fog in Piccadilly, and it
became positively black and in the last degree oppressive East
of Temple Bar. I found the passages and staircases of the Court
House flaringly lighted with gas, and the Court itself similarly
illuminated. I *think* that until I was conducted by officers into
the Old Court and saw its crowded state, I did not know that
the Murderer was to be tried that day. I *think* that until I was
so helped into the Old Court with considerable difficulty, I did
not know into which of the two Courts sitting, my summons
would take me. But this must not be received as a positive assertion, for I am not completely satisfied in my mind on either
point.

I took my seat in the place appropriated to Jurors in waiting,
and I looked about the Court as well as I could through the
cloud of fog and breath that was heavy in it. I noticed the black
vapour hanging like a murky curtain outside the great windows,
and I noticed the stifled sound of wheels on the straw or tan
that was littered in the street; also, the hum of the people gathered there, which a shrill whistle, or a louder song or hail than
the rest, occasionally pierced. Soon afterwards the Judges, two in
number, entered and took their seats. The buzz in the Court was
awfully hushed. The direction was given to put the Murderer
to the bar. He appeared there. And in that same instant I recognised in him, the first of two men who had gone down Piccadilly.

If my name had been called then, I doubt if I could have answered to it audibly. But it was called about sixth or eighth in
the panel, and I was by that time able to say "Here!" Now,
observe. As I stepped into the box, the prisoner, who had been
looking on attentively but with no sign of concern, became violently agitated, and beckoned to his attorney. The prisoner's wish
to challenge me was so manifest, that it occasioned a pause,
during which the attorney, with his hand upon the dock, whispered with his client, and shook his head. I afterwards had it from
that gentleman, that the prisoner's first affrighted words to him
were, *"At all hazards challenge that man!"* But, that as he would
give no reason for it, and admitted that he had not even known

my name until he heard it called and I appeared, it was not done.

Both on the ground already explained, that I wish to avoid reviving the unwholesome memory of that Murderer, and also because a detailed account of his long trial is by no means indispensable to my narrative, I shall confine myself closely to such incidents in the ten days and nights during which we, the Jury, were kept together, as directly bear on my own curious personal experience. It is in that, and not in the Murderer, that I seek to interest my reader. It is to that, and not to a page of the Newgate Calendar, that I beg attention.

I was chosen Foreman of the Jury. On the second morning of the trial, after evidence had been taken for two hours (I heard the church clock strike), happening to cast my eyes over my brother-jurymen, I found an inexplicable difficulty in counting them. I counted them several times, yet always with the same difficulty. In short, I made them one too many.

I touched the brother-juryman whose place was next me, and I whispered to him, "Oblige me by counting us." He looked surprised by the request, but turned his head and counted. "Why," says he, suddenly, "we are Thirt——; but no, it's not possible. No. We are twelve."

According to my counting that day, we were always right in detail, but in the gross we were always one too many. There was no appearance—no figure—to account for it; but I had now an inward foreshadowing of the figure that was surely coming.

The Jury were housed at the London Tavern. We all slept in one large room on separate tables, and we were constantly in the charge and under the eye of the officer sworn to hold us in safe-keeping. I see no reason for suppressing the real name of that officer. He was intelligent, highly polite, and obliging, and (I was glad to hear) much respected in the City. He had an agreeable presence, good eyes, enviable black whiskers, and a fine sonorous voice. His name was Mr. Harker.

When we turned into our twelve beds at night, Mr. Harker's bed was drawn across the door. On the night of the second day, not being disposed to lie down, and seeing Mr. Harker sitting on his bed, I went and sat beside him, and offered him a pinch of snuff. As Mr. Harker's hand touched mine in taking it from my box, a peculiar shiver crossed him, and he said: "Who is this!"

Following Mr. Harker's eyes and looking along the room, I saw again the figure I expected—the second of the two men who had gone down Piccadilly. I rose, and advanced a few steps; then stopped, and looked round at Mr. Harker. He was quite unconcerned, laughed, and said in a pleasant way, "I thought for a moment we had a thirteenth juryman, without a bed. But I see it is the moonlight."

Making no revelation to Mr. Harker, but inviting him to take a walk with me to the end of the room, I watched what the figure did. It stood for a few moments by the bedside of each of my eleven brother-jurymen, close to the pillow. It always went to the right-hand side of the bed, and always passed out crossing the foot of the next bed. It seemed from the action of the head, merely to look down pensively at each recumbent figure. It took no notice of me, or of my bed, which was that nearest to Mr. Harker's. It seemed to go out where the moonlight came in, through a high window, as by an aërial flight of stairs.

Next morning at breakfast, it appeared that everybody present had dreamed of the murdered man last night, except myself and Mr. Harker.

I now felt as convinced that the second man who had gone down Piccadilly was the murdered man (so to speak), as if it had been borne into my comprehension by his immediate testimony. But even this took place, and in a manner for which I was not at all prepared.

On the fifth day of the trial, when the case for the prosecution was drawing to a close, a miniature of the murdered man, missing from his bedroom upon the discovery of the deed, and afterwards found in a hiding-place where the Murderer had been seen digging, was put in evidence. Having been identified by the witness under examination, it was handed up to the Bench, and thence handed down to be inspected by the Jury. As an officer in a black gown was making his way with it across to me, the figure of the second man who had gone down Piccadilly, impetuously started from the crowd, caught the miniature from the officer, and gave it to me with its own hands, at the same time saying in a low and hollow tone—before I saw them in miniature, which was in a locket—"*I was younger then, and my face was not then drained of blood.*" It also came between me and the brother juryman to whom I would have given the miniature, and between him and the brother juryman to whom he would have given it, and so passed it on through the whole of our number, and back into my possession. Not one of them, however, detected this.

At table, and generally when we were shut up together in Mr. Harker's custody, we had from the first naturally discussed the day's proceedings a good deal. On that fifth day, the case for the prosecution being closed, and we having that side of the question in a completed shape before us, our discussion was more animated and serious. Among our number was a vestry-man—the densest idiot I have ever seen at large—who met the plainest evidence with the most preposterous objections, and who was sided with by two flabby parochial parasites; all the three empanelled from a district so delivered over to Fever that they ought to have been upon their own trial, for five hundred Murders. When these mischievous blockheads were at their loudest, which was towards midnight while some of us were already pre-paring for bed, I again saw the murdered man. He stood grimly behind them, beckoning to me. On my going towards them and striking into the conversation, he immediately retired. This was the beginning of a separate series of appearances, confined to that long room in which *we* were confined. Whenever a knot of my brother jurymen laid their heads together, I saw the head of the murdered man among theirs. Whenever their comparison of notes was going against him, he would solemnly and irresistibly beckon to me.

It will be borne in mind that down to the production of the minature on the fifth day of the trial, I had never seen the Ap-pearance in Court. Three changes occurred, now that we entered on the case for the defence. Two of them I will mention to-gether, first. The figure was now in Court continually, and it never there addressed itself to me, but always to the person who was speaking at the time. For instance. The throat of the mur-dered man had been cut straight across. In the opening speech for the defence, it was suggested that the deceased might have cut his own throat. At that very moment, the figure with its throat in the dreadful condition referred to (this it had con-cealed before) stood at the speaker's elbow, motioning across and across its windpipe, now with the right hand, now with the left, vigorously suggesting to the speaker himself, the impossibility of such a wound having been self-inflicted by either hand. For another instance. A witness to character, a woman, deposed to the prisoner's being the most amiable of mankind. The figure at that instant stood on the floor before her, looking her full in the face, and pointing out the prisoner's evil countenance with an extended arm and an outstretched finger.

The third change now to be added, impressed me strongly, as the most marked and striking of all. I do not theorise upon it; I accurately state it, and there leave it. Although the Appearance was not itself perceived by those whom it addressed, its coming close to such persons was invariably attended by some trepidation or disturbance on their part. It seemed to me as if it were prevented by laws to which I was not amenable, from fully revealing itself to others, and yet as if it could, invisibly, dumbly and darkly, overshadow their minds. When the leading counsel for the defence suggested that hypothesis of suicide and the figure stood at the learned gentleman's elbow, frightfully sawing at its severed throat, it is undeniable that the counsel faltered in his speech, lost for a few seconds the thread of his ingenious discourse, wiped his forehead with his handkerchief, and turned extremely pale. When the witness to character was confronted by the Appearance, her eyes most certainly did follow the direction of its pointed finger, and rest in great hesitation and trouble upon the prisoner's face. Two additional illustrations will suffice. On the eighth day of the trial, after the pause which was every day made early in the afternoon for a few minutes' rest and refreshment, I came back into Court with the rest of the Jury, some little time before the return of the Judges. Standing up in the box and looking about me, I thought the figure was not there, until, chancing to raise my eyes to the gallery, I saw it bending forward and leaning over a very decent woman, as if to assure itself whether the Judges had resumed their seats or not. Immediately afterwards, that woman screamed, fainted, and was carried out. So with the venerable, sagacious, and patient Judge who conducted the trial. When the case was over, and he settled himself and his papers to sum up, the murdered man entering by the Judges' door, advanced to his Lordship's desk, and looked eagerly over his shoulder at the pages of his notes which he was turning. A change came over his Lordship's face; his hand stopped; the peculiar shiver that I knew so well, passed over him; he faltered, "Excuse me, gentlemen, for a few moments. I am somewhat oppressed by the vitiated air;" and did not recover until he had drunk a glass of water.

Through all the monotony of six of those interminable ten days—the same Judges and others on the bench, the same Murderer in the dock, the same lawyers at the table, the same tones of question and answer rising to the roof of the court, the same scratching of the Judge's pen, the same ushers going in and out, the same lights kindled at the same hour when there had been any natural light of day, the same foggy curtain outside the great windows when it was foggy, the same rain pattering and dripping when it was rainy, the same footmarks of turnkeys and prisoner day after day on the same sawdust, the same keys locking and unlocking the same heavy doors—through all the wearisome montony which made me feel as if I had been Foreman of the Jury for a vast period of time, and Piccadilly had flourished coevally with Babylon, the murdered man never lost one trace of his distinctness in my eyes, nor was he at any moment less distinct than anybody else. I must not omit, as a matter of fact, that I never once saw the Appearance which I call by the name of the murdered man, look at the Murderer. Again and again I wondered, "Why does he not?" But he never did.

Nor did he look at me, after the production of the miniature, until the last closing minutes of the trial arrived. We retired to consider, at seven minutes before ten at night. The idiotic vestryman and his two parochial parasites gave us so much trouble, that we twice returned into Court, to beg to have certain extracts from the Judge's notes re-read. Nine of us had not the smallest doubt about those passages, neither, I believe, had any one in Court; the dunder-headed triumvirate however, having no idea but obstruction, disputed them for that very reason. At length we prevailed, and finally the Jury returned into Court at ten minutes past twelve.

The murdered man at that time stood directly opposite the Jury-box, on the other side of the Court. As I took my place, his eyes rested on me, with great attention; he seemed satisfied, and slowly shook a great grey veil, which he carried on his arm for the first time, over his head and whole form. As I gave in our verdict "Guilty," the veil collapsed, all was gone, and his place was empty.

The Murderer being asked by the Judge, according to usage, whether he had anything to say before sentence of Death should be passed upon him, indistinctly muttered something which was described in the leading newspapers of the following day as "a few rambling, incoherent, and half-audible words, in which he was understood to complain that he had not had a fair trial, because the Foreman of the Jury was prepossessed against him." The remarkable declaration that he really made, was this : "*My Lord, I knew I was a doomed man when the Foreman of my Jury came into the box. My Lord, I knew he would never let me off, because, before I was taken, he somehow got to my bedside in the night, woke me, and put a rope round my neck.*"

VII

TO BE TAKEN AND TRIED

There can hardly be seen anywhere, a prettier village than Cumner, standing on the brow of a hill which commands one of the finest views in England, and flanked by its broad breezy common, the air of which is notorious for clearness and salubrity. The high road from Dring, for the most part shut in by the fences of gentlemen's seats, opens out when it reaches this common, and, separating from the Tenelms road, ascends in a north-westerly direction till it comes in sight of Cumner. Every step is against the collar, yet so gradual is the ascent, that you scarcely realise it until, turning, you behold the magnificent panorama spread around and beneath.

The village consists chiefly of one short street of somewhat straggling houses, among which you observe its little post-office, its police station, its rustic public-house (the Dunstan Arms), whose landlord also holds the general shop across the way; and its two or three humble lodging-houses. Facing you as you enter the street, which is a cul-de-sac, is the quaint old church, standing not more than a bow-shot from the Rectory. There is something primitive and almost patriarchal in this quiet village, where the pastor lives surrounded by his flock, and can scarcely move from his own gate without finding himself in the midst of them.

Cumner Common is skirted on three sides by dwellings, varying in size and importance, from the small butcher's shop standing in its own garden, and under the shadow of its own apple-trees, to the pretty white house where the curate lodges, and the more pretentious abodes of those who are, or consider themselves, gentry. It is bounded on the east by the low stone wall and gateway of Mr. Malcomson's domain; the modest dwelling of Simon Eade, that gentleman's bailiff, half covered with creepers, the autumnal hues of which might rival the brightest specimen's of American foliage; lastly, by the high brick wall (with its door in the centre), which completely shuts in Mr. Gibbs's "place." On the south side runs the high road to Tenelms, skirting the great Southhanger property, of which Sir Oswald Dunstan is proprietor.

Hardly could the pedestrian tourist, on his way from Dring, fail to pause at the rustic stile nearly opposite the blacksmith's forge, and, resting upon it, gaze down on the magnificent prospect of wood and water spread at his feet—a prospect to which two ancient cedars form no inappropriate foreground. That stile is not often crossed, for the footpath from it leads only to the farm called the Plashetts; but it is very constantly used as a resting-place. Many an artist has sketched the view from it; many a lover has whispered tender words to his mistress beside it; many a weary tramp has rested his or her feet on the worn stone beneath.

This stile was once the favourite resort of two young lovers, inhabitants of the district, and soon to be united. George Eade, the only son of Mr. Malcolmson's bailiff, was a stalwart good-looking young fellow of some six-and-twenty, who worked for that gentleman under his father, and was in receipt of liberal wages. Honest, steady, and fond of self-cultivation, he was capable, if not clever—persevering, if not rapid—an excellent specimen of an honest English peasant. But he had certain peculiarities of disposition and temper, which served to render him considerably less popular than his father. He was reserved; feeling strongly, but with difficulty giving expression to his feelings; susceptible to, and not easily forgiving, injuries; singularly addicted to self-accusation and remorse. His father, a straightforward open-hearted man of five-and-forty, who had raised himself by sheer merit from the position of a labourer to that of the trusted manager of Mr. Malcolmson's property, was highly respected by that gentleman, and by the whole countryside. His mother, feeble in health, but energetic of spirit, was one of the most excellent of women.

This couple, like many of their class, had married imprudently early, and had struggled through many difficulties in consequence: burying, one after another, three sickly children in the little churchyard at Cumner where they hoped one day themselves to lie. On the one son that remained to them their affections were centred. The mother, especially, worshipped her George with an admiring love that partook of idolatry. She was not without some of the weaknesses of her sex. She was jealous; and when she discovered the flame which had been kindled in the heart of her son by the soft blue eyes of Susan Archer, her feelings towards that rosy-cheeked damsel were not those of perfect charity. True, the Archers were people who held themselves high, occupying a large farm under Sir Oswald Dunstan; and they were known to regard Susan's attachment as a decided lowering of herself and them. That attachment had sprung up, as is not unfrequently the case, in the hop-gardens. The girl had been ailing for some time, and her shrewd old doctor assured her father that there was no tonic so efficacious as a fortnight's hop-picking in the sunny September weather. Now there were but few places to which so distinguished a belle as Susan could be permitted to go for such a purpose; but her family knew and respected the Eades, and to Mr. Malcolmson's hop-grounds she was accordingly sent. The tonic prescribed produced the desired effect. She lost her ailments; but she lost her heart too.

George Eade was good looking, and up to that time had never cared for woman. The love he conceived for the gentle, blue-eyed girl was of that all-absorbing character which natures stern and concentrated like his, are fitted to feel, and to feel but once in a lifetime. It carried all before it. Susan was sweet tempered and simple hearted, of a yielding disposition, and, though not unconscious of her beauty, singularly little spoilt by the consciousness. She gave her whole heart to the faithful earnest man whom she reverenced as her superior in moral strength, if not in outward circumstances. They exchanged no rings on the balmy evening which witnessed their plighted faith, but he took from her hat the garland of hops she had laughingly twisted round it, and looking down upon her sweet face with a great love in his brown eyes, whispered, "I shall keep this whilst I live, and have it buried with me when I die!"

But, there was a certain Geoffrey Gibbs, the owner of the "Place" on Cumner Common, who had paid, and was still paying, marked attention to the beautiful Susan. This man, originally in trade, had chanced, some years before, to see in the news-papers a notice that if he would apply to a certain lawyer in London, he would hear of something greatly to his advantage. He did so, and the result was, his acquisition of a comfortable independence, left him by a distant kinsman whom he had never so much as seen. This windfall changed his whole prospects and manner of life, but not his character, which had always been that of an unmitigated snob. In outward circumstances, however, he was a gentleman living on his income, and, as such, the undoubted social superior of the Archers, who were simply tenant-farmers. Hence their desire that Susan should favour his suit. Some people were of opinion, that he had no serious intention of marrying the girl; and Susan herself always encouraged this notion; adding, that were he ten times as rich, and a hundred times as devoted as he represented himself to be, she would die rather than accept the cross-grained monster.

He *was* frightful; less from defects of feature than from utter disproportion of form, and a sinister expression of countenance, far worse than actual ugliness. His legs were as short as his body and hands were long, while his head would have been well suited to the frame of a Hercules; giving him a top-heavy appearance that was singularly ungraceful. His eyebrows were shaggy and overhanging, his eyes small and malicious looking, his nose was beak-shaped, his mouth immense, with thick sensual lips. He wore huge false-looking chains, outrageous shirt-pins and neck-cloths, and cutaway sporting coats of astounding colours. He was a man who delighted in frightening inoffensive females, in driving within an inch of a lady's pony-carriage, or in violently galloping past some timid girl on horseback, and chuckling at her scared attempts to restrain her plunging steed. Like all bullies, he was of course a coward at heart.

Between this man and George Eade a keen hatred existed. George despised as well as detested Gibbs. Gibbs envied as much as he abhorred the more fortunate peasant, who was beloved where he met with nothing but coldness and rebuffs.

Susan's heart was indeed wholly George's, yet it was only when her health had again begun to fail, that her father was frightened into a most unwilling consent to their union; which consent no sooner became known to Mr. Malcolmson, than he voluntarily raised the young man's wages, and undertook to put in repair for him a cottage of his own, not far from that of Simon Eade.

But, when the news of the approaching marriage reached the ears of Gibbs, his jealous fury was aroused to the utmost. He rushed down to the Plashetts, and closeting himself with Mr. Archer, made brilliant offers of settlement on Susan, if she would consent even now to throw over her lover, and become his wife. But he only succeeded in distressing the girl, and tantalising her father. Willingly, indeed, would the latter have acceded to his wishes, but he had passed his solemn word to George, and Susan held him to it. No sooner, however, was Gibbs gone, than the old man burst into loud lamentations over what he called her self-sacrifice; and her eldest brother coming in, joined in reproaching her for refusing prospects so advantageous. Susan was weak, and easily influenced. She was cut to the heart by their cruel words, and went out to meet her lover with her spirits depressed, and her eyes red and swollen. George, shocked at her appearance, listened with indignation to her agitated recital of what had passed.

"Keep your carriage, indeed!" he exclaimed, with bitter scorn. "Does your father make more count of a one-horse shay than of true love such as mine? And a fellow like Gibbs, too! That I wouldn't trust a dog with!"

"Father don't see it so," the girl sobbed out. "Father says he'd make a very good husband, once we was married. And I'd be a lady, and dress fine, and have servants! Father thinks so much of that!"

"So it seems; but don't you be led by him, Susan, darling! 'Tisn't riches and fine clothes that makes folks' happiness—'tis better things! See here, my girl——" He stopped short, and faced her with a look of unutterable emotion. "I love ye so true, that if I thought—if I thought it'd be for your good to marry this fellow—if I thought ye'd be happier with him than with me, I'd—I'd give ye up, Susan! Yes—and never come near ye more! I would indeed!"

He paused, and, raising his hand with a gesture that had in it a rude solemnity very impressive, repeated once more, "*I would indeed!* But ye'd not be happy with Geoffrey Gibbs. Ye'd be miserable—ill-used, perhaps. He ain't a man to make any woman happy—I'm as sure o' that, as that I stand here. He's bad at heart—downright cruel. And I!—what I promise, I'll act up to—O! steady. I'll work for you, and slave for you, and—and love you true!"

He drew her towards him as he spoke, and she, reassured by his words, nestled lovingly to his side. And so they walked on for some moments in silence.

"And, darling," he added, presently, "I've that trust—that faith—in me—that once we're married, and you're mine—safe—so's no one can come between us, I'll get on; and who knows but ye may ride in your carriage yet. Folks do get on, when they've a mind to, serious."

She looked up at him with fond admiring eyes. She honoured him for his strength, all the more because of her own weakness.

"I don't want no carriage," she murmured; "I want nothing but you, George. 'Tisn't I, you know, that wish things different—'tis father——"

The moon had risen, the beautiful bright September moon, nearly at the full; and its light shone on the lovers as they retraced their steps through the silent Southhanger woods—how solemn and lovely at that hour!—towards Susan's home. And before they had reached the gate of the Plashetts, her sweet face was again bright with smiles, and it had been agreed between them that to avoid a repetition of such attempts on the part of Gibbs, and such scenes with her father, she should propose to go to her aunt's, Miss Jane Archer's, at Ormiston, for a fortnight of the three weeks, that yet remained before the marriage should take place.

She acted on this idea, and George took advantage of her absence to attend a sale on the other side of the county, and procure certain articles of furniture required for their new home. Once away, he obtained leave to prolong his stay with a friend till the time of Susan's return. It was pleasanter for him not to be at home at this period. His mother seemed to grow more averse to his marriage, the nearer it approached; declaring that no good could possibly come of union with a girl who had been too much waited upon and flattered, to make a good wife for a plain hard-working man. These remarks, indescribably galling to the lover because not wholly without foundation, had given rise to more than one dispute between his mother and him, which had not tended to diminish the half-unconscious dislike the good woman felt towards her future daughter-in-law.

When George returned home after his fortnight's holiday, he found, instead of the expected letter from his betrothed announcing her arrival at the Plashetts, one addressed to him in a strange hand, and containing the following words :

"George Eade, you are being done. Look to G. G.
                                        "A WELL-WISHER."

Perplexed at so mysterious a communication, he was somewhat annoyed to find that Gibbs had quitted Cumner from the very day after his own departure, and was still absent. This struck his as remarkable; but Susan had written him only a week before, a letter so full of tenderness that he could not bring himself to entertain a single doubt of her truth. But on the very next morning, his mother handed him a letter from Farmer Archer, enclosing one from his sister, informing him that her niece had left her house clandestinely two days before, to be married to Mr. Gibbs. It appeared that the girl had gone, as on previous occasions, to spend the day with a cousin, and that not returning at night, it was concluded she had settled to sleep there. The next morning had brought, instead of herself, the announcement of her marriage.

On reading this news, George was at first conscious of but one feeling. Utter incredulity. There must be some error somewhere; the thing could not be. While his father, with tears in his honest eyes, exhorted him to bear up like a man under this blow, and his mother indignantly declared that a girl who could so conduct herself was indeed a good riddance, he sat silent and half stupefied. Such a breach of faith seemed, to his earnest and loyal nature, simply impossible.

Another half-hour brought confirmation that could not be doubted. James Wilkins, Mr. Gibbs's man-servant, came grinning and important, with a letter for George, which had been enclosed in one from his master to himself. It was from Susan, and signed with her new name.

"I know," it said, "that for what I have done, I shall be without excuse in your eyes—that you will hate and despise me as much as you have hitherto loved and trusted me. I know that I have behaved to you very, very bad, and I don't ask you to forgive me. I know you can't. But I do ask you to refrain from vengeance. It can't bring back the past. Oh, George! If ever you cared for me, listen to what I entreat now. Hate and despise me—I don't expect no other—but don't you revenge my ill conduct on anyone. Forget all about me—that's the best thing for both of us. It would have been better if we had never beheld one another."

Much more followed in the same strain—weak, self-accusing, fearful of consequences—wholly unworthy of George.

He gazed at the letter, holding it in those strong sinewy hands that would have toiled for her so hard and so faithfully. Then, without a word, he held it out to his father, and left the room. They heard him mount the narrow stairs, lock himself into his little garret, and they heard no more.

After a while his mother went to him. Although personally relieved at her son's release, that feeling was entirely absorbed in tender and loving pity for what she knew must be his sufferings. He was sitting by the little casement, a withered branch of hops upon his knee. She went and laid her cheek to his.

"Have patience, lad!" she said, with earnest feeling. "Try—try—to have faith, and comfort'll be sent ye in time. It's hard to bear, I know—dreadful hard and bitter—but for the poor parents' sakes who loves ye so dear, try and bear it."

He looked up at her with cold tearless eyes. "I will," he said, in a hard voice. "Don't ye see I *am* trying?"

His glance was dull and hopeless. How she longed that tears would come and relieve his bursting heart!

"She wasn't worthy of ye, my boy. I always told ye——"

But he stopped her with a stern gesture.

"Mother! Not a word o' that, nor of her, from this hour. What she's done ain't so very bad after all. *I'm* all right—*I* am. Father and you shan't see no difference in me, leastways, not if you'll forbear naming of her ever, ever again. She's turned my heart to stone, that's all! No great matter!"

He laid his hand on his broad chest and heaved a great gasp-sigh. "This morning I had a heart o' flesh here," he said; "now it's a cold, heavy stone. But it's no great matter."

"Oh, don't ye speak like that, my lad!" his mother cried, bursting into tears, and throwing her arms around him. "It kills me to hear ye!"

But he gently unwound those arms, and kissing her on the cheek, led her to the door. "I must go to work now," he said; and, descending the stairs before her, he quitted the cottage with a firm step.

From that hour no one heard him speak of Susan Gibbs. He never inquired into the circumstances of her stay at Ormiston;

H

he never spoke of them, nor of her, to her relations or to his own. He avoided the former; he was silent and reserved with the latter. Susan appeared to be, for him, as though she had never been.

And from that hour he was an altered being. He went about his work as actively, and did it as carefully, as ever; but it was done sternly, doggedly, like an imperative but unwelcome duty. No man ever saw a smile upon his lips; no jocular word ever escaped them. Grave and uncompromising, he went his ungenial way, seeking for no sympathy, and bestowing none, avoiding all companionship save that of his parents;—a sad and solitary man.

Meanwhile, Mr. Gibbs's "Place" on Cumner Common was advertised as to be let; strangers hired it, and for nearly three years nothing was seen of him or his wife. Then news arrived one day that they were to be expected shortly, and quite a ferment of expectation was created in the little village. They came, and certain rumours that had reached it from time to time were found to have only too much foundation in truth.

For it had oozed out, as such things do ooze, that Gibbs shamefully ill used his pretty wife, and that the marriage, which on his side had been one of love, had turned out miserably. Her father and brothers, who had been to see them more than once, had been strangely reserved on the subject of those visits, and it was generally understood that the old farmer lamented his daughter's marriage now, as much as he had formerly longed for it. No one wondered, when they saw her. She was the shadow of her former self; still lovely, but broken, cowed, pale; all the bloom faded; all the spirit crushed out of her. No smile was ever seen upon those pretty lips now, except when she played with her boy, a fair-haired little fellow, the image of herself. But even in her intercourse with this child she was sternly restricted, and her tyrant would not unfrequently dismiss him with an oath, and forbid her to follow him to his nursery.

In spite of their being such near neighbours, the Gibbses had been some time in the place before George met his former love. He never went to Cumner church (nor to any, indeed), and she never quitted her own house, except to drive with her husband, or walk through the Southhanger Woods to her father's. George might have beheld her driving past his father's door with a highstepping horse that always seemed on the point of running away; but he never looked at her, nor replied to his mother's remarks respecting her and her smart turn-out. Yet though he resolutely kept the door of his own lips, he could not close the lips of other people, or his own ears. Do what he would, the Gibbses and their doings pursued him still. His master's labourers gossiped about the husband's brutality; the baker's boy had no end of stories to tell, of the oaths he had heard, and even the blows he had witnessed, when "Gibbs was more than usual excited with drink." The poor frightened wife was understood to have declared that but for her dread of what he might be driven to do in his fury, she would go before a magistrate and swear the peace against him. George could not close his ears to all this; and men said that the expression of his eyes on those occasions was not good to look upon.

One Sunday, the Eades were sitting over their frugal one o'clock dinner, when they heard the sound of a carriage driving furiously past. Mrs. Eade caught up her stick, and, in spite of her lameness, hobbled to the window.

"I thought so!" she cried. "It's Gibbs driving to Tenelms, and drunk again, seemingly. See how he's flogging of the horse. And he's got the little lad, too! He'll not rest till he've broken that child's neck, or the mother's. Simmons declares——"

She stopped, suddenly aware of her son's breath upon her cheek. He had actually come to the window, and now, leaning over her, was gazing sternly at the figures in the carriage, flying down the hill towards the Tenelms road.

"I wish he might break his own neck!" George muttered between his teeth.

"Oh, George! George! don't name such things," Mrs. Eade cried, with a pale shocked face. "It ain't Christian. We've all need of repentance, and our times is in His hand."

"If ye frequented church, my lad, 'stead of keeping away, as I grieve to see ye do," his father said, severely, "ye'd have better feelings in your heart. *They'll* never prosper ye, mark my words."

George had returned to his seat, but he rose again as his father said this. "Church!" he cried, in a loud harsh voice—"I was going there once, and it wasn't permitted. I'll go there no more. D'ye think," he continued, while his white lips trembled with uncontrollable emotion—"d'ye think, because I'm quiet, and do my work reg'lar, d'ye think I've forgotten? *Forgotten!*" He brought his clenched fist down upon the table with startling violence. "I tell ye when I forget, I'll be lying stark and stiff in

my coffin! Let be—let be!" as his mother tried to interrupt
him; "ye mean well, I know, but women haven't the judgment
to tell when to speak, and when to hold hard. Ye'd best never
name that scoundrel 'fore me again, nor yet church." With that,
he went from the room and from the house.

Mrs. Eade fretted sadly over these evidences of George's rancorous and ungodly disposition. To her, he seemed to be on the
high road to perdition, and she ended by sending to Mr. Murray,
the rector, to beg he would be pleased to look in upon her some
morning soon, as she was greatly troubled in her mind. But
Mr. Murray was at that time ill, and nearly a fortnight elapsed
before he was able to answer her summons. Meanwhile, other
events occurred.

It was notorious that one of Mrs. Gibbs's greatest trials was
about her boy, whom her husband persisted in driving out, at
the risk, as everyone thought, of his life. Fearful had been the
scenes between the parents on this account; but the more she
wept and implored, the more he resisted her entreaties. One day,
to frighten her still more, he placed the little fellow, with the
whip in his hand, on the carriage-seat alone, and stood at his
door himself, loosely holding the reins, and jeering at his wife,
who in an agony of terror kept beseeching him to get in, or let
her do so. Suddenly the report of a gun was heard in a neighbouring field; the horse took fright, and started off wildly, jerking the reins from the hands of the half-intoxicated Gibbs; the
whip fell from the hands of the child on the animal's back, still
further exciting it; and the boy, thrown with violence to the
bottom of the carriage, lay half stunned by the shock.

George was close by when this occurred. He threw himself on
the flying horse, and, seizing the bearing-rein with his whole
strength, held on like grim death, in spite of being half dragged,
half borne, along in its headlong flight. At last the animal, getting
its legs entangled in the long trailing reins, fell with fearful violence, and lay stunned and motionless. George was thrown to
the ground, but escaped with a few trifling bruises. The child
at the bottom of the carriage, though frightened and screaming,
was altogether uninjured. In less than five minutes half the village
was collected on the spot, inquiring, congratulating, applauding;
and Susan, with her rescued child clinging to her bosom, was
covering George's hands with passionate tears and kisses.

"Bless you! Bless you a thousand times!" she cried, sobbing

hysterically. "You've saved my darling's life! He might have been killed but for you! How can I ever——"

But a rough hand shoved her aside. "What are you after now?" Gibbs's furious voice was heard to cry, with a shocking oath. "Leave that fellow alone, or I'll——! Are you making a fool of yourself this way, because he's lamed the horse so that he'll have to be shot?"

The poor thing sank down on the bank and broke into a fit of hysterical weeping; whilst a murmur of "Shame, shame!" rose among the bystanders.

George Eade had turned coldly from Susan when she rushed up to him, and had striven to withdraw his hands from her grasp; but now, confronting Gibbs, he said, "It'll be a good deed done, whoever shoots that brute of yours, and it'd be better still to shoot *you* as a man would a mad dog!"

All heard the words. All trembled at his look as he uttered them. The whole of the pent-up rage and resentment of the last three years seemed concentrated in that one look of savage and unutterable hatred.

Mr. Murray found poor Mrs. Eade very suffering, when, two mornings after, he called to congratulate her on her son's escape. She had not closed her eyes since the accident. George's look and words, as they had been described to her, haunted her. The good clergyman could give her but scant comfort. He had tried again and again to reason with and soften her son, but ineffectually. George answered him, with a certain rude respect, that as long as he did his work properly, and injured no man, he had a right to decide for himself in matters concerning only himself; and one of his fixed decisions was never again to see the inside of a church.

"It's a hard trial, my good friend," said Mr. Murray, "a hard and mysterious trial. But I say to you, *have faith*. There is a hidden good in it, that we can't see now."

"It'd be strange if I wasn't thankful for his being spared," Mrs. Eade replied. "It'd be worse than anything to have the dear lad took, revengeful and unforgiving as he is now. But you see, sir——"

She was stopped in her eager speech by a knock at the door. The son of Mr. Beach, the neighbouring butcher, peeped in. He scraped a bow on seeing the clergyman sitting with her, and looked from one to the other with a doubtful demeanour.

"I don't want nothing this morning, thank you, Jim," Mrs. Eade said. Then, struck with the peculiar expression on the young man's face, she added: "Ain't Mr. Beach so well this morning? You look all nohow."

"I'm—I'm a bit flustered," the youth replied, wiping his steaming forehead; "I've just been seeing *him*, and it gave me such a turn!"

"Him! who?"

"Sure! Haven't ye heard, sir? Gibbs have been found dead in Southanger Woods—murdered last night. They say——"

"Gibbs murdered!"

There was a pause of breathless horror.

"They've been carrying his corpse to the Dunstan Arms, and I see it."

Mrs. Eade turned so deadly faint that the clergyman called out hurriedly for Jemima, the servant girl. But Jemima had run out wildly on hearing the appalling intelligence, and was now midway between her master's house and the Gibbs's, listening to a knot of people, all wondering, surmising, gazing with scared eyes at that door in the high wall, the threshold of which its master would never cross again, except feet foremost.

The Eades' parlour was soon full to overflowing. Most of the dwellers on the common had congregated there—why, perhaps none would have cared to explain. Simon Eade came in among the first, and was doing his best to soothe and restore the poor fainting woman, who could hardly as yet realise what had occurred. In the midst of the confusion—the questioning, the describing of the position of the body, the rifled pockets, the dreadful blow from behind, the number of hours since the deed was done—in the midst of all this, steps were heard outside, and George came into the midst of them.

Then a sudden hush succeeded to the Babel of sound, which he could not but have heard as he crossed the threshold. There was something ominous in that silence.

No need to ask if he knew. His face, pale as death, haggard, streaming with perspiration, proved all too plainly he was aware of the ghastly horror. But his first words, low, and uttered half unconsciously, were long after remembered:

"I wish I'd been found dead in that wood 'stead of Gibbs!"

Various circumstances arose, one after another, that united to

surround George with a kind of network of suspicion. Simon
Eade sustained himself like a man, with a proud confidence in
the innocence of his boy, touching even those who could not
share it; and with a pious trust that Providence would yet see
that innocence proved. But the poor feeble mother, shaken by
ill health, half crazed by the remembrance of words and looks
she would give the world to forget, could do little but weep, and
utter broken supplications to Heaven.

George offered no resistance on his apprehension. Sternly, but
without eagerness, he declared his innocence, and from that
moment he kept entire silence. His features worked convulsively
when he wrung his father's hand on parting, and gazed on the
pale face of his mother, who had swooned away on seeing the
police; but he soon recovered his self-possession, and accompanied the officers with a steady step, and a fixed, though gloomy
countenance.

The body of the deceased had been discovered about ten A.M.
by a farmer going to the Plashetts, who had been attracted to
the spot by the howls of Gibbs's dog. The corpse lay among
the underwood, at a short distance from the footpath leading
from the stile so often mentioned, through the wood to the Plashetts, and had apparently been dragged that short distance. Evidences of a fierce struggle were visible on and around the footpath, and some blood also : which appeared to have flowed from
a wound in the back of the head of the deceased, who
must have been struck from behind, by some heavy, though not
blunt, instrument. When found, he had been dead, according to
the medical testimony, some eleven or twelve hours. The pockets
were turned inside out, and the watch and a purse had been
taken, as well as a seal ring.

Gibbs's two servants, James and Bridget Williams, deposed
that their master had quitted his own house on the night of the
murder, at twenty minutes past eight, being unusually sober;
that he had set his watch, the last thing, by the kitchen clock,
and had observed that he should go to the Dunstan Arms first,
and afterwards to the Plashetts. That his not returning that night
had occasioned no uneasiness, as he was in the habit of frequently
absenting himself until morning, and had his latch-key always
with him.

On the other hand, Simon Eade, his wife, and servant girl,
all deposed that George returned home on the night of the

murder, at nine o'clock, having been out since tea-time; that there was nothing unusual in either his manner or appearance; that he supped, and afterwards remained with his parents till ten, when the whole family retired to bed; and that he came down next morning in the sight of Jemima, who had herself risen somewhat earlier than usual.

On his left wrist was found a recent cut, which he stated had been caused by his clasp-knife slipping, as he was cutting his bread and cheese. In the same manner he sought to account for certain marks of blood on the inside of his coat sleeves and on his trousers. The only article belonging to the deceased that was found in his possession was a small lead pencil, marked with the initials "G. G." and three notches; these Job Brettle, the blacksmith, swore Gibbs had handed him the pencil to cut, on the afternoon of the murder. He (Brettle) noticed both notches and initials at the time, and could swear that the pencil in the prisoner's possession was the pencil he had cut. George maintained that he had picked it up on the common, and that he had no idea to whom it belonged.

It came out in cross-examination that a more desperate quarrel than ever, had taken place on the morning of the murder, between Mr. and Mrs. Gibbs; after which, she had been heard to declare that she could support that life no longer, and would apply for help to one who would not refuse it. That she had sent a letter soon after to George Eade, by the son of a neighbouring cottager, and had gone out herself at night, a few minutes after her husband, returning again in a quarter of an hour, more or less, when she had retired to her bedroom, and had not again quitted it until news was brought next morning of the discovery of the corpse.

When questioned by the coroner as to where she had been overnight, no reply could be elicited from her; but she fainted so frequently while under examination, that her evidence was singularly broken and incoherent.

George admitted having gone to the Southanger Woods at about twenty minutes to eight on the night of the murder; but he refused to assign any special reason for going there, declaring that he had not remained there more than a quarter of an hour at most. He stated that, as he was re-crossing the stile, he saw Gibbs and his dog at a distance, making directly for it. The moon shone almost as bright as day, and he recognised him distinctly.

To avoid meeting him, he took the Dring road, and walked nearly as far as the turnpike, when he turned about, and so reached home at nine o'clock without having met a soul.

The following were (briefly) the points in the prisoner's favour :

1. The evidence of three credible witnesses that he returned home at nine o'clock, and sat down to supper without any appearance of hurry or agitation.

2. The shortness of the time in which to commit such a deed, and effectually to conceal the property taken from the deceased.

3. The high moral character born by the prisoner up to that time.

The points against him were :

1. The cut on his wrist, and marks of blood on his clothes.

2. Gibbs's pencil, found upon him.

3. The absence of testimony corroborative of his own account of his doings during the thirty minutes that intervened between Gibbs's leaving the Dunstan Arms (where he had gone straight from home) and his (George's) own return to his father's.

4. The bitter animosity he was known to have cherished against the deceased, and certain words he had been heard to utter respecting him, indicating a desire for his life.

By the evidence of the landlord of the Dunstan Arms, it appeared that Gibbs had left his place to proceed to the Plashetts, at a few minutes before half-past eight o'clock. Now, it would take some four or five minutes' moderate walking for one leaving the public-house, to reach the spot where Gibbs's body was found; thus reducing the period for the murder to be committed in (if committed by George at that time) to three or four and twenty minutes, if he ran home at his full speed, or to nineteen or twenty minutes, if he walked at an average pace.

The demeanour of the prisoner before the magistrates, was stern, and even defiant; but he betrayed no emotion. He was fully committed for trial at the approaching assizes.

Meanwhile, opinion respecting him was greatly divided in Cumner. He had never been a popular man, and his extreme reserve during the last three years had alienated many who, at the period of his great trouble, had been disposed to sympathise with him. And, although he had always held a high place in public estimation, the impression that he was a man of unusually fierce passions, and implacable resentment, had gained ground of late. In short, not a few of those who knew him best, believed that, worked up to savage fury by the sufferings of the woman he had once so fondly loved, and by long brooding over his own wrongs, he had revenged both himself and her by taking the life of his enemy. He might, it was thought, have easily slipped out of his father's house in the dead of night, have waylaid and murdered Gibbs as he was returning from the Plashetts, and have secreted or destroyed the property in order to throw suspicion off the right scent.

His trial will long be remembered in those parts; as well from the intense excitement it occasioned in that particular locality, as from the strong interest manifested about it throughout the kingdom. The most eminent counsel were engaged on his behalf; and Mr. Malcolmson, who never could believe in his guilt, spared neither pains nor expense to aid his cause. He was perfectly calm when he stood in the dock, the one object on which countless eyes were eagerly riveted; but the change that had taken place in his outward seeming, struck even the most indifferent beholder with compassion, and possibly did more to impress the jury in his favour, than even the eloquence of his counsel, wonderful as that proved. For, his sufferings must have been intense. He had grown years older, during the last few weeks. His hair had thinned; his clothes hung upon his attenuated frame. He, once so ruddy and vigorous, stood there wan, haggard, drooping. Even the expression of his countenance had altered; it was stern no more.

A sound like one vast sobbing sigh went through the crowded court when the verdict, Not Guilty, was heard; but no applause, no public mark of joy or gratulation. And silently, with downcast eyes, like a doomed man, George Eade returned with one parent to the home where the other sat praying for his release.

It had been expected that, if acquitted, he would leave Cumner, and seek his fortunes elsewhere. But it was consistent with the character of the man, to brave the opinion of his fellows, and he did so in this instance. On the first Sunday, to the surprise of all, he made his appearance in church, sitting apart from the rest of the congregation, as though unwilling to obtrude himself upon them; from that time his attendance was invariable. Nor was this the only change observable in his conduct. His moroseness had passed away. He had become subdued, patient, manifesting a touching gratitude to those who treated him with common civility, as though he felt himself unworthy of their notice; unremitting in his devotion to his parents; working hard all the day; sometimes puzzling over a book at night; never alluding to the past—never forgetting it; melancholy—more melancholy than ever; but no longer bitter nor resentful. Such had George Eade become; and when men saw him at a distance, they followed him with their eyes, and asked one another in a whisper, "Did he do it?"

He and Susan never met. She long lay dangerously ill at her father's house, whither she had removed after the tragical event. And the old farmer was fitly punished for his sordid coveting of Gibbs's wealth, when it was found that the latter had settled only fifty pounds a year upon his wife, to be forfeited altogether if she should make a second marriage.

It was about a twelvemonth after these events that, one bright moonlight night, as Mr. Murray was sitting in his library alone, his servant entered to inform him that a stranger, who gave his name as Luke Williams, desired to speak with him. It was past ten o'clock, and the clergyman's hours were early and regular.

"Tell him to call to-morrow morning," said he; "this is not a fit hour for business."

"I did tell him so, sir," the man replied; "but he declared his was a business that would not wait an hour."

"Is he a beggar?"

"He didn't beg, sir; but he looks shocking, quite shocking——"

"Show him in."

The man entered; truly a shocking object. Pale, hollow-eyed, cadaverous, with a racking cough that caused him to pant and gasp for breath, he looked like one in the last stage of consumption. He gazed at Mr. Murray with a strange and mournful expression, and Mr. Murray gazed at him.

"Well?"

The stranger glanced at the servant.

"Leave the room, Robert."

Robert did so, but remained in close proximity outside.

"This is a strange hour at which to disturb me. Have you something to say?"

"It *is* a strange hour, sir, for coming; but my reason for coming is stranger."

The man turned to the window, the curtains of which were not drawn, and gazed at the full October moon, which lighted up the quaint old church hard by, the humble gravestones, the quiet home scene, and shed a solemn glory over all.

"Well?" Mr. Murray asked once more.

But the man's eyes were fixed on the sky.

"Yes," he said, shuddering, "it shone like that—like that—the night of the—murder. It did indeed. It shone on his face—Gibbs's—as he lay there—it shone on his open eyes—I couldn't get them to shut; do what I would, they would stare at me. I've never seen moonlight like that since, till to-night. And I'm come to give myself up to you. I always felt I should, and it's better done and over. Better over."

"You murdered Gibbs? You?"

"I did. I've been there to-night, to look at the place. I felt I must see it again; and I saw his eyes, as plain as I see you, open, with the moonlight shining on them. Ah, a horrible sight!"

"You look very wild and ill. Perhaps——"

"You doubt me. I wish *I* could doubt. See here."

With a trembling emaciated hand he drew from his pocket the watch, seal ring, and purse that had belonged to Gibbs; and laid them on the table. Mr. Murray knew them.

"I used the money," said the man, faintly. "There were but a few shillings, and I was in great want."

Then he sank down on a chair with a dreadful groan.

Mr. Murray gave him a restorative, and after a time he rallied With his hollow eyes still gazing at the moonlight, and with that ever-recurring shudder, he faltered out at intervals the following story.

He and Gibbs had been formerly associated in disreputable money transactions, which had ended in his own ruin. Being in abject distress, he had, on the promise of a considerable bribe, agreed to aid Gibbs in a plot to obtain possession of Susan's person. When she and George had separated for the fortnight previous to their contemplated marriage, the two confederates had followed her to Ormiston, and, concealing themselves in a low part of the town, had kept close watch upon her movements. Ascertaining that she was to spend the day with a cousin, they sent a woman, a creature of their own, to waylay her on her road, with a message purporting to come from George Eade, imploring her to hasten to him immediately, as he was injured by an accident on the railroad, and might have but a few hours to live. Appalled by such intelligence, the poor girl hurried to the place where the woman led her, entered without a shadow of suspicion a lonely house in the suburbs, and found herself in the presence of Gibbs and Williams, who, instantly securing the door, informed her that this subterfuge had been resorted to in order to get her into the power of the former. They told her that she was now in a place where screams would not be heeded, even if heard, and whence she would find it impossible to escape, and that she would not be quitted night or day by them or their female assistant, until she should consent to become the wife of Gibbs, who added, with furious oaths, that had her union with George Eade taken place, he would have shot him down on his way from church.

Wild with terror and astonishment, helpless, bewildered, the girl resisted longer than might have been expected in one naturally weak. But finding herself incessantly watched, trembling, too, for her life (for Gibbs stood over her with a loaded pistol and the most furious threats), she was frightened at last into writing, at his dictation, the letters to her aunt and lover, announcing her marriage; though that event did not really take place till nearly three weeks later, when, worn out, and almost stupefied into acquiescence, she was married in due form. Even then, Williams declared that she would have resisted still, but for her fears for her lover's safety. His life seemed to be dearer to her than her own happiness, and Gibbs had sworn so vehemently that his life should be the immediate forfeit of his union with her, that she felt that union would be impossible. She married, therefore, offering herself up as a kind of ransom for the man she loved. Then Williams claimed his reward.

But his worthless confederate was not one to fulfil honestly any promise involving the sacrifice of money. He paid the first of three instalments agreed upon; but constantly shirked the payment of the others, until at last, Williams finding himself in immediate danger of arrest, made his way down to the neighbourhood of Cumner, and lurking about the Southanger Woods, the deep recesses of which were well calculated for concealment, watched his opportunity, and accosted Gibbs one evening as he was driving home from Tenelms alone. That worthy, though, as usual, half drunk, recognised him at once, and swearing at him for an impudent beggar, did his best to drive his horse over him. Infuriated by such treatment, Williams wrote him a letter, declaring that if he failed to bring, on a certain night to a certain spot in Southanger Woods, every shilling of the sum he had promised to pay, he (Williams) would the very next morning go before the nearest magistrate and reveal the whole plot of Susan's abduction and marriage.

Alarmed by this threat, Gibbs answered the appointment, but without bringing the money; indeed, it soon became clear that he had no more intention of paying it than before. Williams, exasperated beyond endurance by these repeated disappointments, and rendered desperate by want, swore he would at least possess himself of whatever money or valuables the other had about him. Gibbs resisted with fury, and a fierce struggle ensued, during which he repeatedly endeavoured to stab his opponent with his clasp-knife. At length Williams prevailed, and throwing all his strength into one supreme effort, hurled Gibbs to the ground, the back of whose head striking with fearful violence against a tree, he was killed by the force of the blow. Appalled by his own act, and by the probable consequences to himself, Williams hastily dragged the body from the footpath, rifled the pockets, and hurried away from the scene. The church clock struck ten as he emerged from Southanger Woods; he walked all that night, rested the next day in an old outhouse, and succeeded in reaching London undiscovered. But he was, almost immediately afterwards, arrested for debt, and had remained in prison until within the last few days, when he was released chiefly because he was believed to be dying of consumption. And he *was* dying, he added, despairingly. For, since that fearful night, the victim's upturned eyes had followed him everywhere—everywhere—and his life had been a burden to him.

Such was the tale, told in broken whispers in the dead of night, to the clergyman, by that miserable man : a tale impossible to doubt, and triumphantly proving the innocence of one who had been too long suspected. Before twelve o'clock next day, the whole village was ringing with the news of Williams's confession, which spread like wildfire.

George bore his triumph, as he had borne unjust suspicion. The man's character had been strangely purified in the furnace of that affliction. The awful fate of his enemy, overtaking him with the suddenness of a chastisement from Heaven, had struck George at the time with a strange compassion, as well as self-upbraiding. For, though guiltless of Gibbs's death, he was not guiltless of many and eager longings for it; and he would have given worlds to have forgiven him, as he hoped himself to be forgiven. Hence his first sad and self-accusing words in his father's house, after hearing of the murder.

It may be mentioned, by the way, that the object of the letter he had received from Susan on the morning of the fatal day, had been to implore him to call upon her father that very afternoon, and induce him to take immediate steps for effecting her separation from her husband, of whom she went in fear of her life, and by whom she was watched too closely to be able to assist herself. And as her letters were liable to be opened, she entreated George to meet her in Southanger Woods that night, in order to inform her of the result of his negotiation (which was never even entered into, as the farmer happened to be from home). Finding, however, that Gibbs was bound to the Plashetts from the public-house, she had rushed out hastily to warn George of the circumstances, and so prevent a meeting between the two, which was very near taking place.

Susan fully confirmed the testimony of Williams as to the circumstances of her abduction. That wretched man survived his confession little more than a week, and died in prison, penitent.

And once more George and Susan met. At that interview he took from his bosom a little silken bag, in which was a bunch of withered hops, so dried by time, that they almost crumbled beneath his touch. And he held them up to her.

There is a cottage on Cumner Common, not far from Simon Eade's, the walls of which are covered with roses and clematis. There you may see Susan, if not as beautiful as of yore, still fair; and happy now, with her brown-eyed baby in her arms; and, if you choose your hour, you may catch George, too, coming in to dinner or to tea, stalwart, handsome, with a bright cheery look on his honest English face, that will do you good to look upon.

VIII

TO BE TAKEN FOR LIFE

Sophy read through the whole of the foregoing several times over, and I sat in my seat in the Library Cart (that's the name we give it) seeing her read, and I was as pleased and as proud as a Pug-Dog with his muzzle black-leaded for an evening party and his tail extra curled by machinery. Every item of my plan was crowned with success. Our reunited life was more than all that we had looked forward to. Content and joy went with us as the wheels of the two carts went round, and the same stopped with us when the two carts stopped.

But I had left something out of my calculations. Now, what had I left out? To help you to a guess, I'll say, a figure. Come. Make a guess, and guess right. Nought? No. Nine? No. Eight? No. Seven? No. Six? No. Five? No. Four? No. Three? No. Two? No. One? No. Now I'll tell you what I'll do with you. I'll say it's another sort of figure altogether. There. Why then, says you, it's a mortal figure. No nor yet a mortal figure. By such means you get yourself penned into a corner, and you can't help guessing a *im*mortal figure. That's about it. Why didn't you say so sooner?

Yes. It was a immortal figure that I had altogether left out of my calculations. Neither man's nor woman's, but a child's. Girl's, or boy's? Boy's. "I says the sparrow, with my bow and arrow." Now you have got it.

We were down at Lancaster, and I had done two nights' more than fair average business (though I cannot in honour recommend them as a quick audience) in the open square there, near the end of the street where Mr. Sly's King's Arms and Royal Hotel stands. Mim's travelling giant otherwise Pickleson happened at the self-same time to be a trying it on in the town. The genteel lay was adopted with him. No hint of a van. Green baize alcove leading up to Pickleson in a Auction Room. Printed poster "Free list suspended, with the exception of that proud boast of an enlightened country, a free press. Schools admitted by private arrangement. Nothing to raise a blush in the cheek of youth or shock the most fastidious." Mim swearing most horrible and terrific in a pink calico pay-place, at the slackness of the public. Serious hand-bill in the shops, importing that it was all but impossible to come to a right understanding of the history of David, without seeing Pickleson.

I went to the Auction Room in question, and I found it entirely empty of everything but echoes and mouldiness, with the single exception of Pickleson on a piece of red drugget. This suited my purpose, as I wanted a private and confidential word with him, which was: "Pickleson. Owing much happiness to you, I put you in my will for a fypunnote; but, to save trouble here's fourpunten down, which may equally suit your views, and let us so conclude the transaction." Pickleson, who up to that remark had had the dejected appearance of a long Roman rushlight that couldn't anyhow get lighted, brightened up at his top extremity and made his acknowledgments in a way which (for him) was parliamentary eloquence. He likewise did add, that, having ceased to draw as a Roman, Mim had made proposals for his going in as a conwerted Indian Giant worked upon by The Dairyman's Daughter. This, Pickleson, having no acquaintance with the tract named after that young woman, and not being willing to couple gag with his serious views, had declined to do, thereby leading to words and the total stoppage of the unfortunate young man's beer. All of which, during the whole of the interview, was confirmed by the ferocious growling of Mim down below in the pay-place, which shook the giant like a leaf.

But what was to the present point in the remarks of the travelling giant otherwise Pickleson, was this: "Doctor Marigold" —I give his words without a hope of conweying their feebleness—"who is the strange young man that hangs about your carts?"—"The strange young *man*?" I gives him back, thinking that he meant her, and his languid circulation had dropped a syllable. "Doctor," he returns, with a pathos calculated to draw a tear from even a manly eye, "I am weak, but not so weak yet as that I don't know my words. I repeat them, Doctor. The strange young man." It then appeared that Pickleson being forced to stretch his legs (not that they wanted it) only at times when he couldn't be seen for nothing, to wit in the dead of the night and towards daybreak, had twice seen hanging about my carts, in that same town of Lancaster where I had been only two nights, this same unknown young man.

It put me rather out of sorts. What it meant as to particulars I no more foreboded then, than you forebode now, but it put me rather out of sorts. Howsoever, I made light of it to Pickleson, and I took leave of Pickleson advising him to spend his legacy in getting up his stamina, and to continue to stand by his religion. Towards morning I kept a look-out for the strange young man, and what was more—I saw the strange young man. He was well dressed and well looking. He loitered very nigh my carts, watching them like as if he was taking care of them, and soon

I

after daybreak turned and went away. I sent a hail after him, but he never started or looked round, or took the smallest notice.

We left Lancaster within an hour or two, on our way towards Carlisle. Next morning at daybreak, I looked out again for the strange young man. I did not see him. But next morning I looked out again, and there he was once more. I sent another hail after him, but as before he gave not the slightest sign of being anyways disturbed. This put a thought into my head. Acting on it, I watched him in different manners and at different times not necessary to enter into, till I found that this strange young man was deaf and dumb.

The discovery turned me over, because I knew that a part of that establishment where she had been, was allotted to young men (some of them well off), and I thought to myself "If she favours him, where am I, and where is all that I have worked and planned for?" Hoping—I must confess to the selfishness—that she might *not* favour him. I set myself to find out. At last I was by accident present at a meeting between them in the open air, looking on leaning behind a fir-tree without their knowing of it. It was a moving meeting for all the three parties concerned. I knew every syllable that passed between them, as well as they did. I listened with my eyes, which had come to be as quick and true with deaf and dumb conversation, as my ears with the talk of people that can speak. He was a going out to China as clerk in a merchant's house, which his father had been before him. He was in circumstances to keep a wife, and he wanted her to marry him and go along with him. She persisted, no. He asked if she didn't love him? Yes, she loved him dearly, dearly, but she could never disappoint her beloved good noble generous and I don't-know-what-all father (meaning me, the Cheap Jack in the sleeved waistcoat), and she would stay with him, Heaven bless him, though it was to break her heart! Then she cried most bitterly, and that made up my mind.

While my mind had been in an unsettled state about her favouring this young man, I had felt that unreasonable towards Pickleson, that it was well for him he had got his legacy down. For I often thought "If it hadn't been for this same weak-minded giant, I might never have come to trouble my head and wex my soul about the young man." But, once that I knew she loved him—once that I had seen her weep for him—it was a different thing. I made it right in my mind with Pickleson on the spot, and I shook myself together to do what was right by all.

She had left the young man by that time (for it took a few minutes to get me thoroughly well shook together), and the young man was leaning against another of the fir-trees—of which there was a cluster—with his face upon his arm. I touched him on the back. Looking up and seeing me, he says, in our deaf and dumb talk : "Do not be angry."

"I am not angry, good boy. I am your friend. Come with me."

I left him at the foot of the steps of the Library Cart, and I went up alone. She was drying her eyes.

"You have been crying, my dear."

"Yes, father."

"Why ?"

"A head-ache."

"Not a heart-ache?"

"I said a head-ache, father."

"Doctor Marigold must prescribe for that head-ache."

She took up the book of my Prescriptions, and held it up with a forced smile; but seeing me keep still and look earnest, she softly laid it down again, and her eyes were very attentive.

"The Prescription is not there, Sophy."

"Where is it ?"

"Here, my dear."

I brought her young husband in, and I put her hand in his, and my only further words to both of them were these : "Doctor Marigold's last prescription. To be taken for life." After which I bolted.

When the wedding come off, I mounted a coat (blue, and bright buttons), for the first and last time in all my days, and I give Sophy away with my own hand. There were only us three and the gentleman who had had charge of her for those two years. I give the wedding dinner of four in the Library Cart. Pigeon pie, a leg of pickled pork, a pair of fowls, and suitable garden-stuff. The best of drinks. I give them a speech, and the gentlemen give us a speech, and all our jokes told, and the whole went off like a sky-rocket. In the course of the entertainment I explained to Sophy that I should keep the Library Cart as my living-cart when not upon the road, and that I should keep all her books for her just as they stood, till she come back to claim them. So she went to China with her young husband, and it was a parting sorrowful and heavy, and I got the boy I had another service, and so as of old when my child and wife were gone, I went plodding along alone, with my whip over my shoulder, at the old horse's head.

Sophy wrote me many letters, and I wrote her many letters. About the end of the first year she sent me one in an unsteady hand: "Dearest father, not a week ago I had a darling little daughter, but I am so well that they let me write these words to you. Dearest and best father, I hope my child may not be deaf and dumb, but I do not yet know." When I wrote back, I hinted the question; but as Sophy never answered that question, I felt it to be a sad one, and I never repeated it. For a long time our letters were regular, but then they got irregular through Sophy's husband being moved to another station, and through my being always on the move. But we were in one another's thoughts, I was equally sure, letters or no letters.

Five years, odd months, had gone since Sophy went away. I was still the King of the Cheap Jacks, and at a greater heighth of popularity than ever. I had had a first-rate autumn of it, and on the twenty-third of December, one thousand eight hundred and sixty-four, I found myself at Uxbridge, Middlesex, clean sold out. So I jogged up to London with the old horse, light and easy, to have my Christmas-Eve and Christmas-Day alone by the fire in the Library Cart, and then to buy a regular new stock of goods all round, to sell 'em again and get the money.

I am a neat hand at cookery, and I'll tell you what I knocked up for my Christmas-Eve dinner in the Library Cart. I knocked up a beefsteak pudding for one, with two kidneys, a dozen oysters, and a couple of mushrooms, thrown in. It's a pudding to put a man in good humour with everything, except the two bottom buttons of his waistcoat. Having relished that pudding and cleared away, I turned the lamp low, and sat down by the light of the fire, watching it as it shone upon the backs of Sophy's books.

Sophy's books so brought up Sophy's self, that I saw her touching face quite plainly, before I dropped off dozing by the fire. This may be a reason why Sophy, with her deaf and dumb child in her arms, seemed to stand silent by me all through my nap. I was on the road, off the road, in all sorts of places, North and South and West and East, Winds liked best and winds liked least, Here and there and gone astray, Over the hills and far away, and still she stood silent by me, with her silent child in her arms. Even when I woke with a start, she seemed to vanish, as if she had stood by me in that very place only a single instant before.

I had started at a real sound, and the sound was on the steps of the cart. It was the light hurried tread of a child, coming clambering up. That tread of a child had once been so familiar to me, that for half a moment I believed I was a going to see a little ghost.

But the touch of a real child was laid upon the outer handle of the door, and the handle turned and the door opened a little way, and a real child peeped in. A bright little comely girl with large dark eyes.

Looking full at me, the tiny creature took off her mite of a straw hat, and a quantity of dark curls fell about her face. Then she opened her lips, and said in a pretty voice :

"Grandfather !"

"Ah my God !" I cries out. "She can speak !"

"Yes, dear grandfather. And I am to ask you whether there was ever any one that I remind you of ?"

In a moment Sophy was round my neck as well as the child, and her husband was wringing my hand with his face hid, and we all had to shake ourselves together before we could get over it. And when we did begin to get over it, and I saw the pretty child a talking, pleased and quick and eager and busy, to her mother, in the signs that I had first taught her mother, the happy and yet pitying tears fell rolling down my face.

THE FIRST POOR TRAVELLER'S STORY

In the year one thousand seven hundred and ninety-nine, a relative of mine went limping down, on foot, to the town of Chatham. He was a poor traveller, with not a farthing in his pocket.

My relative went down to Chatham, to enlist in a cavalry regiment, if a cavalry regiment would have him; if not, to take King George's shilling from any corporal or sergeant who would put a bunch of ribbons in his hat. His object was, to get shot; but, he thought he might as well ride to death as be at the trouble of walking.

My relative's Christian name was Richard, but he was better known as Dick. He dropped his own surname on the road down, and took up that of Doubledick. He was passed as Richard Doubledick; age twenty-two; height, five foot ten; native place, Exmouth; which he had never been near in his life. There was no cavalry in Chatham when he limped over the bridge here with half a shoe to his dusty foot, so he enlisted into a regiment of the line, and was glad to get drunk and forget all about it.

You are to know that this relative of mine had gone wrong and run wild. His heart was in the right place, but it was sealed up. He had been betrothed to a good and beautiful girl whom he had loved better than she—or perhaps even he—believed; but, in an evil hour, he had given her cause to say to him, solemnly, "Richard, I will never marry any other man. I will live single for your sake, but Mary Marshall's lips;" her name was Mary Marshall; "never address another word to you on earth. Go, Richard! Heaven forgive you!" This finished him. This took him down to Chatham. This made him Private Richard Doubledick, with a determination to be shot.

There was not a more dissipated and reckless soldier in Chatham barracks, in the year one thousand seven hundred and ninety-nine, than Private Richard Doubledick. He associated with the dregs of every regiment, he was as seldom sober as he could be, and was constantly under punishment. It became clear to the whole barracks, that Private Richard Doubledick would very soon be flogged.

Now, the Captain of Richard Doubledick's company was a young gentleman not above five years his senior, whose eyes had an expression in them which affected Private Richard Doubledick in a very remarkable way. They were bright, handsome, dark eyes—what are called laughing eyes generally, and, when serious, rather steady than severe—but, they were the only eyes now left in his narrowed world that Private Richard Doubledick could not stand. Unabashed by evil report and punishment, defiant of everything else and everybody else, he had but to know that those eyes looked at him for a moment, and he felt ashamed. He could not so much as salute Captain Taunton in the street, like any other officer. He was reproached and confused —troubled by the mere possibility of the captain's looking at him. In his worst moments he would rather turn back and go any distance out of his way, than encounter those two handsome, dark, bright eyes.

One day, when Private Richard Doubledick came out of the Black Hole, where he had been passing the last eight-and-forty hours, and in which retreat he spent a good deal of his time, he was ordered to betake himself to Captain Taunton's quarters. In the stale and squalid state of a man just out of the Black Hole, he had less fancy than ever for being seen by the Captain; but, he was not so mad yet as to disobey orders, and consequently went up to the terrace overlooking the parade-ground, where the officers' quarters were: twisting and breaking in his hands as he went along, a bit of the straw that had formed the decorative furniture of the Black Hole.

"Come in!" cried the Captain, when he knocked with his knuckles at the door. Private Richard Doubledick pulled off his cap, took a stride forward, and felt very conscious that he stood in the light of the dark bright eyes.

There was a silent pause. Private Richard Doubledick had put the straw in his mouth, and was gradually doubling it up into his windpipe and choking himself.

"Doubledick," said the Captain, "do you know where you are going to?"

"To the Devil, Sir?"

"Yes," returned the Captain. "And very fast."

Private Richard Doubledick turned the straw of the Black Hole in his mouth, and made a miserable salute of acquiescence.

"Doubledick, since I entered his Majesty's service, as a boy of seventeen, I have been pained to see many men of promise going that road; but, I have never been so pained to see a man determined to make the shameful journey, as I have been, ever since you joined the regiment, to see you."

Private Richard Doubledick began to find a film stealing over the floor at which he looked; also to find the legs of the Captain's breakfast-table turning crooked, as if he saw them through water.

"I am only a common soldier, sir," said he. "It signifies very little what such a poor brute comes to."

"You are a man," returned the Captain, with grave indignation, "of education and superior advantages; and if you say that, meaning what you say, you have sunk lower than I had believed. How low that must be, I leave you to consider: knowing what I know of your disgrace, and seeing what I see."

"I hope to get shot soon, sir," said Private Richard Doubledick; "and then the regiment, and the world together, will be rid of me."

The legs of the table were becoming very crooked. Doubledick, looking up to steady his vision, met the eyes that had so strong an influence over him. He put his hand before his own eyes, and the breast of his disgrace-jacket swelled as if it would fly asunder.

"I would rather," said the young Captain, "see this in you, Doubledick, than I would see five thousand guineas counted out upon this table for a gift to my good mother. Have you a mother?"

"I am thankful to say she is dead, sir."

"If your praises were sounded from mouth to mouth through the whole regiment, through the whole army, through the whole country, you would wish she had lived, to say with pride and joy, 'He is my son!'"

"Spare me, sir," said Doubledick. "She would never have heard any good of me. She would never have had any pride and joy in owning herself my mother. Love and compassion she might have had, and would have always had, I know; but not—— Spare me, sir! I am a a broken wretch, quite at your mercy!" And he turned his face to the wall, and stretched out his imploring hand.

"My friend——" began the captain.

"God bless you, sir!" sobbed Private Richard Doubledick.

"You are at the crisis of your fate. Hold your course unchanged a little longer, and you know what must happen. *I* know even better than you can imagine, that after that has happened, you are lost. No man who could shed those tears, could bear those marks."

"I fully believe it, sir," in a low, shivering voice, said Private Richard Doubledick.

"But a man in any station can do his duty, and, in doing it, can earn his own respect, even if his case should be so very unfortunate and so very rare, that he can earn no other man's. A common soldier, poor brute though you called him just now, has this advantage in the stormy times we live in, that he always does his duty before a host of sympathising witnesses. Do you doubt that he may so do it as to be extolled through a whole regiment, through a whole army, through a whole country? Turn while ye may yet retrieve the past, and try."

"I will! I ask for only one witness, sir."

"I understand you. I will be a watchful and a faithful one."

I have heard from Private Richard Doubledick's own lips, that he dropped down upon his knee, kissed the officer's hand, arose, and went out of the light of the dark bright eyes, an altered man.

In that year, one thousand seven hundred and ninety-nine, the French were in Egypt, in Italy, in Germany, where not? Napoleon Buonaparte had likewise begun to stir against us in India, and most men could read the signs of the great troubles that were coming on. In the very next year, when we formed an alliance with Austria against him, Captain Taunton's regiment was on service in India. And there was not a finer non-commissioned officer in it—no, nor in the whole line—than Corporal Richard Doubledick.

In eighteen hundred and one, the Indian Army were on the coast of Egypt. Next year was the year of the proclamation of the short peace, and they were recalled. It had then become well-known to thousands of men, that wherever Captain Taunton with the dark bright eyes, led—there, close to him, ever at his side, firm as a rock, true as the sun, and brave as Mars, would be certain to be found, while life beat in their hearts, that famous soldier, Sergeant Richard Doubledick.

Eighteen hundred and five, besides being the great year of Trafalgar, was a year of hard fighting in India. That year saw such wonders done by a Sergeant-Major, who cut his way single-handed through a solid mass of men, recovered the colours of his regiment which had been seized from the hand of a poor boy shot through the heart, and rescued his wounded captain, who was down, and in a very jungle of horses' hoofs and sabres— saw such wonders done, I say, by this brave Sergeant-Major, that he was specially made the bearer of the colours he had won; and Ensign Richard Doubledick had risen from the ranks.

Sorely cut up in every battle, but always reinforced by the bravest of men—for, the fame of following the old colours, shot through and through, which Ensign Richard Doubledick had saved, inspired all breasts—this regiment fought its way through the Peninsular War, up to the Investment of Badajos in eighteen hundred and twelve. Again and again it had been cheered through the British ranks until the tears had sprung into men's eyes at the mere hearing of the mighty British voice so exultant in their valour; and there was not a drummer-boy but knew the legend, that wherever the two friends, Major Taunton with the dark bright eyes, and Ensign Richard Doubledick who was de-voted to him, were seen to go, there the boldest spirits in the English army became wild to follow.

One day, at Badajos—not in the great storming, but in repel-ling a hot sally of the besieged upon our men at work in the trenches, who had given way, the two officers found themselves hurrying forward, face to face, against a party of French infantry who made a stand. There was an officer at their head, encourag-ing his men,—a courageous, handsome, gallant officer of five and thirty—whom Doubledick saw hurriedly, almost momentarily, but saw well. He particularly noticed this officer waving his sword, and rallying his men with an eager and excited cry, when they fired in obedience to his gesture, and Major Taunton dropped.

It was over in ten minutes more, and Doubledick returned to the spot where he had laid the best friend man ever had, on a coat spread upon the wet clay. Major Taunton's uniform was opened at the breast, and on his shirt were three little spots of blood.

"Dear Doubledick, I am dying."

"For the love of Heaven, no!" exclaimed the other, kneeling down beside him, and passing his arm round his neck to raise his head. "Taunton! My preserver, my guardian angel, my witness! Dearest, truest, kindest of human beings! Taunton! For God's sake!"

The bright dark eyes—so very, very dark now, in the pale face—smiled upon him; and the hand he had kissed thirteen years ago, laid itself fondly on his breast.

"Write to my mother. You will see Home again. Tell her how we became friends. It will comfort her, as it comforts me."

He spoke no more, but faintly signed for a moment towards his hair as it fluttered in the wind. The Ensign understood him. He smiled again when he saw that, and gently turning his face over on the supporting arm as if for rest, died, with his hand upon the breast in which he had revived a soul.

No dry eye looked on Ensign Richard Doubledick, that melancholy day. He buried his friend on the field, and became a lone, bereaved man. Beyond his duty he appeared to have but two remaining cares in life; one, to preserve the little packet of hair he was to give to Taunton's mother; the other, to encounter that French officer who had rallied the men under whose fire Taunton fell. A new legend now began to circulate among our troops; and it was, that when he and the French officer came face to face once more, there would be weeping in France.

The war went on—and through it went the exact picture of the French officer on the one side, and the bodily reality upon the other—until the Battle of Toulouse was fought. In the returns sent home, appeared these words: "Severely wounded, but not dangerously, Lieutenant Richard Doubledick."

At Midsummer time in the year eighteen hundred and fourteen, Lieutenant Richard Doubledick, now a browned soldier, seven and thirty years of age, came home to England, invalided. He brought the hair with him, near his heart. Many a French officer had he seen, since that day; many a dreadful night, in searching with men and lanterns for his wounded, had he relieved French officers lying disabled; but, the mental picture and the reality had never come together.

Though he was weak and suffered pain, he lost not an hour

in getting down to Frome in Somersetshire, where Taunton's mother lived. In the sweet, compassionate words of the most compassionate body of books, "he was the only son of his mother, and she was a widow."

It was a Sunday evening, and the lady sat at her quiet garden-window, reading the Bible; reading to herself, in a trembling voice, that very passage in it as I have heard him tell.—He heard the words; "Young man, I say unto thee, arise!"

He had to pass the window; and the bright dark eyes of his debased time seemed to look at him. Her heart told her who he was; she came to the door, quickly, and fell upon his neck.

"He saved me from ruin, made me a human creature, won me from infamy and shame. O God, for ever bless him! As He will, He will!"

"He will!" the lady answered. "I know he is in Heaven!" Then she piteously cried, "But, O, my darling boy, my darling boy!"

Never, from the hour when Private Richard Doubledick enlisted at Chatham, had the Private, Corporal, Sergeant, Sergeant-Major, Ensign, or Lieutenant, breathed his right name, or the name of Mary Marshall, or a word of the story of his life, into any ear, except his reclaimer's. That previous scene in his existence was closed. He had firmly resolved that his expiation should be, to live unknown; to disturb no more the peace that had long grown over his old offences; to let it be revealed when he was dead, that he had striven and suffered, and had never forgotten; and then, if they could forgive him and believe him—well, it would be time enough—time enough!

But, that night, remembering the words he had cherished for two years, "Tell her how we became friends. It will comfort her, as it comforts me," he related everything. It gradually seemed to him, as if in his maturity he had recovered a mother; it gradually seemed to her, as if in her bereavement she had found a son. During his stay in England, the quiet garden into which he had slowly and painfully crept, a stranger, became the boundary of his home; when he was able to rejoin his regiment in the spring, he left the garden, thinking was this indeed the first time he had ever turned his face towards the old colours with a woman's blessing!

He followed them—so ragged, so scarred and pierced now, that they would scarcely hold together—to Quatre Bras, and

Ligny. He stood beside them, in an awful stillness of many men, shadowy through the mist and drizzle of a wet June forenoon, on the field of Waterloo. And down to that hour, the picture in his mind of the French officer had never been compared with the reality.

The famous regiment was in action early in the battle, and received its first check in many an eventful year, when he was seen to fall. But, it swept on to avenge him, and left behind it no such creature in the world of consciousness, as Lieutenant Richard Doubledick.

Through pits of mire and pools of rain; along deep ditches, once roads, that were pounded and ploughed to pieces by artillery, heavy waggons, tramp of men and horses, and the struggle of every wheeled thing that could carry wounded soldiers; jolted among the dying and the dead, so disfigured by blood and mud as to be hardly recognisable for humanity; undisturbed by the moaning of men and the shrieking of horses, which, newly taken from the peaceful pursuits of life, could not endure the sight of the stragglers lying by the wayside, never to resume their toilsome journey; dead, as to any sentient life that was in it, and yet alive; the form that had been Lieutenant Richard Doubledick, with whose praises England rang, was conveyed to Brussels. There, it was tenderly laid down in hospital. And there it lay, week after week, through the long bright summer days, until the harvest, spared by war, had ripened and was gathered in.

Over and over again, the sun arose and set upon the crowded city; over and over again, the moonlight nights were quiet on the plains of Waterloo; and all that time was a blank to what had been Lieutenant Richard Doubledick. Rejoicing troops marched into Brussels, and marched out; brothers and fathers, sisters, mothers, and wives, came thronging there, drew their lots of joy or agony, and departed; so many times a day the bells rang; so many times, the shadows of the great buildings changed; so many lights sprang up at dusk; so many feet passed here and there upon the pavements; so many hours of sleep and cooler air of night succeeded;—indifferent to all, a marble face lay on a bed, like the face of a recumbent statue on the tomb of Lieutenant Richard Doubledick.

Slowly labouring, at last, through a long heavy dream of confused time and place, presenting faint glimpses of army surgeons whom he knew, and of faces that had been familiar to his youth

—dearest and kindest among them, Mary Marshall's, with a solicitude upon it more like reality than anything he could discern—Lieutenant Richard Doubledick came back to life. To the beautiful life of a calm autumn-evening sunset. To the peaceful life of a fresh quiet room with a large window standing open; a balcony beyond, in which were moving leaves and sweet-smelling flowers; beyond again, the clear sky, with the sun full in his sight, pouring its golden radiance on his bed.

It was so tranquil and so lovely, that he thought he had passed into another world. And he said in a faint voice, "Taunton, are you near me?"

A face bent over him. Not his; his mother's.

"I came to nurse you. We have nursed you, many weeks. You were moved here, long ago. Do you remember nothing?"

"Nothing."

The lady kissed his cheek, and held his hand, soothing him.

"Where is the regiment? What has happened? Let me call you mother. What has happened, mother?"

"A great victory, dear. The war is over, and the regiment was the bravest in the field."

His eyes kindled, his lips trembled, he sobbed, and the tears ran down his face. He was very weak: too weak to move his hand.

"Was it dark just now?"

"No."

"It was only dark to me? Something passed away, like a black shadow. But, as it went, and the sun—O the blessed sun, how beautiful it is!—touched my face, I thought I saw a light white cloud pass out at the door. Was there nothing that went out?"

She shook her head, and, in a little while, he fell asleep: she still holding his hand, and soothing him.

From that time, he recovered. Slowly, for he had been desperately wounded in the head, and had been shot in the body; but, making some little advance every day. When he had gained sufficient strength to converse as he lay in bed, he soon began to remark that Mrs. Taunton always brought him back to his own history. Then, he recalled his preserver's dying words, and thought, "it comforts her."

One day, he awoke out of a sleep, refreshed, and asked her to read to him. But, the curtain of the bed softening the light, which she always drew back when he awoke, that she might see him from her table at the bedside where she sat at work, was held undrawn; and a woman's voice spoke, which was not hers.

"Can you bear to see a stranger?" it said softly. "Will you like to see a stranger?"

"Stranger!" The voice awoke old memories, before the days of Private Richard Doubledick.

"A stranger now, but not a stranger once. Richard, dear Richard, lost through so many years—my name——"

He cried out her name, "Mary!" and she held him in her arms.

"I am not breaking a rash vow, Richard. These are not Mary Marshall's lips that speak. I have another name."

She was married.

"I have another name, Richard. Did you ever hear it?"

"Never!"

He looked into her face, so pensively beautiful, and wondered at the smile upon it through her tears.

"Think again, Richard. Are you sure you never heard my altered name?"

"Never!"

"Don't move your head to look at me, dear Richard. Let it lie here, while I tell my story. I loved a generous, noble man; loved him with my whole heart; loved him for years and years; loved him faithfully, devotedly; loved him with no hope of return; loved him, knowing nothing of his highest qualities—loved him, not even knowing that he was alive. He was a brave soldier. He was honoured and beloved by thousands and thousands, when the mother of his dear friend found me, and showed me that in all his triumphs he had never forgotten me. He was wounded in a great battle. He was brought, dying, here into Brussels. I came to watch and tend him, as I would have joyfully gone, with such a purpose, to the dreariest ends of the earth. When he knew no one else he knew me. When he suffered most, he bore his sufferings barely murmuring, content to rest his head where yours rests now. When he lay at the point of death, he married me, that he might call me Wife before he died. And the name, my dear love, that I took on that forgotten night——"

"I know it now!" he sobbed. "The shadowy remembrance strengthens. It is come back. I thank Heaven that my mind is quite restored! My Mary, kiss me; lull this weary head to rest, or I shall die of gratitude. His parting words are fulfilled. I see Home again!"

Well! They were happy. It was a long recovery but they were happy through it all. The snow had melted on the ground, and the birds were singing in the leafless thickets of the early spring, when those three were first able to ride out together, and when people flocked about the open carriage to cheer and congratulate Captain Richard Doubledick.

But, even then, it became necessary for the Captain, instead of returning to England, to complete his recovery in the climate of Southern France. They found a spot upon the Rhone, within a ride of the old town of Avignon and within view of its broken bridge, which was all they could desire; they lived there, together, six months; then returned to England. Mrs. Taunton growing old after three years—though not so old as that her bright dark eyes were dimned—and remembering that her strength had been benefited by the change, resolved to go back for a year to those parts. So, she went with a faithful servant, who had often carried her son in his arms: and she was to be rejoined and escorted home, at the year's end, by Captain Richard Doubledick.

She wrote regularly to her children (as she called them now), and they to her. She went to the neighbourhood of Aix; and there, in their own chateau near the farmer's house she rented, she grew into intimacy with a family belonging to that part of France. The intimacy began in her often meeting among the vineyards a pretty child: a girl, with a most compassionate heart, who was never tired of listening to the solitary English lady's stories of her poor son and the cruel wars. The family were as gentle as the child, and at length she came to know them so well, that she accepted their invitation to pass the last month of her residence abroad, under their roof. All this intelligence she wrote home, piecemeal as it came about, from time to time; and, at last, enclosed a polite note from the head of the chateau, soliciting, on the occasion of his approaching mission to that neighbourhood, the honour of the company of cet homme si justement célèbre, Monsieur le Capitaine Richard Doubledick.

Captain Doubledick; now a hardy, handsome man in the full vigour of life, broader across the chest and shoulders than he had ever been before; dispatched a courteous reply, and followed it in person. Travelling through all that extent of country after three years of Peace, he blessed the better days on which the world

K

had fallen. The corn was golden, not drenched in unnatural red; was bound in sheaves for food, not trodden underfoot by men in mortal fight. The smoke rose up from peaceful hearths, not blazing ruins. The carts were laden with the fair fruits of the earth, not with wounds and death. To him who had so often seen the terrible reverse, these things were beautiful indeed, and they brought him in softened spirit to the old chateau near Aix, upon a deep blue evening.

It was a large chateau of the genuine old ghostly kind, with round towers and extinguishers and a high leaden roof, and more windows than Aladdin's Palace. The lattice blinds were all thrown open, after the heat of the day, and there were glimpses of rambling walls and corridors within. Then, there were immense outbuildings fallen into partial decay, masses of dark trees, terrace-gardens, balustrades; tanks of water, too weak to play and too dirty to work; statues, weeds, and thickets of iron-railing that seemed to have overgrown themselves like the shrubberies, and to have branched out in all manner of wild shapes. The entrance doors stood open, as doors often do in that country when the heat of the day is past; and the Captain saw no bell or knocker, and walked in.

He walked into a lofty stone hall, refreshingly cool and gloomy after the glare of a Southern day's travel. Extending along the four sides of this hall, was a gallery, leading to suites of rooms; and it was lighted from the top. Still, no bell was to be seen.

"Faith," said the Captain, halting, ashamed of the clanking of his boots, "this is a ghostly beginning!"

He started back, and felt his face turn white. In the gallery, looking down at him, stood the French officer : the officer whose picture he had carried in his mind so long and so far. Compared with the original, at last—in every lineament how like it was!

The French officer moved, and disappeared, and Captain Richard Doubledick heard his steps coming quickly down into the hall. He entered through an archway. There was a bright, sudden look upon his face. Much such a look as it had worn in that fatal moment.

Monsieur le Capitaine Richard Doubledick? Enchanted to receive him! A thousand apologies! The servants were all out in the air. There was a little fête among them in the garden. In effect, it was the fête day of my daughter, the little cherished and protected of Madame Taunton.

He was so gracious and so frank, that Monsieur le Capitaine Richard Doubledick could not withhold his hand. "It is the hand of a brave Englishman," said the French officer, retaining it while he spoke. "I could respect a brave Englishman, even as my foe; how much more as my friend! I, also, am a soldier."

"He has not remembered me, as I have remembered him; he did not take such note of my face, that day, as I took of his," thought Captain Richard Doubledick. "How shall I tell him!"

The French officer conducted his guest into a garden, and presented him to his wife: an engaging and beautiful woman, sitting with Mrs. Taunton in a whimsical old-fashioned pavilion. His daughter, her fair young face beaming with joy, came running to embrace him; and there was a boy-baby to tumble down among the orange-trees on the broad steps, in making for his father's legs. A multitude of children-visitors were dancing to sprightly music; and all the servants and peasants about the chateau were dancing too. It was a scene of innocent happiness that might have been invented for the climax of the scenes of Peace which had soothed the captain's journey.

He looked on, greatly troubled in his mind, until a resounding bell rang, and the French officer begged to show him his rooms. They went upstairs into the gallery from which the officer had looked down; and Monsieur le Capitaine Richard Doubledick was cordially welcomed to a grand outer chamber, and a smaller one within, all clocks, and draperies, and hearths, and brazen dogs, and tiles, and cool devices, and elegance, and vastness.

"You were at Waterloo," said the French officer.

"I was. And at Badajos."

Left alone with the sound of his own stern voice in his ears, he sat down to consider, What shall I do, and how shall I tell him? At that time, many deplorable duels had been fought between English and French officers, arising out of the recent war; and these duels, and how to avoid this officer's hospitality, were the uppermost thought in Captain Richard Doubledick's mind.

He was thinking, and letting the time run out in which he should have dressed for dinner, when Mrs. Taunton spoke to him outside the door, asking if he could give her the letter he had brought from Mary? "His mother above all," the Captain thought. "How shall I tell *her*?"

"You will form a friendship with your host, I hope," said Mrs.

Taunton, whom he hurriedly admitted, "that will last for life. He is so true-hearted and so generous, Richard, that you can hardly fail to esteem one another. If He had been spared," she kissed (not without tears) the locket in which she wore his hair, "he would have appreciated him with his own magnanimity, and would have been truly happy that the evil days were past, which made such a man his enemy."

She left the room; and the Captain walked, first to one window whence he could see the dancing in the garden; then, to another window whence he could see the smiling prospect and the peaceful vineyards.

"Spirit of my departed friend," said he, "is it through thee, these better thoughts are rising in my mind! Is it thou who hast shown me, all the way I have been drawn to meet this man, the blessings of the altered time! Is it thou who has sent thy stricken mother to me, to stay my angry hand! Is it from thee the whisper comes, that this man did his duty as thou didst— and as I did, through thy guidance, which has wholly saved me, here on earth—and that he did no more!"

He sat down, with his head buried in his hands, and, when he rose up, made the second strong resolution of his life: That neither to the French officer, nor to the mother of his departed friend, nor to any soul while either of the two was living, would he breathe what only he knew. And when he touched that French officer's glass with his own, that day at dinner, he secretly forgave him in the name of the Divine Forgiver of injuries.

MRS. LIRRIPER'S LODGINGS

I

HOW MRS. LIRRIPER CARRIED ON THE BUSINESS

WHOEVER would begin to be worried with letting Lodgings that wasn't a lone woman with a living to get is a thing inconceivable to me my dear, excuse the familiarity but it comes natural to me in my own little room when wishing to open my mind to those that I can trust and I should be truly thankful if they were all mankind but such is not so, for have but a Furnished bill in the window and your watch on the mantelpiece and farewell to it if you turn your back for but a second however gentemanly the manners, nor is being of your own sex any safeguard as I have reason in the form of sugar-tongs to know, for that lady (and a fine woman she was) got me to run for a glass of water on the plea of going to be confined, which certainly turned out true but it was in the Station-House.

Number Eighty-one Norfolk Street Strand—situated midway between the City and St. James's and within five minutes' walk of the principal places of public amusement—is my address. I have rented this house many years as the parish rate-books will testify and I could wish my landlord was as alive to the fact as I am myself, but no bless you not half a pound of paint to save his life nor so much my dear as a tile upon the roof though on your bended knees.

My dear you never have found Number Eighty-one Norfolk Street Strand advertised in Bradshaw's Railway Guide and with the blessing of Heaven you never will or shall so find it. Some there are who do not think it lowering themselves to make their names that cheap and even going the lengths of a portrait of the house not like it with a blot in every window and a coach and four at the door, but what will suit Wozenham's lower down on the other side of the way will not suit me, Miss Wozenham having her opinions and me having mine, though when it comes to systematic underbidding capable of being proved on oath in a court of justice and taking the form of "If Mrs. Lirriper names eighteen shilling a week, I name fifteen and six" it then comes to a settlement between yourself and your conscience supposing for the sake of argument your name to be Wozenham which I am well aware it is not or my opinion of you would be greatly lowered, and as to airy bedrooms and a night-porter in constant attendance the less said the better, the bedrooms being stuffy and the porter stuff.

It is forty years ago since me and my poor Lirriper got married at St. Clement's Danes where I now have a sitting in a very pleasant pew with genteel company and my own hassock and being partial to evening service not too crowded. My poor Lirriper was a handsome figure of a man with a beaming eye and a voice as mellow as a musical instrument made of honey and steel, but he had ever been a free liver being in the commercial travelling line and travelling what he called a limekiln road— "a dry road, Emma my dear," my poor Lirriper says to me "where I have to lay the dust with one drink or another all day long and half the night, and it wears me Emma"—and this led to his running through a good deal and might have run through the turnpike too when that dreadful horse that never would stand still for a single instant set off, but for its being night and the gate shut and consequently took his wheel my poor Lirriper and the gig smashed to atoms and never spoke afterwards. He was a handsome figure of a man and a man with a jovial heart and a sweet temper, but if they had come up then they never could have given you the mellowness of his voice, and indeed I consider photographs wanting in mellowness as a general rule and making you look like a new-ploughed field.

My poor Lirriper being behindhand with the world and being buried at Hatfield church in Hertfordshire, not that it was his native place but that he had a liking for the Salisbury Arms where we went upon our wedding-day and passed as happy a fortnight as ever happy was, I went round to the creditors and I says "Gentlemen I am acquainted with the fact that I am not answerable for my late husband's debts but I wish to pay them for I am his lawful wife and his good name is dear to me. I am going into the Lodgings gentlemen as a business and if I prosper

every farthing that my late husband owed shall be paid for the
sake of the love I bore him, by this right hand." It took a long
time to do but it was done, and the silver cream-jug which is
between ourselves and the bed and the mattress in my room
up-stairs (or it would have found legs so sure as ever the Furnished
bill was up) being presented by the gentlemen engraved "To Mrs.
Lirriper a mark of grateful respect for her honourable conduct"
gave me a turn which was too much for my feelings, till Mr.
Betley which at that time had the parlours and loved his joke
says "Cheer up Mrs. Lirriper, you should feel as if it was only
your christening and they were your godfathers and godmothers
which did promise for you." And it brought me round, and I
don't mind confessing to you my dear that I then put a sand-
wich and a drop of sherry in a little basket and went down to
Hatfield churchyard outside the coach and kissed my hand and
laid it with a kind of a proud and swelling love on my husband's
grave, though bless you it had taken me so long to clear his name
that my wedding ring was worn quite fine and smooth when I
laid it on the green green waving grass.

I am an old woman now and my good looks are gone but
that's me my dear over the plate-warmer and considered like in
the times when you used to pay two guineas on ivory and took
your chance pretty much how you came out, which made you
very careful how you left it about afterwards because people
were turned so red and uncomfortable by mostly guessing it was
somebody else quite different, and there was once a certain person
that had put his money in a hop business that came in one
morning to pay his rent and his respects being the second floor
that would have taken it down from its hook and put it in his
breast pocket—you understand my dear—for the L, he says, of
the original—only there was no mellowness in *his* voice and I
wouldn't let him, but his opinion of it you may gather from his
saying to it "Speak to me Emma!" which was far from a rational
observation no doubt but still a tribute to its being a likeness,
and I think myself it *was* like me when I was young and wore
that sort of stays.

But it was about the Lodgings that I was intending to hold
forth and certainly I ought to know something of the business
having been in it so long, for it was early in the second year
of my married life that I lost my poor Lirriper and I set up
at Islington directly afterwards and afterwards came here, being

two houses and eight and thirty years and some losses and a deal of experience.

Girls are your first trial after fixtures and they try you even worse than what I call the Wandering Christians, though why *they* should roam the earth looking for bills and then coming in and viewing the apartments and stickling about terms and never at all wanting them or dreaming of taking them being already provided, is a mystery I should be thankful to have explained if by any miracle it could be. It's wonderful they live so long and thrive so on it but I suppose the exercise makes it healthy, knocking so much and going from house to house and up and down stairs all day, and then their pretending to be so particular and punctual is a most astonishing thing, looking at their watches and saying "Could you give me the refusal of the rooms till twenty minutes past eleven the day after to-morrow in the forenoon, and supposing it to be considered essential by my friend from the country could there be a small iron bedstead put in the little room upon the stairs?" Why when I was new to it my dear I used to consider before I promised and to make my mind anxious with calculations and to get quite wearied out with disappointments, but now I says "Certainly by all means" well knowing it's a Wandering Christian and I shall hear no more about it, indeed by this time I know most of the Wandering Christians by sight as well as they know me, it being the habit of each individual revolving round London in that capacity to come back about twice a year, and it's very remarkable that it runs in families and the children grow up to it, but even were it otherwise I should no sooner hear of the friend from the country which is a certain sign than I should nod and say to myself You're a Wandering Christian, though whether they are (as I *have* heard) persons of small property with a taste for regular employment and frequent change of scene I cannot undertake to tell you.

Girls as I was beginning to remark are one of your first and your lasting troubles, being like your teeth which begin with convulsions and never cease tormenting you from the time you cut them till they cut you, and then you don't want to part with them which seems hard but we must all succumb or buy artificial, and even where you get a will nine times out of ten you'll get a dirty face with it and naturally lodgers do not like good society to be shown in with a smear of black across

the nose or a smudgy eyebrow. Where they pick the black up
is a mystery I cannot solve, as in the case of the willingest girl
that ever came into a house half starved poor thing, a girl so
willing that I called her Willing Sophy down upon her knees
scrubbing early and late and ever cheerful but always smiling
with a black face. And I says to Sophy "Now Sophy my good
girl have a regular day for your stoves and keep the width of
the Airy between yourself and the blacking and do not brush your
hair with the bottoms of the saucepans and do not meddle with
the snuffs of the candles and it stands to reason that it can
no longer be" yet there it was and always on her nose, which
turning up and being broad at the end seemed to boast of it
and caused warning from a steady gentleman and excellent
lodger with breakfast by the week but a little irritable and use
of a sitting-room when required, his words being "Mrs. Lirriper
I have arrived at the point of admitting that the Black is a man
and a brother, but only in a natural form and when it can't be
got off." Well consequently I put poor Sophy on to other work
and forbid her answering the door or answering a bell on any
account but she was so unfortunately willing that nothing would
stop her flying up the kitchen stairs whenever a bell was heard to
tingle. I put it to her "Oh Sophy Sophy for goodness goodness
sake where does it come from?" To which that poor unlucky
willing mortal bursting out crying to see me so vexed replied
"I took a deal of black into me ma'am when I was a small child
being much neglected and I think it must be, that it works
out," so it continuing to work out of that poor thing and not
having another fault to find with her I says, "Sophy, what do
you seriously think of my helping you away to New South Wales
where it might not be noticed?" Nor did I ever repent the money
which was well spent, for she married the ship's cook on the
voyage (himself a Mulotter) and did well and lived happy, and
so far as ever I heard it was *not* noticed in a new state of society
to her dying day.

In what way Miss Wozenham lower down on the other side
of the way reconciled it to her feelings as a lady (which she is
not) to entice Mary Anne Perkinsop from my service is best
known to herself, I do not know and I do not wish to know how
opinions are formed at Wozenham's on any point. But Mary
Anne Perkinsop although I behaved handsomely to her and she
behaved unhandsomely to me was worth her weight in gold as

overawing lodgers without driving them away, for lodgers would be far more sparing of their bells with Mary Anne than I ever knew them be with Maid or Mistress, which is a great triumph especially when accompanied with a cast in the eye and a bag of bones, but it was the steadiness of her way with them through her father's having failed in Pork. It was Mary Anne's looking so respectable in her person and being so strict in her spirits that conquered the tea-and-sugarest gentleman (for he weighed them both in a pair of scales every morning) that I have ever had to deal with and no lamb grew meeker, still it afterwards came round to me that Miss Wozenham happening to pass and seeing Mary Anne take in the milk of a milkman that made free in a rosy-faced way (I think no worse of him) with every girl in the street but was quite frozen up like the statue at Charing Cross by her, saw Mary Anne's value in the lodging business and went as high as one pound per quarter more, consequently Mary Anne with not a word betwixt us says "If *you* will provide yourself Mrs. Lirriper in a month from this day *I* have already done the same," which hurt me and I said so, and she then hurt me more by insinuating that her father having failed in Pork had laid her open to it.

My dear I do assure you it's a harassing thing to know what kind of girls to give the preference to, for if they are lively they get bell'd off their legs and if they are sluggish you suffer from it yourself in complaints and if they are sparkling-eyed they get made love to and if they are smart in their persons they try on your Lodger's bonnets and if they are musical I defy you to keep them away from bands and organs, and allowing for any difference you like in their heads their heads will be always out of window just the same. And then what the gentlemen like in girls the ladies don't, which is fruitful hot water for all parties, and then there's temper though such a temper as Caroline Maxey's I hope not often. A good-looking black-eyed girl was Caroline and a comely-made girl to your cost when she did break out and laid about her, as took place first and last through a new-married couple come to see London in the first floor and the lady very high and it *was* supposed not liking the good looks of Caroline having none of her own to spare, but anyhow she did try Caroline though that was no excuse. So one afternoon Caroline comes down into the kitchen flushed and flashing, and she says to me "Mrs. Lirriper that woman in the first has aggravated me past bearing," I says "Caroline keep your temper," Caroline says with a curdling laugh "Keep my temper? You're right Mrs. Lirriper, so I will. Capital D her!" bursts out Caroline (you might have struck me into the centre of the earth with a feather when she said it) "I'll give her a touch of the temper that *I* keep!" Caroline downs with her hair my dear, screeches and rushes upstairs, I following as fast as my trembling legs could bear me, but before I got into the room the dinner cloth and pink and white service all dragged off upon the floor with a crash and the new married couple on their backs in the fire-grate, him with the shovel and tongs and a dish of cucumber across him and a mercy it was summer-time. "Caroline" I says "be calm," but she catches off my cap and tears it in her teeth as she passes me, then pounces on the new married lady makes her a bundle of ribbons takes her by the two ears and knocks the back of her head upon the carpet Murder screaming all the time Policemen running down the street and Wozenham's windows (judge of my feelings when I came to know it) thrown up and Miss Wozenham calling out from the balcony with crocodile's tears "It's Mrs. Lirriper been overcharging somebody to madness —she'll be murdered—I always thought so—Pleeseman save her!" My dear four of them and Caroline behind the chiffoniere attacking with the poker and when disarmed prize fighting with her double fists, and down and up and up and down and dreadful! But I couldn't bear to see the poor young creature roughly handled and her hair torn when they got the better of her, and I says "Gentlemen Policemen pray remember that her sex is the sex of your mothers and sisters and your sweethearts, and God bless them and you!" And there she was sitting down on the ground handcuffed, taking breath against the skirting-board and them cool with their coats in strips, and all she says was "Mrs. Lirriper I am sorry as ever I touched *you*, for you're a kind motherly old thing," and it made me think that I had often wished I had been a mother indeed and how would my heart have felt if I had been the mother of that girl! Well you know it turned out at the Police-office that she had done it before, and she had her clothes away and was sent to prison, and when she was to come out I trotted off to the gate in the evening with just a morsel of jelly in that little basket of mine to give her a mite of strength to face the world again, and there I met with a very decent mother waiting for her son through bad company and a stubborn one he was with his half boots not laced. So out came Caroline and I says "Caroline come along with me and sit down under the wall where it's retired and eat a little trifle that I have brought with me to do you good" and she throws her arms round my neck and says sobbing "Oh why were you never a mother when there are such mothers as there are!" she says, and in half a minute more she begins to laugh and says "Did I really tear your cap to shreds?" and when I told her "You certainly did so Caroline" she laughed again and said while she patted my face "Then why do you wear such queer old caps you dear old thing? If you hadn't worn such queer old caps I don't think I should have done it even then." Fancy the girl! Nothing could get out of her what she was going to do except O she would do well enough, and we parted she being very thankful and kissing my hands, and I never more saw or heard of that girl, except that I shall always believe that a very genteel cap which was brought anonymous to me one Saturday night in an oilskin basket by a most impertinent young sparrow of a monkey whistling with dirty shoes on the clean steps and playing the harp on the Airy railings with a hoop-stick came from Caroline.

What you lay yourself open to my dear in the way of being the object of uncharitable suspicions when you go into the Lodging business I have not the words to tell you, but never was I so dishonourable as to have two keys nor would I willingly think it even of Miss Wozenham lower down on the other side of the way sincerely hoping that it may not be, though doubtless at the same time money cannot come from nowhere and it is not reason to suppose that Bradshaws put it in for love be it blotty as it may. It *is* a hardship hurting to the feelings that Lodgers open their minds so wide to the idea that you are trying to get the better of them and shut their minds so close to the idea that they are trying to get the better of you, but as Major Jackman says to me "I know the ways of this circular world Mrs. Lirriper, and that's one of 'em all round it" and many is the little ruffle in my mind that the Major has smoothed, for he is a clever man who has seen much. Dear dear, thirteen years have passed though it seems but yesterday since I was sitting with my glasses on at the open front parlour window one evening in August (the parlours being then vacant) reading yesterday's paper my eyes for print being poor though still I am thankful to say a long sight at a dis-

tance, when I hear a gentleman come posting across the road and
up the street in a dreadful rage talking to himself in a fury and
d'ing and c'ing somebody. "By George!" says he out loud and
clutching his walking-stick, "I'll go to Mrs. Lirriper's. Which is
Mrs. Lirriper's?" Then looking round and seeing me he flourishes
his hat right off his head as if I had been the queen and he says
"Excuse the intrusion Madam, but pray Madam can you tell
me at what number in this street there resides a well-known and
much-respected lady by the name of Lirriper?" A little flustered
though I must say gratified I took off my glasses and curtseyed
and said "Sir, Mrs. Lirriper is your humble servant." "As-tonish-
ing!" says he. "A million pardons! Madam, may I ask you to
have the kindness to direct one of your domestics to open the door
to a gentleman in search of apartments, by the name of Jackman?" I had never heard the name but a politer gentleman I
never hope to see, for says he "Madam I am shocked at your
opening the door yourself to no worthier a fellow than Jemmy
Jackman. After you Madam. I never precede a lady." Then he
comes into the parlours and he sniffs and he says "Hah! These
are parlours! Not musty cupboards" he says "but parlours, and
no smell of coal-sacks." Now my dear it having been remarked
by some inimical to the whole neighbourhood that it always smells
of coal-sacks which might prove a drawback to Lodgers if encouraged, I says to the Major gently though firmly that I think
he is referring to Arundel or Surrey or Howard but not Norfolk.
"Madam" says he "I refer to Wozenham's lower down over the
way—Madam you can form no notion what Wozenham's
is—Madam it is a vast coal-sack, and Miss Wozenham has the
principles and manners of a female heaver—Madam from the
manner in which I have heard her mention you I know she has
no appreciation of a lady, and from the manner in which she has
conducted herself towards me I know she has no appreciation
of a gentleman—Madam my name is Jackman—should you
require any other reference than what I have already said, I
name the Bank of England—perhaps you know it!" Such was
the beginning of the Major's occupying the parlours and from
that hour to this the same and a most obliging Lodger and punctual in all respects except one irregular which I need not particularly specify, but made up for by his being a protection and at
all times ready to fill in the papers of the Assessed Taxes and
Juries and that, and once collared a young man with the drawing-

room clock under his cloak, and once on the parapets with his own hands and blankets put out the kitchen chimney and afterwards attending the summons made a most eloquent speech against the Parish before the magistrates and saved the engine, and ever quite the gentleman though passionate. And certainly Miss Wozenham's detaining the trunks and umbrella was not in a liberal spirit though it may have been according to her rights in law or an act *I* would myself have stooped to, the Major being so much the gentleman that though he is far from tall he seems almost so when he has his shirt frill out and his frock-coat on and his hat with the curly brims, and in what service he was I cannot truly tell you my dear whether Militia or Foreign, for I never heard him even name himself as Major but always simple "Jemmy Jackman" and once soon after he came when I felt it my duty to let him know that Miss Wozenham had put it about that he was no Major and I took the liberty of adding "which you are sir" his words were "Madam at any rate I am not a Minor, and sufficient for the day is the evil thereof" which cannot be denied to be the sacred truth, nor yet his military ways of having his boots with only the dirt brushed off taken to him in the front parlour every morning on a clean plate and varnishing them himself with a little sponge and a saucer and a whistle in a whisper so sure as ever his breakfast is ended, and so neat his ways that it never soils his linen which is scrupulous though more in quality than quantity, neither that nor his moustachios which to the best of my belief are done at the same time and which are as black and shining as his boots, his head of hair being a lovely white.

It was the third year nearly up of the Major's being in the parlours that early one morning in the month of February when Parliament was coming on and you may therefore suppose a number of impostors were about ready to take hold of anything they could get, a gentleman and lady from the country came in to view the Second, and I well remember that I had been looking out of window and had watched them and the heavy sleet driving down the street together looking for bills. I did not quite take to the face of the gentleman though he was good-looking too but the lady was a very pretty young thing and delicate, and it seemed too rough for her to be out at all though she had only come from the Adelphi Hotel which would not have been much above a quarter of a mile if the weather had been less severe. Now it did so happen my dear that I had been forced to put five shillings weekly additional on the second in consequence of a loss from running away full-dressed as if going out to a dinner-party, which was very artful and had made me rather suspicious taking it along with Parliament, so when the gentleman proposed three months certain and the money in advance and leave then reserved to renew on the same terms for six months more, I says I was not quite certain but that I might have engaged myself to another party but would step down stairs and look into it if they would take a seat. They took a seat and I went down to the handle of the Major's door that I had already began to consult finding it a great blessing, and I knew by his whistling in a whisper that he was varnishing his boots which was generally considered private, however he kindly calls out "If it's you, Madam, come in," and I went in and told him.

"Well, Madam," says the Major rubbing his nose—as I did fear at the moment with the black sponge but it was only his knuckle, he being always neat and dexterous with his fingers—"well, Madam, I suppose you would be glad of the money?"

I was delicate of saying "Yes" too out, for a little extra colour rose into the Major's cheeks and there was irregularity which I will not particularly specify in a quarter which I will not name.

"I am of opinion, Madam," says the Major "that when money is ready for you—when it is ready for you Mrs. Lirriper—you ought to take it. What is there against it, Madam, in this case up-stairs?"

"I really cannot say there is anything against it sir, still I thought I would consult you."

"You said a newly-married couple, I think, Madam?" says the Major.

I says "Ye-es. Evidently. And indeed the young lady mentioned to me in a casual way that she had not been married many months."

The Major rubbed his nose again and stirred the varnish round and round in its little saucer with his piece of sponge and took to his whistling in a whisper for a few moments. Then he says, "You would call it a Good Let, Madam?"

"Oh certainly a Good Let sir."

"Say they renew for the additional six months. Would it put you about very much Madam if—if the worst was to come to the worst?" said the Major.

"Well I hardly know," I says to the Major. "It depends upon circumstances. Would *you* object Sir for instance?"

"I?" says the Major. "Object? Jemmy Jackman? Mrs. Lirriper close with the proposal."

So I went up-stairs and accepted, and they came in next day which was Saturday and the Major was so good as to draw up a Memorandum of an agreement in a beautiful round hand and expressions that sounded to me equally legal and military, and Mr. Edson signed it on the Monday morning and the Major called upon Mr. Edson on the Tuesday and Mr. Edson called upon the Major on the Wednesday and the Second and the parlours were as friendly as could be wished.

The three months paid for had run out and we had got without any fresh overtures as to payment into May my dear, when there came an obligation upon Mr. Edson to go a business expedition right across the Isle of Man, which fell quite unexpected on that pretty little thing and is not a place that according to my views is particularly in the way to anywhere at any time but that may be a matter of opinion. So short a notice was it that he was to go next day, and dreadfully she cried poor pretty and I am sure I cried too when I saw her on the cold pavement in the sharp east wind—it being a very backward spring that year—taking a last leave of him with her pretty bright hair blowing this way and that and her arms clinging round his neck and him saying "There there there! Now let me go Peggy." And by that time it was plain that what the Major had been so accommodating as to say he would not object to happening in the house, would happen in it, and I told her as much when he was gone while I comforted her with my arm up the staircase, for I says "You will soon have others to keep up for my pretty and you must think of that."

His letter never came when it ought to have come and what she went through morning after morning when the postman brought none for her the very postman himself compassionated when she ran down to the door, and yet we cannot wonder at its being calculated to blunt the feelings to have all the trouble of other people's letters and none of the pleasure and doing it oftener in the mud and mizzle than not and at a rate of wages more resembling Little Britain than Great. But at last one morning when she was too poorly to come running down stairs he says to me with a pleased look in his face that made me next to love the man in his uniform coat though he was dripping wet "I have taken you first in the street this morning Mrs. Lirriper, for here's the one for Mrs. Edson." I went up to her bedroom with it fast as ever I could go, and she sat up in bed when she saw it and kissed it and tore it open and then a blank stare came upon her. "It's very short!" she says lifting her large eyes to my face. "O Mrs. Lirriper it's very short!" I says "My dear Mrs. Edson no doubt that's because your husband hadn't time to write more just at that time." "No doubt, no doubt," says she, and put her two hands on her face and turns round in her bed.

I shut her softly in and I crept down stairs and I tapped at the Major's door, and when the Major having his thin slices of bacon in his own Dutch oven saw me he came out of his chair and put me down on the sofa. "Hush!" says he, "I see something's the matter. Don't speak—take time." I says "O Major I am afraid there's cruel work up-stairs." "Yes yes" says he "I had begun to be afraid of it—take time." And then in opposition to his own words he rages out frightfully, and says "I shall never forgive myself Madam, that I, Jemmy Jackman, didn't see it all that morning—didn't go straight up-stairs when my boot-sponge was in my hand—didn't force it down his throat—and choke him dead with it on the spot!"

The Major and me agreed when we came to ourselves that just at present we could do no more than take on to suspect nothing and use our best endeavours to keep that poor young creature quiet, and what I ever should have done without the Major when it got about among the organ-men that quiet was our object is unknown, for he made lion and tiger war upon them to that degree that without seeing it I could not have believed it was in any gentleman to have such a power of bursting out with fire-irons walking-sticks water-jugs coals potatoes off his table the very hat off his head, and at the same time so furious in foreign languages that they would stand with their handles half turned fixed like the Sleeping Ugly—for I cannot say Beauty.

Ever to see the postman come near the house now gave me such a fear that it was a reprieve when he went by, but in about another ten days or a fortnight he says again "Here's one for Mrs. Edson.—Is she pretty well?" "She is pretty well postman, but not well enough to rise so early as she used" which was so far gospel-truth.

L

I carried the letter in to the Major at his breakfast and I says tottering "Major I have not the courage to take it up to her."

"It's an ill-looking villain of a letter," says the Major.

"I have not the courage Major" I says again in a tremble "to take it up to her."

After seeming lost in consideration for some moments the Major says, raising his head as if something new and useful had occurred to his mind "Mrs. Lirriper, I shall never forgive myself that I, Jemmy Jackman, didn't go straight up-stairs that morning when my boot-sponge was in my hand—and force it down his throat—and choke him dead with it."

"Major" I says a little hasty "you didn't do it which is a blessing, for it would have done no good and I think your sponge was better employed on your own honourable boots."

So we got to be rational, and planned that I should tap at her bedroom door and lay the letter on the mat outside and wait on the upper landing for what might happen, and never was gunpowder and cannon-balls or shells or rockets more dreaded than that dreadful letter was by me as I took it to the second floor.

A terrible loud scream sounded through the house the minute after she had opened it, and I found her on the floor lying as if her life was gone. My dear I never looked at the face of the letter which was lying open by her, for there was no occasion.

Everything I needed to bring her round the Major brought up with his own hands, besides running out to the chemist's for what was not in the house and likewise having the fiercest of all his many skirmishes with a musical instrument representing a ball-room I do not know in what particular country and company waltzing in and out at folding-doors with rolling eyes. When after a long time I saw her coming to, I slipped on the landing till I heard her cry, and then I went in and says cheerily "Mrs. Edson you're not well my dear and it's not to be wondered at," as if I had not been in before. Whether she believed or disbelieved I cannot say and it would signify nothing if I could, but I stayed by her for hours and then she God ever blesses me! and says she will try to rest for her head is bad.

"Major," I whispers, looking in at the parlours, "I beg and pray of you don't go out."

The Major whispers "Madam, trust me I will do no such a thing. How is she?"

I says "Major the good Lord above us only knows what burns and rages in her poor mind. I left her sitting at her window. I am going to sit at mine."

It came on afternoon and it came on evening. Norfolk is a delightful street to lodge in—provided you don't go lower down—but of a summer evening when the dust and waste paper lie in it and stray children play in it and a kind of a gritty calm and bake settles on it and a peal of church-bells is practising in the neighbourhood it is a trifle dull, and never have I seen it since at such a time and never shall I see it evermore at such a time without seeing the dull June evening when that forlorn young creature sat at her open corner window on the second and me at the my open corner window (the other corner) on the third. Something merciful, something wiser and better far than my own self, had moved me while it was yet light to sit in my bonnet and shawl, and as the shadows fell and the tide rose I could sometimes—when I put out my head and looked at her window below—see that she leaned out a little looking down the street. It was just settling dark when I saw *her* in the street.

So fearful of losing sight of her that it almost stops my breath while I tell it, I went down stairs faster than I ever moved in all my life and only tapped with my hand at the Major's door in passing it and slipping out. She was gone already. I made the same speed down the street and when I came to the corner of Howard-street I saw that she had turned it and was there plain before me going towards the west. O with what a thankful heart I saw her going along!

She was quite unacquainted with London and had very seldom been out for more than an airing in our own street where she knew two or three little children belonging to neighbours and had sometimes stood among them at the end of the street looking at the water. She must be going at hazard I knew, still she kept the by-streets quite correctly as long as they would serve her, and then turned up into the Strand. But at every corner I could see her head turned one way, and that way was always the river way.

It may have been only the darkness and quiet of the Adelphi that caused her to strike into it but she struck into it much as readily as if she had set out to go there, which perhaps was the case. She went straight down to the Terrace and along it and looked over the iron rail, and I often woke afterwards in my own bed with the horror of seeing her doing it. The desertion of the wharf below and the flowing of the high water there seemed to settle her purpose. She looked about as if to make out the way down, and she struck out the right way or the wrong way—I don't know which, for I don't know the place before or since—and I followed her the way she went.

It was noticeable that all this time she never once looked back. But there was now a great change in the manner of her going, and instead of going at a steady quick walk with her arms folded before her,—among the dark dismal arches she went in a wild way with her arms opened wide, as if they were wings and she was flying to her death.

We were on the wharf and she stopped. I stopped. I saw her hands at her bonnet-strings, and I rushed between her and the brink and took her round the waist with both my arms. She might have drowned me, I felt then, but she could never have got quit of me.

Down to that moment my mind had been all in a maze and not half an idea had I had in it what I should say to her, but the instant I touched her it came to me like magic and I had my natural voice and my senses and even almost my breath.

"Mrs. Edson!" I says "My dear! Take care. How ever did you lose your way and stumble on a dangerous place like this? Why you must have come here by the most perplexing streets in all London. No wonder you are lost, I am sure. And this place too! Why I thought nobody ever got here, except me to order my coals and the Major in the parlours to smoke his cigar!"—for I saw that blessed man close by, pretending to it.

"Hah—Hah—Hum!" coughs the Major.

"And good gracious me" I says, "why here he is!"

"Halloa! who goes there!" says the Major in a military manner.

"Well!" I says, "if this don't beat everything! Don't you know us Major Jackman?"

"Halloa!" says the Major. "Who calls on Jemmy Jackman?" (and more out of breath he was, and did it less like life, than I should have expected).

"Why here's Mrs. Edson Major" I says, "strolling out to cool her poor head which has been very bad, has missed her way and got lost, and Goodness knows where she might have got to but for me coming here to drop an order into my coal merchant's letter-box and you coming here to smoke your cigar!—And you really are not well enough my dear" I says to her "to be half so far from home without me.—And your arm will be very acceptable I am sure Major" I says to him "and I know she may lean upon it as heavy as she likes." And now we had both got her—thanks be Above!—one on each side.

She was all in a cold shiver and she so continued till I laid her on her own bed, and up to the early morning she held me by the hand and moaned and moaned "O wicked, wicked, wicked!" But when at last I made believe to droop my head and be overpowered with a dead sleep, I heard that poor young creature give such touching and such humble thanks for being preserved from taking her own life in her madness that I thought I should have cried my eyes out on the counterpane and I knew she was safe.

Being well enough to do and able to afford it, me and the Major laid our little plans next day while she was asleep worn out, and so I says to her as soon as I could do it nicely:

"Mrs. Edson my dear, when Mr. Edson paid me the rent for these further six months——"

She gave a start and I felt her large eyes look at me, but I went on with it and with my needlework.

"——I can't say that I am quite sure I dated the receipt right. Could you let me look at it?"

She laid her frozen cold hand upon mine and she looked through me when I was forced to look up from my needlework, but I had taken the precaution of having on my spectacles.

"I have no receipt" says she.

"Ah! Then he has got it" I says in a careless way. "It's of no great consequence. A receipt's a receipt."

From that time she always had hold of my hand when I could spare it which was generally only when I read to her, for of course she and me had our bits of needlework to plod at and neither of us was very handy at those little things, though I am still rather proud of my share in them too considering. And though she took to all I read to her, I used to fancy that next to what was taught upon the Mount she took most of all to His gentle compassion for us poor women and to His young life and to how His mother was proud of him and treasured His sayings in her heart. She had a grateful look in her eyes that never never never will be out of mine until they are closed in my

last sleep, and when I chanced to look at her without thinking
of it I would always meet that look, and she would often offer
me her trembling lip to kiss, much more like a little affectionate
half-broken-hearted child than ever I can imagine any grown
person.

One time the trembling of this poor lip was so strong and her
tears ran down so fast that I thought she was going to tell me
all her woe, so I takes her two hands in mine and I says:

"No my dear not now, you had best not try to do it now.
Wait for better times when you have got over this and are strong,
and then you shall tell me whatever you will. Shall it be
agreed?"

With our hands still joined she nodded her head many times,
and she lifted my hands and put them to her lips and to her
bosom.

"Only one word now my dear" I says. "Is there any one?"

She looked inquiringly "Any one?"

"That I can go to?"

She shook her head.

"No one that I can bring?"

She shook her head.

"No one is wanted by *me* my dear. Now that may be considered past and gone."

Not much more than a week afterwards—for this was far on
in the time of our being so together—I was bending over at
her bedside with my ear down to her lips, by turns listening for
her breath and looking for a sign of life in her face. At last it
came in a solemn way—not in a flash but like a kind of pale
faint light brought very slow to the face.

She said something to me that had no sound in it, but I saw
she asked me:

"Is this death?"

And I says "Poor dear poor dear, I think it is."

Knowing somehow that she wanted me to move her weak
right hand, I took it and laid it on her breast and then folded
her other hand upon it, and she prayed a good good prayer and
I joined in it poor me though there were no words spoke. Then
I brought the baby in its wrappers from where it lay, and I
says:

"My dear this is sent to a childless old woman. This is for
me to take care of."

The trembling lip was put up towards my face for the last time, and I dearly kissed it.

"Yes my dear" I says. "Please God! Me and the Major."

I don't know how to tell it right, but I saw her soul brighten and leap up, and get free and fly away in the grateful look.

*   *   *

So this is the why and wherefore of its coming to pass my dear that we called him Jemmy, being after the Major his own godfather with Lirriper for a surname being after myself, and never was a dear child such a brightening thing in a Lodgings or such a playmate to his grandmother as Jemmy to this house and me, and always good and minding what he was told (upon the whole) and soothing for the temper and making everything pleasanter except when he grew old enough to drop his cap down Wozenham's Airy and they wouldn't hand it up to him, and being worked into a state I put on my best bonnet and gloves and parasol with the child in my hand and I says "Miss Wozenham I little thought ever to have entered *your* house but unless my grandson's cap is instantly restored, the laws of this country regulating the property of the Subject shall at length decide betwixt yourself and me, cost what it may." With a sneer upon her face which did strike me I must say as being expressive of two keys but it may have been a mistake and if there is any doubt let Miss Wozenham have the full benefit of it as is but right, she rang the bell and she says "Jane, is there a street-child's old cap down our Airy?" I says "Miss Wozenham before your housemaid answers that question you must allow me to inform you to your face that my grandson is *not* a street-child and is *not* in the habit of wearing old caps. In fact" I says "Miss Wozenham I am far from sure that my grandson's cap may not be newer than your own" which was perfectly savage in me, her lace being the commonest machine-make washed and torn besides, but I had been put into a state to begin with fomented by impertinence. Miss Wozenham says red in the face "Jane you heard my question, is there any child's cap down our Airy?" "Yes Ma'am" says Jane "I think I did see some such rubbish a lying there." "Then" says Miss Wozenham "let these visitors out, and then throw up that worthless article out of my premises." But here the child who had been staring at Miss Wozenham with all his eyes and more, frowns down his little eyebrows purses up his little mouth puts his chubby legs far apart turns his little dimpled fists round and round slowly over one another like a little coffee-mill, and says to her "Oo impdent to mi Gran, me tut oor hi!" "Oh!" said Miss Wozenham looking down scornfully at the Mite "this is not a street-child is it not! Really!" I bursts out laughing and I says "Miss Wozenham if this an't a pretty sight to you I don't envy your feelings and I wish you good day. Jemmy come along with Gran." And I was still in the best of humours though his cap came flying up into the street as if it had been just turned on out of the water-plug, and I went home laughing all the way, all owing to that dear boy.

The miles and miles that me and the Major have travelled with Jemmy in the dusk betwen the lights are not to be calculated, Jemmy driving on the coach-box which is the Major's brass-bound writing desk on the table, me inside in the easy-chair and the Major Guard up behind with a brown-paper horn doing it really wonderful. I do assure you my dear that sometimes when I have taken a few winks in my place inside the coach and have come half awake by the flashing light of the fire and have heard that precious pet driving and the Major blowing up behind to have the change of horses ready when we got to the Inn, I have half believed we were on the old North Road that my poor Lirriper knew so well. Then to see that child and the Major both wrapped up getting down to warm their feet and going stamping about and having glasses of ale out of the paper match-boxes on the chimney-piece is to see the Major enjoying it fully as much as the child I am very sure, and it's equal to any play when Coachee opens the coach-door to look in at me inside and say "Wery 'past that 'tage.—'Prightened old lady?"

But what my inexpressible feelings were when we lost that child can only be compared to the Major's which were not a shade better, through his straying out at five years old and eleven o'clock in the forenoon and never heard of by word or sign or deed till half-past nine at night, when the Major had gone to the Editor of the Times newspaper to put in an advertisement, which came out next day four and twenty hours after he was found, and which I mean always carefully to keep in my lavender drawer as the first printed account of him. The more the day got on, the more I got distracted and the Major too and both of us made worse by the composed ways of the police though very civil and obliging and what I must call their obstinacy in not entertaining the idea that he was stolen. "We mostly find Mum" says the sergeant who came round to comfort me, which he didn't at all and he had been one of the private constables in Caroline's time to which he referred in his opening words when he said "Don't give way to uneasiness in your mind Mum, it'll all come as right as my nose did when I got the same barked by that young woman in your second floor"—says this sergeant "we mostly find Mum as people ain't over anxious to have what I may call second-hand children. *You'll* get him back Mum." "O but my dear good sir" I says clasping my hands and wringing them and clasping them again "he is such an uncommon child!" "Yes Mum" says the sergeant, "we mostly find that too Mum. The question is what his clothes were worth." "His clothes" I says "were not worth much sir for he had only got his playing-dress on, but the dear child!——" "All right Mum" says the sergeant. "*You'll* get him back, Mum. And even if he'd had his best clothes on, it wouldn't come to worse than his being found wrapped up in a cabbage-leaf, a shivering in a lane." His words pierced my heart like daggers and daggers, and me and the Major ran in and out like wild things all day long till the Major returning from his interview with the Editor of the Times at night rushes into my little room hysterical and squeezes my hand and wipes his eyes and says "Joy joy—officer in plain clothes came up on the steps as I was letting myself in—compose your feelings—Jemmy's found." Consequently I fainted away and when I came to, embraced the legs of the officer in plain clothes who seemed to be taking a kind of a quiet inventory in his mind of the property in my little room with brown whiskers, and I says "Blessings on you sir where is the Darling!" and he says "In Kennington Station House." I was dropping at his feet Stone at the image of that Innocence in cells with murderers when he adds "He followed the Monkey." I says deeming it slang language "Oh sir explain for a loving grandmother what Monkey!" He says "him in the spangled cap with the strap under the chin, as won't keep on—him as sweeps the crossings on a round table and don't want to draw his sabre more than he can help." Then I understood it all and most thankfully thanked him, and me and the Major and him drove over to Kennington and there we found our boy lying quite comfortable before a blazing fire having sweetly played himself to sleep upon a small accordion nothing like so big as a flat iron which they had been so kind as to lend him for the purpose and which it appeared had been stopped upon a very young person.

My dear the system upon which the Major commenced and as I may say perfected Jemmy's learning when he was so small that if the dear was on the other side of the table you had to look under it instead of over it to see him with his mother's own bright hair in beautiful curls, is a thing that ought to be known to the Throne and Lords and Commons and then might obtain some promotion for the Major which he well deserves and would be none the worse for (speaking between friends) L. S. D.-ically. When the Major first undertook his learning he says to me:

"I'm going Madam" he says "to make our child a Calculating Boy."

"Major" I says, "you terrify me and may do the pet a permanent injury you would never forgive yourself."

"Madam," says the Major, "next to my regret that when I had my boot-sponge in my hand, I didn't choke that scoundrel with it—on the spot——"

"There! For Gracious sake," I interrupts, "let his conscience find him without sponges."

"——I say next to that regret, Madam," says the Major would be the regret with which my breast," which he tapped, "would be surcharged if this fine mind was not early cultivated. But mark me Madam," says the Major holding up his forefinger "cultivated on a principle that will make it a delight."

"Major" I says "I will be candid with you and tell you openly that if ever I find the dear child fall off in his appetite I shall know it is his calculations and shall put a stop to them at two minutes' notice. Or if I find them mounting to his head" I says, "or striking any ways cold to his stomach or leading to anything approaching flabbiness in his legs, the result will be the same, but Major you are a clever man and have seen much and you love the child and are his own godfather, and if you feel a confidence in trying try."

"Spoken Madam" says the Major "like Emma Lirriper. All I have to ask Madam, is, that you will leave my godson and myself to make a week or two's preparations for surprising you, and that you will give me leave to have up and down any small articles not actually in use that I may require from the kitchen."

"From the kitchen Major?" I says half feeling as if he had a mind to cook the child.

"From the kitchen" says the Major, and smiles and swells, and at the same time looks taller.

So I passed my word and the Major and the dear boy were shut up together for half an hour at a time through a certain while, and never could I hear anything going on betwixt them but talking and laughing and Jemmy clapping his hands and screaming out numbers, so I says to myself "it has not harmed him yet" nor could I on examining the dear find any signs of it anywhere about him which was likewise of great relief. At last one day Jemmy brings me a card in joke of the Major's neat writing "The Messrs. Jemmy Jackman" for we had given him the Major's other name too "request the honour of Mrs. Lirriper's company at the Jackman Institution in the front parlour this evening at five, military time, to witness a few slight feats of elementary arithmetic." And if you'll believe me there in the front parlour at five punctual to the moment was the Major behind the Pembroke table with both leaves up and a lot of things from the kitchen tidily set out on old newspapers spread atop of it, and there was the Mite stood up on a chair with his rosy cheeks flushing and his eyes sparkling clusters of diamonds.

"Now Gran" says he, "oo tit down and don't oo touch ler poople"—for he saw with every one of those diamonds of his that I was going to give him a squeeze.

"Very well sir" I says "I am obedient in this good company I am sure." And I sits down in the easy-chair that was put for me, shaking my sides.

But picture my admiration when the Major going on almost as quick as if he was conjuring sets out all the articles he names, and says, "Three saucepans, an Italian iron, a hand-bell, a toasting-fork, a nutmeg grater, four pot-lids, a spice-box, two egg-cups, and a chopping-board—how many?" and when that Mite instantly cries "Fifteen, tut down tive and carry ler 'toppin-board" and then claps his hands draws up his legs and dances on his chair!

My dear with the same astonishing ease and correctness him and the Major added up the tables chairs and sofy, the picters fender and fire-irons their own selves me and the cat and the eyes in Miss Wozenham's head, and whenever the sum was done Young Roses and Diamonds claps his hands and draws up his legs and dances on his chair.

The pride of the Major! ("*Here's* a mind Ma'am!" he says to me behind his hand.)

Then he says aloud, "We now come to the next elementary rule: which is called——"

"Umtraction!" cries Jemmy.

"Right" says the Major. "We have here a toasting-fork, a potato in its natural state, two pot-lids, one egg-cup, a wooden spoon, and two skewers, from which it is necessary for commercial purposes to subtract a sprat-gridiron, a small pickle-jar, two lemons, one pepper-castor, a blackbeetle-trap, and a knob of the dresser-drawer—what remains?"

"Toatin-fork!" cries Jemmy.

"In numbers how many?" says the Major.

"One!" cries Jemmy.

("*Here's* a boy, Ma'am?" says the Major to me, behind his hand.)

Then the Major goes on:

"We now approach the next elementary rule: which is entitled——"

"Tickleication" cries Jemmy.

"Correct" says the Major.

But my dear to relate to you in detail the way in which they multiplied fourteen sticks of firewood by two bits of ginger and a larding-needle, or divided pretty well everything else there was on the table by the heater of the Italian iron and a chamber candlestick, and got a lemon over, would make my head spin round and round and round as it did at the time. So I says "if you'll excuse my addressing the chair Professor Jackman I think the period of the lecture has now arrived when it becomes necessary that I should take a god hug of this young scholar." Upon which Jemmy calls out from his station on the chair "Gran oo open oor arms and me'll make a 'pring into 'em." So I opened my arms to him as I had opened my sorrowful heart when his poor young mother lay a dying, and he had his jump and we had a good long hug together and the Major prouder than any peacock says to me behind his hand, "You need not let him know it Madam" (which I certainly need not for the Major was quite audible) "but he is a boy!"

In this way Jemmy grew and grew and went to day-school and continued under the Major too, and in summer we were as happy as the days were long and in winter we were as happy as the days were short and there seemed to rest a Blessing on the Lodgings for they as good as Let themselves and would have done it if there had been twice the accommodation, when sore and hard against my will I one day says to the Major

"Major you know what I am going to break to you. Our boy must go to boarding-school."

It was a sad sight to see the Major's countenance drop, and I pitied the good soul with all my heart.

"Yes Major" I says "though he is as popular with the Lodgers as you are yourself and though he is to you and me what only you and me know, still it is in the course of things and Life is made of partings and we must part with our Pet."

Bold as I spoke, I saw two Majors and half a dozen fireplaces, and when the poor Major put one of his neat bright-varnished boots upon the fender and his elbow on his knee and his head upon his hand and rocked himself a little to and fro, I was dreadfully cut up.

"But" says I clearing my throat "you have so well prepared him Major—he has had such a Tutor in you—that he will have none of the first drudgery to go through. And he is so clever besides that he'll soon make his way to the front rank."

"He is a boy" says the Major—having sniffed—"that has not his like on the face of the earth."

"True as you say Major, and it is not for us merely for our own sakes to do anything to keep him back from being a credit and an ornament wherever he goes and perhaps even rising to be a great man, is it Major? He will have all my little savings when my work is done (being all the world to me) and we must try to make him a wise man and a good man, mustn't we Major?"

"Madam" says the Major rising "Jemmy Jackman is becoming an older file than I was aware of, and you put him to shame. You are thoroughly right Madam. You are simply and undeniably right.—And if you'll excuse me, I'll take a walk."

So the Major being gone out and Jemmy being at home, I got the child into my little room here and I stood him by my chair and I took his mother's own curls in my hand and I spoke to him loving and serious. And when I had reminded the darling how that he was now in his tenth year and when I had said to him about his getting on in life pretty much what I had said to the Major I broke to him how that we must have this same parting, and there I was forced to stop for there I saw of a sudden the well remembered lip with its tremble, and it so brought back that time! But with the spirit that was in him he controlled it soon and he says gravely nodding through his tears, "I understand Gran—I know it *must* be, Gran—go on Gran, don't be afraid of *me*." And when I had said all that ever I could think of, he turned his bright steady face to mine and he says just a little broken here and there "You shall see Gran that I can be a man and that I can do anything that is grateful and loving to you—and if I don't grow up to be what you would like to have me—I hope it will be—because I shall die." And with that he sat down by me and I went on to tell him of the school of which I had excellent recommendations and where it was and how many scholars and what games they played as I had heard and what length of holidays, to all of which he listened bright and clear. And so it came that at last he says "And now dear Gran let me kneel down here where I have been used to say my prayers and let me fold my face for just a minute in your gown and let me cry, for you have been more than father— more than mother—more than brothers sisters friends—to me!" And so he did cry and I too and we were both much the better for it.

From that time forth he was true to his word and ever blithe and ready, and even when me and the Major took him down into Lincolnshire he was far the gayest of the party though for sure and certain he might easily have been that, but he really was and put life into us only when it came to the last Good-by, he says with a wistful look "You wouldn't have me not really sorry would you Gran?" and when I says "No dear, Lord forbid!" he says "I am glad of that!" and ran in out of sight.

But now that the child was gone out of the Lodgings the Major fell into a regularly moping state. It was taken notice of by all the Lodgers that the Major moped. He hadn't even the same air of being rather tall that he used to have, and if he varnished his boots with a single gleam of interest it was as much as he did.

One evening the Major came into my little room to take a cup of tea and a morsel of buttered toast and to read Jemmy's newest letter which had arrived that afternoon (by the very same postman more than middle-aged upon the Beat now), and the letter raising him up a little I says to the Major:

"Major you mustn't get into a moping way."

The Major shook his head. "Jemmy Jackman Madam," he says with a deep sigh, "is an older file than I thought him."

"Moping is not the way to grow younger Major."

"My dear Madam," says the Major, "is there *any* way of growing younger?"

Feeling that the Major was getting rather the best of that point I made a diversion to another.

"Thirteen years! Thir-teen years! Many lodgers have come and gone, in the thirteen years that you have lived in the parlours Major."

"Hah!" says the Major warming. "Many Madam, many."

"And I should say you have been familiar with them all?"

"As a rule (with its exceptions like all rules) my dear Madam" says the Major, "they have honoured me with their acquaintance, and not unfrequently with their confidence."

Watching the Major as he drooped his white head and stroked his black moustachios and moped again, a thought which I think must have been going about looking for an owner somewhere dropped into my old noddle if you will excuse the expression.

"The walls of my Lodgings" I says in a casual way—for my dear it is of no use going straight at a man who mopes—"might have something to tell, if they could tell it."

The Major neither moved nor said anything but I saw he was attending with his shoulders my dear—attending with his shoulders to what I said. In fact I saw that his shoulders were struck by it.

"The dear boy was always fond of story-books" I went on, like as if I was talking to myself. "I am sure this house—his own home—might write a story or two for his reading one day or another."

The Major's shoulders gave a dip and a curve and his head came up in his shirt-collar. The Major's head came up in his shirt-collar as I hadn't seen it come up since Jemmy went to school.

"It is unquestionable that in intervals of cribbage and a friendly rubber, my dear Madam," says the Major, "and also over what used to be called in my young times—in the salad days of Jemmy Jackman—the social glass, I have exchanged many a reminiscence with your Lodgers."

My remark was—I confess I made it with the deepest and artfullest of intentions—"I wish our dear boy had heard them!"

"Are you serious Madam?" asks the Major starting and turning full round.

"Why not Major?"

"Madam" says the Major, turning up one of his cuffs, "they shall be written for him."

"Ah! Now you speak" I says giving my hands a pleased clap. "Now you are in a way out of moping Major!"

"Between this and my holidays—I mean the dear boy's" says the Major turning up his other cuff, "a good deal may be done towards it."

"Major you are a clever man and you have seen much and not a doubt of it."

"I'll begin," says the Major looking as tall as ever he did, "to-morrow."

My dear the Major was another man in three days and he was himself again in a week and he wrote and wrote and wrote with his pen scratching like rats behind the wainscot, and whether he had many grounds to go upon or whether he did at all romance I cannot tell you, but what he has written is in the left-hand glass closet of the little bookcase close behind you, and if you'll put your hand in you'll find it come out heavy in lumps sewn together and being beautifully plain and unknown Greek and Hebrew to myself and me quite wakeful, I shall take it as a favour if you'll read out loud and read on.

II

HOW THE FIRST FLOOR WENT TO CROWLEY CASTLE

I have come back to London, Major, possessed by a family-story that I have picked up in the country. While I was out of town, I visited the ruins of the great old Norman castle of Sir Mark Crowley, the last baronet of his name, who has been dead nearly a hundred years. I stayed in the village near the castle, and thence I bring back some of the particulars of the tale I am going to tell you, derived from old inhabitants who heard them from their fathers;—no longer ago.

We drove from our little sea-bathing place, in Sussex, to see the massive ruins of Crowley Castle, which is the show-excursion of Merton. We had to alight at a field gate: the road further on being too bad for the slightly-built carriage, or the poor tired Merton horse: and we walked for about a quarter of a mile through uneven ground, which had once been an Italian garden; and then we came to a bridge over a dry moat, and went over the groove of a portcullis that had once closed the massive entrance, into an empty space surrounded by thick walls, draperied with ivy, unroofed, and open to the sky. We could judge of the beautiful tracery that had been in the windows, by the remains of the stonework here and there; and an old man—"ever so old," he called himself when we inquired his exact age—who scrambled and stumbled out of some lair in the least devastated part of the ruins at our approach, and who established himself as our guide, showed us a scrap of glass yet lingering in what was the window of the great drawing-room not above seventy years ago. After he had done his duty, he hobbled with us to the neighbouring church, where the knightly Crowleys lie buried: some commemorated by ancient brasses, some by altar-tombs, some by fine Latin epitaphs, bestowing upon them every virtue under the sun. He had to take the church-key back to the adjoining parsonage at the entrance of the long straggling street which forms the village of Crowley. The castle and the church were on the summit of a hill, from which we could see the distant line of sea beyond the misty marshes. The village fell away from the church and parsonage, down the hill. The aspect of the place was little, if at all, changed, from its aspect in the year 1772.

But I must begin a little earlier. From one of the Latin epitaphs I learnt that Amelia Lady Crowley died in 1756, deeply regretted by her loving husband, Sir Mark. He never married again, though his wife had left him no heir to his name or his estate—only a little tiny girl—Theresa Crowley. This child would inherit her mother's fortune, and all that Sir Mark was free to leave; but this little was not much; the castle and all the lands going to his sister's son, Marmaduke, or as he was usually called Duke, Brownlow. Duke's parents were dead, and his uncle was his guardian, and his guardian's house was his home. The lad was some seven or eight years older than his cousin; and probably Sir Mark thought it not unlikely that his daughter and his heir might make a match. Theresa's mother had had some foreign blood in her, and had been brought up in France—not so far away but that its shores might be seen by any one who chose to take an easy day's ride from Crowley Castle for the purpose.

Lady Crowley had been a delicate elegant creature, but no great beauty, judging from all accounts; Sir Mark's family were famous for their good looks; Theresa, an unusually lucky child, inherited the outward graces of both her parents. A portrait which I saw of her, degraded to a station over the parlour chimney-piece in the village inn, showed me black hair, soft yet arch grey eyes with brows and lashes of the same tint as her hair, a full pretty pouting passionate mouth, and a round slender throat. She was a wilful little creature, and her father's indulgence made her more wayward. She had a nurse, too, a French bonne, whose mother had been about my lady from her youth, who had followed my lady to England, and who had died there. Victorine had been in attendance on the young Theresa from her earliest infancy, and almost took the place of a parent in power and affection—in power, as to ordering and arranging almost what she liked, concerning the child's management—in love, because they speak to this day of the black year when virulent smallpox was rife in Crowley, and when, Sir Mark being far away on some diplomatic mission—in Vienna, I fancy—Victorine shut herself up with Miss Theresa when the child was taken ill with the disease, and nursed her night and day. She only succumbed to the dreadful illness when all danger to the child was over. Theresa came out of it with unblemished beauty; Victorine barely escaped with life, and was disfigured for life.

This disfigurement put a stop to much unfounded scandal which had been afloat respecting the French servant's great influence over Sir Mark. He was, in fact, an easy and indolent man, rarely excited to any vehemence of emotion, and who felt it to be a point of honour to carry out his dead wife's wish that Victorine should never leave Theresa, and that the management of the child should be confided to her. Only once had there been a struggle for power between Sir Mark and the bonne, and then she had won the victory. And no wonder, if the old butler's account were true; for he had gone into the room unawares, and had found Sir Mark and Victorine at high words; and he said that Victorine was white with rage, that her eyes were blazing with passionate fire, that her voice was low, and her words were few, but that, although she spoke in French, and he the butler only knew his native English, he would rather have been sworn at by a drunken grenadier with a sword in his hand, than have had those words of Victorine's addressed to him.

Even the choice of Theresa's masters was left to Victorine. A little reference was occasionally made to Madame Hawtrey, the parson's wife and a distant relation of Sir Mark's, but, seeing that, if Victorine chose so to order it, Madam Hawtrey's own little daughter Bessy would have been deprived of the advantages resulting from gratuitous companionship in all Theresa's lessons, she was careful how she opposed or made an enemy of Mademoiselle Victorine. Bessy was a gentle quiet child, and grew up to be a sensible sweet-tempered girl, with a very fair share of English beauty; fresh-complexion, brown-eyed, round-faced, with a stiff though well-made figure, as different as possible from Theresa's slight lithe graceful form. Duke was a young man to these two maidens, while they to him were little more than children. Of course he admired his cousin Theresa the most—who would not?—but he was establishing his first principles of morality for himself, and her conduct towards Bessy sometimes jarred against his ideas of right. One day, after she had been tyrannising over the self-contained and patient Bessy so as to make the latter cry—and both the amount of the tyranny and the crying were unusual circumstances, for Theresa was of a generous nature when not put out of the way—Duke spoke to his cousin :

"Theresa ! You had no right to blame Bessy as you did. It was as much your fault as hers. You were as much bound to remember Mr. Dawson's directions about the sums you were to do for him, as she was."

The girl opened her great grey eyes in surprise. She to blame !

"What does Bessy come to the castle for, I wonder? They pay nothing—we pay all. The least she can do, is to remember for me what we are told. I shan't trouble myself with attending to Mr. Dawson's directions; and if Bessy does not like to do so, she can stay away. She already knows enough to earn her bread as a maid : which I suppose is what she'll have to come to."

The moment Theresa had said this, she could have bitten her tongue out for the meanness and rancour of the speech. She saw pain and disappointment clearly expressed on Duke's face; and, in another moment, her impulses would have carried her to the opposite extreme, and she would have spoken out her self-reproach. But Duke thought it his duty to remonstrate with her, and to read her a homily, which, however true and just, weakened the effect of the look of distress on his face. Her wits were called into play to refute his arguments; her head rather than her heart took the prominent part in the controversy; and it ended unsatisfactorily to both; he, going away with dismal though unspoken prognostics touching what she would become as a woman if she were so supercilious and unfeeling as a girl; she, the moment his back was turned, throwing herself on the floor and sobbing as if her heart would break. Victorine heard her darling's passionate sobs, and came in.

"What hast thou, my angel! Who has been vexing thee,— tell me, my cherished?"

She tried to raise the girl, but Theresa would not be raised; neither would she speak till she chose, in spite of Victorine's entreaties. When she chose, she lifted herself up, still sitting on the floor, and putting her tangled hair off her flushed tear-stained face, said:

"Never mind, it was only something Duke said; I don't care for it now." And refusing Victorine's aid, she got up, and stood thoughtfully looking out of window.

"That Duke!" exclaimed Victorine. "What business has that Mr. Duke to go vex my darling? He is not your husband yet, that he should scold you, or that you should mind what he says."

Theresa listened and gained a new idea; but she gave no outward sign of attention, or of her now hearing for the first time how that she was supposed to be intended for her cousin's wife. She made no reply to Victorine's caresses and speeches; one might almost say she shook her off. As soon as she was left to herself, she took her hat, and going out alone, as she was wont, in the pleasure-grounds, she went down the terrace steps, crossed the bowling-green, and opened a little wicket-gate which led into the garden of the parsonage. There, were Bessy and her mother, gathering fruit. It was Bessy whom Theresa sought; for there was something in Madam Hawtrey's silky manner that was always rather repugnant to her. However, she was not going to shrink from her resolution because Madam Hawtrey was there. So she went up to the startled Bessy, and said to her, as if she were reciting a prepared speech: "Bessy, I behaved very crossly to you; I had no business to have spoken to you as I did."—"Will you forgive me?" was the pre-determined end of this confession; but somehow, when it came to that, she could not say it with Madam Hawtrey standing by, ready to smile and to curtsey as soon as she could catch Theresa's eye. There was no need to ask forgiveness though; for Bessy had put down her half filled basket, and came softly up to Theresa, stealing her brown soil-stained little hand into the young lady's soft white one, and looking up at her with loving brown eyes.

"I am so sorry, but I think it was the sums on page 108. I have been looking and looking, and I am almost sure."

Her exculpatory tone caught her mother's ear, although her words did not.

"I am sure, Miss Theresa, Bessy is so grateful for the privileges of learning with you! It is such an advantage to her! I often tell her, 'Take pattern by Miss Theresa, and do as she does, and try and speak as she does, and there'll not be a parson's daughter in all Sussex to compare with you.' Don't I, Bessy?"

Theresa shrugged her shoulders—a trick she had caught from Victorine—and, turning to Bessy, asked her what she was going to do with those gooseberries she was gathering? And as Theresa spoke, she lazily picked the ripest out of the basket, and ate them.

"They are for a pudding," said Bessy. "As soon as we have gathered enough, I am going in to make it."

"I'll come and help you," said Theresa, eagerly. "I should so like to make a pudding. Our Monsieur Antoine never makes gooseberry puddings."

Duke came past the parsonage an hour or so afterwards : and, looking in by chance through the open casement windows of the kitchen, saw Theresa pinned up in a bib and apron, her arms all over flour, flourishing a rolling-pin, and laughing and chattering with Bessy similarly attired. Duke had spent his morning ostensibly in fishing; but in reality in weighing in his own mind what he could do or say to soften the obdurate heart of his cousin. And here it was, all inexplicably right, as if by some enchanter's wand!

The only conclusion Duke could come to was the same that many a wise (and foolish) man had come to before his day :

"Well! Women are past my comprehension, that's all!"

When all this took place, Theresa was about fifteen; Bessy was perhaps six months older; Duke was just leaving Oxford. His uncle, Sir Mark, was excessively fond of him; yes! and proud, too, for he had distinguished himself at college, and every one spoke well of him. And he, for his part, loved Sir Mark, and, unspoiled by the fame and reputation he had gained at Christ Church, paid respectful deference to Sir Mark's opinions.

As Theresa grew older, her father supposed that he played his cards well in singing Duke's praises on every possible occasion. She tossed her head, and said nothing. Thanks to Victorine's revelations, she understood the tendency of her father's speeches. She intended to make her own choice of a husband when the time came; and it might be Duke, or it might be some one else. When Duke did not lecture or prose, but was sitting his horse so splendidly at the meet, before the huntsman gave the blast, "Found;" when Duke was holding his own in discourse with other men; when Duke gave her a short sharp word of command on any occasion; then she decided that she would marry him, and no one else. But when he found fault, or stumbled about awkwardly in a minuet, or talked moralities against duelling, then she was sure that Duke should never be her husband. She wondered if he knew about it; if any one had told him, as Victorine had told her; if her father had revealed his thoughts and wishes to his nephew, as plainly as he had done to his daughter? This last query made her cheeks burn; and, on days when the suspicion had been brought by any chance prominently before her mind, she was especially rude and disagreeable to Duke.

He was to go abroad on the grand tour of Europe, to which young men of fortune usually devoted three years. He was to have a tutor, because all young men of his rank had tutors; else he was quite wise enough, and steady enough, to have done without one, and probably knew a good deal more about what was best to be observed in the countries they were going to visit, than Mr. Roberts, his appointed bear-leader. He was to come back full of historical and political knowledge, speaking French and Italian like a native, and having a smattering of barbarous German, and he was to enter the House as a county member, if possible—as a borough member at the worst; and was to make a great success; and then, as every one understood, he was to marry his cousin Theresa.

He spoke to her father about it, before starting on his travels. It was after dinner in Crowley Castle. Sir Mark and Duke sat alone, each pensive at the thought of the coming parting.

"Theresa is but young," said Duke, breaking into speech after a long silence, "but if you have no objection, uncle, I should like to speak to her before I leave England, about my—my hopes."

Sir Mark played with his glass, poured out some more wine, drank it off at a draught, and then replied:

"No, Duke, no. Leave her in peace with me. I have looked forward to having her for my companion through these three years; they'll soon pass away" (to age, but not to youth), "and I should like to have her undivided heart till you come back. No, Duke! Three years will soon pass away, and then we'll have a royal wedding."

Duke sighed, but said no more. The next day was the last. He wanted Theresa to go with him to take leave of the Hawtreys at the Parsonage, and of the villagers; but she was wilful, and would not. He remembered, years afterwards, how Bessy's gentle peaceful manner had struck him as contrasted with Theresa's, on that last day. Both girls regretted his departure. He had been so uniformly gentle and thoughtful in his behaviour to Bessy, that, without any idea of love, she felt him to be her pattern of noble chivalrous manhood; the only person, except her father, who was steadily kind to her. She admired his sentiments, she esteemed his principles, she considered his long evolvement of his ideas as the truest eloquence. He had lent her books, he had directed her studies; all the advice and information which Theresa had rejected had fallen to Bessy's lot, and she had received it thankfully.

Theresa burst into a passion of tears as soon as Duke and his suite were out of sight. She had refused the farewell kiss her father had told her to give him, but had waved her white handkerchief out of the great drawing-room window (that very window in which the old guide showed me the small piece of glass still lingering). But Duke had ridden away with slack rein and downcast head, without looking back.

His absence was a great blank in Sir Mark's life. He had never sought London much as a place of residence; in former days he had been suspected of favouring the Stuarts; but nothing could be proved against him, and he had subsided into a very tolerably faithful subject of King George the Third. Still, a cold shoulder having been turned to him by the court party at one time, he had become prepossessed against the English capital. On the contrary, his wife's predilections and his own tendencies had always made Paris a very agreeable place of residence to him.

To Paris he at length resorted again, when the blank in his life oppressed him; and from Paris, about two years after Duke's departure, he returned after a short absence from home, and suddenly announced to his daughter and the household that he had taken an apartment in the Rue Louis le Grand for the coming winter, to which there was to be an immediate removal of his daughter, Victorine, and certain other personal attendants and servants.

Nothing could exceed Theresa's mad joy at this unexpected news. She sprang upon her father's neck, and kissed him till she was tired—whatever he was. She ran to Victorine, and told her to guess what "heavenly bliss" was going to befal them, dancing round the middle-aged woman until she, in her spoilt impatience, was becoming angry, when, kissing her, she told her, and ran off to the Parsonage, and thence to the church, bursting in upon morning prayers—for it was All Saints' Day, although she had forgotten it—and filliping a scrap of paper on which she had hastily written, "We are going to Paris for the winter—all of us," rolled into a ball, from the castle pew to that of the parson. She saw Bessy redden as she caught it, put it into her pocket unread, and, after an apologetic glance at the curtained seat in which Theresa was, go on with her meek responses. Theresa went out by the private door in a momentary fit of passion. "Stupid cold-blooded creature!" she said to herself. But that afternoon Bessy came to the castle, so sorry—and so losing her own sorrow in sympathy with her friend's gladness, that Theresa took her into favour again. The girls parted with promises of correspondence, and with some regret : the greatest on Bessy's side. Some grand promises of Paris fashion, and presents of dress, Theresa made in her patronising way; but Bessy did not seem to care much for them—which was fortunate, for they were never fulfilled.

Sir Mark had an idea in his head of perfecting Theresa's accomplishments and manners by Parisian masters and Parisian society. English residents in Venice, Florence, Rome, wrote to their friends at home about Duke. They spoke of him as of what we should, at the present day, call a "rising young man." His praises ran so high, that Sir Mark began to fear lest his handsome nephew, fêted by princes, courted by ambassadors, made love to by lovely Italian ladies, might find Theresa too country-bred for his taste.

Thus had come about, the engaging of the splendid apartment in the Rue Louis le Grand. The street itself is narrow, and now-a-days we are apt to think the situation close; but in those days it was the height of fashion; for, the great arbiter of fashion, the Duc de Richelieu, lived there, and, to inhabit an apartment in that street, was in itself a mark of bon ton. Victorine seemed almost crazy with delight when they took possession of their new abode. "This dear Paris! This lovely France! And now I see my young lady, my darling, my angel, in a room suited to her beauty and her rank: such as my lady her mother would have planned for her, if she had lived." Any allusion to her dead mother always touched Theresa to the quick. She was in her bed, under the blue silk curtains of an alcove, when Victorine said this,—being too much fatigued after her journey to respond to Victorine's rhapsodies; but now she put out her little hand and gave Victorine's a pressure of gratitude and pleasure. Next day she wandered about the rooms and admired their splendour almost to Victorine's content. Her father, Sir Mark, found a handsome carriage and horses for his darling's use; and also found that not less necessary article—a married lady of rank who would take his girl under her wing. When all these preliminary arrangements were made, who so wildly happy as Theresa! Her carriage was of the newest fashion, fit to vie with any on the Cours de la Reine, the then fashionable drive. The box at the Grand Opéra, and at the Français, which she shared with Madame la Duchesse de G., was the centre of observation; Victorine was in her best humour, Theresa's credit at her dressmaker's was unlimited, her indulgent father was charmed with all she did and said. She had masters, it is true; but, to a rich and beautiful young lady, masters were wonderfully complaisant, and with them as with all the world, she did what she pleased. Of Parisian society, she had enough and more than enough. The duchess went everywhere, and Theresa went too. So did a certain Count de la Grange: some relation or connexion of the duchess: handsome, with a south of France handsomeness: with delicate features, marred by an over-softness of expression, from which (so men said) the tiger was occasionally seen to peep forth. But, for elegance of dress and demeanour he had not his fellow in Paris—which of course meant, not in the world.

Sir Mark heard rumours of this man's conduct, which were not pleasing to him; but when he accompanied his daughter into society, the count was only as deferential as it became a gentleman to be to so much beauty and grace. When Theresa was taken out by the duchess to the opera, to balls, to petits soupers, without her father, then the count was more than deferential; he was adoring. It was a little intoxicating for a girl brought up in the solitude of an English village, to have so many worshippers at her feet all at once, in the great gay city; and the inbred coquetry of her nature came out, adding to her outward grace, if taking away from the purity and dignity of her character. It was Victorine's delight to send her darling out arrayed for conquest; her hair delicately powdered, and scented with maréchale; her little "mouches" put on with skill; the tiny half-moon patch, to lengthen the already almond-shaped eye; the minute star to give the effect of a dimple at the corner of her scarlet lips; the silver gauze looped up over the petticoat of blue brocade, distended over a hoop, much as gowns are worn in our days; the coral onaments of her silver dress, matching with the tint of the high heels to her shoes. And, at night, Victorine was never tired of listening and questioning; of triumphing in Theresa's triumphs; of invariably reminding her that she was bound to marry the absent cousin, and return to the half-feudal state of the old castle in Sussex.

Still, even now, if Duke had returned from Italy, all might have gone well; but when Sir Mark, alarmed by the various proposals he received for Theresa's hand from needy French noblemen, and by the admiration she was exciting everywhere, wrote to Duke, and urged him to join them in Paris on his return from his travels, Duke answered that three months were yet unexpired of the time allotted for the grand tour; and that he was anxious to avail himself of that interval to see something of Spain. Sir Mark read this letter aloud to Theresa, with many expressions of annoyance as he read. Theresa merely said, "Of course, Duke does what he likes," and turned away to see some new lace brought for her inspection. She heard her father sigh over a re-perusal of Duke's letter, and she set her teeth in the anger she would not show in acts or words. That day the Count de Grange met with gentler treatment from her than he had done for many days—than he had done since her father's letter to Duke had been sent off to Genoa. As ill fortune would have it, Sir Mark had occasion to return to England at this time, and he, guileless himself, consigned Theresa and her maid Victorine, and her man Felix, to the care of the duchess for three weeks. They were to reside at the Hôtel de G. during this time. The duchess welcomed them in her most caressing manner, and showed Theresa the suite of rooms, with the little private staircase, appropriated to her use.

The Count de Grange was an habitual visitor at the house of his cousin the duchess, who was a gay Parisian, absorbed in her life of giddy dissipation. The count found means of influencing Victorine in his favour; not by money; so coarse a bribe would have had no power over her; but by many presents, accompanied with sentimental letters, breathing devotion to her charge, and extremest appreciation of the faithful friend whom Theresa looked upon as a mother, and whom for this reason he, the count, revered and loved. Intermixed, were wily allusions to his great possessions in Provence, and to his ancient lineage:—the one mortgaged, the other disgraced. Victorine, whose right hand had forgotten its cunning in the length of her dreary vegetation at Crowley Castle, was deceived, and became a vehement advocate of the dissolute Adonis of the Paris saloons, in his suit to her darling. When Sir Mark came back, he was dismayed and shocked beyond measure by finding the count and Theresa at his feet, entreating him to forgive their stolen marriage—a marriage which, though incomplete as to its legal forms, was yet too complete to be otherwise than sanctioned by Theresa's nearest friends. The duchess accused her cousin of perfidy and treason. Sir Mark said nothing. But his health failed from that time, and he sank into an old querulous grey-haired man.

There was some ado, I know not what, between Sir Mark and the count regarding the control and disposition of the fortune which Theresa inherited from her mother. The count gained the victory, owing to the different nature of the French laws from the English; and this made Sir Mark abjure the country and the city he had loved so long. Henceforward, he swore, his foot should never touch French soil; if Theresa liked to come and see him at Crowley Castle, she should be as welcome as a daughter of the house ought to be, and ever should be; but her husband should never enter the gates of the house in Sir Mark's lifetime.

For some months he was out of humour with Duke, because of his tardy return from his tour and his delay in joining them in Paris: through which, so Sir Mark fancied, Theresa's marriage had been brought about. But—when Duke came home, depressed

in spirits and submissive to his uncle, even under unjust blame—
Sir Mark restored him to favour in the course of a summer's
day, and henceforth added another injury to the debtor side of
the count's reckoning.

Duke never told his uncle of the woeful ill-report he had heard
of the count in Paris, where he had found all the better part
of the French nobility pitying the lovely English heiress who had
been entrapped into a marriage with one of the most disreputable
of their order, a gambler and a reprobate. He could not leave
Paris without seeing Theresa, whom he believed to be as yet
unacquainted with his arrival in the city, so he went to call
upon her one evening. She was sitting alone, splendidly dressed,
ravishingly beautiful; she made a step forward to meet him,
hardly heeding the announcement of his name; for she had recognised a man's tread, and fancied it was her husband, coming to
accompany her to some grand reception. Duke saw the quick
change from hope to disappointment on her mobile face, and she
spoke out at once her reason. "Adolphe promised to come and
fetch me; the princess receives to-night. I hardly expected a visit
from you, cousin Duke," recovering herself into a pretty proud
reserve. "It is a fortnight, I think, since I heard you were in
Paris. I had given up all expectation of the honour of a visit
from you!"

Duke felt that, as she had heard of his being there, it would be
awkward to make excuses which both she and he must know
to be false, or explanations the very truth of which would be
offensive to the loving, trusting, deceived wife. So, he turned
the conversation to his travels, his heart aching for her all the
time, as he noticed her wandering attention when she heard any
passing sound. Ten, eleven, twelve o'clock; he would not leave
her. He thought his presence was a comfort and a pleasure to her.
But when one o'clock struck, she said some unexpected business
must have detained her husband, and she was glad of it, as she
had all along felt too much tired to go out: and besides, the
happy consequence of her husband's detention had been that
long talk with Duke.

He did not see her again after this polite dismissal, nor did he
see her husband at all. Whether through ill chance, or carefully
disguised purpose, it did so happen that he called several times,
he wrote several notes requesting an appointment when he might
come with the certainty of finding the count and countess at

home, in order to wish them farewell before setting out for England. All in vain. But he said nothing to Sir Mark of all this. He only tried to fill up the blank in the old man's life. He went between Sir Mark and the tenants to whom he was unwilling to show himself unaccompanied by the beautiful daughter, who had so often been his companion in his walks and rides, before that ill-omened winter in Paris. He was thankful to have the power of returning the long kindness his uncle had shown him in childhood; thankful to be of use to him in his desertion; thankful to atone in some measure for his neglect of his uncle's wish that he should have made a hasty return to Paris.

But it was a little dull after the long excitement of travel, after associating with all that was most cultivated and seeing all that was most famous, in Europe, to be shut up in that vast magnificent dreary old castle, with Sir Mark for a perpetual companion —Sir Mark, and no other. The parsonage was near at hand, and occasionally Mr. Hawtrey came in to visit his parishioner in his trouble. But Sir Mark kept the clergyman at bay; he knew that his brother in age, his brother in circumstances (for had not Mr. Hawtrey an only child and she a daughter?), was sympathising with him in his sorrow, and he was too proud to bear it; indeed, sometimes he was so rude to his old neighbour, that Duke would go next morning to the Parsonage, to soothe the smart.

And so—and so—gradually, imperceptibly, at last his heart was drawn to Bessy. Her mother angled and angled skilfully; at first scarcely daring to hope; then remembering her own descent from the same stock as Duke, she drew herself up, and set to work with fresh skill and vigour. To be sure, it was a dangerous game for a mother to play; for her daughter's happiness was staked on her success. How could simple country-bred Bessy help being attracted to the courtly handsome man, travelled and accomplished, good and gentle, whom she saw every day, and who treated her with the kind familiarity of a brother; while he was not a brother, but in some measure a disappointed man, as everybody knew? Bessy was a daisy of an English maiden; pure good to the heart's core and most hidden thought; sensible in all her accustomed daily ways, yet not so much without imagination as not to desire something beyond the narrow range of knowledge and experience in which her days had hitherto been passed. Add to this her pretty figure, a bright healthy complexion, lovely teeth, and quite enough of beauty in her other features to have rendered her the belle of a country town, if her lot had been cast in such a place; and it is not to be wondered at, that, after she had been secretly in love with Duke with all her heart for nearly a year, almost worshipping him, he should discover that, of all the women he had ever known—except perhaps the lost Theresa —Bessy Hawtrey had it in her power to make him the happiest of men.

Sir Mark grumbled a little; but now-a-days he grumbled at everything, poor disappointed, all but childless, old man! As to the vicar he stood astonished and almost dismayed. "Have you thought enough about it, Mr. Duke?" the parson asked. "Young men are apt to do things in a hurry, that they repent at leisure. Bessy is a good girl, a good girl, God bless her: but she has not been brought up as your wife should have been: at least as folks will say your wife should have been. Though I may say for her she has a very pretty sprinkling of mathematics. I taught her myself, Mr. Duke."

"May I go and ask her myself? I only want your permission," urged Duke.

"Aye, go! But perhaps you'd better ask Madam first. She will like to be told everything as soon as me."

But Duke did not care for Madam. He rushed through the open door of the Parsonage, into the homely sitting-rooms, and softly called for Bessy. When she came, he took her by the hand and led her forth into the field-path at the back of the orchard, and there he won his bride to the full content of both their hearts.

All this time the inhabitants of Crowley Castle and the quiet people of the neighbouring village of Crowley, heard but little of "The Countess", as it was their fashion to call her. Sir Mark had his letters from her, it is true, and he read them over and over again, and moaned over them, and sighed, and put them carefully away in a bundle. But they were like arrows of pain to him. None knew their contents; none, even knowing them, would have dreamed, any more than he did, for all his moans and sighs, of the utter wretchedness of the writer. Love had long since vanished from the habitation of that pair; a habitation, not a home, even in its brightest days. Love had gone out of the window, long before poverty had come in at the door: yet that grim visitant who never tarries in tracking a disreputable gambler, had now arrived. The count lost the last remnants of his character as a man who played honourably, and thenceforth—that being pretty nearly the only sin which banished men from good society in those days—he had to play where and how he could. Theresa's money went as her poor angry father had foretold. By-and-by, and without her consent, her jewel-box was rifled; the diamonds round the locket holding her mother's picture were wrenched and picked out by no careful hand. Victorine found Theresa crying over the poor relics;—crying at last, without disguise, as if her heart would break.

"Oh, mamma! mamma! mamma!" she sobbed out, holding up the smashed and disfigured miniature as an explanation of her grief. She was sitting on the floor, on which she had thrown herself in the first discovery of the theft. Victorine sat down by her, taking her head upon her breast, and soothing her. She did not ask who had done it; she asked Theresa no question which the latter would have shrunk from answering; she knew all in that hour, without the count's name having passed the lips of either of them. And from that time she watched him as a tiger watches his prey.

When the letters came from England, the three letters from Sir Mark and the affianced bride and bridegroom, announcing the approaching marriage of Duke and Bessy, Theresa took them straight to Victorine. Theresa's lips were tightened, her pale cheeks were paler. She waited for Victorine to speak. Not a word did the Frenchwoman utter; but she smoothed the letters one over the other, and tore them in two, throwing the pieces on the ground, and stamping on them.

"Oh, Victorine!" cried Theresa, dismayed at passion that went so far beyond her own, "I never expected it—I never thought of it—but, perhaps, it was but natural."

"It was not natural; it was infamous! To have loved you once, and not to wait for chances, but to take up with that mean poor girl at the Parsonage. Pah! and *her* letter! Sir Mark is of my mind though, I can see. I am sorry I tore up his letter. He feels, he knows, that Mr. Duke Brownlow ought to have waited, waited, waited. Some one waited fourteen years, did he not? The count will not live for ever."

Theresa did not see the face of wicked meaning as those last words were spoken.

Another year rolled heavily on its course of wretchedness to

Theresa. That same revolution of time brought increase of peace and joy to the English couple, striving humbly, striving well, to do their duty as children to the unhappy and deserted Sir Mark. They had their reward in the birth of a little girl. Yet, close on the heels of this birth, followed a great sorrow. The good parson died, after a short sudden illness. Then came the customary trouble after the death of a clergyman. The widow had to leave the Parsonage, the home of a lifetime, and seek a new resting-place for her declining years.

Fortunately for all parties, the new vicar was a bachelor; no other than the tutor who had accompanied Duke on his grand tour; and it was made a condition that he should allow the widow of his predecessor to remain at the Parsonage as his house-keeper. Bessy would fain have had her mother at the castle, and this course would have been infinitely preferred by Madam Haw-trey, who, indeed, suggested the wish to her daughter. But Sir Mark was obstinately against it; nor did he spare his caustic remarks on Madam Hawtrey, even before her own daughter. He had never quite forgiven Duke's marriage, although he was per-sonally exceedingly fond of Bessy. He referred this marriage, in some part, and perhaps to no greater extent than was true, to madam's good management in throwing the young people together; and he was explicit in the expression of his opinion.

Poor Theresa! Every day she more and more bitterly rued her ill-starred marriage. Often and often she cried to herself, when she was alone in the dead of night, "I cannot bear it—I cannot bear it!" But again in the daylight her pride would help her to keep her woe to herself. She could not bear the gaze of pitying eyes; she could not bear even Victorine's fierce sympathy. She might have gone home like a poor prodigal to her father, if Duke and Bessy had not, as she imagined, reigned triumphant in her place, both in her father's heart and in her father's home. And all this while, that father almost hated the tender attentions which were rendered to him by those who were not his Theresa, his only child, for whose presence he yearned and longed in silent misery. Then again (to return to Theresa), her husband had his fits of kindness towards her. If he had been very fortunate in play, if he had heard other men admire her, he would come back for a few moments to his loyalty, and would lure back the poor tortured heart, only to crush it afresh. One day—after a short time of easy temper, caresses, and levity—she found out something, I know not what, in his life, which stung her to the quick. Her sharp wits and sharper tongue spoke out most cutting insults; at first he smiled, as if rather amused to see how she was ransacking her brain to find stabbing speeches; but at length she touched some sore; he scarcely lost the mocking smile upon his face, but his eyes flashed lurid fire, and his heavy closed hand fell on her white shoulder with a terrible blow!

She stood up, facing him, tearless, deadly white. "The poor old man at home!" was all she said, trembling, shivering all over, but with her eyes fixed on his coward face. He shrank from her look, laughed aloud to hide whatever feeling might be hidden in his bosom, and left the room. She only said again, "The poor old man—the poor old deserted, desolate man!" and felt about blindly for a chair.

She had not sat down a minute though, before she started up and rang her bell. It was Victorine's office to answer it; but Theresa looked almost surprised to see her. "You!—I wanted the others—I want them all! They shall all see how their master treats his wife! Look here!" She pushed the gauze neckerchief from her shoulder—the mark was there red and swollen. "Bid them all come here—Victorine, Amadée, Jean, Adèle, all—I will be justified by their testimony, whatever I do!" Then she fell to shaking and crying.

Victorine said nothing, but went to a certain cupboard where she kept medicines and drugs of which she alone knew the properties, and there she mixed a draught, which she made her mistress take. Whatever its nature was, it was soothing. Theresa leaned back in her chair, still sobbing heavily from time to time, until at last she dropped into a kind of doze. Then Victorine softly lifted the neckerchief, which had fallen into its place, and looked at the mark. She did not speak; but her whole face was a fearful threat. After she had looked her fill, she smiled a deadly smile. And then she touched the soft bruised flesh with her lips, much as though Theresa were the child she had been twenty years ago. Soft as the touch was Theresa shivered, and started and half awoke. "Are they come?" she murmured; "Amadée, Jean, Adèle?" but without waiting for an answer she fell asleep again.

Victorine went quietly back to the cupboard where she kept her drugs, and stayed there, mixing something noiselessly. When she had done what she wanted, she returned to her mistress's bedroom, and looked at her, still sleeping. Then she began to

N

arrange the room. No blue silk curtains and silver mirrors, now, as in the Rue Louis le Grand. A washed-out faded Indian chintz, and an old battered toilette service of Japan-ware; the disorderly signs of the count's late presence; an emptied flask of liqueur.

All the time Victorine arranged this room she kept saying to herself, "At last! At last!" Theresa slept through the daylight, slept late into the evening, leaning back where she had fallen in her chair. She was so motionless that Victorine appeared alarmed. Once or twice she felt her pulse, and gazed earnestly into the tear-stained face. Once, she very carefully lifted one of the eyelids, and holding a lighted taper near, peered into the eye. Apparently satisfied, she went out and ordered a basin of broth to be ready when she asked for it. Again she sat in deep silence; nothing stirred in the closed chamber; but in the street the carriages began to roll, and the footmen and torch-bearers to cry aloud their masters' names and titles, to show what carriage in that narrow street below, was entitled to precedence. A carriage stopped at the hotel of which they occupied the third floor. Then the bell of their apartment rang loudly—rang violently. Victorine went out to see what it was that might disturb her darling —as she called Theresa to herself—her sleeping lady as she spoke of her to her servants.

She met those servants bringing in their master, the count, dead. Dead with a sword-wound received in some infamous struggle. Victorine stood and looked at him. "Better so," she muttered. "Better so. But, monseigneur, you shall take this with you, withersoever your wicked soul is fleeing." And she struck him a stroke on his shoulder, just where Theresa's bruise was. It was as light a stroke as well could be; but this irreverence to the dead called forth indignation even from the hardened bearers of the body. Little recked Victorine. She turned her back on the corpse, went to her cupboard, took out the mixture she had made with so much care, poured it out upon the bare wooden floor, and smeared it about with her foot.

A fortnight later, when no news had come from Theresa for many weeks, a poor chaise was seen from the castle windows lumbering slowly up the carriage road to the gate. No one thought much of it; perhaps it was some friend of the housekeeper's; perhaps it was some humble relation of Mrs. Duke's (for many such had found out their cousin since her marriage). No one noticed the shabby carriage much, until the hall-porter was startled by the sound of the great bell pealing, and, on opening wide the hall-doors, saw standing before him the Mademoiselle Victorine of old days—thinner, sallower, in mourning. In the carriage sat Theresa, in the deep widow's weeds of those days. She looked out of the carriage-window wistfully, in beyond Joseph, the hall-porter.

"My father!" she cried eagerly, before Victorine could speak. "Is Sir Mark—well?" ("alive" was her first thought, but she dared not give the word utterance.)

"Call Mr. Duke!" said Joseph, speaking to some one unseen. Then he came forward. "God bless you, Miss! God bless you! And this day of all days! Sir Mark is well—leastways he's sadly changed. Where's Mr. Duke? Call him! My young lady's fainting!"

And this was Theresa's return home. None ever knew how much she had suffered since she had left home. If any one had known, Victorine would never have stood there dressed in that mourning. She put it on, sorely against her will, for the purpose of upholding the lying fiction of Theresa's having been a happy prosperous marriage. She was always indignant if any of the old servants fell back into the once familiar appellation of Miss Theresa. "The countess," she would say, in lofty rebuke.

What passed between Theresa and her father at that first interview no one ever knew. Whether she told him anything of her married life, or whether she only soothed the tears he shed on seeing her again, by sweet repetition of tender words and caresses—such as are the sugared pabulum of age as well as of infancy—no one ever knew. Neither Duke nor his wife ever heard her allude to the time she had passed in Paris, except in the most cursory and superficial manner. Sir Mark was anxious to show her that all was forgiven, and would fain have displaced Bessy from her place as lady of the castle, and made Theresa take the headship of the house, and sit at table where the mistress ought to be. And Bessy would have given up her onerous dignities without a word; for Duke was always more jealous for his wife's position than she herself was, but Theresa declined to assume any such place in the household, saying, in the languid way which now seemed habitual to her, that English housekeeping, and all the domestic arrangements of an English country house were cumbrous and wearisome to her; that if Bessy would continue to act as she had done hitherto, and would so forestal what must be her natural duties at some future period, she, Theresa, should be infinitely obliged.

Bessy consented, and in everything tried to remember what Theresa liked, and how affairs were ordered in the old Theresa days. She wished the servants to feel that "the countess" had equal rights with herself in the management of the house. But she, to whom the housekeeper takes her accounts—she in whose hands the power of conferring favours and privileges remains de facto—will always be held by servants as the mistress; and Theresa's claims soon sank into the background. At first, she was broken-spirited, too languid, to care for anything but quiet rest in her father's companionship. They sat sometimes for hours hand in hand; or they sauntered out on the terraces, hardly speaking, but happy; because they were once more together, and once more on loving terms. Theresa grew strong during this time of gentle brooding peace. The pinched pale face of anxiety lined with traces of suffering, relaxed into the soft oval; the light came into the eyes, the colour came into the cheeks.

But, in the autumn after Theresa's return, Sir Mark died; it had been a gradual decline of strength, and his last moments were passed in her arms. Her new misfortune threw her back into the wan worn creature she had been when she first came home, a widow, to Crowley Castle; she shut herself up in her rooms, and allowed no one to come near her but Victorine. Neither Duke nor Bessy was admitted into the darkened rooms, which she had hung with black cloth in solemn funeral state.

Victorine's life since her return to the castle had been anything but peaceable. New powers had arisen in the housekeeper's room. Madam Brownlow had her maid, far more exacting than Madam Brownlow herself; and a new housekeeper reigned in the place of her who was formerly but an echo of Victorine's opinions. Victorine's own temper, too, was not improved by her four years abroad, and there was a general disposition among the servants to resist all her assumption of authority. She felt her powerlessness after a struggle or two, but treasured up her vengeance. If she had lost power over the household, however, there was no diminution of her influence over her mistress. It was her device at last that lured the countess out of her gloomy seclusion.

Almost the only creature Victorine cared for, beside Theresa, was the little Mary Brownlow. What there was of softness in her woman's nature, seemed to come out towards children; though, if the child had been a boy instead of a girl, it is probable that Victorine might not have taken it into her good graces. As it was, the French nurse and the English child were capital friends; and when Victorine sent Mary into the countess's room, and bade her not to be afraid, but ask the lady in her infantine babble to come out and see Mary's snow-man, she knew that the little one, for her sake, would put her small hand into Theresa's, and thus plead with more success, because with less purpose, than any one else had been able to plead. Out came Theresa, colourless and sad, holding Mary by the hand. They went, unobserved as they thought, to the great gallery-window, and looked out into the court-yard; then Theresa returned to her rooms. But the ice was broken, and before the winter was over, Theresa fell into her old ways, and sometimes smiled, and sometimes even laughed, until chance visitors again spoke of her rare beauty and her courtly grace.

It was noticeable that Theresa revived first out of her lassitude to an interest in all Duke's pursuits. She grew weary of Bessy's small cares and domestic talk—now about the servants, now about her mother and the Parsonage, now about the parish. She questioned Duke about his travels, and could enter into his appreciation and judgment of foreign nations; she perceived the latent powers of his mind; she became impatient of their remaining dormant in country seclusion. She had spoken of leaving Crowley Castle, and of finding some other home, soon after her father's death; but both Duke and Bessy had urged her to stay with them, Bessy saying, in the pure innocence of her heart, how glad she was that, in the probably increasing cares of her nursery, Duke would have a companion so much to his mind.

About a year after Sir Mark's death, the member for Sussex died, and Theresa set herself to stir up Duke to assume his place. With some difficulty (for Bessy was passive: perhaps even opposed to the scheme in her quiet way), Theresa succeeded, and Duke was elected. She was vexed at Bessy's torpor, as she called it, in the whole affair; vexed as she now often was with Bessy's sluggish interest in all things beyond her immediate ken. Once, when Theresa tried to make Bessy perceive how Duke might shine and rise in his new sphere, Bessy burst into tears, and said, "You speak as if his presence here were nothing, and his fame in London everything. I cannot help fearing that he will leave off caring for all the quiet ways in which we have been so happy ever since we were married."

"But when he is here," replied Theresa, "and when he wants to talk to you of politics, of foreign news, of great public interests, you drag him down to your level of woman's cares."

"Do I?" said Bessy. "Do I drag him down? I wish I was cleverer; but you know, Theresa, I was never clever in anything but housewifery."

Theresa was touched for a moment by this humility.

"Yet, Bessy, you have a great deal of judgment, if you will but exercise it. Try and take an interest in all he cares for, as well as making him try and take an interest in home affairs."

But, somehow, this kind of conversation too often ended in dissatisfaction on both sides; and the servants gathered, from induction rather than from words, that the two ladies were not on the most cordial terms; however friendly they might wish to be, and might strive to appear. Madam Hawtrey, too, allowed her jealousy of Theresa to deepen into dislike. She was jealous because, in some unreasonable way, she had taken it into her head that Theresa's presence at the castle was the reason why she was not urged to take up her abode there on Sir Mark's death: as if there were not rooms and suites of rooms enough to lodge a wilderness of dowagers in the building, if the owner so wished. But Duke had certain ideas pretty strongly fixed in his mind; and one was a repugnance to his mother-in-law's constant company. But he greatly increased her income as soon as he had it in his power, and left it entirely to herself how she should spend it.

Having now the means of travelling about, Madam Hawtrey betook herself pretty frequently to such watering-places as were in vogue at that day, or went to pay visits at the houses of those friends who occasionally came lumbering up in shabby vehicles to visit their cousin Bessy at the castle. Theresa cared little for Madam Hawtrey's coldness; perhaps, indeed, never perceived it. She gave up striving with Bessy, too; it was hopeless to try to make her an intellectual ambitious companion to her husband. He had spoken in the House; he had written a pamphlet that made much noise; the minister of the day had sought him out, and was trying to attach him to the government. Theresa, with her Parisian experience of the way in which women influenced politics, would have given anything for the Brownlows to have taken a house in London. She longed to see the great politicians, to find herself in the thick of the struggle for place and power, the brilliant centre of all that was worth hearing and seeing in the kingdom. There had been some talk of this same London house; but Bessy had pleaded against it earnestly while Theresa sat by in indignant silence, until she could bear the discussion no longer; going off to her own sitting-room, where Victorine was at work. Here her pent-up words found vent—not addressed to her servant, but not restrained before her :

"I cannot bear it—to see him cramped in by her narrow mind, to hear her weak selfish arguments, urged because she feels she would be out of place beside him. And Duke is hampered with this woman : he whose powers are unknown even to himself, or he would put her feeble nature on one side, and seek his higher atmosphere. How he would shine! How he does shine! Good Heaven! To think——"

And here she sank into silence, watched by Victorine's furtive eyes.

Duke had excelled all he had previously done by some great burst of eloquence, and the country rang with his words. He was to come down to Crowley Castle for a parliamentary recess, which occurred almost immediately after this. Theresa calculated the hours of each part of the complicated journey, and could have told to five minutes when he might be expected; but the baby was ill and absorbed all Bessy's attention. She was in the nursery by the cradle in which the child slept, when her husband came riding up to the castle gate. But Theresa was at the gate; her hair all out of powder, and blowing away into dishevelled curls, as the hood of her cloak fell back; her lips parted with a breathless welcome; her eyes shining out love and pride. Duke was but mortal. All London chanted his rising fame; and here in his home Theresa seemed to be the only preson who appreciated him.

The servants clustered in the great hall; for it was now some length of time since he had been at home. Victorine was there, with some headgear for her lady; and when, in reply to his inquiry for his wife, the grave butler asserted that she was with young master, who was, they feared, very seriously ill, Victorine said, with the familiarity of an old servant, and as if to assuage Duke's anxiety : "Madam fancies the child is ill, because she can think of nothing but him, and perpetual watching has made her nervous." The child, however, was really ill; and after a brief greeting to her husband, Bessy returned to her nursery, leaving Theresa to question, to hear, to sympathise. That night she gave way to another burst of disparaging remarks on poor motherly homely Bessy, and that night Victorine thought she read a deeper secret in Theresa's heart.

The child was scarcely ever out of its mother's arms; but the illness became worse, and it was nigh unto death. Some cream had been set aside for the little wailing creature, and Victorine had unwittingly used it for the making of a cosmetic for her mistress. When the servant in charge of it reproved her, a quarrel began as to their respective mistress's right to give orders in the household. Before the dispute ended, pretty strong things had been said on both sides.

The child died. The heir was lifeless; the servants were in whispering dismay, and bustling discussion of their mourning; Duke felt the vanity of fame, as compared to a baby's life. Theresa was full of sympathy, but dared not express it to him; so tender was her heart becoming. Victorine regretted the death in her own way. Bessy lay speechless, and tearless; not caring for loving voices, nor for gentle touches; taking neither food nor drink; neither sleeping nor weeping. "Send for her mother," the doctor said; for Madam Hawtrey was away on her visits, and the letters telling her of her grandchild's illness had not reached her in the slow-delaying cross-country posts of those days. So she was sent for; by a man riding express, as a quicker and surer means than the post.

Meanwhile, the nurses, exhausted by their watching, found the care of little Mary by day, quite enough. Madam's maid sat up with Bessy for a night or two; Duke striding in from time to time through the dark hours to look at the white motionless face, which would have seemed like the face of one dead, but for the long-quivering sighs that came up from the over-laden heart. The doctor tried his drugs, in vain, and then he tried again. This night, Victorine at her own earnest request, sat up instead of the maid. As usual, towards midnight, Duke came stealing in with shaded light. "Hush!" said Victorine, her finger on her lips. "She sleeps at last." Morning dawned faint and pale, and still she slept. The doctor came, and stole in on tip-toe, rejoicing in the effect of his drugs. They all stood around the bed; Duke, Theresa, Victorine. Suddenly the doctor—a strange change upon him, a strange fear in his face—felt the patient's pulse, put his ear to her open lips, called for a glass—a feather. The mirror was not dimmed, the delicate fibres stirred not. Bessy was dead.

I pass rapidly over many months. Theresa was again overwhelmed with grief, or rather, I should say, remorse; for now that Bessy was gone, and buried out of sight, all her innocent virtues, all her feminine homeliness, came vividly into Theresa's mind—not as wearisome, but as admirable, qualities of which she had been too blind to perceive the value. Bessy had been her own old companion too, in the happy days of childhood, and of innocence. Theresa rather shunned than sought Duke's company now. She remained at the castle, it is true, and Madam Hawtrey, as Theresa's only condition of continuing where she was, came to live under the same roof. Duke felt his wife's death deeply, but reasonably, as became his character. He was perplexed by Theresa's bursts of grief, knowing, as he dimly did, that she and Bessy had not lived together in perfect harmony. But he was much in London now; a rising statesman; and when, in autumn, he spent some time at the castle, he was full of admiration for the strangely patient way in which Theresa behaved towards the old lady. It seemed to Duke that in his absence Madam Hawtrey had assumed absolute power in his household, and that the high-spirited Theresa submitted to her fantasies with even more docility than her own daughter would have done. Towards Mary, Theresa was always kind and indulgent.

Another autumn came; and before it went, old ties were renewed, and Theresa was pledged to become her cousin's wife.

There were two people strongly affected by this news when it was promulgated; one—and this was natural under the circumstances—was Madam Hawtrey; who chose to resent the marriage as a deep personal offence to herself as well as to her daughter's memory, and who sternly rejecting all Theresa's entreaties, and Duke's invitation to continue her residence at the castle, went off into lodgings in the village. The other person strongly affected by the news was Victorine.

From being a dry active energetic middle-aged woman, she now, at the time of Theresa's engagement, sank into the passive languor of advanced life. It seemed as if she felt no more need of effort, or strain, or exertion. She sought solitude; liked nothing better than to sit in her room adjoining Theresa's dressing-room, sometimes sunk in a reverie, sometimes employed on an intricate piece of knitting with almost spasmodic activity. But wherever Theresa went, thither would Victorine go. Theresa had imagined that her old nurse would prefer being left at the castle, in the soothing tranquillity of the country, to accompanying her and her husband to the house in Grosvenor-square, which they had taken for the parliamentary season. But the mere offer of a choice seemed to irritate Victorine inexpressibly. She looked upon the proposal as a sign that Theresa considered her as superannuated —that her nursling was weary of her, and wished to supplant her services by those of a younger maid. It seemed impossible to dislodge this idea when it had once entered into her head, and it led to frequent bursts of temper, in which she violently upbraided Theresa for her ingratitude towards so faithful a follower.

One day, Victorine went a little further in her expressions than usual, and Theresa, usually so forbearing towards her, turned at last. "Really, Victorine!" she said, "this is misery to both of us. You say you never feel so wicked as when I am near you; that my ingratitude is such as would be disowned by fiends; what can I, what must I do? You say you are never so unhappy as when you are near me; must we, then, part? Would that be for your happiness?"

"And is that what it has come to!" exclaimed Victorine. "In my country they reckon a building secure against wind and storm and all the ravages of time, if the first mortar used has been tempered with human blood. But not even our joint secret, though it was tempered well with blood, can hold our lives together! How much less all the care, all the love, that I lavished upon you in the days of my youth and strength!"

Theresa came close to the chair in which Victorine was seated. She took hold of her hand and held it fast in her own. "Speak, Victorine," said she, hoarsely, "and tell me what you mean. *What* is our joint secret? And what do you mean by its being secret of blood? Speak out. I WILL know."

"As if you do not know!" replied Victorine, harshly. "You don't remember my visits to Bianconi, the Italian chemist in the Marais, long ago?" She looked into Theresa's face, to see if her words had suggested any deeper meaning than met the ear. No; Theresa's look was stern, but free and innocent.

"You told me you went there to learn the composition of certain unguents, and cosmetics, and domestic medicines."

"Ay, and paid high for my knowledge, too," said Victorine, with a low chuckle. "I learned more than you have mentioned, my lady countess. I learnt the secret nature of many drugs—to speak plainly, I learnt the art of poisoning. And," suddenly standing up, "it was for your sake I learnt it. For your service—you— who would fain cast me off in my old age. For you!"

Theresa blanched to a deadly white. But she tried to move neither feature nor limb, nor to avert her eyes for one moment from the eyes that defied her. "For my service, Victorine?"

"Yes! The quieting draught was all ready for your husband, when they brought him home dead."

"Thank God his death does not lie at your door!"

"Thank God?" mocked Victorine. "The wish for his death does lie at your door; and the intent to rid you of him does lie at my door. And I am not ashamed of it. Not I! It was not for myself I would have done it, but because you suffered so. He had struck you, whom I had nursed on my breast."

"Oh, Victorine!" said Theresa, with a shudder. "Those days are past. Do not let us recall them. I was so wicked because I was so miserable; and now I am so happy, so inexpressibly happy, that—do let me try to make you happy too!"

"You ought to try," said Victorine, not yet pacified; "can't you see how the incomplete action once stopped by Fate, was tried again, and with success; and how you are now reaping the benefit of my sin, if sin it was?"

"Victorine! I do not know what you mean!" But some terror must have come over her, she so trembled and so shivered.

"Do you not indeed? Madame Brownlow, the country girl from Crowley Parsonage, needed sleep, and would fain forget the little child's death that was pressing on her brain. I helped the doctor to his end. She sleeps now, and she has met her baby before this, if priests' tales are true. And you, my beauty, my queen, you reign in her stead! Don't treat the poor Victorine as if she were mad, and speaking in her madness. I have heard of tricks like that being played, when the crime was done, and the criminal of use no longer."

That evening, Duke was surprised by his wife's entreaty and petition that she might leave him, and return with Victorine and her other personal servants to the seclusion of Crowley Castle. She, the great London toast, the powerful enchantress of society, and most of all, the darling wife and true companion, with this sudden fancy for this complete retirement, and for leaving her husband when he was first fully entering into the comprehension of all that a wife might be! Was it ill health? Only last night she had been in dazzling beauty, in brilliant spirits; this morning only, she had been so merry and tender. But Theresa denied that she was in any way indisposed; and seemed suddenly so unwililng to speak of herself, and so much depressed, that Duke saw nothing for it but to grant her wish and let her go. He missed her terribly. No more pleasant tête-à-tête breakfasts, enlivened by her sense and wit, and cheered by her pretty caressing ways. No gentle secretary now, to sit by his side through long long hours, never weary. When he went into society, he no longer found his appearance watched and waited for by the loveliest woman there. When he came home from the House at night, there was no one to take an interest in his speeches, to be indignant at all that annoyed him, and charmed and proud of all the admiration he had won. He longed for the time to come when he would be able to go down for a day or two to see his wife; for her letters appeared to him dull and flat after her bright companionship. No wonder that her letters came out of a heavy heart, knowing what she knew.

She scarcely dared to go near Victorine, whose moods were becoming as variable as though she were indeed the mad woman she had tauntingly defied Theresa to call her. At times she was miserable because Theresa looked so ill, and seemed so deeply unhappy. At other times she was jealous because she fancied Theresa shrank from her and avoided her. So, wearing her life out with passion, Victorine's health grew daily worse and worse during that summer.

Theresa's only comfort seemed to be little Mary's society. She seemed as though she could not lavish love enough upon the motherless child, who repaid Theresa's affection with all the pretty demonstrativeness of her age. She would carry the little three-year-old maiden in her arms when she went to see Victorine, or would have Mary playing about in her dressing-room, if the old French-woman, for some jealous freak, would come and arrange her lady's hair with her trembling hands. To avoid giving offence to Victorine, Theresa engaged no other maid; to shun over-much or over-frank conversation with Victorine, she always had little Mary with her when there was a chance of the French waiting-maid coming in. For, the presence of the child was a holy restraint even on Victorine's tongue; she would sometimes check her fierce temper, to caress the little creature playing at her knees; and would only dart a covert bitter sting at Theresa under the guise of a warning against ingratitude, to Mary.

Theresa drooped and drooped in this dreadful life. She sought out Madam Hawtrey, and prayed her to come on a long visit to the castle. She was lonely, she said, asking for madam's company as a favour to herself. Madam Hawtrey was difficult to persuade; but the more she resisted, the more Theresa entreated; and, when once madam was at the castle, her own daughter had never been so dutiful, so humble a slave to her slightest fancy as was the proud Theresa now.

Yet, for all this, the lady of the castle drooped and drooped, and when Duke came down to see his darling he was in utter dismay at her looks. Yet she said she was well enough, only tired. If she had anything more upon her mind, she refused him her confidence. He watched her narrowly, trying to forestal her smallest desires. He saw only tender affection for Mary, and thought he had never seen so lovely and tender a mother to another woman's child. He wondered at her patience with Madam Hawtrey, remembering how often his own stock had been exhausted by his mother-in-law, and how the brilliant Theresa had formerly scouted and flouted at the vicar's wife. With all this renewed sense of his darling's virtues and charms, the idea of losing her was too terrible to bear.

He would listen to no pleas, to no objections. Before he returned to town, where his presence was a political necessity, he sought the best medical advice that could be had in the neighbourhood. The doctors came; they could make but little out of Theresa, if her vehement assertion were true that she had nothing on her mind. Nothing.

"Humour him at least, my dear lady!" said the doctor, who had known Theresa from her infancy, but who, living at the distant country town, was only called in on the Olympian occasions of great state illnesses. "Humour your husband, and perhaps do yourself some good too, by consenting to his desire that you should have change of air. Brighthelmstone is a quiet village by the sea-side. Consent, like a gracious lady, to go there for a few weeks."

So, Theresa, worn out with opposition, consented, and Duke

made all the arrangements for taking her, and little Mary, and the necessary suite of servants, to Brighton, as we call it now. He resolved in his own mind that Theresa's personal attendant should be some woman young enough to watch and wait upon her mistress, and not Victorine, to whom Theresa was in reality a servant. But of this plan, neither Theresa nor Victorine knew anything until the former was in the carriage with her husband some miles distant from the castle. Then he, a little exultant in the good management by which he supposed he had spared his wife the pain and trouble of decision, told her that Victorine was left behind, and that a new accomplished London maid would await her at her journey's end.

Theresa only exclaimed "O! What will Victorine say?" and covered her face, and sat shivering and speechless.

What Victorine did say, when she found out the trick, as she esteemed it, that had been played upon her, was too terrible to repeat. She lashed herself up into an ungoverned passion; and then became so really and seriously ill that the servants went to fetch Madam Hawtrey in terror and dismay. But when that lady came, Victorine shut her eyes, and refused to look at her. "She has got her daughter in her hand! I will not look!" Shaking all the time she uttered these awe-stricken words, as if she were in an ague-fit. "Bring the countess back to me. Let *her* face the dead woman standing there, I will not do it. They wanted her to sleep—and so did the countess, that she might step into her lawful place. Theresa, Theresa, where are you? You tempted me. What I did, I did in your service. And you have gone away, and left me alone with the dead woman! It was the same drug as the doctor gave, after all—only he gave little, and I gave much. My lady the countess spent her money well, when she sent me to the old Italian to learn his trade. Lotions for the complexion, and a discriminating use of poisonous drugs. I discriminated, and Theresa profited; and now she is his wife, and has left me here alone with the dead woman. Theresa, Theresa, come back and save me from the dead woman!"

Madam Hawtrey stood by, horror-stricken. "Fetch the vicar," said she, under her breath, to a servant.

"The village doctor is coming," said some one near. "How she raves! Is it delirium?"

"It is no delirium," said Bessy's mother. "Would to Heaven it were!"

Theresa had a happy day with her husband at Brighthelm-stone before he set off on his return to London. She watched him riding away, his servant following with his portmanteau. Often and often did Duke look back at the figure of his wife, waving her handkerchief, till a turn of the road hid her from his sight. He had to pass through a little village not ten miles from his home, and there a servant, with his letters and further luggage, was to await him. There he found a mysterious, imperative note, requiring his immediate presence at Crowley Castle. Something in the awe-stricken face of the servant from the castle, led Duke to question him. But all he could say was, that Victorine lay dying, and that Madam Hawtrey had said that after that letter the master was sure to return, and so would need no luggage. Something lurked behind, evidently. Duke rode home at speed. The vicar was looking out for him. "My dear boy," said he, relapsing into the old relations of tutor and pupil, "prepare yourself."

"What for?" said Duke, abruptly; for the being told to prepare himself, without being told for what, irritated him in his present mood. "Victorine is dead?"

"No! She says she will not die until she has seen you, and got you to forgive her, if Madam Hawtrey will not. But first read this: it is a terrible confession, made by her before me, a magistrate, believing herself to be on the point of death!"

Duke read the paper—containing little more in point of detail than I have already given—the horrible words taken down in the short-hand in which the vicar used to write his mild prosy sermons: his pupil knew the character of old. Duke read it twice. Then he said: "She is raving, poor creature!" But for all that, his heart's blood ran cold, and he would fain not have faced the woman, but would rather have remained in doubt to his dying day.

He went up the stairs three steps at a time, and then turned and faced the vicar, with a look like the stern calmness of death. "I wish to see her alone." He turned out all the watching women, and then he went to the bedside where Victorine sat, half propped up with pillows, watching all his doings and his looks, with her hollow awful eyes. "Now, Victorine, I will read this paper aloud to you. Perhaps your mind has been wandering; but you understand me now?" A feeble murmur of assent met his listening ear.

"If any statement in this paper be not true, make me a sign. Hold up your hand—for God's sake hold up your hand. And if you can do it with truth in this, your hour of dying, Lord have mercy upon you; but if you cannot hold up your hand, then Lord have mercy upon me!"

He read the paper slowly; clause by clause he read the paper. No sign; no uplifted hand. At the end she spoke, and he bent his head to listen. "The Countess—Theresa you know—she who has left me to die alone—she"—then mortal strength failed and Duke was left alone in the chamber of death.

He stayed in the chamber many minutes, quite still. Then he left the room, and said to the first domestic he could find, "The woman is dead. See that she is attended to." But he went to the vicar, and had a long long talk with him. He sent a confidential servant for little Mary—on some pretext, hardly careful, or plausible enough; but his mood was desperate, and he seemed to forget almost everything but Bessy, his first wife, his innocent girlish bride.

Theresa could ill spare her little darling, and was perplexed by the summons; but an explanation of it was to come in a day or two. It came.

"Victorine is dead; I need say no more. She could not carry her awful secret into the next world, but told all. I can think of nothing but my poor Bessy, delivered over to the cruelty of such a woman. And you, Theresa, I leave you to your conscience, for you have slept in my bosom. Henceforward I am a stranger to you. By the time you receive this, I, and my child, and that poor murdered girl's mother, will have left England. What will be our next step I know not. My agent will do for you what you need."

Theresa sprang up and rang her bell with mad haste. "Get me a horse!" she cried, "and bid William be ready to ride with me for his life—for my life—along the coast, to Dover!"

They rode and they galloped through the night, scarcely staying to bait their horses. But when they came to Dover, they looked out to sea upon the white sails that bore Duke and his child away. Theresa was too late, and it broke her heart. She lies buried in Dover churchyard. After long years Duke returned to England; but his place in parliament knew him no more, and his daughter's husband sold Crowley Castle to a stranger.

III

HOW THE SIDE-ROOM WAS ATTENDED BY A DOCTOR

How the Doctor found his way into our society, none of us can tell. It did not occur to us to inquire into the matter at the time, and now the point is lost in the dim obscurity of the past. We only know that he appeared suddenly and mysteriously. It was shortly after we had formed our Mutual Admiration Society, in this very room in Mrs. Lirriper's Lodgings. We were discussing things in general in our usual amiable way, admiring poets, worshipping heroes, and taking all men and all things for what they seemed. We were young and ingenuous, pleased with our own ideas, and with each other's; full of belief and trust in all things good and noble, and with no hatred, save for what was false, and base, and mean. In this spirit we were commenting with indignation upon a new heresy with regard to the age of the world, when a strange voice broke in upon our conversation.

"I beg your pardon; you are wrong. The age of the world is exactly three millions eight hundred and ninety-seven thousand four hundred and twenty-five years, eight months, fourteen days, nine hours, thirty-five minutes, and seventeen seconds."

At the first sound of this mysterious voice we all looked up, and perceived standing on the hearth-rug before the fire by which you sit, Major, a little closely-knit, middle-aged man, dressed in black. He had a hooked nose, piercing black eyes, and a grizzled beard, and his head was covered with a shock of crisp dark hair. Our first impulse was to resent the stranger's interference as an impertinence, and to demand what business he had in that room in Mrs. Lirriper's house, sacred to the social meetings of the Mutual Admiration Society? But we no sooner set eyes upon him than the impulse was checked, and we remained for a minute or so gazing upon the stranger in silence. We saw at a glance that he was no mere meddling fool. He was considerably older than any of us there present, his face beamed with intelligence, his eyes sparkled with humour, and his whole expression was that of a man confident of mental strength and superiority. The look on his face seemed to imply that he had reckoned us all up in an instant. So much were we impressed by the stranger's appear-

o

ance, that we quite forgot the queries which had naturally occurred to us when he interrupted our conversation : Who are
you? Where do you belong? How did you come here? It was
allowable for a member of the society to introduce a friend; but
none of us had introduced him, and we were the only members
in the room. None of us had seen him enter, nor had we been
conscious of his presence until we heard his voice. On comparing
notes afterwards, it was found that the same thought had flitted
across all our minds. Had he come down the chimney? Or up
through the floor? But at the time, as we saw no smoke and smelt
no brimstone, we dismissed the suspicion for the more natural
explanation that some member had introduced him, and had
gone away, leaving him there. I was mentally framing a civil
question with the view of elucidating this point, when the
stranger, who spoke with a foreign accent, again addressed us.

"I trust," he said, "I am not intruding upon your society; but
the subject of your discussion is one that I have studied deeply,
and I was betrayed into a remark by—by my enthusiasm : I beg
you will pardon me."

He said this so affably, and with so much dignified politeness
of an elderly kind, that we were all disarmed, and protested, in
a body, that there was no occasion for any apology. And it followed upon this, in some sort of insensible way, that the stranger
came and took a seat among us, and spent the evening with us,
proving a match for us in the airy gaiety of our discussions, and
more than a match for us in all kinds of knowledge. We were
all charmed with the stranger, and he appeared to be highly
pleased with us. When he went away he shook hands with us
with marked cordiality and warmth, and left us his card. It bore
this inscription :

DOCTOR GOLIATH, PH.D.

After this, the doctor regularly frequented our society, and we
took his coming as a matter of course; being quite content to
accept his great learning and numerous accomplishments as a
certificate of his eligibility for membership in our fraternity. It
was no wonder that we came to look upon the doctor as a great
personage. His fund of knowledge was inexhaustible. He seemed
to know everything—not generally and in a superficial manner—
but particularly and minutely. It was not, however, by making
a parade of his knowledge that he gave us this impression. He let

it out incidentally, as occasion required. If language were the topic, the doctor, by a few off-hand remarks, made it plain to us that he was acquainted with almost every language under the sun. He spoke English with an accent which partook of the character of almost every modern tongue. If law came up, he could discourse of codes and judgments with the utmost familiarity, citing act, chapter, and section, as if the whole study of his life had been law. So with politics, history, geology, chemistry, mechanics, and even medicine. Nothing came amiss to Doctor Goliath. He was an animated Cyclopædia of universal knowledge. But there was nothing of the pedant about him. He treated his learning as bagatelle; he threw off his knowledge as other people throw off jokes; he was only serious when he mixed a salad, brewed a bowl of punch, or played a game of piquet. He was not at all proud of being able to translate the Ratcatcher's Daughter into six languages, including Greek and Arabic; but he believed he was the only man on the face of the earth who knew the exact proportions of oil and vinegar requisite for the proper mixture of a potato-salad. It was impossible to resist the spell of Doctor Goliath's wonderful character. He was learned in the highest degree; yet he had all the reckless jollity of a schoolboy, and could talk nonsense and make sport of wisdom and philosophy better than any of us. He took our society by storm; he became an oracle; we quoted him as an authority, and spoke of him as *the* doctor, as if there were no other doctor on the face of the earth.

Shortly before the doctor's appearance among us, we, the members of the Mutual Admiration Society, had sworn eternal friendship. We had vowed ever to love each other, ever to believe in each other, ever to be true and just and kindly towards each other, and never to be estranged one from another either by prosperity or adversity. As a sign and symbol of our brotherhood, we had agreed to call each other by familiar and affectionate abbreviations of our christian names; and, in pursuance of this amiable scheme, we had arranged to present each other with loving cups. As we were a society of little wealth, except in the matter of loving kindness and mutual admiration, it was resolved that the cups should be fashioned of pewter, of the measure of one quart, and each with two handles. The order was given, the loving-cups were made, and each bore an inscription in this wise : "To Tom from Sam, Jack, Will, Ned, Charley, and Harry, a token of Friendship;" this inscription being only varied as regarded the relative positions of donors and recipient. The cups were all ready, and nothing remained to be done but to pay the money and bring them away from the shop of our Benvenuto Cellini, which was situated in the parish of St. Martin's-in-the-Fields. A delay, however, occurred, owing to circumstances which I need not particularise further than to say, that they were circumstances over which we had no control.

This delay, owing to the obduracy of these uncontrollable circumstances, continued for some weeks, when, one evening, Tom came in with a large brown paper parcel under his arm. It was a parcel of strange and unwonted aspect.

"Ha! ha!" cried the doctor, "what have we here? Say, my Tom, is it something to eat, something to drink, something perchance to smoke? For in such things only doth my soul delight."

"I don't believe you when you say that, doctor," said Tom, quite seriously; for Tom had fallen more prostrate than any of us before the doctor's great character.

"Not believe me?" cried the doctor. "I mean it. Man, sir, is an animal whose only misfortune is, that he is endowed with the accursed power of thinking. If I were not possessed by this evil spirit of Thought, do you know what I would do?"

Tom could form no idea what he would do.

"Well, then," said the doctor, "I would lie all day in the sun, and eat potato-salad out of a trough!"

"What! like a pig?" Tom exclaimed.

"Yes, like a pig," said the doctor. "I never see a pig lying on clean straw, with his snout poked into a delightful mess of barley-meal and cabbage-leaves, but I become frightfully envious!"

"Oh, doctor!" we all exclaimed in chorus.

"Fact. I say to myself, How much better off, how much happier, is this pig than I! To obtain my potato-salad, without which life would be a blank, I have to do a deed my soul abhors. I have to work. The pig has no work to do for that troughful of barley-meal and cabbage-leaves. Because I am an animal endowed with the power of thought and reason, I was sent to school and taught to read. See what misfortune, what misery, that has brought upon me! You laugh, but am I not driven to read books, and parliamentary debates, and leading articles? I was induced the other day to attend a social congress. If I had been a pig, I should not to have had to endure that."

"Ah, but, doctor," said Tom, "the pig has no better part."

The doctor burst into a yell of exultation.

"What! The pig no better part? Ha! ha! Sir, the better part of pig is pork. The butcher comes to me, and to the pig alike; but what remains of me when he has done his fell work? You put me in a box and screw me down, and stow me away out of sight; and you pretend to grieve for me. But the pig—you eat him, and rejoice in earnest! And that reminds me that I shall have a pork-chop for supper. By the way, is it a lettuce you have in that paper parcel, Tom?"

"It is not a lettuce, doctor."

"Not a lettuce! Ha! I see something glitter—precious metal —gold? no, silver! to obtain which, in a commensurate quantity, I would commit crimes—murder!"

"Oh, doctor," said Tom, "you are giving yourself a character which you don't deserve."

"Am I?" said the doctor. "You don't know me. And after all, what is murder? Nothing. You kill two or three of your fellow-creatures—a dozen for that matter; what then? There are plenty more. Do you know what is the population of the earth? I will tell you. Exactly one thousand three hundred millions eight hundred and ninety-nine thousand six hundred and twenty souls. How many murders are committed in the course of a year do you imagine? You think only those you read of in the newspapers. Bah! An intimate knowledge of the subject enables me to inform you that the number of murders committed in Great Britain and Ireland, and the Channel Islands, annually, amounts to fifteen thousand seven hundred and forty-five. It is one of the laws of nature for keeping down the population. Every man who commits a murder, obeys this law."

Tom's hair was beginning to stand on end, for the doctor said all this with a terrible fierceness of manner. His strange philosophy was not without its effect upon the rest of us. We had been accustomed to a good deal of freedom in our discussions, but we had never ventured upon anything so audacious as this.

"Come, Tom," said the doctor, "unveil your treasure, and let me see if it be worth my while lying in wait for you in the dark lanes as you go home to-night."

"Well, no, it isn't, doctor," said Tom, "for the article is only of pewter." And Tom uncovered his loving-cup. Circumstances had relented in Tom's case, and he had gone and paid for his own loving-cup.

"Pewter!" said the doctor. "Bah! it is not worth my while; but if it had been silver, now, why then I might——" And the doctor put on a diabolical expression, that seemed to signify highway robbery accompanied with violence, and murder followed by immediate dissection. Presently the doctor noticed the inscription. "Ha! ha!" he said, "what is this? An inscription! 'To Tom, from Sam, Jack, Will, Ned, Charley, and Harry—a token of Friendship.' Friendship? Ha! ha! 'tis but a name, an empty name, a mockery, a delusion, and a snare. I tell you there is no such thing in the world."

"Oh, don't say that, doctor!" cried Tom, looking quite hurt.

"Ah," returned the doctor, "you will find it out. I have always found it out; and since I formed my first friendship and was deceived—it is now—let me see how many years?—one thousand eight hundred and—but no matter."

The doctor paused, as if oppressed with painful recollections.

"Ned," said Sam, leaning across to me, "do you know what I think the doctor is?"

"No," I said.

"Well," he said, "hang'd if I don't think he is the Wandering Jew. Look at his boots!"

I looked at his boots. They were not neat boots: that was all I perceived about them.

"Don't you observe," said Sam, "how flat and trodden down they are? The doctor has done a deal of walking in those boots. Mark their strange and ancient shape! Look at the dust upon them—it is the dust of centuries!"

The doctor was roaring with laughter at the idea of our mutual presentation scheme, and was calling us "innocents," and Tom's loving-cup a "mug."

Tom was getting red in the face and looking ashamed. In fact, we were all looking rather sheepish; for it had never struck us until now, how silly and sentimental we all were. We said nothing to the doctor about the six other loving-cups that were waiting to be paid for and claimed; and when Tom, with a face as red as a coal, covered up his "mug" as the doctor called it and put it away, we were glad to change the subject, to escape from our embarrassment. We were so thoroughly ashamed of ourselves, that we endeavoured to redeem our characters in the eyes of the doctor, by plunging recklessly into any depth of cynical opinion that he chose to sound. And the doctor, in the course of time, led us to the very bottom of the pit of cynicism. As we listened to him, and held converse with him day after day, we began to see how very green and unsophisticated we had all been. We came to know that the poets and heroes whom we had worshipped were nothing but humbugs and pretenders; that the great statesmen whom we had believed in and admired, were blunderers or traitors; that the mighty potentates whose power and sagacity we had extolled, were tyrannical miscreants, or puppets in the hands of others; that the philanthropists whom all men praised, were conceited self-seeking hypocrites; that the patriots whose names we had reverenced in common with all the world, were scoundrels of the deepest dye. The doctor's influence led us on insensibly, step by step. How could we resist it? It was a fascination. He knew everything, could prove everything, and had such a store of facts that we had never heard of in support of his conclusions, that it was impossible, with our limited knowledge, to withstand him. We were shocked at first; but, as the revolution proceeded, we got used to the sight of blood, and saw the heads of our heroes fall, with the utmost indifference. At length we came to revel in it, and sought for new victims, that we might demolish them and do our despite upon them. The doctor led the way more boldly as we advanced. He hinted darkly at crimes in which he had had a hand, and at crimes which he would yet commit when the opportunity arrived. Whenever a murder was committed, the doctor was the friend and advocate of the murderer, and vowed fierce vengeance against the judge and jury who condemned him to be hanged. When news of war and disaster came, he rubbed his hands and gloated over it with glee, because he had prophesied what would happen through the imbecility and treason of infamous scoundrels who called themselves statesmen and generals.

From a Mutual Admiration Society, we became a Society of iconoclasts. Tom, and Jack, and Sam, and Harry, and the rest of us, who had begun by swearing eternal friendship, were now bitter disputants, despising each other's mental qualities, calling each duffers behind each other's backs, and laughing all the old modest pretensions to scorn. The loving-cups had faded out of memory. I passed the shop of our Benvenuto Cellini, the pewterer, one day, and saw the whole six exposed in the window for sale. I called upon Tom, to show him an article demolishing a popular author whom we had once idolised, and I noticed his loving-cup stowed away under the table with a waste-paper-basket and a spittoon. It had grown dull and battered like a public-house pot, and was filled with short black pipes, and matches, and ends of cigars, and rubbish. I kicked it playfully with my foot, and laughed; and Tom blushed and put it away out of sight.

Our society, in its new form, prospered exceedingly. We became famous for the freedom of our speech and the audacity of our opinions. Our company was much sought after, and we were proud of our originality and independence. We spent all our leisure hours together, and our defiant discussions kept us in a constant state of mental intoxication. But a sober moment arrived.

Tom and I sat together, one gloomy day, alone. We were solemn and moody, and smoked in silence. At length Tom said:

"Ned, I passed the shop to-day, and saw those six loving-cups in the window."

I replied, fretfully, "Bother the loving-cups!"

"No," said Tom, "I have other thoughts at this present moment; I have had them often, but have smothered them—smothered them ruthlessly, Ned; but they have always come to life again. They are very lively to-night—owing, perhaps, to the fog, or the state of my liver, or the state of my conscience—and I can't smother them."

"What do you mean, Tom?"

"You remember when we ordered the cups?"

"Yes."

"The doctor came among us shortly afterwards."

"He did."

"And we didn't carry out our intention."

"No. You paid for yours, Tom, and brought it away, but the rest are still unredeemed pledges of affection."

"Exactly," said Tom; "and that was owing to the doctor. He laughed at us. He made us ashamed of ourselves. He made me ashamed of myself. But I had paid for my cup, and brought it away, and the thing was done. If I had not done it when I did, I should never have done it. What were we ashamed of?"

"Silliness," I said.

"No, kindliness and good feeling, which we can't have too much of in this short journey."

I did not answer. Tom went on.

"This doctor has upset us all. He has changed our nature. He has turned the milk of human kindness that was in us, sour. He is a very fascinating person, I grant; but who is he? None of us know. He came among us mysteriously; we accepted him without question. Yet we don't know anything about him. We don't know what he is; what he does; where he lives; or even what country he belongs to."

"Well?"

"Well, I sometimes think he is the devil. He is very pleasant, but he is diabolical in all his views and opinions, nevertheless. If he is not the devil, he has, at any rate, played the devil with *us*. I feel it at quiet moments like these, when we are not excited and bandying flippant jokes and unbelieving sarcasms."

I smoked for a few moments in silence, and I then said:

"I feel it, too, exactly as you do, Tom. I have wished to say so often, only—only I didn't like."

"Ned that is exactly what I have felt. Suppose we take courage now."

"Suppose we do," I said.

"Very well, then," said Tom. "Let us find out who this Doctor Goliath is, what he is, and all about him."

Tom had scarcely said the words when the doctor came in. He had a small bag in his hand, and a parcel under his arm.

"I am not going to stay this evening," he said. "I have work to do—work that the world will hear of. Ha?" And he contracted his brows darkly, and laid his finger on his nose in a portentous manner.

"Good night," he said; "if I survive, well and good; if not, remember me—but as to that, I don't imagine for a moment that you will do anything of the sort. You will say 'poor wretch,' and then go on with your jokes and your sport. 'Tis the way of this vile world, which has been a huge mistake from the beginning. Farewell."

"Ned," said Tom, "let us follow him."

We did so. We followed him into the Strand and on to the bridge, where he had an altercation with the toll-keeper. We could hear the words "swindle," "imposition," "highway robbery;" and we saw the doctor's face under the lamp glaring savagely at the man. At length he flung down his halfpenny, and walked hurriedly on, but stopped abruptly at the first recess, turned into it, and looked over the parapet at the river. We had long seriously entertained the suspicion—among many others of a like kind—that the doctor knew something about the mysterious, and as yet undiscovered, murder, which is associated with that spot. He had hinted at it himself often.

"Look!" said Tom. "Fascination draws him to the scene of his crime.—I almost wish he would throw himself over."

But the doctor did no such thing. After looking down at the river for a few moments, he leaped off the stone ledge, and passed on. We followed at a safe distance, and kept him in sight through a great many narrow and gloomy streets, where our only guide was the dark figure moving like a shadow before us. At length the doctor turned up a narrow passage, and disappeared. We ran forward to the entrance, but the passage was completely dark, and we could see nothing. We hesitated for a moment, but immediately summoned up courage and followed, groping our way in the dark with the assistance of the wall. On coming out at the other end of this dark tunnel, we found ourselves in a triangular court lighted by a single gas-lamp placed at the apex of the triangle. There seemed to be no entrance to it save by the narrow passage through which we had passed. All these strange and mysterious characteristics of the place we were enabled to see at a glance, by the aid of the one gas-lamp that stood like a mark of admiration in the corner. And that glance took in the cloudy figure of the doctor standing at a door in the darkest nook of the court, knocking. He was admitted before we reached the spot, but we had marked the house. It was number thirteen.

"An ogglesome number," said Tom. And there was an ogglesome plaster head over the doorway—a head, with a leer upon its face, and a reckoning-up expression, just like the doctor's. It seemed to be laughing at the fool's errand we had come upon.

I said, "What are we to do now?"

"Well, really, I don't know," said Tom.

"Stop," I cried; "I see a bill in the window. What does it say?"

Tom suggested, "Mangling done," as being most appropriate to a house inhabited by Doctor Goliath.

But it was not mangling. It was "Lodgings to Let for a Single Gentleman."

"Let us knock," I said, "and inquire about the lodgings, and ascertain what sort of a place it is."

We saw a light pass into the first floor. That was evidently the doctor's room, and he had gone up-stairs. We waited a little, and then knocked. The door was opened by an elderly lady of exceedingly benignant aspect, who wore the remnants of a smile upon her face. The smile was evidently not intended for us, but we took it as if it were, and reciprocated with a smiling inquiry about the lodgings. Would we step in and look at them? They were two rooms down stairs: a sitting-room and a bed-room. As the elderly lady, with a candle in her hand, was leading the way along the passage, the doctor called from above,

"Mrs. Mavor, I want you here directly."

"Excuse me a moment, gentlemen," said Mrs. Mavor; "the doctor, my first-floor lodger, has just come in, and wants his coffee. Pray take a seat in the parlour."

Mrs. Mavor left us, and went up-stairs, and the next moment we heard the doctor saying in loud and angry tones:

"Where is my spider? How dare you sweep away my spider with your murderous broom?"

"Oh, the nasty thing!" we heard Mrs. Mavor begin to say, but the doctor would not let her speak.

"Nasty thing! That's *your* opinion. What do you suppose that spider's opinion is of *you*, when you come and bring his house about his ears in the midst of his industry? How would you like it? Let me tell you that spider had as much right to live as you have; more—more! He was industrious, which you are not; he had a large family to support, which you have not; and if he did spread a net to catch the flies, don't you hang up 'Lodgings to Let,' and take in single young men, like myself, and *do* for them? You are a heartless, wicked woman, Mrs. Mavor."

Mrs. Mavor came down almost immediately, laughing.

"That's my first-floor lodger, Doctor Goliath," she said; "he has strange ways in some things, and pretends to get in an awful temper if any one touches his pets; but he is such a good kind soul!"

Tom and I began to stare.

"He has been with me now over seven years," Mrs. Mavor continued, "and he has behaved so well to me, and has been so kind to me when I have been ill, that nothing should induce me to take any person into the house that might disturb him or put him out of his ways. If the doctor were to leave Povis-place, I am sure I don't know what all the neighbours and the poor people about here would do; for he doctors them when they are ill, and he advises them when they are well, and he writes letters for them, and gets up subscriptions for them when there's any misfortune; and the children—they're all wild after him! Very often you'll see him here in the place, when he has been the gentlest and best of friends to their fathers and mothers, playing games with them, and a score of romping boys and girls on the top of his back—but *he* don't mind; he's so good natured, and so fond of children!"

Tom and I were opening our eyes wider and wider. The doctor called again: "Mrs. Mavor, bring me a ball of worsted, and let it be nice and soft."

Mrs. Mavor went up-stairs with the worsted, and came back again smiling.

"He has got his dumb pets round him now," she said, "and one of them has had an accident, and he can't bear to see the poor creature suffer. He is so tender-hearted!"

Tom and I were speechless. The doctor's pets, what could they be? Imps?

I said to Mrs. Mavor, that we had heard of Doctor Goliath, that he was a very learned and skilful man, and that we would like to have a peep at him, if she would permit us. Mrs. Mavor hesitated. He would be angry, she said, if he knew it. We put it upon our admiration for the man, and she consented; but we were only to peep through the door, and were not to make a noise.

We went up-stairs quietly to the doctor's landing. His door was ajar, and we could see nearly half the room through the crack, without being seen. If it had been possible to open our eyes any wider, we should have done it now.

For, the doctor was seated at a table on which his tea-things were laid. A canary-bird sat perched upon his head, a kitten was sporting at his feet, and he himself was occupied in binding up the leg of a guinea-pig.

"Poor little thing!" he was saying. "I am so sorry, so sorry; but never mind. There, there! I will bind up its poor little leg, and it will get well and run about as nicely as ever. Ah, little cat; now you know what I told you about that canary-bird. If you kill that canary-bird, I shall kill you. That is the law of Moses, little cat: it is a cruel law, I think, but I am afraid I should have to put it in force; for I love that little bird, and I love you, too, little cat, so you will not kill my pretty canary, will you? Sweet, sweet!" and the bird, perched upon the doctor's head, was answering "Sweet, sweet!"

Mrs. Mavor was behind us, calling to us in a loud whisper to come away. We astonished Mrs. Mavor and her lodger both. We walked right into the doctor's room.

He started at the sound of our footsteps; and when he saw us he turned pale with anger.

"What means this—this unwarrantable—this impertinent intrusion?"

He poured such a volley of angry words upon us that we were confused, and scarcely knew how to act. I saw that the only course was to take the bull by the horns.

"Doctor," I said, "you are an old humbug."

"What do you mean; what do you mean, sir? How dare you!" returned the doctor.

"And I say so too," struck in the mild Tom, who had never before been known to speak so bold; "doctor, you are an old humbug."

"Well, upon my word," said the doctor, "the audacity of this proceeding——"

"Who taught us to be audacious, doctor?" Tom asked, before he could finish the sentence.

The doctor gave way. He laughed, and he looked sheepish— as sheepish as we had looked when he discovered our loving-cup scheme. He scarcely knew what to say, and he put on a fierce look again, and called Mrs. Mavor.

"How dare you allow strangers to enter my room in this manner? Take that bird and that mischievous cat and that nasty guinea-pig, away, directly."

"It's of no use, doctor," said Tom; "we have found you out, and you can't deceive us any more. I have thought until now that you were an incarnate fiend, but I find you belong to the other side." Tom evidently meant that the doctor was a sort of angel, but he did not use the word; being probably struck with incongruity of associating an angelic embodiment with a wide-awake hat and Blucher boots.

The doctor laughed: which encouraged Tom to address a moral lesson, and the doctor's conduct, to Mrs. Mavor.

"To all of us, Mrs. Mavor, he has made himself out a dia-bolical person: fierce, bloodthirsty, cruel. We had made a little

Paradise among ourselves, and he entered it, like the beguiling serpent, and made us all wicked and unhappy. What did he do it for?"

Mrs. Mavor, seeing that the doctor was getting the worst of it, plucked up courage and spoke out. "He does it everywhere beyond the boundaries of Povis-place, and I'll tell you what he does it for. *He is ashamed of being good, and kind, and tender-hearted!*"

"A pretty thing to be ashamed of," said Tom. "I've half a mind to punch his head!"

"No, don't," said the doctor, laughing. "Sit down and have a cup of coffee, and then Mrs. Mavor will come and join us in a game of whist, and we'll have a potato-salad for supper, and I'll brew such a bowl of punch as I flatter myself no man on the face of the earth besides myself———"

"Doctor," said Tom again, "you're a humbug."

We told all to the society, and the next time the doctor came among us at Mrs. Lirriper's here, he was received with shouts of derisive welcome.

The doctor gave a party in Povis-place, and we were all invited. There was so much victuals, there were so many bottles of German wine, and there was so large a number of guests, that Mrs. Mavor's small tenement was in some danger of bursting. If I remember rightly, the provisions were on the scale of a ham and two fowls and a dozen of hocheimer, to each guest: to say nothing of the potato-salad, which was made in a bran-new wash-hand basin, purchased for the occasion.

And after supper there was a presentation. The loving-cups had been redeemed; and one more was added to the number; and there they were, all bright and glittering—having been rubbed up expressly for the occasion—in a row upon the table. And the extra one was inscribed, "To the Doctor, from Tom, Ned, Sam, Will, Jack, Charley, and Harry, a Token of Friendship and Esteem."

Though our old heroes and idols are all set up on their pedestals long ago, Major, we are still given to cynical and audacious talk in our society, which is still held in my rooms here. But it deceives no one; and when the doctor tries to be fierce, he blushes at the feeble and foolish attempt he is making to conceal the tenderness of the kindest heart that ever beat.

IV

HOW THE SECOND FLOOR KEPT A DOG

Mrs. Lirriper rather objects to dogs, you say, Major? Very natural in a London house. Shall I tell you why I hope she will not object to *my* dog, Major? Help yourself. So I will.

"Ah, but, to goodness, look you, will her bite?" exclaimed an old Welshwoman, as she pulled her big hat further on her head, and looked askance at the big black dog which the man sitting next her had just hauled on to the coach-roof.

"It isn't a her, and he won't bite," was the sententious reply of the dog's master.

Not a pleasant-looking man, this; tall and thin, whiskerless and sallow faced; his head looking more like a bladder of lard surmonuted by a scratch-wig, than anything human : dressed all in black, with a stiff shiny hat, beaver gloves, and thick lustre-less Wellington boots. He had enormous collars encircling his face and growing peakedly out of a huge black silk cravat; he had a black satin waistcoat and a silver watch-guard, and an umbrella in a shiny oilskin case, and a hard slippery cold black cowskin bag, with J. M. upon it in staring white letters; and he looked very much like what he was—Mr. John Mortiboy, junior partner in the house of Crump and Mortiboy, Manchester warehouse-men, Friday-street, Cheapside, London.

What brought Mr. John Mortiboy into Wales to spend his holiday, or what induced such a pillar of British commerce to encumber himself with a dog, is no business of ours, Major. All I know, is, that he had been set down at the Barberth-road station, had dragged the black cow-skin bag from under his seat, had released the dog from a square bare receptacle which the animal had filled with howls, and had mounted himself and his dog on to the top of the coach travelling toward the little watering-place of Penethly. The dog, a big black retriever, lay on the coach-roof with his fine head erect, now gazing round the landscape, now dropping his cold muzzle between his paws and taking snatches of sleep. His master sat on the extreme edge of the seat, with one Wellington boot very much displayed and dangling in the air, and he, the Wellington boot's owner, appar-ently deriving much enjoyment from the suction of his umbrella-handle. He cast his big eyes round him now and then at certain portions of the scenery pointed out by the coachman, and expressed his opinion that it was "handsome," but beyond that never vouchsafed a word until the coach drew up at the Royal Inn at Penethly, when he went at once round to the stables and superintended the preparation of a meal for his dog, then ordered a "point steak well beat, potatoes, and a pint of sherry," to be ready for him in an hour's time; inquired the way to Albion Villa; and set off for Albion Villa accompanied by his dog Beppo.

I don't think Mr. John Mortiboy was much wanted at Albion Villa, nor that he was exactly the kind of man who would have suited its inmates. They were little conscious of the approach of his hard creaking boots, striding over the ill-paved High-street of the little town, and were enjoying themselves after their own simple fashion. The blinds were down, the candles were lighted, and Mrs. Barford was pretending to be knitting, but really enjoying a placid sleep; Ellen, her eldest daughter, was reading a magazine; Kate, her youngest, was making some sketches under the observant tuition of a slim gentleman with a light beard, who apparently took the greatest interest in his pupil. Upon this little group the clang of the gate bell, the creaking of Mr. John Mortiboy's boots, and the strident tones of Mr. John Mortiboy's voice, fell uncomfortably. "Say Mr. John Mortiboy, of London," he exclaimed, while yet in the little passage outside. The startled Welsh servant having obeyed him, he followed close upon her heels into the room.

"Servant, ladies!" said he, with a short circular nod, "servant, Mrs. Barford! Best to explain matters wholesale. You wonder who I am. You're sister-in-law to my uncle, Jonas Crump. I'm my uncle's partner in Friday-street. Done too much; rather baked in the head—heavy consignments and sitting up late at night poring over figures. The doctor recommended change of air; uncle Crump recommended Penethly, and mentioned you. I came down here, and have taken the liberty of calling. Down, Beppo! Don't mind him, miss, he won't hurt you."

"Oh! I'm not afraid of the *dog*!" said Ellen, with a slight start at Mr. Mortiboy's general manner, and at his calling her "Miss." Kate looked on in wonder, and the slim gentleman with the light beard confided to the said beard, the word "Brute."

"We're—very—pleased to see you, Mr. Mortiboy," said Mrs. Barford, "and—and hope that you will soon recover your health in our quiet village. I'm sure anything that we can—can do—my daughters, Miss Ellen, Miss Kate Barford; a friend of ours, Mr. Sandham—we shall be most happy to——" As Mrs. Barford's voice died away in the contemplation of the happiness before her, the young ladies and Mr. Sandham bowed, and Mr. Mortiboy favoured them with a series of short nods. Then he said, abruptly turning to the slim gentleman, "In the army, sir?"

"No, sir, I am not!" retorted the slim gentleman, with great promptitude.

"Beg pardon, no offence! Volunteer, perhaps? Hair, you know, beard, et cætera, made me think you were in the military line. Many young gents now-a-days are volunteers!"

"Mr. Sandham is an artist," said Mrs. Barford, interposing in dread lest there should be an outbreak.

"Oh ah!" said Mr. Mortiboy. "Bad trade that—demand not equal to supply, is it? Too many hands employed; barely bread and cheese, I'm told, for any but the top-sawyers."

"Sir!" said Mr. Sandham, in a loud tone of voice, and fiercely.

"Edward!" said Miss Kate, beneath her breath, appealingly.

"Won't you take some refreshment, Mr. Mortiboy?" asked Mrs. Barford, warningly. "We're just going to supper."

"No, thank you, mam," said Mr. Mortiboy. "I've a steak and potatoes waiting for me at the Royal, after which I shall turn in at once, as I'm done up by my journey. Good night, ladies all! Good night to you, sir! I'll look you up to-morrow morning, and if any of you want to go for a turn, I shall be proud to beau you about. Good night!" And beckoning his dog, Mr. Mortiboy took his departure.

Scarcely had the door closed behind him, than the long-restrained comments began.

"A pleasant visitor uncle Crump has sent us, mamma!" said Kate.

"Uncle Crump, indeed! Who never sent us anything before, except a five-pound note when poor papa died!" exclaimed Ellen.

"But you won't, will you, mamma, you won't be put upon in this way? You won't have this horrid man running in and out at all times and seasons, and——"

"And *beau*-ing us about! The vulgar wretch!" interrupted Kate.

"My dears! my dears!" said Mrs. Barford, "it strikes me that some one has been teaching you very strong language."

P

"Not I, Mrs. Barford," said Mr. Sandham; "absolve me from that; though I must own that if ever I saw a man who wanted kicking——"

"Nonsense, Mr. Sandham. This gentleman is imbued with certain London peculiarities, no doubt; but I dare say there's good in him. There must be, or he would never be the partner of such an upright man as Jonas Crump."

"Upright man! Pooh!" said Kate; and then the supper came in, and the subject dropped.

At nine o'clock next morning, just as the breakfast-things had been cleared, and Mrs. Barford was going through her usual interview with the cook, Kate, who was sitting in the little bay-window, started and exclaimed: "Oh, mamma! Here's this horrid man!"

Ellen peeped over her shoulder, and said, "I think he looks, if possible, more dreadful by daylight than by candlelight!"

Mr. John Mortiboy, utterly unconscious of the effect he was producing, unlatched the garden-gate, and then for the first time looking up, nodded shortly and familiarly at the sisters. "How do, young ladies?" he called from the garden. "Fine morning this; fresh and all that sort of thing! I feel better already. When a London man's a little overdone, nothing sets him up so soon, as a sniff of the briny."

And then he took a great gulp, as if to swallow as much fresh air as possible, and entered the house, followed by his dog.

"Did you hear him, Nelly?" asked Kate. "The wretch! I'm sure *I* won't be seen walking with him, in his nasty black clothes, like an undertaker!"

"He has a chimney-pot hat on, and has brought his umbrella! Fancy! At the sea!" said Ellen.

"Good morning, Mrs. Barford," said Mr. Mortiboy; "domestic arrangements, eh? I understand. If you've no objection, I'll do myself the pleasure of cutting my mutton with you to-day. And mutton it will be, I suppose! Can't get any beef here, I understand, except on Friday, which is killing-day for the barracks. Bad arrangement that; wants alteration."

"Hadn't you better alter it then, Mr. Mortiboy," said Kate; "superintending the butcher will be a pleasant way of spending your holiday."

"Joking, miss, eh? Well, I don't mind. But ain't you coming

out, young ladies, for a mouthful of air. I suppose the old lady don't move so early."

"If you refer to mamma," said Ellen, frigidly, "she never goes out until just before dinner."

"Ah, I thought not. Old folks must wait until the air is what they call warmed by the sun. But that won't hinder our taking a turn, I suppose. Where's Whiskerandos?"

"If, as I presume, you mean Mr. Sandham, the gentleman who was here last night, I cannot inform you, Mr. Mortiboy," said Kate, with a very flushed face, and a slightly trembling voice; "but I would advise you not to let him hear you joking about him, as he is rather quick-tempered."

"Oh, indeed?" exclaimed Mr. Mortiboy, "a fire-eater is he? Well, there's no duelling now, you know. Any nonsense of that sort,—give a man in charge of a policeman, or summons him before a magistrate, and get him bound over."

Just at this moment Mrs. Barford came in and told the girls to get their hats on, and show Mr. Mortiboy the prettiest spots in the village, the Castle Hill, the ruined Abbey, and the Smuggler's Leap. To these places they went, Mr. Mortiboy discoursing the whole way of the badness of the roads, and of what improvements might be made if they had a properly constituted local board of health at Penethly; declaring that the cries of "Milford oysters," and "fresh haddick," were entirely unconstitutional and illegal, as no one had a right to shout in the public streets; that there ought to be proper stands provided for the car-drivers; and that a regular police supervision was urgently demanded. He did not think much of the Abbey ruins, and he laughed in scorn at the story of the Smuggler's Leap. As they were on their homeward way, coming round the Castle Hill, they met Mr. Sandham, very ruddy and fresh, and shiny, and with a couple of towels in his hand. He took off his wide-awake as he approached the ladies, and bowed slightly to Mr. Mortiboy.

"Ah, Mr. Sandham!" said Ellen, with an admonitory finger, "you have been bathing again by St. Catherine's Rock, after all the warning we gave you!"

"My dear Ellen," interposed Kate, with a petulant air, "how can you? If Mr. Sandham chooses to risk his life after what he has been told, it surely is nothing to us!"

"Now, Miss Kate, Miss Kate, that's not fair!" said Sandham; "you know," he added, dropping his voice, "that every word of yours would have weight with me, but the tide was slack this morning, and really there is no other place where a swimmer can really enjoy a bath. You are a swimmer, Mr. Mortiboy?"

"Yes, sir," replied that gentleman. "Yes, sir, I can manage it. I've had lessons at Peerless Pool and the Holborn Baths, and can keep up well enough. But I don't like it. I don't see much fun in what are absurdly called the 'manly exercises.' Twenty years ago, young men used to like driving coaches; now I can't conceive duller work than holding a bunch of thick leather reins in your hand, steering four tired horses, sitting on a hard seat, and listening to the conversation of an uneducated coachman. I never ride, because I hate bumping up and down on a hard saddle and rubbing the skin off my body; I never play cricket, because in the hot weather I like to keep quiet and cool, and not toil in the sun; and as to going out shooting and stumping over miles of stubble in September, lugging a big gun and tiring myself to death, I look upon that as the pursuit of a maniac! I am a practical man!"

"You are indeed!" said Kate, as she dropped gradually behind with Mr. Sandham, and left the practical man and her sister Ellen to lead the way to the house.

It is unnecessary to recount the sayings and doings of Mr. John Mortiboy during the next few days. It is enough that he spent the greater portion of them with the Barford family, and that he so elaborated his ideas of practicality, and so inveighed against everything that was not absolutely useful in a mercantile point of view—including, in a measure, art, poetry, music, and the domestic affections—that he incurred the unmitigated hatred of the young ladies, and even fell to zero in Mrs. Barford's estimation.

It was about the fifth morning after the intrusion of this utterly incongruous element into the society of Albion Villa, that Ellen and Kate strolled out immediately after breakfast with the view of escaping the expected visit of their persecutor, and made their way to the Castle Hill. The night had been tempestuous, and from their window they had noticed that a heavy sea was running: they consequently were not surprised to see a little group of people gathered on the heights looking towards St. Catherine's Rock: a huge mass of granite surmounted by an old ruin, round which, when it was insulated at high water, the tide always swept with a peculiar and dangerous swirl. But when they joined the group, among which were several of their friends, they found that the concourse were regarding, with interest mingled with fright, the movements of a swimmer who had rounded the extremity of Catherine's, and was seen making for the shore.

"He'll never do it," said Captain Calthorp, an old half-pay dragoon, who had been tempted by the cheapness of Penethly to pitch his tent there; "he'll never do it, by Jove! Yes! Well struggled, sir; he made a point there—hold on, now, and he's in."

"Who is it?" asked the coast-guard lieutenant, who was standing by. "Any one we know?"

"I can't tell at this distance!" said Captain Calthorp, "though it looks like——stay! There's one of your look-out men on the height, with a glass; give him a hail!"

"Yoho! Morgan!" cried the lieutenant. "Ay, ay, sir!" was the man's ready response, though the glass was never moved. "Bring that glass down here!" "Ay, ay, sir," and in two minutes the old coast-guard man was by his officer's side. He saluted and handed the glass, but as he did so he said, in an under tone, "God help the gentleman, he's done! Ah, look you now, poor thing, nothing can save him."

"What!" cries the lieutenant, clapping the glass to his eye. "By Jove, you're right! he's in a bad way, and it—why it's the artist-chap, that friend of the Barfords'!"

"Who?" screamed Kate, rushing up at the moment. "*Who* did you say, Mr. Lawford? Oh, for God's sake, save him! Save him, Mr. Lawford! Save him, Captain Calthorp!"

"My dear young lady," said the last-named gentleman, "I am sure Lawford didn't know *you* were here, or he wouldn't——"

"This is no time for ceremony, Captain Calthorp," said Ellen; "for Heaven's sake, let some effort be made to save my sister's— to save Mr. Sandham!"

"My dear Miss Barford," said Lawford, who had been whispering with Morgan, "I fear no mortal aid can avail the poor dear fellow now. Before we could descend the rock, and launch a boat, with the tide ebbing at the rate it now is——"

"Hur would have been swep' round Cath'rine's, and away out to sea!" said Morgan.

"Oh, help him!" screamed Kate. "Oh, how cruel! how cowardly! Oh, help him, Mr. Lawford!" She lifted up her hands piteously to the lieutenant. "Oh, Mr. Mortiboy," she exclaimed, as that gentleman came slowly sauntering up the hill with Beppo at his heels, "for God's sake, save Mr. Sandham!"

"Save—Mr. Sandham—my dear young lady; I don't exactly comprehend!" began Mr. Mortiboy, looking vaguely in the direction of her outstretched hand; then suddenly, "Good Lord! is that his head? There! Down there!"

"Yes!" whispered Ellen Barford; "yes! They say he will be whirled away before a boat could be launched—they say he is lost now!"

"Not at all! Not yet, at least!" replied Mortiboy, excited, but without much perceptible alteration of manner. "While there's life there's hope, you know, Miss B., and even yet we may—— Here, Beppo! Hi, man! hi! Good boy!" The dog came, leaping round his master. "Hi! ho! Not here! There! there Look, boy!" catching him by the collar, and pointing down to where Sandham's head was a mere speck on the water. "Look, man! Look, old boy! He sees it, by Jove!" as the dog uttered a low growl, and became restive. "In, old man! In, fine fellow! In, Beppo! Look! Noble dog, in he goes!"

In he went, with one bound over the low stone wall, then quickly down the sloping slippery boulders, then with a plunge into the sea—lost sight of for a moment, rising to view again, paddling off straight for the drowning man. The swift current whirled him in eddies here and there, but still the brave dog persevered; the spectators held their breath, as they saw him bearing down upon the black speck, which was every second growing smaller and smaller, and receding further and further from the land. But the dog made grand progress, the strong sucking under-current helped him, and he arrived at Sandham's side just in time for the drowning man to fling his arm round the dog's neck, and to feel his shoulder seized by the dog's teeth. They saw this from the shore, and then Kate Barford fainted.

But the work was only half done: the dog turned round, and battled bravely for the shore, but he was encumbered by his burden, and now the current was against him. He strove and strove, but the way he made was small, and every foot was gained with intense struggling and exertion. "By Jove! He'll never do it," cried Lieutenant Lawford, with the glass at his eye; and, as he said the words, old Morgan, the preventive-man, added through his teeth, "Hur must be helped, at any cost," and sped away down the rock, shaping his course to where a small pleasure-boat lay high and dry on the sand. "I'm with you, governor," cried John Mortiboy; "I can't feather, but I pull a strongish oar;" and he followed the old man as best he could. The boat was reached, and pushed by main force to the water's edge, where Mortiboy entered it, and old Morgan ran in, waist-deep, to give it the starting shove, and then leaped in to join his comrade. On they pulled, Morgan with a measured steady stroke, Mortiboy with fevered strong jerks that sent the boat's head now to the right, now to the left: when old Morgan, suddenly looking over his shoulder, called out, "Hur's done! Hur's sinking now, both on 'em!" Mortiboy looked round too; they were still some ten boats' length from the objects of their pursuit, and both dog and man were vanishing. "Not yet!" cried he; and in an instant he had torn off the black coat and the Wellington boots, and had flung himself, as nobly as his own dog, into the sea.

A very few strokes brought him to Sandham; he seized him by the hair of his head, and battled bravely with the waves; the dog, recognising his master, seemed to take fresh courage, and the trio floated until old Morgan dragged them one by one into the boat. When they reached the shore, all Penethly was on the beach, cheering with all its might: they lifted out Mr. Sandham, insensible but likely to recover, and they administered a very stiff glass of grog to Mr. Mortiboy, who was shivering like an aspen-leaf, but who received even greater warmth from a warm pressure of Ellen Barford's hand, and a whispered "God bless you, Mr. Mortiboy!" than from the grog—though he took that, too, like a man whom it comforted. As for Beppo, I don't know what the fishing population would not have done for him, but that he positively refused to stir from Sandham's side. As they carried the artist up to his lodgings the dog buried his nose in the pendent hand, and did not leave until he had seen his charge safely placed in bed.

Mr. Sandham was, in his own words, "All right" next day, but Mr. Mortiboy, unaccustomed to exercise and damp, fell ill, and was confined to his bed for several weeks:—would have never left it, I think, but for the care and attention of his three nurses from Albion Villa. Of these, Ellen was the most constant and the most regular, and the patient always seemed better under her care.

"He is making progress, Kate," she said one night to her sister. "He is a good patient. You know, as he would say himself, he is so practical."

"God bless his practicality, Nell," said Kate, with tears in her eyes. "Think what it did for us!"

Three years have passed since then, Major, and a family group is going to be gathered in a large square room built as a kind of excrescence to a very pretty villa in Kensington. This is to be the studio of Mr. Sandham, A.R.A. But as the mortar and plaster are extraordinarily slow in drying (when were they not, Major?), Mr. Sandham, A.R.A., come up from Wales with the family group, to take possession, has established the group at the excellent Lodgings of the excellent Mrs. Lirriper, and he, the owner of said studio, is smoking a pipe with a worthy Major, and smoothing with his slippered foot the rough curly back of his dog Beppo, who is stretched in front of the fire. Mrs. Sandham, formerly Kate Barford, is working at a baby's frock, and asking now and then the advice of her sister, who is frilling a little cap. (There they are, Major. Don't tell them that I said so.)

"How late John is to-night, Ellen," says old Mrs. Barford, from her place in the chimney-corner. (You hear her, Major?)

"Always at Christmas-time, dear mother," says Ellen. (There she is, Major.) "Since uncle Crump's death, you know, John's business is trebled, and it all hangs on him, dear old fellow!"

"He will be late for supper, Nelly," says Sandham. "(—Excuse me, Major.)"

"No he won't, Ned!" cries a cheery voice at the door as John Mortiboy appears; "no he won't. He's never late for anything good. Don't you know, he's a practical man?"

—Mr. Mortiboy, Major Jackman, Major, Mr. Mortiboy!

V

HOW THE THIRD FLOOR KNEW THE POTTERIES

I am a plain man, Major, and you may not dislike to hear a plain statement of facts from me. Some of those facts lie beyond my understanding. I do not pretend to explain them. I only know that they happened as I relate them, and that I pledge myself for the truth of every word of them.

I began life roughly enough, down among the Potteries. I was an orphan; and my earliest recollections are of a great porcelain manufactory in the country of the Potteries, where I helped about the yard, picked up what halfpence fell in my way, and slept in a harness-loft over the stable. Those were hard times; but things bettered themselves as I grew older and stronger, especially after George Barnard had come to be foreman of the yard.

George Barnard was a Wesleyan—we were mostly dissenters in the Potteries—sober, clear-headed, somewhat sulky and silent, but a good fellow every inch of him, and my best friend at the time when I most needed a good friend. He took me out of the yard, and set me to the furnace-work. He entered me on the books at a fixed rate of wages. He helped me to pay for a little cheap schooling four nights a week; and he led me to go with him on Sundays to the chapel down by the river-side, where I first saw Leah Payne. She was his sweetheart, and so pretty that I used to forget the preacher and everybody else, when I looked at her. When she joined in the singing, I heard no voice but hers. If she asked me for the hymn-book, I used to blush and tremble. I believe I worshipped her, in my stupid ignorant way; and I think I worshipped Barnard almost as blindly, though after a different fashion. I felt I owed him everything. I knew that he had saved me, body and mind; and I looked up to him as a savage might look up to a missionary.

Leah was the daughter of a plumber, who lived close by the chapel. She was twenty, and George about seven or eight-and-thirty. Some captious folks said there was too much difference in their ages; but she was so serious-minded, and they loved each other so earnestly and quietly, that, if nothing had come between them during their courtship, I don't believe the question of disparity would ever have troubled the happiness of their married lives. Something did come, however; and that something was a Frenchman, called Louis Laroche. He was a painter on porcelain, from the famous works at Sèvres; and our master, it was said, had engaged him for three years certain, at such wages as none of our own people, however skilful, could hope to command. It was about the beginning or middle of September when he first came among us. He looked very young; was small, dark, and well made; had little white soft hands, and a silky moustache; and spoke English nearly as well as I do. None of us liked him; but that was only natural, seeing how he was put over the head of every Englishman in the place. Besides, though he was always smiling and civil, we couldn't help seeing that he thought himself ever so much better than the rest of us; and that was not pleasant. Neither was it pleasant to see him strolling about the town, dressed just like a gentleman, when working hours were over; smoking good cigars, when we were forced to be content with a pipe of common tobacco; hiring a horse on Sunday afternoons, when we were trudging a-foot; and taking his pleasure as if the world was made for him to enjoy, and us to work in.

"Ben, boy," said George, "there's something wrong about that Frenchman."

It was on a Saturday afternoon, and we were sitting on a pile of empty seggars against the door of my furnace-room, waiting till the men should all have cleared out of the yard. Seggars are deep earthen boxes in which the pottery is put, while being fired in the kiln.

I looked up, inquiringly.

"About the Count?" said I, for that was the nickname by which he went in the pottery.

George nodded, and paused for a moment with his chin resting on his palms.

"He has an evil eye," said he; "and a false smile. Something wrong about him."

I drew nearer, and listened to George as if he had been an oracle.

"Besides," added he, in his slow quiet way, with his eyes fixed straight before him as if he was thinking aloud, "there's a young look about him that isn't natural. Take him just at sight, and you'd think he was almost a boy; but look close at him—see the little fine wrinkles under his eyes, and the hard lines about his mouth, and then tell me his age, if you can! Why, Ben boy, he's as old as I am, pretty near; ay, and as strong, too. You stare; but I tell you that, slight as he looks, he could fling you over his shoulder as if you were a feather. And as for his hands, little and white as they are, there are muscles of iron inside them, take my word for it."

"But, George, how can you know?"

"Because I have a warning against him," replied George, very gravely. "Because, whenever he is by, I feel as if my eyes saw clearer, and my ears heard keener, than at any other times. Maybe it's presumption, but I sometimes feel as if I had a call to guard myself and others against him. Look at the children, Ben, how they shrink away from him; and see there, now! Ask Captain what he thinks of him! Ben, that dog likes him no better than I do."

I looked, and saw Captain crouching by his kennel with his ears laid back, growling audibly, as the Frenchman came slowly down the steps leading from his own workshop at the upper end of the yard. On the last step he paused; lighted a cigar; glanced round, as if to see whether any one was by; and then walked straight over to within a couple of yards of the kennel. Captain gave a short angry snarl, and laid his muzzle close down upon his paws, ready for a spring. The Frenchman folded his arms deliberately, fixed his eyes on the dog, and stood calmly smoking. He knew exactly how far he dared go, and kept just that one foot out of harm's way. All at once he stopped, puffed a mouthful of smoke in the dog's eyes, burst into a mocking laugh, turned lightly on his heel, and walked away; leaving Captain straining at his chain, and barking after him like a mad creature.

Days went by, and I, at work in my own department, saw no more of the Count. Sunday came—the third, I think, after I had talked with George in the yard. Going with George to chapel, as usual, in the morning, I noticed that there was something strange and anxious in his face, and that he scarcely opened his lips to me on the way. Still I said nothing. It was not my place to question him; and I remember thinking to myself that the cloud would all clear off as soon as he found himself by Leah's side, holding the same book, and joining in the same hymn. It did not, however, for no Leah was there, I looked every moment to the door, expecting to see her sweet face coming in; but George never lifted his eyes from his book, or seemed to notice that her place was empty. Thus the whole service went by, and my thoughts wandered continually from the words of the preacher. As soon as the last blessing was spoken, and we were fairly across the threshold, I turned to George, and asked if Leah was ill?

"No," said he, gloomily. "She's not ill."

"Then why wasn't she——?"

"I'll tell you why," he interrupted, impatiently. "Because you've seen her here for the last time. She's never coming to chapel again."

"Never coming to the chapel again?" I faltered, laying my

hand on his sleeve in the earnestness of my surprise. "Why, George, what is the matter?"

But he shook my hand off, and stamped with his iron heel till the pavement rang again.

"Don't ask me," said he, roughly. "Let me alone. You'll know soon enough."

And with this he turned off down a by-lane leading towards the hills, and left me without another word.

I had had plenty of hard treatment in my time; but never, until that moment, an angry look or syllable from George. I did not know how to bear it. That day my dinner seemed as if it would choke me; and in the afternoon I went out and wandered restlessly about the fields till the hour for evening prayers came round. I then returned to the chapel, and sat down on a tomb outside, waiting for George. I saw the congregation go in by twos and threes; I heard the first psalm-tune echo solemnly through the evening stillness; but no George came. Then the service began, and I knew that, punctual as his habits were, it was of no use to expect him any longer. Where could he be? What could have happened? Why should Leah Payne never come to chapel again? Had she gone over to some other sect, and was that why George seemed so unhappy?

Sitting there in the little dreary churchyard with the darkness fast gathering around me, I asked myself these questions over and over again, till my brain ached; for I was not much used to thinking about anything in those times. At last, I could bear to sit quiet no longer. The sudden thought struck me that I would go to Leah, and learn what the matter was, from her own lips. I sprang to my feet, and set off at once towards her home.

It was quite dark, and a light rain was beginning to fall. I found the garden-gate open, and a quick hope flashed across me that George might be there. I drew back for a moment, hesitating whether to knock or ring, when a sound of voices in the passage, and the sudden gleaming of a bright line of light under the door, warned me that some one was coming out. Taken by surprise, and quite unprepared for the moment with anything to say, I shrank back behind the porch, and waited until those within should have passed out. The door opened, and the light streamed suddenly upon the roses and the wet gravel.

"It rains," said Leah, bending forward and shading the candle with her hand.

"And is as cold as Siberia," added another voice, which was not George's, and yet sounded strangely familiar. "Ugh! what a climate for such a flower as my darling to bloom in!"

"Is it so much finer in France?" asked Leah, softly.

"As much finer as blue skies and sunshine can make it. Why, my angel, even your bright eyes will be ten times brighter, and your rosy cheeks ten times rosier, when they are transplanted to Paris. Ah! I can give you no idea of the wonders of Paris— the broad streets planted with trees, the palaces, the shops, the gardens!—it is a city of enchantment."

"It must be, indeed!" said Leah. "And you will really take me to see all those beautiful shops?"

"Every Sunday, my darling—Bah! don't look so shocked. The shops in Paris are always open on Sunday, and everybody makes holiday. You will soon get over these prejudices."

"I fear it is very wrong to take so much pleasure in the things of this world," sighed Leah.

The Frenchman laughed, and answered her with a kiss.

"Good night, my sweet little saint!" and he ran lightly down the path, and disappeared in the darkness. Leah sighed again, lingered a moment, and then closed the door.

Stupified and bewildered, I stood for some seconds like a stone statue, unable to move; scarcely able to think. At length, I roused myself, as it were mechanically, and went towards the gate. At that instant, a heavy hand was laid upon my shoulder, and a hoarse voice close beside my ear, said:

"Who are you? What are you doing here?"

It was George. I knew him at once, in spite of the darkness, and stammered his name. He took his hand quickly from my shoulder.

"How long have you been here?" said he, fiercely. "What right have you to lurk about, like a spy in the dark? God help me, Ben—I'm half mad. I don't mean to be harsh to you."

"I'm sure you don't," I cried, earnestly.

"It's that cursed Frenchman," he went on, in a voice that sounded like the groan of one in pain. "He's a villain. I know he's a villain; and I've had a warning against him ever since the first moment he came among us. He'll make her miserable, and break her heart some day—my pretty Leah—and I loved her so! But I'll be revenged—as sure as there's a sun in heaven, I'll be revenged!"

His vehemence terrified me. I tried to persuade him to go home; but he would not listen to me.

"No, no," he said. "Go home yourself, boy, and let me be. My blood is on fire: this rain is good for me, and I am better alone."

"If I could only do something to help you——"

"You can't," interrupted he. "Nobody can help me. I'm a ruined man, and I don't care what becomes of me. The Lord forgive me! my heart is full of wickedness, and my thoughts are the promptings of Satan. There go—for Heaven's sake, go. I don't know what I say, or what I do!"

I went, for I did not dare refuse any longer; but I lingered awhile at the corner of the street, and watched him pacing to and fro, to and fro in the driving rain. At length I turned reluctantly away, and went home.

I lay awake that night for hours, thinking over the events of the day, and hating the Frenchman from my very soul. I could not hate Leah. I had worshipped her too long and too faithfully for that; but I looked upon her as a creature given over to destruction. I fell asleep towards morning, and woke again shortly after daybreak. When I reached the pottery, I found George there before me, looking very pale, but quite himself, and setting the men to their work the same as usual. I said nothing about what had happened the day before. Something in his face silenced me; but seeing him so steady and composed, I took heart, and began to hope he had fought through the worst of his trouble. By-and-by the Frenchman came through the yard, gay and off-hand, with his cigar in his mouth, and his hands in his pockets. George turned sharply away into one of the workshops, and shut the door. I drew a deep breath of relief. My dread was to see them come to an open quarrel; and I felt that as long as they kept clear of that, all would be well.

Thus the Monday went by, and the Tuesday; and still George kept aloof from me. I had sense enough not to be hurt by this. I felt he had a good right to be silent, if silence helped him to bear his trial better; and I made up my mind never to breathe another syllable on the subject, unless he began.

Wednesday came. I had overslept myself that morning, and came to work a quarter after the hour, expecting to be fined; for George was very strict as foreman of the yard, and treated friends and enemies just the same. Instead of blaming me, however, he called me up, and said:

"Ben, whose turn is it this week to sit up?"

"Mine, sir," I replied. (I always called him "Sir" in working hours.)

"Well, then, you may go home to-day, and the same on Thursday and Friday; for there's a large batch of work for the ovens to-night, and there'll be the same to-morrow night and the night after."

"All right, sir," said I. "Then I'll be here by seven this evening."

"No, half-past nine will be soon enough. I've some accounts to make up, and I shall be here myself till then. Mind you are true to time, though."

"I'll be as true as the clock, sir," I replied, and was turning away when he called me back again.

"You're a good lad, Ben," said he. "Shake hands."

I seized his hand, and pressed it warmly.

"If I'm good for anything, George," I answered with all my heart, "it's you who have made me so. God bless you for it!"

"Amen!" said he, in a troubled voice, putting his hand to his hat.

And so we parted.

In general, I went to bed by day when I was attending to the firing by night; but this morning I had already slept longer than usual, and wanted exercise more than rest. So I ran home; put a bit of bread and meat in my pocket; snatched up my big thorn stick; and started off for a long day in the country. When I came home, it was quite dark and beginning to rain, just as it had begun to rain at about the same time that wretched Sunday evening: so I changed my wet boots, had an early supper and a nap in the chimney-corner, and went down to the works at a few minutes before half-past nine. Arriving at the factory gate, I found it ajar, and so walked in and closed it after me. I remember thinking at the time that it was unlike George's usual caution to leave it so; but it passed from my mind next moment. Having slipped in the bolt, I then went straight over to George's little counting-house, where the gas was shining cheerfully in the window. Here also, somewhat to my surprise, I found the door open, and the room empty. I went in. The threshold and part of the floor was wetted by the driving rain. The wages-book was open on the desk, George's pen stood in the ink, and his hat hung on its usual peg in the corner. I concluded, of course, that he had gone round to the ovens; so, following him, I took down his hat and carried it with me, for it was now raining fast.

The baking-houses lay just opposite, on the other side of the yard. There were three of them, opening one out of the other; and in each, the great furnace filled all the middle of the room. These furnaces are, in fact, large kilns bulit of brick, with an oven closed in by an iron door in the centre of each, and a chimney going up through the roof. The pottery, enclosed in seggars, stands round inside on shelves, and has to be turned from time to time while the firing is going on. To turn these seggars, test the heat, and keep the fires up, was my work at the period of which I am now telling you, Major.

Well! I went through the baking-houses one after the other, and found all empty alike. Then a strange vague uneasy feeling came over me, and I began to wonder what could have become of George. It was possible that he might be in one of the workshops; so I ran over to the counting-house, lighted a lantern, and made a thorough survey of the yards. I tried the doors; they were all locked as usual. I peeped into the open sheds; they were all vacant. I called "George! George!" in every part of the outer premises; but the wind and rain drove back my voice, and no other voice replied to it. Forced at last to believe that he was really gone, I took his hat back to the counting-house, put away the wages-book, extinguished the gas, and prepared for my solitary watch.

The night was mild, and the heat in the baking-rooms intense. I knew, by experience, that the ovens had been overheated, and that none of the porcelain must go in at least for the next two hours; so I carried my stool to the door, settled myself in a sheltered corner where the air could reach me, but not the rain, and fell to wondering where George could have gone, and why he should not have waited till the time appointed. That he had left in haste was clear—not because his hat remained behind, for he might have had a cap with him—but because he had left the book open, and the gas lighted. Perhaps one of the workmen had met with some accident, and he had been summoned away so urgently that he had no time to think of anything; perhaps he would even now come back presently to see that all was right before he went home to his lodgings. Turning these things over in my mind, I grew drowsy, my thoughts wandered, and I fell asleep.

I cannot tell how long my nap lasted. I had walked a great distance that day, and I slept heavily; but I awoke all in a moment, with some sort of terror upon me, and looking up, saw George Barnard sitting on a stool before the oven door, with the firelight full upon his face.

Ashamed to be found sleeping, I started to my feet. At the same instant, he rose, turned away without even looking towards me, and went out into the next room.

"Don't be angry, George!" I cried, following him. "None of the seggars are in. I knew the fires were too strong, and——"

The words died on my lips. I had followed him from the first room to the second, from the second to the third, and in the third—I lost him!

I could not believe my eyes. I opened the end door leading into the yard, and looked out; but he was nowhere in sight. I went round to the back of the baking-houses, looked behind the furnaces, ran over to the counting-house, called him by his name over and over again; but all was dark, silent, lonely, as ever.

Then I remembered how I had bolted the outer gate, and how impossible it was that he should have come in without ringing. Then, too, I began again to doubt the evidence of my own senses, and to think I must have been dreaming.

I went back to my old post by the door of the first baking-house, and sat down for a moment to collect my thoughts.

"In the first place," said I to myself, "there is but one outer gate. That outer gate I bolted on the inside, and it is bolted still. In the next place, I searched the premises, and found all the sheds empty, and the workshop-doors padlocked as usual on the outside. I proved that George was nowhere about, when I came, and I know he could not have come in since, without my knowledge. Therefore it is a dream. It is certainly a dream, and there's an end of it."

And with this I trimmed my lantern and proceeded to test the temperature of the furnaces. We used to do this, I should tell you, by the introduction of little roughly-moulded lumps of common fire-clay. If the heat is too great, they crack; if too little, they remain damp and moist; if just right, they become firm and smooth all over, and pass into the biscuit stage. Well! I took my three little lumps of clay, put one in each oven, waited while I counted five hundred, and then went round again to see the results. The two first were in capital con-

Q

dition, the third had flown into a dozen pieces. This proved that the seggars might at once go into the ovens One and Two, but that number Three had been over-heated, and must be allowed to go on cooling for an hour or two longer.

I therefore stocked One and Two with nine rows of seggars, three deep on each shelf; left the rest waiting till number Three was in a condition to be trusted; and, fearful of falling asleep again, now that the firing was in progress, walked up and down the rooms to keep myself awake. This was hot work, however, and I could not stand it very long; so I went back presently to my stool by the door, and fell to thinking about my dream. The more I thought of it, the more strangely real it seemed, and the more I felt convinced that I was actually on my feet, when I saw George get up and walk into the adjoining room. I was also certain that I had still continued to see him as he passed out of the second room into the third, and that at that time I was even following his very footsteps. Was it possible, I asked myself, that I could have been up and moving, and yet not quite awake? I had heard of people walking in their sleep. Could it be that I was walking in mine, and never waked till I reached the cool air of the yard? All this seemed likely enough, so I dismissed the matter from my mind, and passed the rest of the night in attending to the seggars, adding fresh fuel from time to time to the furnaces of the first and second ovens, and now and then taking a turn through the yards. As for Number Three, it kept up its heat to such a degree that it was almost day before I dared trust the seggars to go in it.

Thus the hours went by; and at half-past seven on Thursday morning, the men came to their work. It was now my turn to go off duty, but I wanted to see George before I left, and so waited for him in the counting-house, while a lad named Steve Storr took my place at the ovens. But the clock went on from half-past seven to a quarter to eight; then to eight o'clock; then to a quarter-past eight—and still George never made his appearance. At length, when the hand got round to half-past eight, I grew weary of waiting, took up my hat, ran home, went to bed, and slept profoundly until past four in the afternoon.

That evening I went down to the factory quite early; for I had a restlessness upon me, and I wanted to see George before he left for the night. This time, I found the gate bolted, and I rang for admittance.

"How early you are, Ben!" said Steve Storr, as he let me in.

"Mr. Barnard's not gone?" I asked, quickly; for I saw at the first glance that the gas was out in the counting-house.

"He's not gone," said Steve, "because he's never been."

"Never been?"

"No: and what's stranger still, he's not been home either, since dinner yesterday."

"But he was here last night."

"Oh yes, he was here last night, making up the books. John Parker was with him till past six; and you found him here, didn't you, at half-past nine?"

I shook my head.

"Well, he's gone, anyhow. Good night!"

"Good night!"

I took the lantern from his hand, bolted him out mechanically, and made my way to the baking-houses like one in a stupor. George gone? Gone without a word of warning to his employer, or of farewell to his fellow-workmen? I could not understand it. I could not believe it. I sat down bewildered, incredulous, stunned. Then came hot tears, doubts, terrifying suspicions. I remembered the wild words he had spoken a few nights back; the strange calm by which they were followed; my dream of the evening before. I had heard of men who drowned themselves for love; and the turbid Severn ran close by—so close, that one might pitch a stone into it from some of the workshop windows.

These thoughts were too horrible. I dared not dwell upon them. I turned to work, to free myself from them, if I could; and began by examining the ovens. The temperature of all was much higher than on the previous night, the heat having been gradually increased during the last twelve hours. It was now my business to keep the heat on the increase for twelve more; after which it would be allowed, as gradually, to subside, until the pottery was cool enough for removal. To turn the seggars, and add fuel to the two first furnaces, was my first work. As before, I found number three in advance of the others, and so left it for half an hour, or an hour. I then went round the yard; tried the doors; let the dog loose; and brought him back with me to the baking-houses, for company. After that, I set my lantern on a shelf beside the door, took a book from my pocket, and began to read.

I remember the title of the book as well as possible. It was called Bowlker's Art of Angling, and contained little rude cuts of all kinds of artificial flies, hooks, and other tackle. But I could not keep my mind to it for two mnutes together; and at last I gave it up in despair, covered my face with my hands, and fell into a long absorbing painful train of thought. A considerable time had gone by thus—maybe an hour—when I was roused by a low whimpering howl from Captain, who was lying at my feet. I looked up with a start, just as I had started from sleep the night before, and with the same vague terror; and saw, exactly in the same place and in the same attitude, with the firelight full upon him—George Barnard!

At this sight, a fear heavier than the fear of death fell upon me, and my tongue seemed paralysed in my mouth. Then, just as last night, he rose, or seemed to rise, and went slowly out into the next room. A power stronger than myself appeared to compel me, reluctantly, to follow him. I saw him pass through the second room—cross the threshold of the third room—walk straight up to the oven—and there pause. He then turned, for the first time, with the glare of the red firelight pouring out upon him from the open door of the furnace, and looked at me, face to face. In the same instant, his whole frame and countenance seemed to glow and become transparent, as if the fire were all within him and around him—and in that glow he became, as it were, absorbed into the furnace, and disappeared!

I uttered a wild cry, tried to stagger from the room, and fell insensible before I reached the door.

When I next opened my eyes, the grey dawn was in the sky; the furnace doors were all closed as I had left them when I last went round; the dog was quietly sleeping not far from my side; and the men were ringing at the gate, to be let in.

I told my tale from beginning to end, and was laughed at, as a matter of course, by all who heard it. When it was found, however, that my statements never varied, and, above all, that George Barnard continued absent, some few began to talk it over seriously, and among those few, the master of the works. He forbade the furnace to be cleared out, called in the aid of a celebrated naturalist, and had the ashes submitted to a scientific examination. The result was as follows:

The ashes were found to have been largely saturated with some kind of fatty animal matter. A considerable portion of those ashes consisted of charred bone. A semi-circular piece of iron, which evidently had once been the heel of a workman's heavy boot, was found, half fused, at one corner of the furnace. Near it, a tibia bone, which still retained sufficient of its original form and texture to render identification possible. This bone, however, was so much charred, that it fell into powder on being handled.

After this, not many doubted that George Barnard had been foully murdered, and that his body had been thrust into the furnace. Suspicion fell upon Louis Laroche. He was arrested, a coroner's inquest was held, and every circumstance connected with the night of the murder was as thoroughly sifted and investigated as possible. All the sifting in the world, however, failed either to clear or to condemn Louis Laroche. On the very night of his release, he left the place by the mail train, and was never seen or heard of there, again. As for Leah, I know not what became of her. I went away myself before many weeks were over, and never have set foot among the Potteries from that hour to this.

VI

HOW THE BEST ATTIC WAS UNDER A CLOUD

Major, you have assured me of your sympathy; you shall receive my confidence. I not only seem—as you have searchingly observed—"under a cloud," but I am. I entered (shall I say like a balloon?) into a dense stratum of cloud, obscuring the wretched earth from view, in the year eighteen hundred and dash, in the sweet summer season, when nature, as has been remarked by some distinguished poet, puts on her gayest garb, and when her countenance is adorned with the sunniest and loveliest of smiles. Ah! what are now those smiles to me? What care I for sunshine or for verdure? For me, summer is no more. For, I must ever remember that it was in the summer that the canker ate its way into my heart's core—that it was in the summer that I parted with my belief in mankind—that it was in summer that I knew for the first time that WOMAN—but this is premature. Pray be seated.

I have no doubt that my appearance and words convey to you, Major, and to all observant persons, that I have an elevated soul. In fact, were it otherwise, how could I be under a cloud? The sordid soul won't blight. To one possessing an elevated soul like myself, the task of keeping accounts at a furrier's (in a large way) could not be otherwise than repugnant. It *was* repugnant, and the rapture of getting a holiday, which was annually accorded me in June—not a busy month in the fur-trade— was something perfectly indescribable. Of course, whenever my vacation time came round, I invariably rushed off to the country; there to indulge my natural tastes and commune with our mother, Nature.

On the particular occasion of which I have now to speak, I had, however, other communings to look forward to, besides those in which nature takes her silent yet eloquent part. I loved— Aha!—Love—Woman—Vertigo—Despair—I beg your pardon —I will be calm. I loved Miss Nuttlebury. Miss Nuttlebury lived in the neighbourhood of Dartford (at a convenient distance from the Powder-Mills), so in the neighbourhood of Dartford (rather further from the Powder-Mills) I determined to spend my vacation. I made arrangements at a certain small roadside inn for my board and lodging.

I was acquainted—nay, I was on friendly terms—with the Nuttleburys. Mr. Nuttlebury, a land surveyor in a rather small way, was an old friend of my father's; so I had access to the house. I had access also, as I thought, to the heart of Mary, which was Miss Nuttlebury's name. If I was mistaken—Aha!— but I am again premature. You are aware, or perhaps you are not aware, that my name is Oliver Cromwell Shrubsole—so called after the great Protector of British rights; the man who, or rather but for whom—but I am again premature, or rather, I should say, on the whole the reverse.

The first days of my residence near Fordleigh, the name of the village where the Nuttleburys dwelt, were happy in the extreme. I saw much of Mary. I walked with Mary, made hay with Mary, observed the moon in Mary's society, and in vain sought to interest Mary in those mysterious shadows which diversify the surface of that luminary. I subsequently endeavoured to interest the fair girl in other matters nearer home—in short, in myself; and I fondly imagined that I succeeded in doing so.

One day, when I had dropped in at the family dinner-hour—

not from base motives, for I was boarded at my inn by contract—
I found the family conversing on a subject which caused me considerable uneasiness. At the moment of my arrival, Mr. Nuttlebury was uttering these words:

"At what time will he be here, then?" (He?)

I listened breathless, after the first salutation had passed, for more; I was not long in ascertaining that "he" was a cousin of Mary's, who was coming down to spend some days at Fordleigh, and whose arrival was anticipated by the whole family with expressions of delight. The younger boy and girl Nuttleburys seemed to be especially rapturous at the prospect of the Beast's arrival, and from this I augured ill. Altogether, I felt that there was a trying scene coming; that my opportunities of converse with my soul's idol would be fewer than they had been, and that general discomfort and misery were about to ensue. I was right.

Oho!—I beg your pardon—I will be calm.

The Beast, "He," arrived in the course of that very afternoon, and I believe I am not speaking too strongly in affirming that we—"he" and I—hated each other cordially from the first moment of our exchanging glances. He was an under-hand looking beast, short of stature; such a creature as any high-souled woman should have abhorred the sight of; but his prospects were good, he having some small situation in the Custom-house, on the strength of which, he gave himself airs, as if he was a member of the government; and when he talked of the country, he spoke of it as "we." Alas! how could I compete with him? What could I talk about, except the fur-trade, and the best method of keeping the moths under? So, having nothing to talk about, I remained sulky and glum and silent: a condition in which a man does not usually tell to advantage in society. I felt that I was not telling to advantage, and this made me hate the beast—whose disgusting name was Huffell—more cordially than before. It affords me a gloomy pleasure to think that I never once lost an opportunity of contradicting him—flat—in the course of that first evening. But, somehow or other, he generally got the best of it: possibly because I had contradicted him for the sake of doing so, and without bestowing a thought upon the rights or wrongs of the matter under discussion. But the worst of it was, that it did appear to me, that Mary—my Mary—seemed to be on the side of Huffell. Her eyes would brighten—or

I thought so—when he triumphed. And what right had she to go and fig herself out like that, in all her finery for Huffell? She never did so for me.

"This must be put a stop to, and promptly," I muttered to myself, as I walked back to my inn in a state of the most intense fury. And to leave him there with the field all to himself! What might he not be saying of me at that moment? Turning me into ridicule, perhaps? I resolved to crush him next day, or perish in the attempt.

Next day I lay in wait for him, and presently I thought my opportunity had come:

"WE shall have to make some change about that appointment of Sir Cornelius," said Huffell, "or he'll have all his family in the office in a week."

"What do you mean by '*we*?'" I asked, with ferocious emphasis.

"I mean government," he answered, coolly.

"Well but *you're* not government," was my dignified reply. "The Custom-house, even as represented by those who hold high positions in it, has as little to do with governing the country as can well be imagined. The higher officials in the Custom-house, are at best rather government servants than government advisers, while the lower——"

"Well, sir, 'the lower?'"

"The less they try to connect themselves with their betters by talking about 'we,' the better for all parties." I said this in a scathing manner, and feeling painfully warm in the forehead.

"You're talking about what you don't understand, sir," said the exciseman, or the tide-waiter, or whatever he was. "*We're* all in the same boat. Pray do you never say 'we' when talking of your master's shop?"

"Master's shop, sir?"

"Oh, I beg your pardon," said he mockingly, "aren't you a cashier in a fur-shop?"

Shop! Fur-shop! I could have seen him—seen him—moth eaten.

"I'll tell you what I'm not, sir," I burst out, losing self-control, "I am not the man to put up with the con-foun-ded impudence of an obscure tide-waiter."

"Tide-waiter!" repeated the beast, starting to his feet.

"Tide-waiter," I calmly reiterated.

At this, the whole family of the Nuttleburys, who had hitherto
appeared to be paralysed, interposed, one screeching out one
thing, another yelling another. But they were all—Mary and
all—against me, and affirmed that I had purposely picked a
quarrel with their relation—which, by-the-by, I rather think I
had. The unpleasantness ended in Mr. Nuttlebury's requesting
me, in so many words, to withdraw.

"After what has occurred there is nothing left for me, but to
do so," I remarked, making towards the door with much
majesty; "but if Mr. Huffell thinks he has heard the last of this,
he is a good deal mistaken. As for you, Mary," I continued;—
but before I could complete my sentence I experienced a sensation of an elderly hand in my coat-collar, and found myself in
the passage, with the room door closed against me. I lost no time
in vacating this ignominious position, and seeking the open air.
Presently I found myself at my desk writing to Dewsnap.

Dewsnap was then my greatest friend. He was, like me, in the
fur business, and was a fine honourable upright noble fellow, as
bold as brass, and always especially sensitive about the point of
honour. To this friend I wrote a long account of all that had
happened; asking his advice. I mentioned at the end of my
letter that I was only restrained by the want of a pair of pistols,
from inviting this wretched being to a hostile meeting.

The next day I passed in retirement, speculating much on what
Dewsnap's answer would be. It was a day of heavy rain, and I
had plenty of time to mourn over my exclusion from the cheerful
abode of the Nuttleburys', and to reflect how much better off
my rival was (sunning himself in my adored one's smiles) than I,
a lonely exile, flattening my nose against the window of a country
inn, and watching the drippings of the roof-drain as they splashed
into the fast-filling water-butt. It is needless to say that I retired
to rest early, and that I was unable to sleep.

I could sleep next morning, however, and did so till a late
hour. I was aroused from a heavy slumber, by a loud knocking
at my door, and the sound of a voice which I seemed to recognise.

"Here, Shrubsole! Hi, Oliver! Let me in. Shrubsole, what a
lazy fellow you are!"

Gracious Heaven, was it possible? Was it the voice of Dewsnap? I rose, unlocked the door, and jumped into bed again.

Yes, it was my friend. He entered erect, vigorous, energetic as
usual, deposited a small carpet-bag near the door, and, retaining

a curious-looking oblong mahogany box under his arm, advanced to greet me.

"What on earth do you do lying in bed at this time of the day?" said Dewsnap, grasping my hand.

"I couldn't sleep till morning came," I answered, passing my hand athwart my brow. "But how did you get away?"

"Oh, I've got a few days' holiday, and am come down to answer your letter in person. Well? How's this affair going on?"

"Do not ask me," I groaned. "It has made me wretched. I know no more. You don't know how fond I was of that girl."

"Well, and you shall have her yet. I'm going to settle it all for you," said Dewsnap, confidently.

"What do you mean to do?" I asked, with some hesitation.

"Do? Why, there's only one thing *to* do!" He rattled the queer-looking mahogany box as though it contained metallic pills.

"What have you got in that box?" I asked.

"There's a pair of pistols in this box," said Dewsnap, proudly, "with either one of which it would almost be a pleasure to find yourself winged."

"Sir?" I observed, sitting up in bed with marked displeasure.

"You mentioned your difficulty about weapons, so I borrowed them of a friend of mine—a gunmaker—and brought them down with me."

"Hang him!" I thought, "how very prompt he has been about it. Amazingly prompt, to be sure.—You think, then," I added, aloud, "that there's no—no other way out of the difficulty?"

"Apology," said Dewsnap, who had now opened the box, and was clicking away with the lock of one of the weapons, with the muzzle directed towards my head—"ample apology on the part of the other side—is the only alternative. Written apology, in fact."

"Ah," I replied, "I don't think the other side will agree to that."

"Then," said my friend, extending his pistol, and aiming at a portrait of the Marquis of Granby hanging over the fireplace: "then we must put a bullet into the exciseman."

(And suppose the exciseman puts a bullet into me, I thought to myself. So erratic is thought!)

"Where does the exciseman live?" inquired my friend, putting on his hat. "There is not a moment to be lost in these cases."

"Wait till I'm dressed," I remonstrated, "and I'll show you. Or you can go after breakfast."

"Not a bit of it. The people down stairs will tell me where to find him. Nuttlebury's, I think you said? I'll be there and back, by the time you're ready for breakfast."

He was out of the room almost before he had done speaking, and I was left to make my toilet and improve my appetite for breakfast with the reflection that the number of such meals in store for me was, perhaps, more limited than I could have wished. Perhaps I a little regretted having put the affair into the hands of my energetic friend. So erratic (I may again remark) is human thought!

I waited some time for my friend, but was obliged at last to begin breakfast without him. As the meal was approaching its termination, I saw him pass the window of the little parlour in which I took my meals, and immediately afterwards he entered the room.

"Well," he said, sitting down at the table and commencing a vigorous attack on the eatables, "it is as I expected. We are driven to extremities."

"What do you mean?" I asked.

"I mean," remarked Dewsnap, chipping away at his egg, "that the other side declines to apologise, and that consequently the other side must be bowled down;—shot."

"Oh dear me," I said—relenting, Major, relenting—"I shouldn't like to do that."

"You wouldn't like to do that? May I ask, Mr. Shrubsole, what you mean by that remark?"

"I mean that, that—is there no other way out of it?"

"Now look here, Shrubsole," said my companion, with a severe air, and suspending for a moment his attack on the breakfast; "you have put this affair in my hands, and you must allow me to carry it through, according to the laws of honour. It is extremely painful to me to be engaged in such an affair" (I couldn't help thinking that he seemed rather to enjoy it), "but, being engaged in it, I shall go through with it to the end. Come! We'll get these things cleared away, and then you shall sit down and write a formal challenge, which I will undertake to deliver in the proper quarter."

Dewsnap was too much for me. He seemed to have all the right phrases at his tongue's end; he was so tremendously well-informed as to what was the right thing to do, and the right thing to say when conducting an affair of this kind, that I could not help asking him whether he had ever been engaged in one before?

"No," he said, "no; but I believe I have a sort of aptitude for the kind of thing. Indeed, I have always felt that I should be in my element in arranging the details of an affair of honour."

"How you would enjoy being a principal, instead of a second!" I said—rather maliciously; for Dewsnap's alacrity aggravated me.

"No, not a bit, my dear fellow. I take such an interest in this affair that I identify myself with you entirely, and quite feel as if I *was* a principal."

(Then you feel a very curious sensation about the pit of the stomach, my boy, I thought to myself. I did not however give the thought expression. I merely mention it as an instance of the erratic nature of thought.)

"By-the-by," remarked Dewsnap, as he pocketed my challenge and prepared to depart, "I forgot to mention that one or two fellows of our acquaintance are coming down."

"One or two fellows?" I repeated, in a highly displeased, nay, crushing tone.

"Yes, Cripps is coming, and Fowler, and perhaps Kershaw, if he can get away. We were talking your affair over, the evening before I left, and they were all so much interested in it—for I predicted from the first, that there must be a meeting—that they're all coming down to see you through it."

How I cursed my own folly in having entrusted the keeping of my honour to this dreadfully zealous friend of mine! I thought, as he marched off erect and fussy with that wretched challenge in his pocket, that there was something positively bloodthirsty about the man. And then those other fellows coming down for the express purpose of seeing somebody shot! For that *was* their purpose, I felt. I fully believed that, if by any fortunate chance there should be no blood shed, those so-called friends of mine would go away disgusted.

The train of reflection into which I had fallen was interrupted at this juncture, by the appearance outside the window, of three human figures. These turned out, on inspection, to be no other than the individuals whose taste for excitement I had been condemning so strongly in my own mind. There they were, Messrs. Cripps, Fowler, and Kershaw, grinning and gesticulating at me through the window, like vulgar unfeeling idiots as they were. And one of them (I think it was Cripps) had the brutality to put himself into the attitude supposed to be the correct one for a duellist, with his left hand behind his back, and his right raised as if to discharge an imaginary pistol.

They were in the room with me directly, large, noisy, and vulgar, laughing and guffawing—making comments on my appearance, asking me if I had made my will, what I had left to each of them, and otherwise conducting themselves in a manner calculated to turn one's milk of human kindness to bitterest gall. How they enjoyed it! When they learned that Dewsnap was actually at that time away on a war mission, and that he might return at any moment with the fatal answer—I say when they heard that, they positively gloated over me. They sat down and stared at me, and every now and then one of them would say, with a low, chuckling giggle, "I say, old fellow! How do you feel about it now?" It was a hideous relief to me when Dewsnap returned with the baleful news that the challenge was accepted, and that the meeting was appointed for the next morning at eight o'clock.

Those ruffians enjoyed themselves that afternoon to the utmost. They had such a pleasure in store for next day, that it gave an added zest to everything they did. It sharpened their appetites, it stimulated their thirst, it imparted to the skittles with which they amused themselves during the afternoon, an additional charm. The evening was devoted to conviviality. Dewsnap, after spending some time in oiling the triggers of the pistols, remarked that now they were in such prime condition, that they would "snap a fellow's head off, almost without his knowing it." This inhuman remark was made at the moment when we were separating for the night.

I passed the greater part of the dark hours, in writing letters of farewell to my relations, and in composing a stinger for Miss Mary Nuttlebury, which I trusted would embitter the whole of her future life. Then I threw myself on my bed—which was not wholly devoid of knobs—and found for a few hours the oblivion I desired.

We were first on the ground. Indeed, it was necessary that we should be, as those three ferocious Anabaptists, Cripps, Fowler, and Kershaw, had to be stowed away in places of concealment whence they could see without being seen; but even when this stowage had been accomplished and the fatal hour had arrived, we were still kept waiting so long that a faint hope—misgiving, I meant to say—began to dawn in my heart that my adversary had been seized with a sudden panic, and had fled at the last moment, leaving me master of the situation, with a bloodless victory.

The sound of voices, and of laughter—laughter!—reached me while I was musing on the prospect of an honourable escape from my perilous position. In another moment my antagonist, still talking and laughing with some one who closely followed him, jumped over a stile at the side of the field in which we awaited him. Grinning in the most impudent manner, my antagonist inquired of his second, who was the village apothecary's assistant, whether he was a good hand at patching up bullet wounds?

It was at this moment that an incident occurred which caused a small delay in our proceedings. One of the Anabaptists— Cripps—had, with a view to concealment, and also perhaps with a view to keeping out of harm's way, perched himself in a tree which commanded a good view of the field of action; but not having used sufficient caution in the choice of his position, he had trusted his weight to a bough which proved unequal to the task of sustaining it. Consequently it happened that just as the seconds were beginning their preliminary arrangements, and during an awful pause, the unlucky Cripps came plunging and crashing to the ground, where he remained seated at the foot of the tree in a state of undignified ruin and prostration.

After this there was a prodigious row and confusion. My opponent having thus discovered that there was one person observing our proceedings from a place of concealment, concluded naturally enough that there might be others. Accordingly a search was promptly instituted, which ended in the unearthing of my two other friends, who were obliged to emerge from their hiding-places in a very humiliated and crestfallen condition. My adversary would not hear of fighting a duel in the presence of so large an audience, and so it ended in the three brutal Anabaptists being—very much to my satisfaction—expelled from the field. The appearance they presented as they retired along the pathway in Indian file, was the most abject thing I have ever beheld.

This little business disposed of, there remained the great affair of the day to settle, and it took a great deal of settlement. There were diversities of opinions about every detail connected with the murderous operations. There were disputes about the number of paces which should separate the combatants, about the length of those paces, about the proper method of loading pistols, about the best way of giving the signal to fire—about everything. But what disgusted me most, was the levity displayed by my opponent, who seemed to think the whole thing a capital joke, sneering and sniggering at everything that was done or said. Does the man bear a charmed life, I asked myself, that he behaves with such sickening flippancy when about to risk it?

At last all these endless preliminaries were settled, and Mr. Huffell and I remained staring defiance at each other with a distance of only twelve paces between us. The beast was grinning even now, and when he was asked for the last time whether he was prepared to make an apology, he absolutely laughed.

It had been arranged that one of the seconds, Huffell's as it happened, should count one, two, three, and that at the word "three" we should both fire (if we could) at the same moment. My heart felt so tight at about this period, that I fancied it must have contracted to half its usual size, and I had a sensation of being light on my legs, and inordinately tall, such as one has after having had a fever.

"One!" said the apothecary, and the monosyllable was followed by quite a long pause.

"Two!"

"Stop!" cried a voice, which I recognised as the voice of my adversary, "I have something to say."

I whisked myself round in a moment, and saw that Mr. Huffell had thrown his weapon down on the ground, and had left the position which had been assigned to him.

"What have you to say, sir?" asked the inexorable Dewsnap, in a severe tone; "whatever it is, you have chosen a most extraordinary moment to say it in."

"I have changed my mind," said Mr. Huffell, in a lachrymose tone; "I think that duelling is sinful, and I consent to apologise."

Astounded as I was at this announcement, I had yet leisure to observe that the apothecary did not look in the least surprised at what had happened.

"You consent to apologise?" asked Dewsnap, "to resign all claim to the lady, to express your deep contrition for the insolent expressions you have made use of towards my friend?"

"I consent," was the reply.

"We must have it all down in writing, mind!" stipulated my uncompromising friend.

"You shall have it all down in writing," said the contrite one.

"Well, this is a most extraordinary and unsatisfactory sort of thing," said Dewsnap, turning to me. "What are we to do?"

"It is unsatisfactory, but I suppose we must accept his apology," I answered, in a leisurely and nonchalant manner. My heart expanded at about this period.

"Has anybody got writing materials about him by chance?" asked my second, in a not very conciliatory tone.

Yes, the apothecary had, and he whipped them out in a moment—a note-book of unusual size, and an indelible ink-pencil.

An apology of the most humble and abject kind was now dictated by my friend Dewsnap, and written down by the crushed and conquered Huffell. When he had affixed his signature to the document, it exactly filled one leaf of the apothcary's memorandum-book. The leaf was torn out and handed to my representative. At that moment the sound of the village-clock striking nine reached us from the distant church.

Mr. Huffell started as if the day were more advanced than he anticipated.

"I believe that the document is regular?" he asked. "If so, there is nothing to detain us in a spot henceforth replete with painful associations. Gentlemen both, good morning."

"Good morning, sir," said Dewsnap, sharply; "and allow me to add, that you have reason to consider yourself an uncommonly lucky young man."

"I do so consider myself, I assure you," retorted the servile wretch.

With that, he took his leave and disappeared over the stile, closely followed by his companion. Again I thought I heard this precious pair explode into fits of laughter as soon as they were on the other side of the hedge.

Dewsnap looked at me, and I looked at Dewsnap, but we could make nothing of it. It was the most inexplicable thing that the man should have gone so far, should have had his finger on the trigger of his pistol, should have waited till the very signal to fire was on the lips of his second, and should then have broken down in that lamentable manner. It really was, as my friend and

I agreed, the most disgraceful piece of cowardice of which we had ever had experience. Another point on which we were agreed, was, that our side had come out of this affair with an amount of honour and glory such as is rarely achieved by the sons of men in this practical and un-romantic age.

And now behold the victor and his friends assembled round the small dining-table at the George and Dragon, and celebrating their triumph by a breakfast! in preparing which all the resources of the establishment were brought into play.

It was a solemn occasion. The moment, I acknowledge, was to me a glorious one. My friends, naturally proud of their associate, and anxious to commemorate in some fitting manner the event of the morning, had invited me to this meal to be provided at their own expense. These dear fellows were no longer my guests. I was theirs. Dewsnap was in the chair—it was of the Windsor pattern—I was placed on his right: while at the other end of the table, which was not very far off, another Windsor chair supported the person of Mr. Cripps, the vice. The viands set before us were of the most recherché description, and when these had been done full justice to, and the chair had called for a bottle of champagne, our hilarity began almost to verge on the boisterous. My own mirth, indeed, was chastened by one pervading thought, of which I never for a moment lost sight. Had I not a secret joy which champagne could neither increase nor diminish? Had not my rival formerly abdicated, and was I not that very day to appear in the presence of Mary Nuttlebury as one who had risked his life for her sake? Yes. I waited impatiently for the hour when these good fellows should take their departure, determining that, the moment they were gone, I would take possession of the field ingloriously vacated by my rival, and would enjoy the fruits of my victory. I was aroused from these reflections by the voice of my friend Dewsnap. It was, however, no longer the familiar acquaintance who spoke, but the official chairman.

Mr. Dewsnap began by remarking that we were met together on an occasion and under circumstances, of a very peculiar— he might almost say of an anomalous—nature. To begin with, here was a social meeting—nay, a convivial meeting, taking place at ten o'clock in the forenoon. That was the first anomaly. And for what was the meeting convened? To commemorate an act belonging to a class of achievements usually associated with a by-

R

gone age, rather than with that in which an inexorable Destiny had cast the lots of the present generation. Here was the second anomaly. Yes, these were anomalies, but anomalies of what a delightful kind! Would there were more such! It was—Mr. Dewsnap went on to say—the fashion of the day to decry the practice of duelling, but he, for his part, had always felt that circumstances might occur in the course of any man's career which would render an appeal to arms desirable—nay, to one who was sensitive on the point of honour, inevitable—and he therefore thought it highly important that the practice of duelling should not wholly fall into desuetude, but should be occasionally revived, as it had been on—on—in short, the present occasion.

At this moment, curiously enough, a faint cheer was heard in the distance. It came, doubtless, from the throats of some of the village-boys, and presently subsided. It was enough, however, to deprive our worthy chair of the thread of his eloquence, so that he was compelled to start again on a new tack.

"Gentlemen," said Mr. Dewsnap, "I must throw myself on your indulgence if my words fail to flow as freely as I could wish. I am, to begin with, gentlemen, powerfully moved, and that alone is enough to deprive me of any small amount of eloquence of which I may at other times be possessed. Likewise, I must frankly own that I am unaccustomed to public speaking at ten o'clock in the morning, and that the day-light puts me out. And yet," continued the chair, "I do not know why this should be so. Do not wedding-breakfasts take place by daylight? And are not speeches made on those occasions? And, after all, why should we not look upon this very meal as, to a certain extent, a wedding-breakfast? You seem surprised, gentlemen, at this inquiry, but I will ask you whether the event we are met together to celebrate—the event of this morning—has not been the first act of a drama which we all hope will terminate in a wedding—the wedding of our noble and courageous friend?"

It was a curious thing that, just when our chairman had got as far as this in his speech, the cheering we had heard before was repeated; though now much more loudly. It was also a curious thing that the bells of the village church, which was not very far off, began to ring a merry peal. There might not be much to concern us, in this, but still it was curious. The attention of Mr. Dewsnap's audience began to wander, and their glances were, from time to time, directed towards the window. Mr. Dewsnap's own attention began also to wander, and the thread of his discourse seemed once more to elude his grasp.

"Gentlemen," he began again, resolved, like a true orator as he was, to avail himself of accident, "I was remarking that this festive meal was, in some sort and by a figure of speech, a kind of wedding-breakfast, and while the words were yet upon my lips, behold the bells of the village church break out into a joyous peal! Gentlemen, there is something almost supernatural about this. It is a happy augury, and as such I accept it."

The bells were becoming quite frantic now, and the cheering was louder.

"And as such I accept it!" repeated Mr. Dewsnap. "Gentlemen, I should not be surprised if this were an ovation offered to our noble and courageous friend. The villagers have heard of his noble and courageous conduct, and are approaching the inn to offer their humble congratulations."

It was quite certain that the villagers were approaching the inn, for the sound of their voices became every moment louder and louder. We all began to be restless under our chairman's eloquence, and when at length the sound of wheels rapidly approaching was added to the cheering and the bell-ringing, I could bear it no longer, and rushed hastily to the window, followed by everybody else in the room, the chair himself included.

A carriage and pair drove swiftly past the window. Major, I sicken while I speak. There was a postilion on the near horse, and on that postilion's jacket was a—Oho!—Excuse me, I beg—a wedding-favour. It was an open carriage, and in it were seated two persons; one, was the gentleman, who had made me that humble apology not much more than an hour ago; the other, was Mary Nuttlebury, now, if I were to believe the evidence of my senses, Mary Huffell. They both laughed when they saw me at the window, and kissed their hands to me as they whirled away.

I became as one frantic. I pushed my friends, who in vain sought to restrain me, on one side. I rushed out into the village street. I yelled after the carriage. I gesticulated at the carriage. I ran after the carriage. But to what purpose? It was over. The thing was done. I had to return to the inn, the laughing-stock of the rude and ignorant populace.

I know no more. I don't know what became of me, how my bill at the inn was defrayed, how I got away. I only know that

I am finally, hopelessly, and irretrievably under a cloud; that all my old companions, and my old habits have become odious to me; and that even the very lodgings in which I formerly resided were so unbearable, owing to the furniture being impregnated with painful associations, that I was obliged to remove and take up my quarters elsewhere. This, sir, is how I came to occupy these rooms, and I may here mention—if indeed the testimonial of a blighted wretch is of any value—that I have no cause to regret my change of abode, and that I regard Mrs. Lirriper as a most unexceptionable person, labouring indeed, as far as I can see, under only one defect. She is A WOMAN.

VII

HOW THE PARLOURS ADDED A FEW WORDS

I have the honour of presenting myself by the name of Jackman. I esteem it a proud privilege to go down to posterity through the instrumentality of the most remarkable boy that ever lived—by the name of JEMMY JACKMAN LIRRIPER—and of my most worthy and most highly respected friend, Mrs. Emma Lirriper, of Eighty-one, Norfolk-street, Strand, in the County of Middlesex, in the United Kingdom of Great Britain and Ireland.

It is not for me to express the rapture with which we received that dear and eminently remarkable boy, on the occurrence of his first Christmas holidays. Suffice it to observe that when he came flying into the house with two splendid prizes (Arithmetic, and Exemplary Conduct), Mrs. Lirriper and myself embraced with emotion, and instantly took him to the Play, where we were all three admirably entertained.

Nor, is it to render homage to the virtues of the best of her good and honoured sex—whom, in deference to her unassuming worth, I will only here designate by the initials E. L.—that I add this record to the bundle of papers with which our, in a most distinguished degree, remarkable boy has expressed himself delighted, before re-consigning the same to the left-hand glass closet of Mrs. Lirriper's little bookcase.

Neither, is it to obtrude the name of the old original superannuated obscure Jemmy Jackman, once (to his degradation) of

Wozenham's, long (to his elevation) of Lirriper's. If I could be consciously guilty of that piece of bad taste, it would indeed be a work of supererogation, now that the name is borne by JEMMY JACKMAN LIRRIPER.

No. I take up my humble pen to register a little record of our strikingly remarkable boy, which my poor capacity regards as presenting a pleasant little picture of the dear boy's mind. The picture may be interesting to himself when he is a man.

Our first re-united Christmas-day was the most delightful one we have ever passed together. Jemmy was never silent for five minutes, except in church-time. He talked as we sat by the fire, he talked when we were out walking, he talked as we sat by the fire again, he talked incessantly at dinner, though he made a dinner almost as remarkable as himself. It was the spring of happiness in his fresh young heart flowing and flowing, and it fertilised (if I may be allowed so bold a figure) my much-esteemed friend, and J—J— the present writer.

There were only we three. We dined in my esteemed friend's little room, and our entertainment was perfect. But everything in the establishment is, in neatness, order, and comfort, always perfect. After dinner, our boy slipt away to his old stool at my esteemed friend's knee, and there, with his hot chestnuts and his glass of brown sherry (really, a most excellent wine!) on a chair for a table, his face outshone the apples in the dish.

We talked of these jottings of mine, which Jemmy had read through and through by that time; and so it came about that my esteemed friend remarked, as she sat smoothing Jemmy's curls:

"And as you belong to the house too, Jemmy,—and so much more than the Lodgers, having been born in it—why, your story ought to be added to the rest, I think, one of these days."

Jemmy's eyes sparkled at this, and he said, "So I think, Gran."

Then, he sat looking at the fire, and then he began to laugh, in a sort of confidence with the fire, and then he said, folding his arms across my esteemed friend's lap and raising his bright face to hers:

"Would you like to hear a boy's story, Gran?"

"Of all things," replied my esteemed friend.

"Would you, godfather?"

"Of all things," I too replied.

"Well then," said Jemmy, "I'll tell you one."

Here, our indisputably remarkable boy gave himself a hug, and laughed again, musically, at the idea of his coming out in that new line. Then, he once more took the fire into the same sort of confidence as before, and began :

"Once upon a time, When pigs drank wine, And monkeys chewed tobaccer, 'Twas neither in your time nor mine, But that's no macker——"

"Bless the child!" cried my esteemed friend, "what's amiss with his brain!"

"It's poetry, Gran," returned Jemmy, shouting with laughter. "We always begin stories that way, at school."

"Gave me quite a turn, Major," said my esteemed friend, fanning herself with a plate. "Thought he was light-headed!"

"In those remarkable times, Gran and Godfather, there was once a boy;—not me, you know."

"No, no," says my respected friend, "not you. Not him, Major, you understand?"

"No, no," says I.

"And he went to school in Rutlandshire——"

"Why not Lincolnshire?" says my respected friend.

"Why not, you dear old Gran? Because *I* go to school in Lincolnshire, don't I?"

"Ah, to be sure!" says my respected friend. "And it's not Jemmy, you understand, Major?"

"No, no," says I.

"Well!" our boy proceeded, hugging himself comfortably, and laughing merrily (again in confidence with the fire), before he again looked up in Mrs. Lirriper's face, "and so he was tremendously in love with his schoolmaster's daughter, and she was the most beautiful creature that ever was seen, and she had brown eyes, and she had brown hair all curling beautifully, and she had a delicious voice, and she was delicious altogether, and her name was Seraphina."

"What's the name of *your* schoolmaster's daughter, Jemmy?" asks my respected friend.

"Polly!" replied Jemmy, pointing his forefinger at her. "There now! Caught you! Ha! ha! ha!"

When he and my respected friend had had a laugh and a hug together, our admittedly remarkable boy resumed with a great relish :

"Well! And so he loved her. And so he thought about her, and dreamed about her, and made her presents of oranges and nuts, and would have made her presents of pearls and diamonds if he could have afforded it out of his pocket-money, but he couldn't. And so her father—O, he WAS a Tartar! Keeping the boys up to the mark, holding examinations once a month, lecturing upon all sorts of subjects at all sorts of times, and knowing everything in the world out of book. And so this boy——"

"Had he any name?" asks my respected friend.

"No he hadn't, Gran. Ha! ha! There now! Caught you again!"

After this, they had another laugh and another hug, and then our boy went on.

"Well! And so this boy he had a friend about as old as himself, at the same school, and his name (for He *had* a name, as it happened) was—let me remember—was Bobbo."

"Not Bob," says my respected friend.

"Of course not," says Jemmy. "What made you think it was, Gran? Well! And so this friend was the cleverest and bravest and best looking and most generous of all the friends that ever were, and so he was in love with Seraphina's sister, and so Seraphina's sister was in love with him, and so they all grew up."

"Bless us!" says my respected friend. "They were very sudden about it."

"So they all grew up," our boy repeated, laughing heartily, "and Boppo and this boy went away together on horseback to seek their fortunes, and they partly got their horses by favour, and partly in a bargain; that is to say, they had saved up between them seven-and-fourpence, and the two horses, being Arabs, were worth more, only the man said he would take that, to favour them. Well! And so they made their fortunes and came prancing back to the school, with their pockets full of gold enough to last for ever. And so they rang at the parents' and visitors' bell (not the back gate), and when the bell was answered they proclaimed, 'The same as if it was scarlet fever! Every boy goes home for an indefinite period!' And then there was a great hurrahing, and then they kissed Seraphina and her sister—each his own love and not the other's on any account—and then they ordered the Tartar into instant confinement."

"Poor man!" said my respected friend.

"Into instant confinement, Gran," repeated Jemmy, trying to look severe and roaring with laughter, "and he was to have nothing to eat but the boys' dinners, and was to drink half a cask of their beer, every day. And so then the preparations were made for the two weddings, and there were hampers, and potted things, and sweet things, and nuts, and postage-stamps, and all manner of things. And so they were so jolly, that they let the Tartar out, and he was jolly too."

"I am glad they let him out," says my respected friend, "because he had only done his duty."

"Oh but hadn't he overdone it though!" cried Jemmy. "Well! And so then this boy mounted his horse, with his bride in his arms, and cantered away, and cantered on and on till he came to a certain place where he had a certain Gran and a certain godfather—not you two, you know."

"No, no," we both said.

"And there he was received with great rejoicings, and he filled the cupboard and the bookcase with gold, and he showered it out on his Gran and his godfather because they were the two kindest and dearest people that ever lived in this world. And so while they were sitting up to their knees in gold, a knocking was heard at the street door, and who should it be but Bobbo, also on horseback with his bride in his arms, and what had he come to say but that he would take (at double rent) all the Lodgings for ever, that were not wanted by this boy and this Gran and this godfather, and that they would all live together, and all be happy! And so they were, and so it never ended!"

"And was there no quarrelling?" asked my respected friend, as Jemmy sat upon her lap, and hugged her.

"No! Nobody ever quarrelled."

"And did the money never melt away?"

"No! Nobody could ever spend it all."

"And did none of them ever grow older?"

"No! Nobody ever grew older after that."

"And did none of them ever die?"

"O no, no, no, Gran!" exclaimed our dear boy, laying his cheek upon her breast, and drawing her closer to him. "Nobody ever died."

"Ah Major, Major," says my respected friend, smiling benignly upon me. "This beats our stories. Let us end with the Boy's story, Major, for the Boy's story is the best that is ever told!"

In submission to which request on the part of the best of women, I have here noted it down as faithfully as my best abilities, coupled with my best intentions, would admit, subscribing it with my name,

J. JACKMAN.

The Parlours.

Mrs. Lirriper's Lodgings.

THE END OF THE CHRISTMAS NUMBER FOR 1863

MRS. LIRRIPER'S LEGACY

I

Ah! It's pleasant to drop into my own easy-chair my dear though a little palpitating what with trotting up-stairs and what with trotting down, and why kitchen-stairs should all be corner stairs is for the builders to justify though I do not think they fully understand their trade and never did, else why the sameness and why not more conveniences and fewer draughts and likewise making a practice of laying the plaster on too thick I am well convinced which holds the damp, and as to chimney-pots putting them on by guess-work like hats at a party and no more know-inging what their effect will be upon the smoke bless you than I do if so much, except that it will mostly be either to send it down your throat in a straight form or give it a twist before it goes there. And what I says speaking as I find of those new metal chimneys all manner of shapes (there's a row of 'em at Miss Wozenham's lodging-house lower down on the other side of the way) is that they only work your smoke into artificial patterns for you before you swallow it and that I'd quite as soon swallow mine plain, the flavour being the same, not to mention the conceit of putting up signs on the top of your house to show the forms in which you take your smoke into your inside.

Being here before your eyes my dear in my own easy-chair in my own quiet room in my own Lodging House Number Eighty-one Norfolk-street Strand London situated midway between the City and St. James's—if anything is where it used to be with these hotels calling themselves Limited but called Un-limited by Major Jackman rising-up everywhere and rising up into flagstaffs where they can't go any higher, but my mind of those monsters is give me a landlord's or landlady's wholesome face when I come off a journey and not a brass plate with an electrified number clicking out of it which it's not in nature can be glad to see me and to which I don't want to be hoisted like molasses at the Docks and left there telegraphing for help with the most ingenious instruments but quite in vain—being here my dear I have no call to mention that I am still in the Lodgings as a business hoping to die in the same and if agreeable to the clergy partly read over at Saint Clement's Danes and concluded in Hatfield churchyard when lying once again by my poor Lirriper ashes to ashes and dust to dust.

Neither should I tell you any news my dear in telling you that the Major is still a fixture in the Parlours quite as much so as the roof of the house, and that Jemmy is of boys the best and brightest and has ever had kept from him the cruel story of his poor pretty young mother Mrs. Edson being deserted in the second floor and dying in my arms, fully believing that I am his born Gran and him an orphan, though what with engineering since he took a taste for it and him and the Major making Locomotives out of parasols broken iron pots and cotton-reels and them absolutely a getting off the line and falling over the table and injuring the passengers almost equal to the originals it really is quite wonderful. And when I says to the Major, "Major can't you by *any* means give us a communication with the guard?" the Major says quite huffy, "No madam it's not to be done," and when I says "Why not?" the Major says, "That is between us who are in the Railway Interest madam and our friend the Right Honourable Vice-President of the Board of Trade" and if you'll believe me my dear the Major wrote to Jemmy at school to consult him on the answer I should have before I could get even that amount of unsatisfactoriness out of the man, the reason being that when we first began with the little model and the working signals beautiful and perfect (being in general as wrong as the real) and when I says laughing "What appointment am I to hold in this undertaking gentlemen?" Jemmy hugs me round the neck and tells me dancing, "You shall be the Public Gran" and consequently they put upon me just as much as ever they like and I sit growling in my easy-chair.

My dear whether it is that a grown man as clever as the Major cannot give half his heart and mind to anything—even a plaything—but must get into right down earnest with it, whether it is so or whether it is not so I do not undertake to say, but Jemmy is far outdone by the serious and believing ways of the Major in the management of the United Grand Junction Lirriper and Jackman Great Norfolk Parlour Line, "For" says my Jemmy with the sparkling eyes when it was christened, "we must have a whole mouthful of name Gran or our dear old Public" and there the young rogue kissed me, "won't stump up." So the Public took the shares—ten at ninepence, and immediately when that was spent twelve Preference at one-and-sixpence—and they were all signed by Jemmy and countersigned by the Major, and between ourselves much better worth the money than some shares I have paid for in my time. In the same holidays the line was made and worked and opened and ran excursions and had collisions and burst its boilers and all sorts of accidents and offences all most regular correct and pretty. The sense of responsibility entertained by the Major as a military style of station-master my dear starting the down train behind time and ringing one of those little bells that you buy with the little coal-scuttles off the tray round the man's neck in the street did him honour, but noticing the Major of a night when he is writing out his monthly report to Jemmy at school of the state of the Rolling Stock and the Permanent Way and all the rest of it (the whole kept upon the Major's sideboard and dusted with his own hands every morning before varnishing his boots) I notice him as full of thought and care as full can be and frowning in a fearful manner, but indeed the Major does nothing by halves as witness his great delight in going out surveying with Jemmy when he has Jemmy to go with, carrying a chain and a measuring tape and driving I don't know what improvements right through Westminster Abbey and fully believed in the streets to be knocking everything upside down by Act of Parliament. As please Heaven will come to pass when Jemmy takes to that as a profession!

Mentioning my poor Lirriper brings into my head his own youngest brother the Doctor though Doctor of what I am sure it would be hard to say unless Liquor, for neither Physic nor Music nor yet Law does Joshua Lirriper know a morsel of except continually being summoned to the County Court and having orders made upon him which he runs away from, and once was taken in the passage of this very house with an umbrella up and the Major's hat on, giving his name with the door-mat round him as Sir Johnson Jones K.C.B. in spectacles residing at the Horse

Guards. On which occasion he had got into the house not a
minute before, through the girl letting him on to the mat when he
sent in a piece of paper twisted more like one of those spills for
lighting candles than a note, offering me the choice between
thirty shillings in hand and his brains on the premises marked
immediate and waiting for an answer. My dear it gave me such
a dreadful turn to think of the brains of my poor dear Lirriper's
own flesh and blood flying about the new oilcloth however unworthy to be so assisted, that I went out of my room here to
ask him what he would take once for all not to do it for life
when I found him in the custody of two gentlemen that I should
have judged to be in the feather-bed trade if they had not announced the law, so fluffy were their personal appearance. "Bring
your chains sir," says Joshua to the littlest of the two in the
biggest hat, "rivet on my fetters!" Imagine my feelings when I
pictered him clanking up Norfolk-street in irons and Miss
Wozenham looking out of window! "Gentlemen" I says all of a
tremble and ready to drop "please to bring him into Major Jackman's apartments." So they brought him into the Parlours, and
when the Major spies his own curly-brimmed hat on him which
Joshua Lirriper had whipped off its peg in the passage for a
military disguise he goes into such a tearing passion that he tips
it off his head with his hand and kicks it up to the ceiling with
his foot where it grazed long afterwards. "Major" I says "be
cool and advise me what to do with Joshua my dead and gone
Lirriper's own youngest brother." "Madam" says the Major "my
advice is that you board and lodge him in a Powder Mill, with
a handsome gratuity to the proprietor when exploded." "Major"
I says "as a Christian you cannot mean your words." "Madam"
says the Major "by the Lord I do!" and indeed the Major besides
being with all his merits a very passionate man for his size had
a bad opinion of Joshua on account of former troubles even
unattended by liberties taken with his apparel. When Joshua
Lirriper hears this conversation betwixt us he turns upon the
littlest one with the biggest hat and says "Come sir! Remove
me to my vile dungeon. Where is my mouldy straw!" My dear
at the picter of him rising in my mind dressed almost entirely
in padlocks like Baron Trenck in Jemmy's book I was so overcome that I burst into tears and I says to the Major, "Major
take my keys and settle with these gentlemen or I shall never
know a happy minute more," which was done several times both

before and since, but still I must remember that Joshua Lirriper has his good feelings and shows them in being always so troubled in his mind when he cannot wear mourning for his brother. Many a long year have I left off my widow's mourning not being wishful to intrude, but the tender point in Joshua that I cannot help a little yielding to is when he writes "One single sovereign would enable me to wear a decent suit of mourning for my much-loved brother. I vowed at the time of his lamented death that I would ever wear sables in memory of him but Alas how shortsighted is man, How keep that vow when penniless!" It says a good deal for the strength of his feelings that he couldn't have been seven year old when my poor Lirriper died and to have kept to it ever since is highly creditable. But we know there's good in all of us—if we only knew where it was in some of us—and though it was far from delicate in Joshua to work upon the dear child's feelings when first sent to school and write down into Lincolnshire for his pocket-money by return of post and got it, still he is my poor Lirriper's own youngest brother and mightn't have meant not paying his bill at the Salisbury Arms when his affection took him down to stay a fortnight at Hatfield church-yard and might have meant to keep sober but for bad company. Consequently if the Major *had* played on him with the garden-engine which he got privately into his room without my knowing of it, I think that much as I should have regretted it there would have been words betwixt the Major and me. Therefore my dear though he played on Mr. Buffle by mistake being hot in his head, and though it might have been misrepresented down at Wozenham's into not being ready for Mr. Buffle in other respects he being the Assessed Taxes, still I do not so much regret it as perhaps I ought. And whether Joshua Lirriper will yet do well in life I cannot say, but I did hear of his coming out at a Private Theatre in the character of a Bandit without receiving any offers afterwards from the regular managers.

Mentioning Mr. Buffle gives an instance of there being good in persons where good is not expected, for it cannot be denied that Mr. Buffle's manners when engaged in his business were not agreeable. To collect is one thing and to look about as if suspicious of the goods being gradually removing in the dead of night by a back door is another, over taxing you have no control but suspecting is voluntary. Allowances too must ever be made for a gentleman of the Major's warmth not relishing being spoke to with a pen in the mouth, and while I do not know that it is more irritable to my own feelings to have a low-crowned hat with a broad brim kept on in-doors than any other hat still I can appreciate the Major's, besides which without bearing malice or vengeance the Major is a man that scores up arrears as his habit always was with Joshua Lirriper. So at last my dear the Major lay in wait for Mr. Buffle and it worrited me a good deal. Mr. Buffle gives his rap of two sharp knocks one day and the Major bounces to the door. "Collector has called for two quarters' Assessed Taxes" says Mr. Buffle. "They are ready for him" says the Major and brings him in here. But on the way Mr. Buffle looks about him in his usual suspicious manner and the Major fires and asks him "Do you see a Ghost sir?" "No sir" says Mr. Buffle. "Because I have before noticed you" says the Major "apparently looking for a spectre very hard beneath the roof of my respected friend. When you find that supernatural agent, be so good as point him out sir." Mr. Buffle stares at the Major and then nods at me. "Mrs. Lirriper sir" says the Major going off into a perfect steam and introducing me with his hand. "Pleasure of knowing her" says Mr. Buffle. "Ah—hum!—Jemmy Jackman sir!" says the Major introducing himself. "Honour of knowing you by sight" says Mr. Buffle. "Jemmy Jackman sir" says the Major wagging his head sideways in a sort of an obstinate fury "presents to you his esteemed friend that lady Mrs. Emma Lirriper of Eighty-one Norfolk-street Strand London in the County of Middlesex in the United Kingdom of Great Britain and Ireland. Upon which occasion sir," says the Major, "Jemmy Jackman takes your hat off." Mr. Buffle looks at his hat where the Major drops it on the floor, and he picks it up and puts it on again. "Sir" says the Major very red and looking him full in the face "there are two quarters of the Gallantry Taxes due and the Collector has called." Upon which if you can believe my words my dear the Major drops Mr. Buffle's hat off again. "This—" Mr. Buffle begins very angry with his pen in his mouth, when the Major steaming more and more says "Take your bit out sir! Or by the whole infernal system of Taxation of this country and every individual figure in the National Debt, I'll get upon your back and ride you like a horse!" which it's my belief he would have done and even actually jerking his neat little legs ready for a spring as it was. "This" says Mr. Buffle without his pen "is an assault and I'll have the law on you." "Sir" replies the Major "if you are a man of honour, your Collector of whateever may be due on the Honourable Assessment by applying to Major Jackman at The Parlours Mrs. Lirriper's Lodgings, may obtain what he wants in full at any moment."

When the Major glared at Mr. Buffle with those meaning words my dear I literally gasped for a teaspoonful of sal volatile in a wine-glass of water, and I says "Pray let it go no further gentlemen I beg and beseech of you!" But the Major could be got to do nothing else but snort long after Mr. Buffle was gone, and the effect it had upon my whole mass of blood when on the next day of Mr. Buffle's rounds the Major spruced himself up and went humming a tune up and down the street with one eye almost obliterated by his hat there are not expressions in Johnson's Dictionary to state. But I safely put the street door on the jar and got behind the Major's blinds with my shawl on and my mind made up the moment I saw danger to rush out screeching till my voice failed me and catch the Major round the neck till my strength went and have all parties bound. I had not been behind the blinds a quarter of an hour when I saw Mr. Buffle approaching with his Collecting-books in his hand. The Major likewise saw him approaching and hummed louder and himself approached. They met before the Airy railings. The Major takes off his hat at arm's length and says "Mr. Buffle I believe?" Mr. Buffle takes off *his* hat at arm's length and says "That is my name sir." Says the Major "Have you any commands for me, Mr. Buffle?" Says Mr. Buffle "Not any sir." Then my dear both of 'em bowed very low and haughty and parted, and whenever Mr. Buffle made his rounds in future him and the Major always met and bowed before the Airy railings, putting me much in mind of Hamlet and the other gentleman in mourning before killing one another, though I could have wished the other gentleman had done it fairer and even if less polite no poison.

Mr. Buffle's family were not liked in this neighbourhood, for when you are a householder my dear you'll find it does not come by nature to like the Assessed, and it was considered besides that a one-horse pheayton ought not to have elevated Mrs. Buffle to that heighth especially when purloined from the Taxes which I myself did consider uncharitable. But they were *not* liked and there was that domestic unhappiness in the family in consequence of their both being very hard with Miss Buffle and one another on account of Miss Buffle's favouring Mr. Buffle's articled young

S

gentleman, that it *was* whispered that Miss Buffle would go either into a consumption or a convent she being so very thin and off her appetite and two close-shaved gentlemen with white bands round their necks peeping round the corner whenever she went out in waistcoats resembling black pinafores. So things stood towards Mr. Buffle when one night I was woke by a frightful noise and a smell of burning, and going to my bedroom window saw the whole street in a glow. Fortunately we had two sets empty just then and before I could hurry on some clothes I heard the Major hammering at the attics' doors and calling out "Dress yourselves!—Fire! Don't be frightened!—Fire! Collect your presence of mind!—Fire! All right—Fire!" most tremenjously. As I opened my bedroom door the Major came tumbling in over himself and me and caught me in his arms. "Major" I says breathless "where is it?" "I don't know dearest madam" says the Major—"Fire! Jemmy Jackman will defend you to the last drop of his blood—Fire! If the dear boy was at home what a treat this would be for him—Fire!" and altogether very collected and bold except that he couldn't say a single sentence without shaking me to the very centre with roaring Fire. We ran down to the drawing-room and put our heads out of window, and the Major calls to an unfeeling young monkey scampering by be joyful and ready to split "Where is it?—Fire!" The monkey answers without stopping "Oh here's a lark! Old Buffle's been setting his house alight to prevent it being found out that he boned the Taxes. Hurrah! Fire!" And then the sparks came flying up and the smoke came pouring down and the crackling of flames and spatting of water and banging of engines and hacking of axes and breaking of glass and knocking at doors and the shouting and crying and hurrying and the heat and altogether gave me a dreadful palpitation. "Don't be frightened dearest madam," says the Major. "—Fire! There's nothing to be alarmed at—Fire! Don't open the street door till I come back—Fire! I'll go and see if I can be of any service—Fire! You're quite composed and comfortable ain't you?—Fire, Fire, Fire!" It was in vain for me to hold the man and tell him he'd be galloped to death by the engines—pumped to death by his over-exertions —wet-feeted to death by the slop and mess—flattened to death when the roofs fell in—his spirit was up and he went scampering off after the young monkey with all the breath he had and none to spare, and me and the girls huddled together at the parlour

windows looking at the dreadful flames above the houses over
the way, Mr. Buffle's being round the corner. Presently what
should we see but some people running down the street straight
to our door, and then the Major directing operations in the
busiest way, and then some more people and then—carried in
a chair similar to Guy Fawkes—Mr. Buffle in a blanket!

My dear the Major has Mr. Buffle brought up our steps and
whisked into the parlour and carted out on the sofy, and then
he and all the rest of them without so much as a word burst
away again full speed, leaving the impression of a vision except
for Mr. Buffle awful in his blanket with his eyes a rolling. In a
twinkling they all burst back again with Mrs. Buffle in another
blanket, which whisked in and carted out on the sofy they all
burst off again and all burst back again with Miss Buffle in
another blanket, which again whisked in and carted out they
all burst off again and all burst back again with Mr. Buffle's
articled young gentleman in another blanket—him a holding
round the necks of two men carrying him by the legs, similar
to the picter of the disgraceful creetur who has lost the fight (but
where the chair I do not know) and his hair having the appearance of newly played upon. When all four of a row, the Major
rubs his hands and whispers me with what little hoarseness he can
get together, "If our dear remarkable boy was only at home what
a delightful treat this would be for him!"

My dear we made them some hot tea and toast and some hot
brandy-and-water with a little comfortable nutmeg in it, and at
first they were scared and low in their spirits but being fully
insured got sociable. And the first use Mr. Buffle made of his
tongue was to call the Major his Preserver and his best of friends
and to say "My for ever dearest sir let me make you known to
Mrs. Buffle" which also addressed him as her Preserver and her
best of friends and was fully as cordial as the blanket would
admit of. Also Miss Buffle. The articled young gentleman's head
was a little light and he sat a moaning "Robina is reduced to
cinders, Robina is reduced to cinders!" Which went more to
the heart on account of his having got wrapped in his blanket
as if he was looking out of a violin-celler-case, until Mr. Buffle
says "Robina speak to him!" Miss Buffle says "Dear George!"
and but for the Major's pouring down brandy-and-water on the
instant which caused a catching in his throat owing to the nutmeg and a violent fit of coughing it might have proved too much

for his strength. When the articled young gentleman got the better of it Mr. Buffle leaned up against Mrs. Buffle being two bundles, a little while in confidence, and then says with tears in his eyes which the Major noticing wiped, "We have not been an united family, let us after this danger become so, take her George." The young gentleman could not put his arm out far to do it, but his spoken expressions were very beautiful though of a wandering class. And I do not know that I ever had a much pleasanter meal than the breakfast we took together after we had all dozed, when Miss Buffle made tea very sweetly in quite the Roman style as depicted formerly at Covent Garden Theatre and when the whole family was most agreeable, as they have ever proved since that night when the Major stood at the foot of the Fire-Escape and claimed them as they came down—the young gentleman headforemost, which accounts. And though I do not say that we should be less liable to think ill of one another if strictly limited to blankets, still I do say that we might most of us come to a better understanding if we kept one another less at a distance.

Why there's Wozenham's lower down on the other side of the street. I had a feeling of much soreness several years respecting what I must still ever call Miss Wozenham's systematic underbidding and the likeness of the house in Bradshaw having far too many windows and a most umbrageous and outrageous Oak which never yet was seen in Norfolk-street nor yet a carriage and four at Wozenham's door, which it would have been far more to Bradshaw's credit to have drawn a cab. This frame of mind continued bitter down to the very afternoon in January last when one of my girls, Sally Rairyganoo which I still suspect of Irish extraction though family represented Cambridge, else why abscond with a bricklayer of the Limerick persuasion and be married in patterns not waiting till his black eye was decently got round with all the company fourteen in number and one horse fighting outside on the roof of the vehicle—I repeat my dear my ill-regulated state of mind towards Miss Wozenham continued down to the very afternoon of January last past when Sally Rairyganoo came banging (I can use no milder expression) into my room with a jump which may be Cambridge and may not, and said "Hurroo Missis! Miss Wozenham's sold up!" My dear when I had it thrown in my face and conscience that the girl Sally had reason to think I could be glad of the ruin of a fellow-creetur, I burst into tears and dropped back in my chair and I says "I am ashamed of myself!"

Well! I tried to settle to my tea but I could not do it what with thinking of Miss Wozenham and her distresses. It was a wretched night and I went up to a front window and looked over at Wozenham's and as well as I could make it out down the street in the fog it was the dismalest of the dismal and not a light to be seen. So at last I says to myself "This will not do," and I puts on my oldest bonnet and shawl not wishing Miss Wozenham to be reminded of my best at such a time, and lo and behold you I goes over to Wozenham's and knocks. "Miss Wozenham at home?" I says turning my head when I heard the door go. And then I saw it was Miss Wozenham herself who had opened it and sadly worn she was poor thing and her eyes all swelled and swelled with crying. "Miss Wozenham" I says "it is several years since there was a little unpleasantness betwixt us on the subject of my grandson's cap being down your Airy. I have overlooked it and I hope you have done the same." "Yes Mrs. Lirriper" she says in a surprise "I have." "Then my dear" I says "I should be glad to come in and speak a word to you." Upon my calling her my dear Miss Wozenham breaks out a crying most pitiful, and a not unfeeling elderly person that might have been better shaved in a nightcap with a hat over it offering a polite apology for the mumps having worked themselves into his constitution, and also for sending home to his wife on the bellows which was in his hand as a writing-desk, looks out of the back parlour and says "The lady wants a word of comfort" and goes in again. So I was able to say quite natural "Wants a word of comfort does she sir? Then please the pigs she shall have it!" And Miss Wozenham and me we go into the front room with a wretched light that seemed to have been crying too and was sputtering out, and I says "Now my dear, tell me all," and she wrings her hands and says "Oh Mrs. Lirriper that man is in possession here, and I have not a friend in the world who is able to help me with a shilling."

It doesn't signify a bit what a talkative old body like me said to Miss Wozenham when she said that, and so I'll tell you instead my dear that I'd have given thirty shillings to have taken her over to tea, only I dursn't on account of the Major. Not you see but what I knew I could draw the Major out like thread and wind him round my finger on most subjects and perhaps even

on that if I was to set myself to it, but him and me had so often
belied Miss Wozenham to one another that I was shamefaced,
and I knew she had offended his pride and never mine, and
likewise I felt timid that that Rairyganoo girl might make things
awkward. So I says "My dear if you could give me a cup of tea
to clear my muddle of a head I should better understand your
affairs." And we had the tea and the affairs too and after all
it was but forty pound, and—There! She's as industrious and
straight a creeter as ever lived and has paid back half of it
already, and where's the use of saying more, particularly when
it ain't the point? For the point is that when she was a kissing
my hands and holding them in hers and kissing them again and
blessing blessing blessing, I cheered up at last and I says "Why
what a waddling old goose I have been my dear to take you
for something so very different!" "Ah but I too" says she "how
have *I* mistaken *you*!" "Come for goodness' sake tell me" I
says "what you thought of me?" "Oh" says she "I thought you
had no feeling for such a hard hand-to-mouth life as mine, and
were rolling in affluence." I says shaking my sides (and very glad
to do it for I had been choking quite long enough) "Only
look at my figure my dear and give me your opinion whether
if I was in affluence I should be likely to roll in it!" That
did it! We got as merry as grigs (whatever *they* are, if you
happen to know my dear—*I* don't) and I went home to
my blessed home as happy and as thankful as could be. But before
I make an end of it, think even of my having misunderstood the
Major! Yes! For next forenoon the Major came into my little
room with his brushed hat in his hand and he begins "My
dearest madam——" and then put his face in his hat as if he
had just come into church. As I sat all in a maze he came out
of his hat and began again. "My esteemed and beloved
friend——" and then went into his hat again. "Major," I cries
out frightened "has anything happened to our darling boy?"
"No, no, no" says the Major "but Miss Wozenham has been here
this morning to make her excuses to me, and by the Lord I can't
get over what she told me." "Hoity toity, Major," I says "you
don't know yet that I was afraid of you last night and didn't
think half as well of you as I ought! So come out of church
Major and forgive me like a dear old friend and I'll never do
so any more." And I leave you to judge my dear whether I ever
did or will. And how affecting to think of Miss Wozenham out

of her small income and her losses doing so much for her poor old father, and keeping a brother that had had the misfortune to soften his brain against the hard mathematics as neat as a new pin in the three back represented to lodgers as a lumber-room and consuming a whole shoulder of mutton when-ever provided!

And now my dear I really am a going to tell you about my Legacy if you're inclined to favour me with your attention, and I did fully intend to have come straight to it only one thing does so bring up another. It was the month of June and the day before Midsummer Day when my girl Winifred Madgers—she was what is termed a Plymouth Sister, and the Plymouth Brother that made away with her was quite right, for a tidier young woman for a wife never came into a house and afterwards called with the beautifullest Plymouth Twins—it was the day before Midsummer Day when Winifred Madgers comes and says to me "A gentleman from the Consul's wishes particular to speak to Mrs. Lirriper." If you'll believe me my dear the Consols at the bank where I have a little matter for Jemmy got into my head, and I says "Good gracious I hope he ain't had any dreadful fall!" Says Winifred "He don't look as if he had ma'am." And I says "Show him in."

The gentleman came in dark and with his hair cropped what I should consider too close, and he says very polite "Madame Lirrwiper!" I says "Yes sir. Take a chair." "I come," says he "frrwom the Frrwench Consul's." So I saw at once that it wasn't the Bank of England. "We have rrweceived," says the gentleman turning his r's very curious and skilful, "frrwom the Mairrwie at Sens, a communication which I will have the honour to rrwead. Madame Lirrwiper understands Frrwench?" "Oh dear no sir!" says I. "Madame Lirriper don't understand anything of the sort." "It matters not," says the gentleman, "I will trrwanslate."

With that my dear the gentleman after reading something about a Department and a Mairie (which Lord forgive me I supposed till the Major came home was Mary, and never was I more puzzled than to think how that young woman came to have so much to do with it) translated a lot with the most obliging pains, and it came to this:—That in the town of Sens in France, an unknown Englishman lay a dying. That he was speechless and without motion. That in his lodging there was a gold watch and a purse containing such and such money and a trunk containing such and such clothes, but no passport and no papers, except that on his table was a pack of cards and that he had written in pencil on the back of the ace of hearts: "To the authorities. When I am dead, pray send what is left, as a last Legacy, to Mrs. Lirriper Eighty-one Norfolk-street Strand London." When the gentleman had explained all this, which seemed to be drawn up much more methodical than I should have given the French credit for, not at that time knowing the nation, he put the document into my hand. And much the wiser I was for that you may be sure, except that it had the look of being made out upon grocery-paper and was stamped all over with eagles.

"Does Madame Lirrwiper" says the gentleman "believe she rrwecognises her unfortunate compatrrwiot?"

You may imagine the flurry it put me into my dear to be talked to about my compatriots.

I says "Excuse me. Would you have the kindness sir to make your language as simple as you can?"

"This Englishman unhappy, at the point of death. This compatrrwiot afflicted," says the gentleman.

"Thank you sir" I says "I understand you now. No sir I have not the least idea who this can be."

"Has Madame Lirrwiper no son, no nephew, no godson, no frrwiend, no acquaintance of any kind in Frrwance?"

"To my certain knowledge" says I "no relation or friend, and to the best of my belief no acquaintance."

"Pardon me. You take Locataires?" says the gentleman.

My dear fully believing he was offering me something with his obliging foreign manners—snuff for anything I knew—I gave a little bend of my head and I says if you'll credit it, "No I thank you. I have not contracted the habit."

The gentleman looks perplexed and says "Lodgers?"

"Oh!" says I laughing. "Bless the man! Why yes to be sure!"

"May it not be a former lodger?" says the gentleman. "Some lodger that you pardoned some rrwent? You have pardoned lodgers some rrwent?"

"Hem! It has happened sir" says I, "but I assure you I can call to mind no gentleman of that description that this is at all likely to be."

In short my dear we could make nothing of it, and the gentleman noted down what I said and went away. But he left me the paper of which he had two with him, and when the Major came in I says to the Major as I put it in his hand "Major here's

Old Moore's Almanack with the hieroglyphic complete, for your opinion."

It took the Major a little longer to read than I should have thought, judging from the copious flow with which he seemed to be gifted when attacking the organ-men, but at last he got through it and stood a gazing at me in amazement.

"Major" I says "you're paralysed."

"Madam" says the Major, "Jemmy Jackman is doubled up."

Now it did so happen that the Major had been out to get a little information about rail-roads and steam-boats, as our boy was coming home for his Midsummer holidays next day and we were going to take him somewhere for a treat and a change. So while the Major stood a gazing it came into my head to say to him "Major I wish you'd go and look at some of your books and maps, and see whereabouts this same town of Sens is in France."

The Major he roused himself and he went into the Parlours and he poked about a little, and he came back to me and he says: "Sens my dearest madam is seventy odd miles south of Paris."

With what I may truly call a desperate effort "Major" I says "we'll go there with our blessed boy!"

If ever the Major was beside himself it was at the thoughts of that journey. All day long he was like the wild man of the woods after meeting with an advertisement in the papers telling him something to his advantage, and early next morning hours before Jemmy could possibly come home he was outside in the street ready to call out to him that we was all a going to France. Young Rosy-cheeks you may believe was as wild as the Major, and they did carry on to that degree that I says "If you two children ain't more orderly I'll pack you both off to bed." And then they fell to cleaning up the Major's telescope to see France with, and went out and bought a leather bag with a snap to hang round Jemmy, and him to carry the money like a little Fortunatus with his purse.

If I hadn't passed my word and raised their hopes, I doubt if I could have gone through with the undertaking but it was too late to go back now. So on the second day after Midsummer Day we went off by the morning mail. And when we came to the sea which I had never seen but once in my life and that when my poor Lirriper was courting me, the freshness of it and the deepness and the airiness and to think that it had been rolling ever since and that it was always a rolling and so few of us minding, made me feel quite serious. But I felt happy too and so did Jemmy and the Major and not much motion on the whole, though me with a swimming in the head and a sinking but able to take notice that the foreign insides appear to be constructed hollower than the English, leading to much more tremenjous noises when bad sailors.

But my dear the blueness and the lightness and the coloured look of everything and the very sentry-boxes striped and the shining rattling drums and the little soldiers with their waists and tidy gaiters, when we got across to the Continent—it made me feel as if I don't know what—as if the atmosphere had been lifted off me. And as to lunch why bless you if I kept a man-cook and two kitchen-maids I couldn't get it done for twice the money, and no injured young woman a glaring at you and grudging you and acknowledging your patronage by wishing that your food might choke you, but so civil and so hot and attentive and every way comfortable except Jemmy pouring wine down his throat by tumblers-full and me expecting to see him drop under the table.

And the way in which Jemmy spoke his French was a real charm. It was often wanted of him, for whenever anybody spoke a syllable to me I says "Noncomprenny, you're very kind but it's no use—Now Jemmy!" and then Jemmy he fires away at 'em lovely, the only thing wanting in Jemmy's French being as it appeared to me that he hardly ever understood a word of what they said to him which made it scarcely of the use it might have been though in other respects a perfect Native, and regarding the Major's fluency I should have been of the opinion judging French by English that there might have been a greater choice of words in the language though still I must admit that if I hadn't known him when he asked a military gentleman in a grey cloak what o'clock it was I should have took him for a Frenchman born.

Before going on to look after my Legacy we were to make one regular day in Paris, and I leave you to judge my dear what a day *that* was with Jemmy and the Major and the telescope and me and the prowling young man at the inn door (but very civil too) that went along with us to show the sights. All along the railway to Paris Jemmy and the Major had been frightening me to death by stooping down on the platforms at stations to inspect the engines underneath their mechanical stomachs, and by creeping in and out I don't know where all, to find improvements for the United Grand Junction Parlour, but when we got out into the brilliant streets on a bright morning they gave up all their London improvements as a bad job and gave their minds to Paris. Says the prowling young man to me "Will I speak Inglis No?" So I says "If you can young man I shall take it as a favour," but after half an hour of it when I fully believed the man had gone mad and me too I says "Be so good as fall back on your French sir," knowing that then I shouldn't have the agonies of trying to understand him which was a happy release. Not that I lost much more than the rest either, for I generally noticed that when he had described something very long indeed and I says to Jemmy "What does he say Jemmy?" Jemmy says looking at him with vengeance in his eye "He is so jolly indistinct!" and that when he had described it longer all over again and I says to Jemmy "Well Jemmy what's it all about?" Jemmy says "He says the building was repaired in seventeen hundred and four, Gran."

Wherever that prowling young man formed his prowling habits I cannot be expected to know, but the way in which he went round the corner while we had our breakfasts and was there again when we swallowed the last crumb was most marvellous, and just the same at dinner and at night, prowling equally at the theatre and the inn gateway and the shop-doors when we bought a trifle or two and everywhere else but troubled with a tendency to spit. And of Paris I can tell you no more my dear than that it's town and country both in one, and carved stone and long streets of high houses and gardens and fountains and statues and trees and gold, and immensely big soldiers and immensely little soldiers and the pleasantest nurses with the whitest caps a playing at skipping-rope with the bunchiest babies in the flattest caps, and clean tablecloths spread everywhere for dinner and people sitting out of doors smoking and sipping all day long and little plays being acted in the open air for little people and every shop a complete and elegant room, and everybody seeming to play at everything in this world. And as to the sparkling lights my dear after dark, glittering high up and low down and on before and on behind and all round, and the crowd of theatres and the crowd of people and the crowd of all sorts, it's pure enchantment. And pretty well the only thing that grated on me was that whether you pay your fare at the railway or whether you change your money at a money-dealer's or whether you take your ticket at the theatre, the lady or gentleman is caged up (I suppose by Government) behind the strongest iron bars having more of a Zoological appearance than a free country.

Well to be sure when I did after all get my precious bones to bed that night, and my Young Rogue came in to kiss me and asks "What do you think of this lovely lovely Paris, Gran?" I says "Jemmy I feel as if it was beautiful fireworks being let off in my head." And very cool and refreshing the pleasant country was next day when we went on to look after my Legacy, and rested me much and did me a deal of good.

So at length and at last my dear we come to Sens, a pretty little town with a great two-towered cathedral and the rooks flying in and out of the loopholes and another tower atop of one of the towers like a sort of a stone pulpit. In which pulpit with the birds skimming below him if you'll believe me, I saw a speck while I was resting at the inn before dinner which they made signs to me was Jemmy and which really was. I had been a fancying as I sat in the balcony of the hotel that an Angel might light there and call down to the people to be good, but I little thought what Jemmy all unknown to himself was a calling down from that high place to some one in the town.

The pleasantest-situated inn my dear! Right under the two towers, with their shadows a changing upon it all day like a kind of a sundial, and country people driving in and out of the court-yard in carts and hooded cabriolets and such-like, and a market outside in front of the cathedral, and all so quaint and like a picter. The Major and me agreed that whatever came of my Legacy this was the place to stay in for our holiday, and we also agreed that our dear boy had best not be checked in his joy that night by the sight of the Englishman if he was still alive, but that we would go together and alone. For you are to understand that the Major not feeling himself quite equal in his wind to to the heighth to which Jemmy had climbed, had come back to me and left him with the Guide.

So after dinner when Jemmy had set off to see the river, the Major went down to the Mairie, and presently came back with a military character in a sword and spurs and a cocked-hat and a yellow shoulder-belt and long tags about him that he must have found inconvenient. And the Major says "The Englishman still lies in the same state dearest madam. This gentleman will conduct us to his lodging." Upon which the military character pulled off his cocked-hat to me, and I took notice that he had shaved his forehead in imitation of Napoleon Bonaparte but not like.

We went out at the court-yard gate and past the great doors of the cathedral and down a narrow High Street where the people were sitting chatting at their shop-doors and the children were at play. The military character went in front and he stopped at a pork-shop with a little statue of a pig sitting up, in the window, and a private door that a donkey was looking out of.

When the donkey saw the military character he came slipping out on the pavement to turn round and then clattered along the passage into a back-yard. So the coast being clear, the Major and me were conducted up the common stair and into the front room on the second, a bare room with a red tiled floor and the outside lattice blinds pulled close to darken it. As the military character opened the blinds I saw the tower where I had seen Jemmy, darkening as the sun got low, and I turned to the bed by the wall and saw the Englishman.

It was some kind of brain fever he had had, and his hair was all gone, and some wetted folded linen lay upon his head. I looked at him very attentive as he lay there all wasted away with his eyes closed, and I says to the Major

"I never saw this face before."

The Major looked at him very attentive too, and he says

"*I* never saw this face before."

When the Major explained our words to the military character, that gentleman shrugged his shoulders and showed the Major the card on which it was written about the Legacy for me. It had been written with a weak and trembling hand in bed, and I knew no more of the writing than of the face. Neither did the Major.

Though lying there alone, the poor creetur was as well taken care of as could be hoped, and would have been quite unconscious of any one's sitting by him then. I got the Major to say that we were not going away at present and that I would come back to-morrow and watch a bit by the bedside. But I got him to add—and I shook my head hard to make it stronger—"We agree that we never saw this face before."

Our boy was greatly surprised when we told him sitting out in the balcony in the starlight, and he ran over some of those stories of former Lodgers, of the Major's putting down, and asked wasn't it possible that it might be this lodger or that lodger. It was not possible and we went to bed.

In the morning just at breakfast-time the military character came jingling round, and said that the doctor thought from the signs he saw there might be some rally before the end. So I says to the Major and Jemmy, "You two boys go and enjoy yourselves, and I'll take my Prayer-Book and go sit by the bed." So I went, and I sat there for some hours, reading a prayer for him poor soul now and then, and it was quite on in the day when he moved his hand.

He had been so still, that the moment he moved I knew of it, and I pulled off my spectacles and laid down my book and rose and looked at him. From moving one hand he began to move both, and then his action was the action of a person groping in the dark. Long after his eyes had opened, there was a film over them and he still felt for his way out into light. But by slow degrees his sight cleared and his hands stopped. He saw the ceiling, he saw the wall, he saw me. As his sight cleared, mine cleared too, and when at last we looked in one another's faces, I started back and I cries passionately :

"O you wicked wicked man ! Your sin has found you out !"

For I knew him, the moment life looked out of his eyes, to be Mr. Edson, Jemmy's father who had so cruelly deserted Jemmy's young unmarried mother who had died in my arms, poor tender creetur, and left Jemmy to me.

"You cruel wicked man ! You bad black traitor !"

With the little strength he had, he made an attempt to turn over on his wretched face to hide it. His arm dropped out of the bed and his head with it, and there he lay before me crushed in body and in mind. Surely the miserablest sight under the summer sun !

"O blessed Heaven" I says a crying, "teach me what to say to this broken mortal ! I am a poor sinful creetur, and the Judgment is not mine."

As I lifted my eyes up to the clear bright sky, I saw the high tower where Jemmy had stood above the birds, seeing that very window; and the last look of that poor pretty young mother when her soul brightened and got free, seemed to shine down from it.

"O man, man, man!" I says, and I went on my knees beside the bed; "if your heart is rent asunder and you are truly penitent for what you did, Our Saviour will have mercy on you yet!"

As I leaned my face against the bed, his feeble hand could just move itself enough to touch me. I hope the touch was penitent. It tried to hold my dress and keep hold, but the fingers were too weak to close.

I lifted him back upon the pillows, and I says to him:

"Can you hear me?"

He looked yes.

"Do you know me?"

He looked yes, even yet more plainly.

"I am not here alone. The Major is with me. You recollect the Major?"

Yes. That is to say he made out yes, in the same way as before.

"And even the Major and I are not alone. My grandson—his godson—is with us. Do you hear? My grandson."

The fingers made another trial to catch at my sleeve, but could only creep near it and fall.

"Do you know who my grandson is?"

Yes.

"I pitied and loved his lonely mother. When his mother lay a dying I said to her, 'My dear this baby is sent to a childless old woman.' He has been my pride and joy ever since. I love him as dearly as if he had drunk from my breast. Do you ask to see my grandson before you die?"

Yes.

"Show me, when I leave off speaking, if you correctly understand what I say. He has been kept unacquainted with the story of his birth. He has no knowledge of it. No suspicion of it. If I bring him here to the side of this bed, he will suppose you to be a perfect stranger. It is more than I can do, to keep from him the knowledge that there is such wrong and misery in the world; but that it was ever so near him in his innocent cradle, I have kept from him, and I do keep from him, and I ever will keep from him. For his mother's sake, and for his own."

He showed me that he distinctly understood, and the tears fell from his eyes.

"Now rest, and you shall see him."

So I got him a little wine and some brandy and I put things straight about his bed. But I began to be troubled in my mind lest Jemmy and the Major might be too long of coming back. What with this occupation for my thoughts and hands, I didn't hear a foot upon the stairs, and was startled when I saw the Major stopped short in the middle of the room by the eyes of the man upon the bed, and knowing him then, as I had known him a little while ago.

There was anger in the Major's face, and there was horror and repugnance and I don't know what. So I went up to him and I led him to the bedside and when I clasped my hands and lifted of them up, the Major did the like.

"O Lord" I says "Thou knowest what we two saw together of the sufferings and sorrows of that young creetur now with Thee. If this dying man is truly penitent, we two together humbly pray Thee to have mercy on him!"

The Major says "Amen!" and then after a little stop I whispers him, "Dear old friend fetch our beloved boy." And the Major, so clever as to have got to understand it all without being told a word, went away and brought him.

Never never never, shall I forget the fair bright face of our boy when he stood at the foot of the bed, looking at his unknown father. And O so like his dear young mother then!

"Jemmy" I says, "I have found out all about this poor gentleman who is so ill, and he did lodge in the old house once. And as he wants to see all belonging to it, now that he is passing away, I sent for you."

"Ah poor man!" says Jemmy stepping forward and touching one of his hands with great gentleness. "My heart melts for him. Poor, poor, man!"

The eyes that were so soon to close for ever, turned to me, and I was not that strong in the pride of my strength that I could resist them.

"My darling boy, there is a reason in the secret history of this fellow-creetur, lying as the best and worst of us must all lie one day, which I think would ease his spirit in his last hour if you would lay your cheek against his forehead and say 'May God forgive you!'"

"O Gran," says Jemmy with a full heart "I am not worthy!" But he leaned down and did it. Then the faltering fingers made out to catch hold of my sleeve at last, and I believe he was a trying to kiss me when he died.

*   *   *   *   *

There my dear! There you have the story of my Legacy in full, and it's worth ten times the trouble I have spent upon it if you are pleased to like it.

You might suppose that it set us against the little French town of Sens, but no we didn't find that. I found myself that I never looked up at the high tower atop of the other tower, but the days came back again when that fair young creetur with her pretty bright hair trusted in me like a mother, and the recollection made the place so peaceful to me as I can't express. And every soul about the hotel down to the pigeons in the court-yard made friends with Jemmy and the Major, and went lumbering away with them on all sorts of expeditions in all sorts of vehicles drawn by rampagious cart-horses—with heads and without—mud for paint and ropes for harness—and every new friend dressed in blue like a butcher, and every new horse standing on his hind legs wanting to devour and consume every other horse, and every man that had a whip to crack crack-crack-crack-crack-cracking it as if it was a schoolboy with his first. As to the Major my dear that man lived the greater part of his time with a little tumbler in one hand and a bottle of small wine in the other, and whenever he saw anybody else with a little tumbler, no matter who it was—the military character with the tags, or the inn servants at their supper in the court-yard, or towns-people a chatting on a bench, or country-people a starting home after market—down rushes the Major to clink his glass against their glasses and cry—Hola! Vive Somebody! or Vive Something! as if he was beside himself. And though I could not quite approve of the Major's doing it, still the ways of the world are the ways of the world varying according to different parts of it, and dancing at all in the open Square with a lady that kept a barber's shop my opinion is that the Major was right to dance his best and to lead off with a power that I did not think was in him, though I was a little uneasy at the Barricading sound of the cries that were set up by the other dancers and the rest of the company, until when I says "What are they ever calling out Jemmy?" Jemmy says "They're calling out Gran, Bravo the Military English! Bravo the Military English!" which was very gratifying

T

to my feelings as a Briton and became the name the Major was known by.

But every evening at a regular time we all three sat out in the balcony of the hotel at the end of the court-yard, looking up at the golden and rosy light as it changed on the great towers, and looking at the shadows of the towers as they changed on all about us ourselves included, and what do you think we did there? My dear if Jemmy hadn't brought some other of those stories of the Major's taking down from the telling of former lodgers at Eighty-one Norfolk-street, and if he didn't bring 'em out with this speech:

"Here you are Gran! Here you are Godfather! More of 'em! *I*'ll read. And though you wrote 'em for me, Godfather, I know you won't disapprove of my making 'em over to Gran; will you?"

"No my dear boy," says the Major. "Everything we have is hers, and we are hers."

"Hers ever affectionately and devotedly J. Jackman, and J. Jackman Lirriper," cries the Young Rogue giving me a close hug. "Very well then Godfather. Look here. As Gran is in the Legacy way just now, I shall make these stories a part of Gran's Legacy. I'll leave 'em to her. What do you say Godfather?"

"Hip hip Hurrah!" says the Major.

"Very well then" cries Jemmy all in a bustle. "Vive the Military English! Vive the Lady Lirriper! Vive the Jemmy Jackman Ditto! Vive the Legacy! Now, you look out, Gran. And you look out, Godfather, *I*'ll read! And I'll tell you what I'll do besides. On the last night of our holiday here when we are all packed and going away, I'll top up with something of my own."

"Mind you do sir" says I.

"Don't you be afraid, Gran" cries Young Sparkles. "Now then! I'm going to read. Once, twice, three and away. Open your mouths and shut your eyes, and see what Fortune sends you. All in to begin. Look out Gran. Look out Godfather!"

So in his lively spirits Jemmy began a reading, and he read every evening while we were there, and sometimes we were about it late enough to have a candle burning quite steady out in the balcony in the still air. And so here is the rest of my Legacy my dear that I now hand over to you in this bundle of papers all in the Major's plain round writing. I wish I could hand you the church towers over too, and the pleasant air and the inn yard and the pigeons often coming and perching on the rail by

Jemmy and seeming to be critical with their heads on one side, but you'll take as you find.

II

I have lived in a common-place way, Major, in common-place times, and should have mighty little to tell of my own life and adventures (if I were put to it) that would be likely to interest any one save myself. But I have a story by me that shall be yours if you please. Of this story I have only to say a very few words. My father had the manuscript of it in his possession as long as I can remember, and he once allowed me, when I began to approach years of discretion, to read it. It was given to him by a very old friend, whom I dimly remember about our house when I was a boy—a French gentleman of obliging manners, and with a melancholy smile. He fades out of the memory of my youthful days very early, and I chiefly remember him because my father told me that he had received this manuscript from him, and that in parting with it the French gentleman had said: "Ah! few people would believe what went on at that time in France, but here's a specimen. I don't expect you to believe it, mind!"

When the time came for examining my deceased father's papers, this paper turned up among the rest. I put it aside, being immersed in business matters at the time, and only came upon it yesterday, in these very lodgings, in the course of a periodical rummage among a great box of papers from my bankers in the Strand hard by. The periodical rummage came to an end directly, and, with the zest naturally derived from a sense that I ought to be doing something else, I read over every word of the manuscript. It is faded and yellow, as you see; and it is odd, as you shall hear. Thus it goes:

It is pretty well known that as the eighteenth century drew towards its close, and as the moment approached when the mighty change which had been long threatening, was actually about to take place—it is well known, I say, that we Parisians had got into a condition of mind, which was about as bad as bad could be. Luxurious, used up, we had for the most part lost all sense of enjoyment; while as to any feeling of duty—Heaven help us! there was little enough of that. What did we believe of man's responsibility? We were here to enjoy ourselves if we could; if we could not—why, there was a remedy.

It was just one of those states of things which all thinking men were able to see, could not possibly last long. A great shock must be at hand, such men said: a constitution so utterly deranged must pass through some serious attack before it would be likely to get better. That "serious attack" came, and the great French Revolution inaugurated a new condition of affairs. What I have to relate, however, has nothing to do with the revolution, but took place some few years before that great convulsion shook the world, and another era began.

It is not to be supposed that men who held the opinions, and led the lives of the better class of Parisians at that time, were happy. Indeed, a frank open-hearted man, who was tolerably content with the world as he found it, and was able and willing to enjoy himself in it, would have been looked upon with contempt by the more enlightened (and miserable) sort, and would have been regarded as a man deficient alike in intellect and "ton." There were few enough of such, however, and the representatives of the morbid class had it all their own way. Of course among these it was not likely that an agency so well calculated to help them out of their difficulties as suicide should be neglected, and it is not too much to say that the sacrifices offered up at that terrible shrine, were beyond all limits of ordinary proportion. It was such a resource to fall back upon, such a quick way out of the difficulty! Was money short? Was a wife troublesome, or a mistress obdurate? Was there a course of east wind setting in? Were pleasures pleasures no longer, while pain was still pain? Was life, for any reason, not worth having: was it a bore, a penance, a hell upon earth? Here was the remedy at hand—get rid of it. As to what lay beyond—pooh! one must take his chance. Perhaps there was nothing. Perhaps there were the Elysian Fields, with endless earthly gratifications, and sempiternal youth and freshness, to make them enjoyable. "Let us be off with all speed," said the weary ones; "who will help us on our way?"

Helpers were not wanting. There were cunning poisons which would dispose of you in a twinkling, and let you know nothing about it. There were baths and lancets, and anybody could seat himself in a warm bath and open one of his own veins and die with decency. Then there were pistols, beautiful little toys all inlaid with silver and mother-of-pearl, and with your own arms let into the butt, and your coronet, if you happened—which was very likely—to be a marquis. And was there not charcoal? The sleep said to be produced by its fumes was of the soundest—no dreams—no waking. But then you must be sure to stop up all the chinks, or you might happen to inhale a breath of air, and so find yourself back among the east winds and creditors, and the rest of the ills of life, with only a congestion of the head for your pains. All the various modes by which our poor little spark of life may be quenched, were in vogue at that time, but there was one particular method of doing the terrible business which was more fashionable than the rest, and of which it is my special business to treat.

There was a certain handsome street in Paris, and in the Faubourg St. Germain, in which there lived a certain learned and accomplished Doctor. We will call this learned man, Dr. Bertrand. He was a man of striking and rather agreeable appearance, with a fine portly figure, and a handsome and strikingly intelligent face; his age was somewhere between forty and fifty; but there was one characteristic about his countenance, which every one who came in contact with him must have felt, though not all would have been able to explain what it was that affected them. His eyes were dead. They never changed, and they rarely moved. The rest of his face was as mobile as the faces of other people in the average, but not so with the eyes. They were of a dull leaden colour, and they actually seemed dead : the idea being further carried out by the livid and unwholesome tints of the skin around those organs. Judged from its hues, the skin might have mortified.

Dr. Bertrand, in spite of his dead eyes, was a personage of cheerful, almost gay, manners, and of an unvarying and amazing politeness. Nothing ever put him out. He was also a man surrounded by impenetrable mystery. It was impossible to get *at* him, or to break down the barriers which his politeness erected around him. Dr. Bertrand had made many discoveries by which the scientific world had profited. He was a rich man, and his pecuniary means had increased lately in a marked degree. The Doctor made no secret of his resources; it was part of his nature to enjoy luxury and splendour, and he lived in both. His house, an hotel of moderate size in the Rue Mauconseil, enclosed in a court-yard of its own, filled with shrubs and flowers, was a model of taste. His dining-room especially was the realised ideal of what such an apartment should be. Pictures, beautiful pictures—not pieces of wall furniture—decorated the walls, and these were lighted up at night in the most artful manner by lamps of enormous power. The floor was padded with the most splendid Persian carpets, the curtains and chairs were of the finest Utrecht velvet, and, in a conservatory outside, always heated to the most luxurious point, a fountain played perpetually : the light trickling of its water making music in the beautiful place.

And well might Dr. Bertrand have so perfect a dining-room in his house. To give dinners was a great part of Dr. Bertrand's business. In certain circles those dinners were highly celebrated, but they were always talked about under the rose. It was whispered that their splendour was fabulous; that the dishes and the wines reached a point of perfection absolutely unknown elsewhere; that the guests were waited upon by servants who knew their business, which is saying much; that they dined seated upon velvet fauteuils, and ate from golden plates; and it was said, moreover, that Dr. Bertrand entered into the spirit of the times, that he was a mighty and experienced chemist, and that it was an understood thing that Dr. Bertrand's guests did not feel life to be all they could wish, and had no desire to survive the night which succeeded their acceptance of his graceful hospitality.

Strange and intolerable imputation ! Who could live under it ? The Doctor could apparently. For he not only lived but throve and prospered under it.

It was a delicate and dainty way of getting out of the difficulties of life, this provided by Dr. Bertrand. You dined in a style of unwonted luxury, and you enjoyed excellent company, the Doctor himself the very best of company. You felt no uneasiness or pain, for the Doctor knew his business better than that; you went home feeling a little drowsy perhaps, just enough so to make your bed seem delightful; you went off to sleep instantly—the Doctor knew to a minute how to time it all—and you woke up in the Elysian Fields. At least that was where you expected to wake up. That, by-the-by, was the only part of the programme which the Doctor could not make sure of.

Now, there arrived at Dr. Bertrand's house one morning, a

letter from a young gentleman named de Clerval, in which an application was made, that the writer might be allowed to partake of the Doctor's hospitality next day. This was the usual form observed, and (as was also usual) a very handsome fee accompanied the letter. A polite answer was returned in due time, enclosing a card of invitation for the following day, and intimating how much the Doctor looked forward to the pleasure of making Monsieur de Clerval's acquaintance.

A dull rainy day at the end of November, was not a day calculated to reconcile to life any one previously disapproving of the same. Everything was dripping. The trees in the Champs Elysées, the eaves of the sentry-boxes, the umbrellas of those who were provided with those luxuries, the hats of those who were not; all were dripping. Indeed, dripping was so entirely a characteristic of the day, that the Doctor, with that fine tact and knowledge of human nature which distinguished him, had, in arranging the evening programme, given orders that the conservatory fountain should be stopped, lest it should affect the spirits of his guests. Dr. Bertrand was always very particular that the spirits of his guests should not be damped.

Alfred de Clerval was something of an exception to the Doctor's usual class of visitors. In his case it was not ennui, nor weariness of life, nor a longing for sensation, that made him one of the Doctor's guests. It was a mixture of pique and vexation, with a real conviction that what he had set his heart upon, as alone capable of bringing him happiness, was out of his reach. He was of a rash impetuous nature, he believed that all his chance of happiness was gone for life, and he determined to quit life. Two great causes ordinarily brought grist to Dr. Bertrand's mill : money troubles, and love troubles. De Clerval's difficulties were of the latter description. He was in a fever of love and jealousy. He was, and had been for some time, the devoted lover of Mademoiselle Thérèse de Farelles : a noted beauty of that day. All had gone smoothly for a time, until a certain Vicomte de Noel, a cousin of the lady's, appeared upon the scene, and Alfred de Clerval becoming jealous, certain unpleasant scenes ensued, and finally a serious quarrel : Mademoiselle de Farelles belonging to that class of persons who are too proud to clear themselves from a false imputation when they might otherwise very easily do so. Throughout, de Clerval had never once seen the Vicomte; indeed, the principal intercourse between this last and Mademoiselle de Farelles, had been by letter, and it was partly this correspondence which had brought the quarrel about.

When de Clerval entered the salon of Dr. Bertrand where the guests were assembled before dinner, he found himself one of eight or ten persons, all about, like himself, to gather round the Doctor's table, with intentions of a desperate kind. Physiognomically they belonged to all manner of types, some being fat in the face, some thin in the face, some florid in the face, and some very pale in the face. In one respect alone there was a similarity among them; they *all* wore a sort of fixed impregnable expression which was intended to be, and to a certain extent was, unfathomable.

It has been said that there was every sort of person in this assembly. Here was, for instance, a fat man with a countenance naturally jovial, plethoric, in want of a little doctoring no doubt, too much of a "bon vivant" assuredly, but why on earth here now? If he had come in the morning to consult the Doctor on his digestion, one could understand; but what does he do here now? That man knows that to-morrow morning it will be proclaimed to the world that he is ruined, and an impostor. His affairs will collapse, like a house made of cards, and he who has an especial affection for social importance, and who has hitherto enjoyed a good position among his fellows, knows that he would never be able to show his face again. True to his sociability and love of company, to the last, he comes to make an end in good society. Surely no other system, but Dr. Bertrand's, would ever have met the views of this unhappy speculator. Honour then to Dr. Bertrand! who provides every class of persons with the means of suicide.

Here, again, is an individual of another description altogether. A dark thin close-shaved man, who has the fixed unfathomable expression more developed than all the others. This morning his valet knocked at his door, and brought him a letter directed to Monsieur, which the fille de chambre had found on Madame's dressing-table. Madame herself was not in the room, there was only the letter lying before the looking-glass. Monsieur read it, and he is here dining with Dr. Bertrand, and his face is deadly white, and he does not speak a word.

Such guests as these and de Clerval were of an exceptional character. The right man in the right place was a tall faded young man, whom Alfred observed leaning against the chimney-piece, too languid to sit, stand, or recline, and so driven to lean. He had a handsome countenance as far as symmetry of feature and proportion went, but the expression was terrible: so blank, so weary, so hopeless, that one really almost felt that his coming there to dine with Dr. Bertrand was the best thing he could do. He was splendidly dressed, and the value of his waistcoat buttons and studs, seemed to prove that it was not poverty which had brought him there: just as the utter vapidity and blankness of his weary face seemed to indicate that he was incapable of such a strength of love as would drive him to this last resource. No, this was a case of ennui: hopeless, final, terrible. Some of his friends had dined with Dr. Bertrand, and it seemed to have answered, as they never bored him again. He thought he would try it, so here he was come to dinner. Others were there, like this one. Men who had already outlived themselves, so to speak—outlived their better selves—their belief, their health, their natural human interest in the things that happen beneath the sun—men whose hearts had gone to the grave long ago, and whose bodies were now to follow.

"We do not go through the ceremony of introduction in these little réunions of ours," whispered the Doctor in de Clerval's ear; "we are all supposed to know each other." This was after the servant had solemnly announced dinner, and when the guests and their entertainers were passing to the salle-à manger.

The room looked charming. The Doctor had not only caused the fountains to be stopped, but had even, to increase the comfort of the scene, directed that the great velvet curtains should be drawn over the entrance to the conservatory. The logs blazed upon the hearth, and the table was covered with glittering candles. For the Doctor well knew the effect of these, and how they add to the gaiety of every scene into which they are introduced.

The guests all took their places round that dreadful board, and perhaps at that moment—always a chilly one, under the circumstances—a serious sense of what they were doing forced itself upon some of them. Certainly Alfred de Clerval shuddered as he sat down to table, and certain good thoughts made a struggle to gain possession of his mind. But the die was cast. He had come to that place with an intent known to everybody present, and he must go through with the intent. He thought, too, that he caught the Doctor's eye fixed upon him. He must be a man—a MAN.

The Doctor seemed a little anxious at about this period of the entertainment, and now and then would sign impatiently to the servants to do their work swiftly. And so the oysters went round, and then some light wine. It was Château Yquem. The Doctor's wine was matchless.

Dr. Bertrand seemed resolved that there should be no pauses in the conversation, and tore himself to tatters—though apparently enjoying himself extremely—in order to keep it going at this time. There was one horrible circumstance connected with the flagging talk. No one alluded to the future. Nobody spoke of to-morrow. It would have been indelicate in the host; in the guests it would have been folly.

"On such a day as this," remarked the Doctor, addressing a distinguished looking spectre at the other end of the table, "you will have missed your drive in the Bois, M. le Baron?"

"No," replied the person addressed, "I was there in the afternoon for two hours."

"But the fog—could you see?"

"I had runners before me with torches. I had the idea that it might prove interesting."

"And, was it?" inquired another spectral personage, looking up suddenly : as if he rather regretted having committed himself to the Doctor's hospitality before trying this new experiment. "*Was* it interesting?"

"Not in the remotest degree," replied the Baron, in an extinguished sort of voice, and to the other's evident satisfaction. "It was impossible to go beyond a foot-pace, nothing but a grey mist was to be seen on all sides, the horses were bewildered and had to be led. In short, it was an experience to make a man commit sui——"

"Allow me strongly to recommend this salmi," cried the Doctor, in a loud voice. "My chef is particularly good at it." The Baron had got upon an awkward tack, and it was necessary to interrupt him. Dr. Bertrand well knew how difficult it was on these occasions to keep that horrid word, which the Baron had so nearly spoken, out of the conversation. Everybody tried to avoid it, but it would come up.

"For my part, I spent the day at the Louvre," said a little man with a green complexion, and all his features out of draw-

ing. He was a gentleman who had hitherto been entirely unsuccessful in putting an end to himself. He had been twice cut
down, and once sewn up when he had had the misfortune to miss
his jugular by the eighth of an inch. He had been saved from
drowning by a passing friend, whom he hated ever afterwards.
He had charcoaled himself, forgetting to stop up the key-hole;
and he had jumped out of window, just in time to be caught
by a passing manure-cart. "I spent the day at the Louvre,"
remarked this unfortunate gentleman; "the effect of the fog upon
some of the pictures was terrible."

"Dear me!" said the gentleman who had before regretted
having missed the Bois in a fog, and who on the whole seemed
to have come to the Doctor's prematurely; "I should like to
have seen that very much, very much indeed. I wonder if there
will be a fog to—to——"

"Tomorrow," he was going to say. The Doctor though the
moment a propitious one for sending round the champagne; and
even in this assembly it did its usual work, and the buzz of talk
followed as it circulated.

"This poulet," said the Doctor, "is a dish on which we pride
ourselves rather." It was curious that the Doctor's guests always
had a disposition to avoid these dishes which he recommended the
most strongly. They knew why they were come, and that was all
very well; but there was something treacherous in recommending
things. But the Doctor was up to this. He had given enough of
these entertainments to enable him to observe how regular this
shyness was in its action, and so he thus paved the way for the
next dish, which was always *the* dish he wanted his guests to
partake of, and which they did partake of almost invariably.
The next dish in this case was a new one, a "curry à l'Anglaise,"
and almost everybody rushed at it headlong. The dish was a
novelty even in England then, and in France wholly unknown.
The Doctor smiled as he raised the champagne to his lips. "There
is a fine tonic quality about these English curries," he remarked.

"And tonics always disagree with my head," said a little man
at the end of the table, who had not yet spoken. And he ate no
more curry.

Alfred de Clerval was, in spite of his sorrows, so far alive to
all that was going on around him as to miss partaking of some
of Dr. Bertrand's favourite dishes. He had also entered into conversation with one of his next neighbours. On his left was the

commercial man, whose exposure was to take place next day; and this gentleman, naturally a bon vivant, was making the most of his time, and committing fearful havoc on the Doctor's dishes and wine. On the right of de Clerval was a gentleman whom Alfred had not observed until they were seated together at table, but he was a remarkable looking man. They talked at first of indifferent matters, or of what went on around them. They *got on* together, as the saying goes. Men are not very particular in forming acquaintances when their duration is likely to be short, and so when the wine had circulated for some time—and every man there partook of it fiercely—these two had got to speak freely, for men who were but friends of an hour.

"You are a young man," said the stranger, after a pause, during which he had observed de Clerval closely; "you are a young man to be dining with Dr. Bertrand."

"The Doctor's hospitality is, I suspect, suited at times to persons of all ages," replied Alfred. "I was going to add, and of both sexes. How is it, by-the-by, that there are no ladies among the Doctor's guests?"

"I suppose he won't have them," retorted the other, with bitterness; "and he is right! They would be going into hysterics in the middle of dinner, and disorganising the Doctor's arrangements, as they do disorder every system of which they form a part, even to the great world itself."

"True enough," thought Alfred to himself. "This man has suffered as I have, from being fool enough to put his happiness in a woman's keeping."

De Clerval stole a look at him. He was a man considerably his own senior. He was a very tall man, and had something of that languid air in all his movements which often belongs to height. His face was deeply marked for his age, but there was a very kind and merciful expression on it, and, though he looked weary and perhaps indolent, his was not by any means a blasé countenance. He looked like a man who has goodness in him, but instinctively and quite independent of any influence wrought by principle. A good nature, kind generous and honourable, was there; but the man had no rudder or compass to steer by. It was a fine new vessel adrift.

In his own terrible position one would say that such an one could have no leisure to think of anything else. A man under such circumstances might be excused for a little egotism, might be expected to be absorbed in himself and his own troubles; but it was not so with this stranger. His eye wandered from time to time round the table, and evidently his mind was largely occupied with speculations as to what the rest of Dr. Bertrand's patients were suffering under. "How curious it would be," he at length remarked to de Clerval, "if we could know what is amiss with each one of the guests assembled here. There is a little man opposite, for instance, who has not spoken once; see, he is writing in a furtive manner in his pocket-book—writing, perhaps, to some one who will be sorry to-morrow to hear what has happened. What on earth brought *him* here? One would have expected that he would have died somewhere in a corner alone. Perhaps he was afraid. There, again, is a man who, to all appearance, is worn out with illness. A fixed pain, perhaps, which is never to be better, and which he can—or will—bear no longer. One would have thought that he would have remained at home. But we all seem afraid to die in solitude, and the Doctor makes everything so very pleasant. Listen; here is a new surprise for us."

Dr. Bertrand was an energetic person, and a man of resource. Not only had he, in consideration of the fog and the rain, caused the fountain to be stopped, and the curtains to be drawn over the entrance to the conservatory, but he had arranged that some musicians should be placed where the flowers used to show, in order that a novel air of luxury might be given to this particular festival. Nor were these common musicians, whose performance might have infused gloom rather than cheerfulness into the assembly. The Doctor had caused performers of choice ability to be selected, and their music now stole gently on the senses of the guests, and produced an effect that was infinitely agreeable.

"How well this man understands his business," remarked de Clerval to his neighbour. "There is something almost great about him."

There is nothing that varies more in its effect upon us than music; according to the circumstances under which we hear it, it will, to a great extent, prove either stimulating or saddening; still more, of course, does the effect depend upon the music selected. In this case, with the talk already started, with the wine circulating incessantly, with lights flashing in all directions, the effect of the music was exciting in the extreme. And then it had been selected with no common skill. It was not touching music, such as makes one think; but it was made up of a selection of vigorous gallant tunes that seemed to stir the blood in the veins, and rather agitate the nerves than soothe them.

The music was an experiment which Dr. Bertrand had not tried before, and he watched the effect of it carefully.

De Clerval and his neighbour were silent for a time, partly because they were listening to the music, and also because, for the moment, it was difficult to hear one another. The Doctor's guests were noisy enough now. The wine—the good wine—was doing its work, and loosening the tied-up tongues. What talk it was! Talk of the gaming-table, and the night revel. The horrid infidelity of the time brayed out by throats through which no word of prayer or song of praise had passed since the days of earliest childhood.

De Clerval and his neighbour were pursuing their conversation, when the attention of both was suddenly drawn to the opposite side of the table.

Behind the Doctor's chair there always stood a middle-aged man whose business it was to remain stationary in that place, and to keep a steady eye upon every one at table, in order that the very first sign of anything going wrong with a guest might be instantly observed and acted on. The Doctor's calculations were generally most accurate; still he was human, and occasionally some peculiarity of constitution on the part of one of his patients would defeat him. Or they might partake of certain dishes in continuous succession, some one or two only of which the Doctor had intended to be eaten consecutively. In short, unpleasant things would take place occasionally, and so this special officer was in attendance.

This individual suddenly bent down and drew his master's attention to a gentleman seated at the other end of the table, over whom there had gathered a certain strange rigidity of figure and face. He had dropped his fork, and now sat bolt upright in his chair, staring straight before him with a fixity of gaze and a drop of the lower jaw which Dr. Bertrand understood perfectly well.

"Peste!" said the Doctor. "How cantankerous some exceptional constitutions are! One never knows where to have them. You must not lose a second; call in the others and remove him. He is of an epileptic constitution. Lose not a moment."

The familiar disappeared for an instant, and returned, accompanied by four noiseless men, who followed him swiftly to the end of the table where the wretched guest was seated. He had already begun to shriek aloud, while his features were distorted horribly, and the foam was gathering on his lips.

"Oh, my life!" he screamed. "My lost life! Give it me—I must have it—a loan—it was only a loan! I have frittered it away. I want it back. Only a little of it, then; a very little would be something. Ah, it is this man!" The Doctor was near him now, and the epileptic made a furious attempt to get at him. "This man has got my life, my misspent life—it is going—going from me at his will—my life—my lost——" The miserable creature was overpowered and fainting, and the four noiseless men carried him away. Still, as they bore him through the door, he lifted up his voice again, and cried aloud for his youth—his lost youth—and said he would use it differently if they would give it back to him.

They could hear his screams for some time after that, even in the Doctor's padded and muffled house. The incident was horrible, and produced a state of excitement in the other guests. The noise and uproar which followed this terrible occurrence were hellish; everybody was up in arms at once, and it was upon the Doctor himself that all the indignation fell. What did he mean by it? He was an impostor. They had been brought there under false pretences. They had understood that what was done in that establishment was done decently, done effectually, done with a consideration for the feelings of the guests, done in a gentlemanlike manner. Here they were, on the contrary, subjected to a scene which was horrible, disgusting, a thing of the hospitals, a horror!

The Doctor bowed before this storm of invectives. He was deeply, abjectly, miserable at what had occurred: such a thing was rare—rare in the extreme. There were people with constitutions that defied all calculation; people who did not know how to live, nor even how to—— Well, he could only express his profound regret. Would they do him the favour to taste this new wine just brought up? It was Lafitte of a celebrated year, and the Doctor drained off a bumper, by way of setting a good example. It was soon followed by the already half-drunken guests, and the noise and uproar became worse than ever.

"Did you observe what that gentleman partook of?" asked Dr. Bertrand of his familiar. "The gentleman who has just made a scene, I mean?"

"By unlucky chance," was the reply, "he partook in succession of three of your most powerfully *seasoned* dishes. I was thinking— but it is not for me to speak——"

"Yes, yes, it is. What were you thinking?"

"I was thinking, monsieur, whether it was judicious to put three preparations of such great strength next to each other."

"Quite true, quite true," answered the Doctor. "I will make a note of the case."

Meanwhile, de Clerval and his neighbour had fallen again into conversation. There seemed about the stranger something like an interest in his companion. It appeared as if he still thought this dining-room of the Doctor's no place for so young a man.

"If I am too young to be here," said de Clerval, "ought not you, who are of maturer years, to be too wise?"

"No," replied the other; "I have reasoned the thing out, and have thought well and carefully of what I am doing. I had one last chance of happiness after many missed or thrown away; the chance has failed me; there is nothing in store; there is nothing possible now that would give me the least satisfaction. The world is of no use to me, and I am of no use in the world."

There was a pause. Perhaps de Clerval felt that under the circumstances there was little room for argument; perhaps he perceived that, to reason against a course which he was himself pursuing, and yet which he felt unaccountably inclined to reason against, was preposterous—at any rate he was silent and the stranger went on :

"It is curious, with regard to certain of one's relatives, how we lose sight of them for a time, a very long time even, and then some circumstance brings one into contact with them, and the intercourse becomes intimate and frequent. It was so with me and my cousin. I had not seen her for years. I had been much away from Paris during those years—in Russia, at Vienna, and elsewhere—engaged in diplomatic service. In all the wild dissipations to be found at the different courts to which I was attached, I engaged with the most dissipated; and when I lately returned to Paris I believed myself to be a totally exhausted man, for whom a veritable emotion was henceforth out of the question. But I was mistaken."

"There is nothing," remarked Alfred, "that men are more frequently mistaken about."

"Well! I was so at any rate," continued the stranger. "After a lapse of many years I met my cousin again, and found in her, qualities so irresistible, so unlike any I had met with in the world, such freshness and truth——"

"There *are* such women on earth," interrupted de Clerval.

"In a word," continued the other, without noticing the interruption, "I came to the conclusion that, could I ally her destiny with mine, there was a new life and a happy one yet in store for me. I believed that I should be able to shake off my old vile garments, get rid of my old bad habits, and—*begin again.* What a vision came up before me of a life in which SHE should lead me and help me, be my guide along a good way better known to her than to me! I determined to make the cast, and that my life should depend on the issue of the throw. It was only yesterday that the cast was made—and the consequence is, that—that I am here."

Alfred was silent; a strange feeling of pity came over him for this man. In spite of his own trouble, there seemed to be a corner in his heart that was sorry yet for his neighbour.

"At that terrible interview," the stranger went on, "I forced the truth from her. Thérèse was not a demonstrative woman. There was a fund of reserve about her which kept her from showing herself to every one. It was a fault, and so was her pride, the besetting sin of those who have never fallen."

From the moment when the name of Thérèse had been mentioned, the attention of Alfred had been drawn with increased fixity to the narrative to which he was listening. It was with greediness that he now caught at every word which followed.

"I forced the truth from her. I believe she spoke it the less unwillingly because it was her wish to save me from any delusion in the matter, and mercifully to deprive me of hope which could never have any real foundation. I besought her to tell me, in the name of Heaven's truth, was there one in the world more favoured—one who possessed the place in her heart which I had sought to occupy? She hesitated, but I pressed her hard and wrung it from her. Yes, there was one: one who held her heart for ever. I was greedy, I would know all: his name: his condition. And I did. I got to know it all—the history of their love—the name of my rival."

"And what was it?" asked Alfred, in a voice that seemed to himself like that of another man.

"Alfred de Clerval."

U

Alfred sprung to his feet, and looked towards the Doctor. "She loves me," he gasped, "and I am *here*!"

The sudden move of de Clerval attracted all attention. "Ah! another!" the guests yelled out. "Another who does not know how to behave himself. Another who is going to scream at us and drive us mad, and die before our very faces!"

"No, no!" cried Alfred. "No, no! not die, but live! I *must* live. All is changed, and I call upon this Doctor here to save me."

"How do you mean that 'all is changed'?" whispered the man whose narration had brought all this about. "Changed by what I have said?"

The noise was so great that de Clerval could not for the moment answer. The self-doomed wretches round the table seemed to feel a horrible jealousy at the idea of an escape. Even the Doctor sought in vain to restore order now.

"Ah, the renegade," cried the guests, "the coward! He is afraid. He has thought better of it! Impostor, what did he ever come among us for!"

"Hold! gentlemen," cried Alfred, in a voice that made the glasses ring; "I am neither coward nor renegade. I came here to die, because I wished to die. And now I wish to live—not from caprice nor fear, but because the circumstances which made me wish to die, are changed; because I have learnt the truth but this moment, learnt it in this room, learnt it at this table, learnt it of this gentleman."

"Tell me," said the stranger, now seizing him by the arm, "what had my story to do with all this? Unless—unless——"

"Monsieur le Vicomte de Noel," replied the other, "I am Alfred de Clerval, and the story you told me was of Thérèse de Farelles. Judge whether I am anxious to live or not."

A frightful convulsion passed over the features of the Vicomte de Noel, and he fell back in his chair.

Meanwhile the uproar continued among Dr. Bertrand's guests.

"We acknowledge nothing," one of the maddened wretches cried, "as a reason for breaking faith with Death. We are all his votaries. We came together in good fellowship to do him honour. Hurrah for Death! Here is a fellow who would turn infidel to our religion. A renegade, I say again, and what should be the fate of renegades!"

"Follow me without a moment's delay," whispered a voice in Alfred's ear. "You are in the greatest danger."

It was the Doctor's familiar spirit who spoke. Alfred turned to follow him. Then he hesitated, and, hastily leaning down, said these words in de Noel's ear :

"For Heaven's sake don't let your life be sacrificed in this horrible way. Follow me, I entreat you."

"Too late! It is over," gasped the dying man. He seemed to make an ineffectual effort to say more, and then he spread his arms out on the table, and his head fell heavily upon them.

"You will be too late in another instant," said the Doctor's servant, seizing Alfred hastily by the arm. As de Clerval passed through the side-door which the man opened, such a rush was made towards the place as plainly showed what a narrow escape he had had. The servant, however, locked and bolted the door in time, and those poor half-poisoned and half-drunken wretches were foiled in their purpose.

And now, that escape effected, and the excitement of the previous moment at an end, a strange weakness and giddiness came over de Clerval, and he sunk upon a large sofa to which he had mechanically found his way. The room was a large one, and dimly lighted by a simple lamp, shaded, which stood upon a bureau or escritoire nearly large enough to occupy one end of the room, and covered with papers, bottles, surgical instruments, and other medical lumber. The room was filled with such matters, and it opened into another and a smaller apartment, in which were crucibles, a furnace, many chemical preparations, and a bath which could be heated at the shortest notice.

"The Doctor will be here himself immediately," said the familiar, approaching de Clerval with a glass, in which was some compound which he had hastily mixed; "meantime, he bade me give you this."

De Clerval swallowed the mixture, and the attendant left the room. No doubt there was work enough for him elsewhere. Before leaving, however, he told Alfred that he must by all means keep awake.

In compliance with these instructions, and feeling an unwonted drowsiness creeping over him, de Clerval proceeded to walk up and down the room. He was not himself. He would stop, almost without knowing it, in the middle of his promenade, become unconscious for a moment, then would be suddenly and

violently roused by finding that his balance was going, and once
he did fall. But he sprang up instantly, feeling that his life depended on it. He set himself mental tasks, tasks of memory, or
he would try to convince himself that he was in possession of his
faculties by reasoning as to where he was, what circumstances
had occurred, and the like. "I am in Dr.—Dr.—study," he would
say to himself. "I know all about it—waiting to see—waiting,
mind, to see—I am waiting—Dr.——" He was falling into a
state of insensibility in spite of all his efforts, when Dr. Bertrand,
whose approach he had not heard, stood there before him. The
sight of the Doctor roused him.

"Doctor, can you save me?"

"First, I must ask *you* a question," replied the Doctor. "It is
about one of the dishes at table—now recollect yourself. The
'Curry à l'Anglaise.' Did you partake of it?"

De Clerval was silent for a moment, making a violent effort
to collect his bewildered faculties.

At last he remembered something that decided him.

"No, I did not. I remember thinking that an English dish
is never good in France, and I let it pass."

"Then," said Dr. Bertrand, "there is good hope. Follow me
into this room."

For a long time Alfred de Clerval's life was in the greatest
danger. Although he had not partaken of that one particular dish
which Dr. Bertrand considered it beyond his power to counter-
act, he had yet swallowed enough that was poisonous, to make
his ultimate recovery exceedingly doubtful. Probably no other
man but he who had so nearly caused his death could have saved
his life. But Dr. Bertrand knew what was wrong—which is not
always the case with doctors—and he also knew how to deal
with that wrong. So, after a long and tedious illness and con-
valescence, Alfred so far recovered as to be able to drop the
Doctor's acquaintance, which he was very anxious to do, and
to take advantage of the information he had gained from the
unfortunate Vicomte de Noel.

Whether Mademoiselle de Farelles was able to pardon the
crime her lover had so nearly committed, in consideration of
the fact that it was love for her which had led him on to attempt
it, I don't know; but my belief is that she did pardon it.

For Dr. Bertrand, his career was a short one. The practices by which he was amassing a large fortune were not long in coming to the knowledge of the police authorities, and in due time it was determined by those who had the power to carry out their conclusions, that it would be for the good of the Doctor's health that the remainder of his life should be passed in the neighbourhood of Cayenne, where, if he chose, he might give dinners to such of the convicts as could be the most easily spared by government.

III

ANOTHER PAST LODGER RELATES
HIS EXPERIENCE AS A POOR RELATION

The evening was raw and there was snow on the streets, genuine London snow, half-thawed, and trodden, and defiled with mud. I remembered it well, that snow, though it was fifteen years since I had last seen its cheerless face. There it lay, in the same old ruts, and spreading the same old snares on the side-paths. Only a few hours arrived from South America viâ Southampton, I sat in my room at Morley's Hotel, Charing Cross, and looked gloomily out at the fountains, walked up and down the floor discontentedly, and fiercely tried my best to feel glad that I was a wanderer no more, and that I had indeed got home at last.

I poked up my fire, and took a long look backward upon my past life, through the embers. I remembered how my childhood had been embittered by dependence, how my rich and respectable uncle, whose ruling passion was vainglory, had looked on my existence as a nuisance, not so much because he was obliged to open his purse to pay for my clothing and education, as because that, when a man, he thought I could reflect no credit upon his name. I remembered how in those days I had a soul for the beautiful, and a certain almost womanish tenderness of heart, which by dint of much sneering had been successfully extracted from me. I remembered my uncle's unconcealed relief at my determination to go abroad and seek my fortune, the cold good-by of my only cousin, the lonely bitter farewell to England hardly sweetened by the impatient hopes that consumed rather than cheered me—the hopes of name and gold, won by my own exertions, with which I should yet wring from those who despised me, the worthless respect which they denied me now.

Sitting there at the fire, I rang the bell, and the waiter came to me : an old man whose face I remembered. I asked him some questions. Yes, he knew Mr. George Rutland; recollected that many years ago he used to stay at Morley's when he came to London. The old gentleman had always stayed there. But Mr. George was too grand for Morley's now. The family always came to town in the spring, but, at this season, "Rutland Hall, Kent," would be pretty sure to be their address.

Having obtained all the information I desired, I began forthwith to write a letter :

"Dear George,—I dare say you will be as much surprised to see my handwriting as you would to behold an apparition from the dead. However, you know I was always a ne'er-do-well, and I have not had the grace to die yet. I am ashamed not to be able to announce myself as having returned home with my fortune made; but mishaps will follow the most hard-working and well-meaning. I am still a young man, even though fifteen of the best years of my life have been lost, and I am willing to devote myself to any worthy occupation. Meantime, I am anxious to see you and yours. A long absence from home and kindred makes one value the grasp of a friendly hand. I shall not wait for your reply to this, but go down to Kent the day after to-morrow, arriving, I believe, about dinner-time. You see I am making myself assured of your welcome for a few weeks, till I have time to look about me.

"I remain, dear George,
"Your old friend and cousin,
"Guy Rutland."

I folded this missive and placed it in its envelope. "I shall find out, once for all, what they are made of," I said, complacently, as I wrote the address, "George Rutland, Esq., Rutland Hall, Kent."

It was about seven on a frosty evening when I arrived at the imposing entrance of Rutland Hall. No Cousin George came rushing out to meet me. "Of course not," I thought; "I am unused to their formal manners in this country. He is lying in wait for me on the mat inside." I was admitted by a solemn person as quietly and mechanically as though my restoration to home and kindred were a thing that had happened regularly in his presence every day since his birth. He ushered me into a grand hall, but no mat supported the impatient feet of the dignified master of the house. "Ah!" said I, "even this, perhaps, were scarcely etiquette. No doubt he stands chafing on the drawing-room hearth-rug, and I have little enough time to make myself presentable before dinner." So, resigning myself to circumstances, I meekly followed a guide who volunteered to conduct me to the chamber assigned to my especial use. I had to travel a considerable distance before I reached it. "Dear me!" I remarked to myself when I did reach it, "I had expected to find the rooms in such a house more elegantly appointed than this!"

I made my toilette, and again submitting myself to my guide, was convoyed to the drawing-room door. All the way down stairs I had been conning pleasant speeches with which to greet my kinsfolk. I am not a brilliant person, but I sometimes succeed in pleasing when I try, and on this occasion I had the desire to do my best.

The drawing-room door was at the distant end of the hall, and my arrival had been so very quiet, that I conceived my expectant entertainers could hardly be aware of my presence in the house. I thought I should give them a surprise. The door opened and closed upon me, leaving me within the room. I looked around me, and saw—darkness there, and nothing more.

Ah, yes, but there was something more! There was a blazing fire which sent eddying swirls of light through the shadows, and right in the blush of its warmth a little figure was lounging in an easy-chair. The little figure was a girl of apparently about fifteen or sixteen years of age, dressed in a short shabby black frock, who was evidently spoiling her eyes by reading by the firelight. She lay with her head thrown back, a mass of fair curly hair being thus tossed over the velvet cushion on which it rested, while she held her book aloft to catch the light. She was luxuriating in her solitude, and little dreaming of interruption.

She was so absorbed in her book, the door had opened and closed so noiselessly, and the room was so large, that I was obliged to make a sound to engage her attention. She started violently then, and looked up with a nervous fearfulness in her face. She dropped her book, sat upright, and put out her hand, eagerly grasping a thing I had not noticed before, and which leaned against the chair—a crutch. She then got up leaning on it and stood before me. The poor little thing was lame, and had two crutches by her.

I introduced myself, and her fear seemed to subside. She asked me to sit down, with a prim little assumption of at-home-ness, which did not sit upon her with ease. She picked up her book and laid it on her lap; she produced a net from the recesses of her chair, and with a blush gathered up the curls and tucked them into its meshes. Then she sat quiet, but kept her hand upon her crutches, as if she was ready at a moment's notice to limp away across the carpet, and leave me to my own resources.

"Thomson thought there was nobody in the room," she said, as if anxious to account for her own presence there. "I always stay in the nursery, except sometimes when they all go out and I get this room to myself. Then I like to read here."

"Mr. Rutland is not at home?" I said.

"No, they are all out dining."

"Indeed! Your papa, perhaps, did not get my letter?"

She blushed crimson.

"I am not a Miss Rutland," she said. "My name is Teecie Ray. I am an orphan. My father was a friend of Mr. Rutland, and he takes care of me for charity."

The last word was pronounced with a certain controlled quiver of the lip. But she went on. "I don't know about the letter, but I heard a gentleman was expected. I did not think it could be to-night, though, as they all went out."

"A reasonable conclusion to come to," I thought, and thereupon began musing on the eagerness of welcome displayed by my affectionate Cousin George. If I were the gentleman expected, they must have received my letter, and in it were fully set forth the day and hour of my proposed arrival. "Ah! George, my dear fellow," I said, "you are not a whit changed!"

Arriving at this conclusion, I raised my glance, and met, full, the observant gaze of a pair of large shrewd grey eyes. My little hostess for the time being was regarding me with such a curiously legible expression on her face, that I could not but read it and be amused. It said plainly: "I know more about you than you think, and I pity you. You come here with expectations which will not be fulfilled. There is much mortification in store for you. I wonder you came here at all. If I were once well outside these gates, I should never limp inside them again. If I knew a road out into the world you come from, I would set out bravely on my crutches. No, not even for the sake of a stolen hour like this, in a velvet chair, would I remain here."

How any one glance could say all this, was a riddle; but it did say all this. The language of the face was as simple to me as though every word had been translated into my ear. Perhaps a certain internal light, kindled long ago, before this little orphan was born, or George Rutland had become owner of Rutland Hall, assisted me in deciphering so much information so readily. However that may be, certain things before surmised became assured facts in my mind, and a quaint bond of sympathy became at once established between me and my companion.

"Miss Ray," I said, "what do you think of a man who, having been abroad for fifteen years, has the impudence to come home without a shilling in his pocket? Ought he not to be stoned alive?"

"I thought how it was," said she, shaking her head, and looking up with another of her shrewd glances. "I knew it, when they put you into such a bad bedroom. They are keeping all the good rooms for the people who are coming next week. The house will be full for Christmas. It won't do," she added, meditatively.

"What won't do?" I said.

"Your not having a shilling in your pocket. They'll sneer at you for it, and the servants will find it out. I have a guinea that old Lady Thornton gave me on my birthday, and if you would take the loan of it I should be very glad. I don't want it at all, and you could pay me back when you are better off."

She said this with such business-like gravity, that I felt obliged to control my inclination to laugh. She had evidently taken me under her protection. Her keen little wits foresaw snares and difficulties besetting my steps during my stay at Rutland Hall, to which my newer eyes, she imagined, must be ignorantly blind. I looked at her with amusement, as she sat there seriously considering my financial interests. I had a fancy to humour this quaint confidential relation that had sprung up so spontaneously between us. I said gravely:

"I am very much obliged to you for your offer, and will gladly take advantage of it. Do you happen to have the guinea at hand?"

She seized her crutches, and limped quickly out of the room. Presently she returned with a little bon-bon box, which she placed in my hand. Opening it, I found one guinea, wrapped up carefully in silver paper.

"I wish it had been more!" she said, wistfully, as I coolly transferred it to my pocket, box and all. "But I so seldom get money!"

At this moment, the solemn person who had escorted me hither and thither before, announced that my dinner was served.

On my return to the drawing-room, I found, to my intense disappointment, that my beneficent bird had flown. Teecie Ray had limped off to the nursery.

Next morning, at breakfast, I was introduced to the family. I found them, on the whole, pretty much what I had expected. My Cousin George had developed into a pompous portly pater-familias; and, in spite of his cool professions of pleasure, was evidently very sorry to see me. The Mamma Rutland just countenanced me, in a manner the most frigidly polite. The grown-up young ladies treated me with the most well-bred negligence. Unless I had been very obtuse indeed, I could scarcely have failed to perceive the place appointed for me in Rutland Hall. I was expected to sit below the salt. I was that dreadful thing— a person of no importance. George amused himself with me for a few days, displaying to me his various fine possessions, and then, on the arrival of grander guests, left me to my own resources. The Misses Rutland endured my escort on their riding expeditions only till more eligible cavaliers appeared. As for the lady of the house, her annoyance at having me quartered indefinitely on her premises, was hardly concealed. The truth was, they were new people in the circle in which they moved, and it did not suit them to have a poor relation coming suddenly among them, calling them "cousin," and making himself at home in the house. For me, I was not blind, though none of these things did it suit me to see. I made myself as comfortable as was possible under the circumstances, took every sneer and snub in excellent part, and was as amiable and satisfied on all occasions as though I believed myself to be the most cherished inmate of the household. That this meanness of mine should provoke their contempt, I had hardly a right to complain of. Nor did I. I accepted this like the rest of their hospitality, and smiled contentedly as the days went on. The gloom which had oppressed me on my first arrival in England had all betaken itself away. How could I feel otherwise than supremely happy at finding myself thus surrounded by my kind relations, thus generously entertained under their hospitable roof?

As I found that the guests at Rutland Hall enjoyed a certain freedom in their choice of amusements, and the disposal of their time, I speedily availed myself of this privilege. I selected my own associates, and I entertained myself as pleased me best. Not finding myself always welcomed in the drawing-room, I contrived, by a series of the most dexterous artifices, to gain the free entrée of the nursery. In this nursery were growing up, some five or six younger branches of the Rutland family. After a certain hour in the day none of the elders ever thought of invading its remote precincts. Five o'clock in the evening was the children's tea-hour, and the pleasantest, I thought, in the twenty-four. Nurse was a staid woman, who knew how to appreciate a little present now and again, and to keep her own counsel on the subject. The children were not pleasant children; they were unruly mischievous little wretches. They conceived a sort of affection for me, because I sometimes brought to the nursery, sundry purchases made during solitary rides; picture-books, tops, dolls, or sweetmeats, procured by means of Teecie Ray's guinea. I suggested as much to Teecie one evening as she sat by, watching the distribution, and she nodded her head in sage satisfaction. She thought that I economised my substance very well. It covered a great many small extravagances, that guinea did.

Whatever might be my position at Rutland Hall, Teecie Ray's was simply intolerable. A spirit less brave must have been cowed and broken by it : a nature less delicate must have been blunted and made coarser. The servants openly neglected her, the children used her as they pleased; wreaked their humours on her, sparing neither blow nor taunt in their passions, and demanding from her at all times whatever service it suited their capricious fancy to need. Nurse, the only one who ever showed a grain of consideration for the orphan, would sometimes shield her from their impish attacks, when she could do so with safety to herself; but she was not permitted to deal with those darlings in the only fashion which would have been at all likely to bring them to reason. As for the elders of the house, Teecie Ray's momentary presence, or the mere mention of her name, was sufficient to ruffle their peace of mind. "What is to be done with that girl?" I heard Mrs. Rutland remark to one of her daughters. "If she were not lame, one might set her to earn her bread in some way; but, as it is——" A shrug of the shoulders, and a certain vinegar-like expression of countenance, which this lady knew how to assume, sufficiently developed the idea thus imperfectly expressed.

And how did Teecie Ray meet all this? She did not complain nor rebel, she did not sulk nor fret. Under that well-worn black frock of hers, she carried a little breastplate of sober determined endurance. When sorely tried, there was never any cowardly submission to be seen in her grave little face, neither was there ever in her manner or words either reproach or remonstrance. She simply endured. Her large patient eyes and mute wise mouth seemed to say, "Whatever I suffer, whatever I long to dare, gratitude shackles my limbs, and seals my lips. I am saved from many things; therefore I am dumb."

The second time I met my little benefactress, was a day or two after our first interview in the drawing-room. I came upon her, one afternoon by chance, limping down a hedge lane which lay to the back of the house, away beyond the gardens, and the kitchen gardens, and the pleasure-grounds. This lane, I found, led to a large meadow, and beyond the meadow there was a wooded hill, and far down at the distant side of the hill there was a river. This was Teecie Ray's favourite ramble, and her one avenue of escape from the torments of the nursery. I immediately began pouring forth a legion of perplexing troubles and difficulties, to all of which she listened with perfect credulity, expressing her sympathy as I went along by an expressive nod of the head, or a shrewd swift glance. Then she gave me her wise little counsel when all was told, and went home, I believe, pondering on my case.

As the days passed, and my relations became more and more involved in their winter gaieties, I found myself more and more thrown upon my own resources for amusement. Occasionally I was included in an invitation, and accepted it; but in general I preferred indulging my fancy for keeping aloof from those who were little charmed with my company. A system of the most unblushing bribery had won for me a warm welcome from the savage tribes in the nursery. Many and many an evening found me walking down that hedged lane in the frosty dusk, with Teecie Ray limping by my side, and talking her grave simple little talk. I had always some fresh puzzle to propose to her, and she was always ready to knit her smooth brows over its solution. Once she stopped short, and struck her little crutches on the snow.

"You ought to go away from here and work," she cried. "Oh, if *I* could!"

A certain Sir Harry arrived at Rutland Hall; I will not trouble myself to think of his second name; it is not worth remembering. He was a wealthy bachelor of high family, and his movements were watched with interest by the lady of the house. This Sir Harry had a fancy for smoking his cigar in the hedged lane, and on more than one occasion he encountered my little benefactress limping on her solitary way, and stared at the pretty fresh face under her old black hat, till it blushed with uncomfortable brilliance. Teecie changed her track like a hunted hare, but Sir Harry scented her out, and annoyed her with his fulsome compliments. The matter reached Mrs. Rutland's ears, and she vented her chagrin on the defenceless little girl. I know not what sorry accusations and reproaches she bestowed upon her during a long private lecture; but, that evening when, at the children's tea-hour, I entered the nursery door with a new ball in my hand for Jack (the youngest and least objectionable of the band), I saw Teecie Ray's face grievously clouded for the first time. It was flushed and swollen with passionate crying. I do not intend to commit to paper certain remarks which I made sotto voce on beholding this disfigurement.

"Come, come, Teecie," I said, while nurse was busy quelling a disturbance which had arisen because "Cousin Guy" had not brought something to every one else as well as Jack; "where is all your philosophy, little mother? You need never preach to me again, if you set me such a bad example."

Teecie said never a word, but stared on into the fire. This wound had cut deep. Sir Harry, and Mrs. Rutland, of Rutland Hall, at that moment I should have dearly loved to knock your two good-for-nothing heads together!

"Teecie," I said, "you have one friend, at any rate, even if he be not a very grand one."

She gave one of her quaint expressive little nods. Translated, it meant: "I understand all that, but I cannot talk just now." By-and-by, however, she brightened up, and went to the table to claim her share of tea and thick bread-and-butter, and I began to mend a bow belonging to Tom. Tom was one of the leaders of the unruly tribes, a regular savage chieftain.

Ere two days more had passed I felt strongly inclined to exercise the horsewhip on this young gentleman's shoulders. Tom, one

fine morning, was seized with an impish inspiration to play a
trick upon Teecie. Stealing her crutches, he walked about the
nursery mimicking her poor little limp, and then marching off
with them, heedless of her entreaties to have them restored,
carried them in triumph out of doors, and smashed them in pieces
with a hatchet. Teecie sat helpless in the din and riot of that
ill-conditioned nursery. Bright bracing days came and found her
a prisoner, looking with longing eyes through the window-panes,
out over the beautiful country lanes. Tom saw her patience with
the most audacious indifference. But why talk about Tom? I
could not help believing, nor do I ever intend to help believing,
that older heads than Tom's plotted the cruel caging of that
bonnie bird.

The bird drooped on its perch; but who cared? Nurse vowed
it was a shame, and showed more kindness than usual to the
prisoner, but I will not venture to decide how much of this tenderness was owing to the odd crown-pieces which found their way
from my hand to hers—all out of the guinea, of course? O yes,
all out of the guinea. And there was another friend who sometimes expressed an interest in Teecie Ray's existence. This was
that Lady Thornton, whose bounty had indirectly furnished me
with pocket-money during my stay at Rutland Hall. The favour
of this old lady I had done my best to win. She was a nice comfortable old lady, and I liked her. It happened that she called
one day during Teecie Ray's imprisonment, to invite the Rutlands
and their visitors, great and small, young and old, to a party to
be given at her house, a few miles distant. I chanced to be alone
in the drawing-room when she arrived, and I seized the opportunity to tell her the story of Teecie's crutches.

"A bad boy!" she said. "A bad, malicious boy! She must
get new crutches before my party."

"Of course she must," I said, very heartily.

The old lady threw back her head, raising her fat chin in a
peculiar sort of way, and looking at me direct through her
spectacles.

"Indeed!" she said. "Pray, young man, what particular interest
do you take in Teecie Ray?"

I smiled. "Oh, Teecie and I are excellent friends," I said.

"Teecie and you!" she repeated. "Pray, are you aware that
Miss Ray is eighteen years of age?"

"Is she indeed? I know nothing about the ages of little girls."

"But Teecie is not a little girl, Mr. Guy Rutland. Teecie **Ray** is a woman, I tell you!"

Teecie Ray a woman! I could not help laughing. What? My little benefactress, my little mother! I am afraid I scandalised Lady Thornton on that occasion by my utter scorn of her proposition. Christina Rutland swept into the room at this crisis, and relieved me in my difficulty. But often afterwards during that day, I laughed when I thought of Lady Thornton's piece of information. Teecie Ray a woman? Preposterous!

One morning, when it wanted but a week of the party, a curious event occurred. The heads of the house met in consultation on the matter, in the library, before breakfast. An extraordinary Thing had arrived from London at Rutland Hall. The Thing was a large wooden case, directed to Teecie Ray. On being eagerly opened, it was found to contain a pair of crutches.

And such a pair of crutches! Light and symmetrical, and fanciful, works of art in their way. Tortoiseshell stems with silver mountings of exquisite workmanship, capped with dainty little cushions of embroidered velvet. Thunder-stricken were the elders of the house. "Who could have done this thing?" was on every lip. Who, indeed? Who outside of Rutland Hall had ever heard of Teecie Ray? These crutches were costly affairs. I knew the conclusion they came to, one and all. They pitched on Sir Harry as the culprit. It was a thorn in their side, and I rubbed my hands in glee.

Having considered the question in their dismay, they decided that Teecie should be kept in ignorance of her mysterious present. It was not fit for her to use, it would fill her mind with absurd ideas. And so, in spite of the arrival of her beautiful new crutches, poor Teecie still sat helpless in the nursery. The wooden case and its contents were hidden away, and no word was spoken of their existence.

I waited a few days to see if the elders would relent, but to no purpose. The bird still pined on its perch. No kindly hand seemed likely to open the cage door and let it fly. There sat Teecie, day after day, in her nursery chair, hemming aprons for nurse, or darning the children's stockings, looking longingly out of the window, and growing pale for want of fresh air. Still never rebelling, never complaining. Meantime the stir of Christmas preparation was agitating all the household, and the children were full of rapture at the prospect of Lady Thornton's Christmas

party. There was great excitement in the nursery about pretty
new dresses, wonderful fussing about ribbons, and muslins, and
fripperies. Teecie alone sat silent in her shabby frock. By-and-by,
her hands were full, bowing up sashes, sewing on tuckers, stitching
rosettes on shoes. She was a nimble little workwoman, and they
kept her busy. Seeing how well a lapful of bright ribbons became
her, I thought it a pity she should not have a gay dress as well as
the rest.

Nobody said, "Teecie, what will you wear?" nor even, "Teecie,
are not you invited too?" No one seemed to expect for a moment
that Teecie could wish to be merry with the rest. How could
she go, she who was lame and had no crutches?

It happened that I had an errand to the nearest town. It was
rather late when, on my return, I called at the best millinery
establishment in the place, and asked for a parcel.

Yes, the parcel was ready. A large flat box. "Would the gentleman like to see the lady's pretty dress?" The box was opened,
and a cloud of some airy fabric shaken out under my eyes. I
cannot, of course, describe it, but it was something white, very
pure and transparent, with something else of pink just blushing
through it. It was very tasteful, I pronounced, trying to look wise.
There was only one fault: "Did it not seem rather long for a
little girl?" I asked, remembering the figure it was to adorn,
with its short skirt just coming to the top of the boots, so well
worn and mended.

"Oh, sir," said the milliner, with dignity, "you said the young
lady was eighteen years of age, and of course we have given
her a flowing skirt!"

It was late in the evening when I reached home. Two merry
carriage-fulls were just departing from the door as I drove up.
A few minutes afterwards, I was in the nursery with the milliner's
parcel in my hands. There sat dear little Cinderella, resting one
flushed cheek on her hand, and contemplating the litter of scraps
of ribbon, fragments of lace, scissors, flowers, and reels of cotton,
which lay scattered around her. She had had a toilsome tiresome
day, and now they had got all they wanted of her, and had left
her to her solitude.

A flash of pleasure sprang to her face when she saw me. "Oh!
I thought you had gone with the rest," she said.

"No," said I, "I have not gone yet, but I am going presently.
I came for you."

"For me!" she echoed in dismay. "You know I could not go. I have no dress, even if I could walk."

"A friend has sent you a dress," I said, "and I will undertake to provide the crutches. Nurse, will you please to take this box, and get Miss Teecie ready as quickly as possible. The carriage is waiting for us at the door."

Teecie flushed very red at first, and I thought she was going to burst out crying, and then she turned pale, and looked frightened. Nurse, to whom I had slipped a munificent Christmas-box, immediately fell into raptures over the pretty dress.

"Come, Teecie," I said, "make haste!" And, trembling between dread and delight, Teecie suffered herself to be carried off to her toilette.

By the time I returned from an exploring expedition, with the wonderful silver-and-tortoise-shell crutches under my arm, Teecie was ready.

Teecie was ready. Those three simple little words mean so much that I feel I must stop and try to translate them into all they are bound to convey. They do not mean that Teecie, the child whom I was wont to call my little benefactress, my little mother, had got on a nice new frock, and was equipped for a juvenile party like other children. But they mean that there, when I came back, stood a beautiful girl by the nursery fire, in a fair sweeping blush-coloured robe. When she turned her head, I saw that the sweet face framed in its childlike curls was the same, but still the old Teecie Ray was gone, and here was (*peccavi* Lady Thornton!) a lovely woman.

We were all three ludicrously amazed at the sudden metamorphose that had taken place. Teecie was too simple not to show that she felt the change in herself, felt it keenly, with a strange delight and a strange shyness. Nurse had so long been accustomed to use her as a child that she stood bewildered. As for me, I was first frightened at what I had done, then enchanted, then foolishly awkward, and almost as shy as Teecie herself.

When I presented the crutches, nurse looked at me as though I must be some prince in disguise, out of the Arabian Nights. It was with a curious feeling that I saw Teecie try them, not limping now, rather gliding over the nursery floor, with the little velvet cushions hidden away amidst clouds of lace and muslin under her round white shoulders, and the airy masses of the fresh tinted gown just crushed back a little by the gleaming silver

x

staves. I don't know why it was that I thought at that moment, with a certain rapture, of a guinea in a little bon-bon box, that lay below in the one shabby portmanteau which I had thought proper to bring with me to Rutland Hall!

Our equipage awaited us. It was too late now to withdraw from what I had undertaken. Teecie and I were soon dashing over the snowy roads to Lady Thornton's. I will not attempt to describe the remainder of that memorable evening, or the sensation caused by our arrival; the wonder and mortification of my kind relations; or the mingled pleasure and displeasure of the hostess, who, while delighted to see her little favourite, took occasion to whisper angrily in my ear, "And pray, sir, how is all this to end?"

The scene was all new and delightful to Teecie, but her dread of Mrs. Rutland's portentous frown would not let her enjoy it. We both felt that a storm would burst over our heads that night, and we were not wrong. None of the family from Rutland Hall took the least notice of us. When the time came for going home, they went off in their two carriages, and Teecie and I drove home as we had come. When we arrived, we found Cousin George and his wife waiting for us in the library, armed to the teeth. I saw it was to be war and no quarter. Mrs. Rutland took Teecie into her clutches, and carried her off, and I was left with George. I need not repeat all that passed between us.

"Sir," he said, "we have suffered your insolent intrusion long enough. You leave this house to-morrow morning."

"Cousin George," I said, "don't put yourself in a passion. I will go to-morrow morning, but upon one condition—that Teecie Ray may come with me, if she will."

He looked at me perfectly aghast. "Do you know," he said, "that she is a penniless friendless orphan, whom I have sheltered through charity?"

"I want to make her my wife," I said, sternly, "if, indeed, I be so fortunate as to have won her affections."

"And after that," he said, with a sneer "how do you propose to live? Upon air, or your friends?"

"Not upon you, George Rutland," I said, looking him steadily in the eyes. "Mark me. I have tried you out. I have sifted you, all in this house, like a handful of wheat. I found you all chaff, but the one golden grain which lies on my palm. I will keep it and treasure it, if I may. God grant I may!"

"Very fine," said George, "*very* fine. Remember, however, that from this moment I wash my hands of you both: you, Guy Rutland, and her, Teecie Ray."

"Amen!" I said, and bade him good night, and turned on my heel and left him.

Early next morning I knocked at the nursery door, and begged of nurse to awake Miss Teecie, and ask her to speak with me in the garden. I then went out to wait for her. It was Christmas morning, the day of peace and good will. What I felt was scarcely peace, as I looked over the calm landscape. And yet I bore no ill will to any man or woman.

Teecie came to me by-and-by; just the same old Teecie, limping over the frosty path in her short shabby frock, and looking half ashamed of her grand new crutches. I felt relieved when I saw her so. I was shy of the dainty lady whom I had called into existence the night before. And yet when I looked more closely, I knew that this was not quite the old Teecie, and that the very same Teecie of a day ago never, never, could come back. Something was altered. Whether the change was in her or me, or in both of us, I did not inquire. The change was not an unpleasant one.

We strolled out of the garden, and into the lane, and we talked earnestly all the way. On our way back I said:

"And you're not afraid of starving with me, Teecie? You'll take the risk?"

One of her old nods was Teecie's answer.

"Go and fetch your hat, then," said I, "and we won't even wait for breakfast. Don't bring anything else with you, not a shred. I have still some halfpence left—out of the guinea, you know—and we'll get all we want."

Teecie fetched her hat and returned, and we set off together. An hour afterwards we were man and wife. We said our prayers side by side in the church, and then we walked back to Rutland Hall, to say good-by to our kinsfolk. I believe they all thought me mad, and her a little fool;—at least until Cousine George received the cheque, which I sent him next day; a cheque to cover the expenses incurred by him through his charity to Teecie Ray. Then they began to wonder, and to waver. I took my wife abroad, and showed her the world. Time and care cured her of her lameness. It was not surprising that on her return to England her kinsfolk should scarcely recognise her—Teecie Rutland, née

Ray—walking without crutches, and the wife of a millionnaire! Half a bride-cake conciliated Lady Thornton, and the wonderful guinea is still in my possession. I call it Teecie's dower. The crutches, the donor of which I beg to assure you, major, was *not* Sir Harry, are also preserved as family curiosities.

IV

ANOTHER PAST LODGER RELATES WHAT LOT HE DREW
AT GLUMPER HOUSE

I F the dietary at Doctor Glumper's could not be pronounced purely Spartan in its principles, it was simply that the Spartan stomach—well disciplined as we know it to have been—would have revolted at such treatment. Salamis demanded other stamina than could be supplied by the washings of a beef-bone. Xerxes was not deified under the immediate inspiration of rice-dumpling.

Doctor Glumper's was not much worse, in its commissariat, my dear Major Jackman, than hundreds of other establishments, at which—in those days—the sons of gentlemen studied and starved. There was enough to live upon, provided we could have fairly eaten what there *was*. Therein lay the difficulty. Our meals, bad enough at the beginning of the week, grew gradually worse towards the end : insomuch that we arrived at the Sabbath, much in the condition of a band of young seafarers, who had been cast away, and were only saved from utter starvation by the opportune arrival of a ship freighted with roast-beef and York-shire pudding.

True, there was a life-boat. It's name, in our case, was "Hannah's Basket." Hannah was the laundress, and, on Saturday afternoon, after delivering the linen, regularly made her appearance in the playground, displaying the bottom of her buck-basket paved with delicacies, carefully selected on the principle of combining the three grand qualities of sweetness, stickiness, and economy.

Elegance and refinement were little thought of, in those days. The boy who brought a silver fork would have been simply regarded as possessed of a jocular turn. As for the spoon and six towels, which, according the the printed terms of Glumper House, seemed absolutely essential to a sound classical education—the spoon found its way into a species of armoury of Mrs. Glumper's, formed of the spoils of the young Philistines, her pupils, prohibited toys, confiscated literature, and so forth; while the towels, absorbed in the general republic of that article, passed into indiscriminate use. Well, we had nothing to say against steel forks. The meat, peradventure, might have proved impervious to any less undaunted metal.

Our Monday's dinner was boiled leg of mutton. One helping. More was not refused; but the ill-concealed impatience with which the application was received, established the custom of contenting ourselves with what was first supplied. The due reward of this pusillanimity appeared on the following day, in the form of half-consumed joints—cold, ghastly, seamed with red murderous streaks, and accompanied by certain masses of ill-washed cabbage, interesting as an entomological study; but, as a viand, repulsive by reason of the caterpillars, whose sodden dull-green corpses I have seen lying in ranks beside the plates of fastidious feeders.

Three days a week, we had rice-pudding—a confection which, by an unfortunate conjuncture of circumstances, I never could from infancy endure; but the great trial of our lives, and stomachs, was reserved for Saturday, when we sat down to what was satirically styled a "beef-steak-pie."

Mean and debased must be the spirit of that bullock who would confess to any share in such a production! Into the composition of that dish beef entered as largely as the flesh of the unicorn into peas-porridge. The very wildness of the rumours that were afloat respecting its actual origin proved how dark, difficult, and mysterious was the inquiry. School tradition pointed to the most grotesque and inharmonious elements, as actually detected in the pie. Substances, in texture, flavour, and appearance, the reverse of bovine, had been over and over again deposed to by the dismayed recipients, who proved their good faith by preferring famine itself to "beef-steak-pie". The utter impossibility of identifying the ingredients, as having pertained to any animal recognised by British cooks, was the terrific feature of the case.

Whatever was the prevailing element of the pie, it was supplemented with minor matters, about which, though they do not appear in any accepted recipe for the dish in question, there could be no dispute.

Sholto Shillito, for instance, who had the appetite of an ogre, boldly swallowed the portion assigned him, but quietly and sternly removed to the side of his plate three fingers and a ligament of the thumb of an ancient dog-skin glove.

Billy Duntze discovered and secreted something that was for several halves preserved in the school as the leg of a flamingo. At all events, it was introduced, so labelled, to every new arrival, on the very first evening of his sojourn among us.

George van Kempen found a pair of snuffers.

Charley Brooksbank remarked a singular protuberance in his portion of pie, and, carefully excavating the same, as if it were a Phœnician relic, brought to light something that looked like the head of a doll that had been afflicted with hydrocephalus. On being cut into, it was green. For the first few weeks of each half— that is, while our pocket-money held out—we got on pretty well. Our pocket-money exhausted, starvation stared us in the face.

The present generation may wonder why we did not try the effect of respectful remonstrance. The times, as I have said, were different then, and besides, the present generation didn't personally know Mrs. Glumper. A fearful woman was Mrs. Glumper. I don't mean that she raved, struck, or demeaned herself in any way not ordinarily witnessed in polite society; but I do mean that she had a cool quiet scorn, a consciousness of a putting-down power, as though an elephant, just tickling the ground with a foot as big as a writing-table, were to show how easily and effectually he might, if he pleased, turn that table upon *you*.

In addition to this overbearing contempt, Mrs. Glumper had a thousand ways of making us uncomfortable, without resorting to overt tyranny; insomuch that to be "out of favour" with that excellent lady was regarded as the climax of school misery.

Not a word have I to say against the doctor. Even *then* I felt him to be a good man. In remembering his character, I believe him to have been one of the best that ever breathed. With the understanding of a sage, he was as simple as a child; *so* simple, that it was matter of genuine astonishment that he retained the coat upon his back; *so* simple, that the circumstances of his having espoused Mrs. G. became almost intelligible. For this guileless act, rumour even supplied the motive. Mrs. Glumper, then Miss

Kittiewinkle, was herself the mistress of an extremely preparatory school, and it was in the cowed and miserable victims of her Muscovite rule that the kind doctor read an invitation of the most pressing kind, to take the mistress under *his*. The consequence of this union of interests was, that the establishment, losing its infantine character, flourished up into a school of seventy boys : only the very smallest of whom were submitted to Mrs. Glumper's immediate dominion.

Affairs were in this unsatisfactory position towards the middle of a certain half. It was precisely the period at which the greatest impecuniosity usually prevailed. Money was tighter than any one could recollect. Hannah's breadstuffs were in a condition of blockade. Could "shirtings" have been exchanged for eatings, Hannah might have done a brisk business in turn-downs, but the old lady was too wary for such traffic.

We held a consultation. The doctor's cow, which sometimes grazed in the playing-field, was incidentally present, and by her sleek contented aspect, excited universal disgust.

"Crib her oilcake !" squeaked a voice from the outer senatorial circle.

"It is well for the honourable felon on the back benches," remarked our president, Jack Rogers, who delighted to give to our consultations the aspect of a grave debate, "that his skull is beyond punching-distance. If the oil cake, lavished on yonder pampered animal, had been vested in trustees, to the sole and separate use, notwithstanding coverture, of *Mrs.* Glumper—I— well, I will go so far as to say this council might have taken into consideration what has fallen from the distinguished thief. But it's Glumper's, and the proposal of the estimable criminal will be received with the contempt it deserves."

A murmur of approval greeted this speech, after which sundry suggestions were offered.

Burned pens (Gus Halfacre remarked) were edible. He *might* say, toothsome.

"My left boot is at the service of the commonwealth," said Frank Lightfoot. "The right, having been recently repaired and thickened, and being devoid of a large nail in the sole (of which I invite the state to take heed), I reserve to myself for the last extremity."

"Thus extremes *will* meet," observed the president. "But this is no reason for jesting. Has anybody anything to propose ?"

"We have always Murrell Robinson," said Sholto Shillito, gloomily, and with an aspect so wolfish, that the young gentleman alluded to—a plump rosy child of eight, who had not yet had time to dwindle—set up a howl of terror.

"It might—humph—yes, it might be politic," said the chairman, thoughtfully. " 'Twould touch her home. If Jezebel Glumper lost a couple, say, of pupils, under the peculiar circumstances glanced at by the honourable senator in the inky corduroys, she might have some—shall I say bowels?—for those of the remainder. But the observation of my honourable friend has suggested to my mind a course of action which, though in some respects similar, and promising the like results, is not open to the same objections. Some fellow must *bolt*, placing on record his reasons for that step."

Jack's proposal, unexpected as it was, met with considerable favour, the only difficulty being to decide who the fugitive should be. Bolting from school by no means implied return to the paternal mansion. Everybody looked inquiringly at his neighbour. No one volunteered.

The chairman surveyed us with mournful severity.

"There was once," he faltered, "an individual, known to you all (except the fifth class)—wept over by some—who, on learning that he might greatly benefit certain public property by jumping into a hole, asked no questions, popped in, and did it. Has our school no Curtius? Must seventy stomachs languish unsatisfied for want of a single heart? Shillito, you greedy young beggar, *you* will go."

Mr. Shillito emphatically invoked benediction on himself, in the event of his doing anything of the kind.

"Percy Pobjoy," said the president, "you are one at odds with fortune. You are penniless—worse, for your week's pay, old chap, is impounded for a month. You have sailed into the extreme north of Mrs. Glumper's favour, and are likely to make it your persistent abode. You detest rice. You have scruples concerning caterpillars. Percival, my friend, three ladies of eminence, whose names and office are fully recorded in your classical dictionary, unanimously select *you* as the party to perform this public service."

Mr. Pobjoy regretted to run counter to the anticipations of *any* lady, but, possessing, as he did, a grandmother who would, he conceived, prove more than a match for the three Destinies—

and he would throw the Furies in—he must deny himself the gratification proposed.

"Then," resumed the president, cheerfully, with the air of having at last secured his man, "I at once address myself to the distinguished senator on the inverted flower-pot. He who licked that bully, the miller's boy, in twelve minutes and a half, will be again our champion. Joles will go."

Mr. Joles somewhat sullenly failed to perceive the analogy between pitching into a cheeky clown, and running away from school. Could the honourable president detect the smallest indication of verdure in his (Mr. J.'s) sinister organ of vision? Such a contingency was, nevertheless, essential to his (Mr. J.'s) adopting the course required of him.

Other honourable senators having, when appealed to, returned answers of a no less discouraging character, there seemed to be but one course remaining—that of drawing lots. A resolution to do this was carried, after some discussion : it being agreed that he on whom the lot might fall should decamp on the morrow, and, having found some secure hiding-place, write to one of his schoolmates, or (perhaps preferably) to his own friends, declaring that the step he had taken was prompted by a reluctance to perish of starvation.

The proposed time was subsequently extended to one week, in order that he who drew the fatal lot might have time to try the effect of a touching appeal to his parents or friends, fairly setting forth the treatment we were experiencing. If this answered, well and good. If not, the honourable gentleman (said our chief) "will cut his lucky this day se'nnight."

Lots were then solemnly drawn, in the primitive Homeric fashion, every boy's name—those of the fifth class excepted—being inscribed in a slip of paper, and flung into a hat. There was a strong feeling in favour of exempting Jack Rogers, our president —the Nestor of the school—who, being near seventeen, and about to leave, would, no doubt, have preferred fighting through the remainder of his term, famish as he might. But the good fellow flounced at the idea, as though it had been an insult, and himself cast in his name.

Carefully following our classic model, the hat was then violently shaken. The lot that, in obedience to a fillip from the Fates, first leaped out and touched the earth, was to decide the question. *Two* flew out, but one of these rested on the shaker's sleeve. There was a decided disinclination to take up the other. It seemed as if nobody had, until this supreme crisis, fully realised the consequences that might ensue from thus abandoning at once both school and home.

My heart, I confess, stood still for a moment, as Jack Rogers stood forward and picked up the paper. Then I felt the blood mount to my cheeks, as our leader slowly read, "Charles Stuart Trelawny."

"Always in luck, Charley!" he continued, laughing; but I think Jack only intended to keep up my spirits. "Write directly, my boy," he added, in a graver tone, "and, take my advice, write bang up to the governor. Treat it as a matter of business. Mamma is safe to put in *her* word."

I wrote at once:

"My dear Papa,—I hope you are quite well. I ain't. You know I'm not greedy, and not so foolish as to expect at school such jolly things as at home. So you must not be angry when I say what I'm *obliged* to say, that we can't eat what Mrs. Glumper says is dinner; and as there's nothing else but slop and a bit of bread, everybody's starving.

"I remain, your dutiful Son,

"C. S. TRELAWNY.

"P.S. If you don't like to speak to Mrs. Glumper, would you mind asking mamma and Agnes, with my love, to send me a big loaf of bread (with Crust, and, if possible, browned) that might last a week?

"Lieut.-Gen. Trelawny, C.B., K.H.,

Penrhyn Court."

I thought this despatch sufficiently businesslike, and waited with some anxiety for the result. If papa only knew what depended on his decision! He *ought* to put faith in me, for I had never been untruthful, and had done myself no more than justice in reminding him that I was no glutton.

It was, I believe, on the fourth day of suspense that a large parcel was brought into the playground, a crowd of curious and expectant youths escorting it, and witnessing its delivery. Small blame to them!

There resided within the limits of that parcel—for, though mighty, it *had* its limits—first, a beef-steak-pie, not only composed of real beef, but enriched with eggs and minor excellences, all trembling in a jellied gravy of surpassing savour. There was, secondly, a chosen company of mince-pies, clinging together from sheer richness, in such wise that a very stoic, if hungry, might be reluctant to "sever such sweet friends," and devour them two at a time.

There was revealed, in the third place, a large apple turnover : so called, I should surmise, because a boy might turn it over and over, and back again, and, after all, find himself unable to determine which looked the more enticing—the sugary, or the buttery side. And, finally, there was a cake, which I can scarcely repent having characterised, at the moment, as 'tremendous!'"

There was no letter, but the augury seemed good. Such ambassadors as pies and turnovers speak with tongues of their own. It was *not* intended that we should perish. We should see the effect of my manly and business-like appeal, perhaps that very day, in an improved bill of fare, and a diminution of caterpillars. As to husbanding our new supplies, such an idea never occurred to any one. Alas, that we could not *all* partake! Lots had to be once more drawn, a lucky party of eighteen, with Jack Rogers and myself, honorary, made extremely short work of the parcel.

Shade follows sunshine. There was no amelioration of the accustomed fare at dinner; but a decided cloud on Mrs. Glumper's haughty brow was interpreted favourably by Jack—a close observer of human nature—as evincing her disgust at the costly reform to which she saw herself committed.

Alas! for once, our leader was wrong. Not that day, nor the following day, nor any other day, so long as that establishment survived, was there any departure from the time-(dis)honoured rules of diet.

It was long before I came into possession of the state papers actually exchanged on this occasion. Premising that my father, busied with his other letters, had handed over mine to my mother, saying, "Do see to this, my dear," here they are :

The Lady Caroline Trelawny to Mrs. Glumper.

"Dear Mrs. Glumper,—I trust that the size of the parcel I forward to my boy, will not alarm you. Charley is growing very rapidly, so rapidly, indeed, that his father drew my attention to

the circumstance, not without some misgiving that he might out-
grow his strength. You may smile at the anxiety that prompts me
to remind one so experienced as yourself in the care of youth,
that good, clean, and sufficient food is more than ever necessary
to my tall boy. He is not a dainty boy, and the conditions I
have mentioned will, I am sure, meet all that he, or I, on his
behalf, could desire. With compliments to Dr. Glumper, I am,
dear Mrs. Glumper, sincerely yours,

"Caroline M. Trelawny."

Mrs. Glumper to the Lady Caroline Trelawny.

"Dear Madam,—Perhaps the most satisfactory answer I can
make to your obliging note will be conveyed in the assurance
that Dr. Glumper, myself, our family, and the masters (except
Monsieur Legourmet, who insists on providing his own meals),
live invariably with, and as, our boys; and that, in the matter of
food, there is neither stint nor compulsion.

"Respectfully yours,

"Jezebel Glumper."

There was, unfortunately, just sufficient colouring of truth in
this to satisfy the consciences of both ladies. They *did* dine, or
rather sit down, with us, and being helped first to the tit-bits, accompanied with hot gravy and et cæteras, at their own cross-table,
got on pretty well. As for the good old doctor, he was the most
innocent of accomplices in promoting our starvation. He simply
did as his wife decreed, caring nothing for himself, and would
have starved with his boys without a murmur.

After it became apparent that our move had failed, all, before
the arrival of the fatal day, passed with me like a curious dream.
I felt as if I no longer belonged to the school, hardly to myself,
and though no verbal reference was made to my impending disappearance, I saw that no one had forgotten it. Significant were
the facts, that Percy Pobjoy, who had owed me eightpence from
time immemorial, borrowed that sum to repay me; and that
another chap, with whom I had had a row, spontaneously asked
my pardon.

Saturday—*the* day—appeared in due course. There remained
but one more meal, one more chance for Mrs. Glumper and for
me.

"If she gives us but a commonly decent feed to-day," muttered

Jack Rogers, pinching my elbow, as we went in, "by Jove, Charley, my boy, we'll stop *your* nefarious plans!"

No such chance. There it was, the flabby mass of rice, helped first, as a good appetite-choking stuff, to relieve the succeeding dish from any undue pressure.

After rice appeared the much-dreaded pie, glaring yellowly, with its course pretentious outside—prototype of many a living humbug—veiling one knows not what of false and vile. O, the contrast to the rich and delicate article—alike only in name— sent by my mother!

The pie was served, and was undergoing the usual suspicious scrutiny, when Mrs. Glumper, with the voice of a herald, proclaimed:

"Master Trelawny will eat every grain of that rice before he receives anything further."

There was a half-audible titter; but I remained firm, and thus ended the last "dinner" at Glumper House.

Jack Rogers put his arm in mine.

"I'm sorry for this, Trelawny," he said.

"I'm *not*," said I, trying to smile, "exc—except for——" I thought of my mother, and broke down.

"We'll have a Palaver, at all events," said Jack.

In a moment, a large concourse assembled under our favourite elm. If the truth must out, I could have dispensed with this ceremony, which somehow imparted a sensation of being present at one's own burial. But Jack Rogers was not to be denied this splendid opportunity of speech-making.

He did speak, in a manner, and at a length, that must have been remembered in the school long after I—its theme—was forgotten there. In his peroration, he observed that the honour and the well-being of Glumper's could not, in this extremity, have been confided to worthier hands. Nor was it this community alone that was to profit by the important step about to be taken. The eyes of every school in Europe were, or would be, if they knew what was going on, fixed on Glumper House. Mr. Trelawny was about to place his foot on the first rung of the ladder of affluence, fame, and power. What pecuniary means, he would frankly ask, were at my disposal?

I replied, with the like openness, "Eightpence."

"The precise amount," resumed Jack, triumphantly, "(within one and tenpence) from whence colossal fortunes spring! 'He

began his immortal career with half-a-crown.' Or, 'The origin.
of this eminent citizen was of the humblest; he commenced life
with two-and-sixpence.' Or, 'Our modern Crœsus began the
battle of life with the moiety of a five-shilling piece. He died worth
TWO MILLIONS sterling!' Such, are among our most familiar
passages in biography. Charles, my boy, again you are in luck."
And he shook my hand warmly.

I ventured incidentally to suggest that I was *not* in possession
of the magical amount required.

"Nay, by George, but you shall be!" exclaimed Jack. "Here's
sixpence towards it. Think of it when you're a confoundedly
crusty old millionaire, and send old Jack a haunch from one of
your deer-parks—the Scotch one. Who'll subscribe to the Trelawny Testimonial?"

Hard up as the good chaps were, so many came forward, that
a sum of about nine-and-sixpence was poured into the hands of
our chief. But Jack's remark had been working strangely in my
mind. Something admonished me to keep strictly to the rule which
had, apparently, prospered so well.

In a few words I thanked my mates, therefore, for their kind
intentions, but declined to take more than was required to make
up the exact fortune-making sum. I would do nothing (I added,
in substance) to risk a failure, nor impair the innate vigour, the
youthful freshness, of half-a-crown, by dabbling with an adoles-
cent amount like ten-and-twopence : a sum entirely unassociated
with any of those encouraging biographies quoted by our president. I would take my half-crown—no more.

As the day was waning, it became necessary to make preparations for my departure. Accordingly, attended by a few faithful
friends, I proceeded to make up a small bundle, such as I could
conveniently carry, leaving the remainder of my possessions at
the disposal of fate. There was one thing I was very loath to
abandon. It was a flower-pot, containing the commencement of
a very promising scarlet-runner. It had been the source of great
interest and consolation. I half resolved to make it the sharer of
my fortunes. But Jack Rogers objected. In vain he taxed his
memory to recal any one instance in which the successful adven-
turer had flung himself upon the world with half-a-crown *and* a
scarlet-runner. If the case of Jack and the Beanstalk were relied
upon, he (Rogers) would only remark that the present age of

inquiry had succeeded in throwing very considerable doubt upon portions of that narrative. This was enough.

About escaping, there was no difficulty. Part of the playing-field was out of sight of the house, and, although it was penal to frequent this portion, and it was the duty of the monitor of the day to report any one so doing, on the present occasion the monitor in person gave me a leg up the wall. There was a last shaking of hands, and a suppressed cheer, when I paused for a moment on the top.

"You'll write that letter to-morrow, then, from—from some-where?" said Jack, mysteriously. (I nodded.) "All right, old boy?"

"Ye-es," I responded. "All right, you know. Hoor——"

Down I dropped——adrift!

That wall seemed to make all the difference. I don't think that, until my feet alighted on the alien ground of Mr. Turfitt's brick-field, I had fully realised the fact of running away. But a runaway I was now; and, to do my boyish courage justice, no thought of returning or seeking the protection of home, ever entered into my imagination. One brief and bitter pang I did experience, as I thought of the probable effect the tidings of my flight might have upon the happy home circle; but I met it with the reflection that the letter I should write must set them at ease as to my personal safety and prospects. In the mean time, it was obviously desirable to get away.

Dr. Glumper's was situated in an open suburb north of London, and therefore, well on the high road to fortune. I set my face straight towards the quarter in which I concluded the City to lie, and trudged on, vaguely wondering what would happen to me when bedtime came.

Suddenly, a bright thought, suggested by the name on a public-house sign, shot across my mind. I had a friend—Philip Con-canen—who resided at Chelsea, nothing of a walk, five miles. Phil had long outgrown Glumper's, though his name and his fame and a very rudely-executed minature of Mrs. G., carved on the inside of his whilom desk, still survived. He was a middle-aged man now—going on, I should think, for nineteen—and had called once at Glumper's in a gig, driving himself. I had been a favourite of Phil's, and felt convinced that he would not only afford me his counsel, but keep *mine*. Well over the first steps of my pilgrimage, I had no fears about the remainder.

Philip was already in business with his father and uncle—wealthy brewers and distillers—whose establishment displayed on its river-face a frontage so imposing as almost to justify the tradition that it had once been mistaken for Chelsea Hospital. On the land side, you merely dived down a dark and narrow lane, sole shaft to the gold mine that lay beyond. Down this passage, as evening fell, I groped my way, and, by great good luck, found Philip in sole command (till Monday morning) of "Concanen Brothers, and Concanen."

Philip gave me a cordial welcome, and, thanks to his old housekeeper, a most heart-reviving supper, and listened to my story with all the kindness and interest I had expected; also with a degree of gravity I had *not* expected. Intercourse with men and vats had already taken off the edge of his romance. There is, in beer, a decided tendency to sap the life of sentiment. In meal, I have since observed, a contrary rule prevails. Your miller's daughter—if he has one—is almost always a heroine.

My friend criticised with some severity the golden visions of Jack Rogers, repudiated belief in the efficacy of half-a-crown as the especial keystone of affluence, and even hinted (though remotely) at the desirability of my making terms with the home authorities, and abandoning my enterprise.

On this point, however, I was firmness itself, and after a lengthened discussion the following convention was agreed to :

That the old housekeeper, Mrs. Swigsby, should be admitted to our complete confidence, with a view to my occupancy of the spare bedroom till Monday. That on that day I should transfer my quarters to Philip's own private smoko-harness room, from whence a side portal and a passage, dark at noon, gave upon Paradise-alley, and thence to the privacy of Jew's-road. That I should retain such refuge until I had enjoyed an opportunity of "feeling my way"—which, indeed, would necessarily occur whenever I crossed the threshold. That on the slightest suspicion of my whereabout becoming known, I should depart, so as to avoid compromising my friend. Lastly, that I should at once write to my parents an assurance of my personal safety.

With some difficulty—owing to Mrs. Swigsby's being a deafer creature than I could have conceived possible—that excellent lady was indoctrinated in the matter, and dismissing from her mind a first idea that I was the nephew of Mr. Arthur Thistlewood, and deeply compromised in certain, then recent, proceedings in Cato-street, promised every assistance. This arranged, I sat down to my letter :

"My dear Papa and Mama,—I hope you are quite well. We ate up the Pie and other Things you so kindly sent, and then began Starving again. Rice, and Catterpillars, and what they call Beefstake-Pie but Isn't, *as usual.* I hoped you would have written to Mrs. Glumper, but perhaps you were Afrade. We held a Counsel, and Settled to run away One by One—till the Dinners get better. We drew Lots, and it Fell to me. I knew you would Approve, for I heard you once say, about Captain Shurker, that it wasn't honourable to Back Out. I have my Second-best suit, some linen, my Bible, and Latin Delectus, and a Sum of Money which is the Beginning of a Fortune. I know what I am Doing—that is, I shall To-morrow—so I hope you won't be angry and kiss Mama and my love to Agnes and I am your Affectionate Dutiful Son,

"C. S. TRELAWNY."

Early on Monday morning, Phil introduced me to my new quarters in the smoko-harness room, where we found Mrs. Swigsby engaged in constructing what she called a "trumpery" bed. From the good lady's demeanour, I could not help fancying that she even now harboured some misgivings concerning me, for she glanced at me now and then as if she expected me to go off like a grenade. It was useless, however, to attempt to enlighten her further. Phil confessed as much, and owned that we must take our chance.

He introduced me to the dark passage and private entrance, and presenting me with the key, took his leave, assuring me that no one would enter the apartment until evening, when he would himself bring me supper, bear me company at that meal, and hear how I had felt my way.

When, a few minutes later, I turned into Jew's-road, the sensation of not belonging to myself came back rather strongly, bringing with it a brother sensation, still less soothing—that of not, for the moment, belonging to anybody else! Nevertheless, I held up my head, and marched on as confidently as if I expected an influential friend to meet me by appointment at the next corner.

How—*how* did people begin? Usually, I thought, with some happy incident. Would any obliging infant, of high birth, do me the favour to be nearly run over? Any stout gentleman—victim

Y

to casual orange-peel—trip and be picked up by me? Any hurrying man of commerce let fall a book containing securities of in-
estimable value, close to my feet? No; most of these things had
had their turn. Fortune scorns to repeat herself. I had a conviction
that I must begin at the foot of the ladder. "He" (some great
man) "once swept a barber's shop," was a legend of my childhood. Where was such a barber?

"Wanted, a Lad."

It came like an answer. Were these characters *real*? If so,
Fortune—though she writes an indifferent hand—has not deserted me. *I* am a lad. And wanted. Behold me!

I entered the establishment. It wasn't a barber's. Greasier.
Pigs' toes, I imagine, prevailed.

"What can I do for *you*, young gentleman?" inquired the
stout white-aproned proprietor, brandishing an immense knife.

"Please, do you want a lad?" I asked.

The man looked at me from head to foot. Then he said:

"We *did*, but unfortnetly we only takes six parlour-boarders
at a time; and the Markiss o' Queerfinch has just grabbed the
last wacancy for his seventeenth son."

"I—I want to be a lad, sir," I faltered.

"Lookee here, young gentleman; if you don't want none of
my trotters, use your own, or you'll get *me* into a scrape as well
as yourself. Now, off with you!"

Twice more, tempted by similar announcements, I ventured
to prefer my claims, but with no better success. One glance at
my exterior seemed to satisfy everybody that I was not the lad
for *them*. Yes, I was too smart! The recent runaway was visible
in my still glossy blue jacket and gilt buttons; not to mention
the snowy turn-down. I was not sorry when evening came, that
I might return home, and recount my adventures to the sympathising Phil.

Philip agreed that I was *not*, perhaps, exactly the sort of
messenger a struggling tripe-seller would select, but suggested that
I might fly at higher game. Why not feel my way among classes
to whom a gentlemanly appearance and manner did *not* form an
insuperable objection?

Why not, indeed? Time was precious. Mrs. Swigsby's misgivings were evidently on the increase. I would do it to-morrow.

"Right, my boy," said Phil, as he bade me good night.
"Straight, now, to the fountain head, you know."

I *didn't* exactly know. Feeling one's way, and going to the fountain head—though admirable as general principles—were, not so easy of application. Where *was* the fountain head?

"In your great banking and commercial firms," Phil had said, over our wine; "always deal with Principals."

My friend evidently assumed that I should seek out parties of this description. Accordingly, selecting from the Directory the names of a very eminent City banking firm, I "felt my way" towards their distant domicile, and found myself in the presence of about fifty clerks—all busily employed. After standing for some time unnoticed, I approached one of the desks.

"Please, sir, I want your head."

"My *what*?" inquired the clerk, with considerable energy. "What do you want with my head?"

I explained that I meant his Principal; the head of the firm: whereupon the clerk smiled languidly.

"Mr. Ingott's down at Goldborough Park," he said, "but if it's anything about the Turkish Loan, we'll send an express. He can be here to-morrow."

I assured him it had nothing to do with the Turkish Loan, or any loan, and that any other partner of the house would do as well.

The clerk nodded, whispered to another clerk, and desiring me to follow, led the way through a labyrinth of desks, into an inner room, where sat an old gentleman reading the paper. He looked at me inquiringly through his gold eye-glasses. The clerk whispered—and——

"Well, my young friend?" said the old banker.

"Pl—please, sir," I blurted out, "do you want a confidential lad?"

The clerk tittered; but the old gentleman, with one look, dismissed him, and proceeded:

"Who sent you hither, my boy, and what do you mean?"

His manner was very kind, so I told him at once, that nobody sent me; that, acting upon advice, I was engaged in feeling my way, and wished to begin by being a lad—a *confidential* lad, if possible; that, with that view, I had come straight to the fountain head; that, being, I must confess, at variance with my friends, I could not mention whence I came, but that he might rely upon my honesty; and that I was prepared, if necessary, to deposit in the hands of the firm a certain sum of money, as an indemnification for any losses that might be incurred through my inexperience.

The old gentleman inquired the amount.

"Two-and-sixpence."

I saw his eye twinkle; then, as if a sudden thought had struck him, he put his hand upon my shoulder and turned me to the light.

"Hem—I thought so," I fancied I heard him mutter. Then he added aloud : "See here, my lad. I cannot make so important an engagement on my own responsibility. I must consult my partners in the firm. Sit down in the messenger's room—that door yonder. In half an hour I will give you your answer."

In the messenger's room I found a respectable-looking youth, eating bread-and-cheese. He offered me some, but I could not eat. Kind as the old gentleman's manner was, there was something in it that gave me uneasiness. It almost seemed as if he knew me.

"Who," I asked the messenger, "is that old gentleman who said he must consult his partners?"

"Sir Edward Goldshore—him that lives at Bilton Abbey, near Penrhyn."

"Penrhyn? General Trelawny's?"

"That, sir, is the ticket. The general often lunches here when he's in town. Consult his partners, did the governor say? Why, they're all out of town but *him*!"

"Don't you," I asked, faintly, "think this room of yours rather hot? I'll—take a run—and—and come back before I'm wanted."

Ere the youth could start any objections I had vanished.

That unlucky day was doomed to an unluckier close. Concanen made his appearance in the harness-room with a somewhat harassed face.

"It's a bore, my dear old fellow, but I fear your camp must be broken up. There's no trusting old Swigsby. You must move on, Charley, my boy, and, if you won't go slick home, like a reasonable chap, feel your way in other quarters."

There was, obviously, no alternative. I marched on the following morning. But Phil's good offices did not cease until he had seen me established in a (very humble) lodging not far distant, but in a locality where I could continue to feel my way without much chance of recognition. The rent—five shillings a week—Phil at first insisted on paying; but, on my representation that the acceptance of any money aid might vitiate my entire future, the kind fellow consented to purchase, at full value, such articles of my wardrobe as would supply me with all that was necessary for an entire week, leaving my half-crown still intact.

Thus was I, for the second time, adrift. Fortune kept steadily aloof. Go whither, ask whom, I would, the same suspicious look invariably greeted me. Whether I brushed my jacket neatly, or tore experimental holes in the elbows, it seemed that I could never hit the desired medium between gentility and vagabondism.

I shall not describe at length those miserable days, nor the steady diminution of my hopes and resources, until the middle of the second week found me, with my rent paid, indeed, but destitute of everything save the clothes I stood in, and *sixpence* !

I had given up in despair all search for employment. Go home I would not. Of Phil I had heard nothing, and I feared to compromise him by any overt communication. What was to be done?

One morning, I was prowling feebly about, *very* hungry, and, every now and then, feeling the sixpence in my jacket-pocket, as though the very sight of a cook-shop might have drawn it forth, when I noticed an old Jew seated on the lower steps of a house. He was not a neat or a well-washed Jew. I don't think that I ever in after life beheld a dirtier; but my attention was drawn to him by the demeanour of a potboy, who, in passing, had muttered, "Old chap's sewn up!" and whistled on two fingers, almost over the man's head, a pæan of congratulation upon the circumstance.

The old Jew looked faintly up. The face, though grimy, was not, I thought, ignoble; and, indifferent whither I strolled, I turned to take another look at him. He was very old, very ragged, and, to all appearance, famine-stricken; at least, I never saw hunger written so legibly in any face, except my own. He made a languid motion with his fingers towards me, like a dying creature, but did not beg, and I passed on my way. Suddenly, the thought shot across me, "Should the old man *die* !"

The sixpence seemed to give a spontaneous leap in my pocket, as though inspired with the same idea. Back I went, wavering, for, if I yielded to charitable impulse, what must I myself do? If he would divide it with me—but how ask a dying man for change? I passed him again.

Either my fancy misled me, or the sixpence gave me a discontented punch in the side. "*But*," I answered, as though in remonstrance with it, "you, are the last hope of my fortune; in giving *you*, I part with millions—'two millions'." A last emphatic punch determined me. I turned once more, walked hastily back, and dropped my two millions into the old man's hand!

How I got through the remainder of that day I hardly know. It was about dusk, when, growing every moment more faint and desponding, I turned to crawl homeward. I was pausing unconsciously before a baker's window, when a hand touched my shoulder. It was my Jew. The old man had changed considerably for the better, and now, of the two, looked far the more alive.

"Good rolls those," said the old Jew, approvingly. "Hungry?"

Almost too weary to speak, I nodded.

"And—and—no money?" asked the old man, with curious eagerness.

I shook my head, and prepared to move away.

"I—I spent that sixpence," resumed the Jew, "but if you don't despise a poor man's haunt, I'll give you a supper, and, if you need it, lodging too. My castle is close at hand."

I looked at him with surprise, and followed him. Falling into a sort of mendicant gait, he shuffled feebly on, and, turning into a dark narrow street, composed of very small tenements indeed, paused at one of the nearest, and struck upon the window-sill with his crutch-stick.

"Take hold of my coat when she opens the door," said the old Jew. "You may find it darkish below."

It *was* darkish, insomuch that the "she" who opened to us was invisible in the gloom, but a silver voice, that was not the Jew's, uttered an exclamation of welcome, and died away, like a spirit's, into some upper region, whither we stumbled in pursuit. A candle-end, dimly flickering in the corner, revealed our conductress in the person of a girl of about fifteen, attired in a thick white robe which covered her from neck to foot, and seemed, so far as I might presume to judge, to be her only garment. The large sleeves were turned back to the elbows, as if she had been engaged in household work, and the inaudibility of her movements was accounted for by her feet being bare. A broad white fillet tied back immense masses of dark brown hair. The face! Boy as I was, and a very sleepy and exhausted one—I was roused at once into a state of stupid ecstasy by one glance at her marvellous beauty. "Is it a woman? Is it a woman?" I remember gasping, as it were, to myself. And as she stood, for a few seconds, motionless, her form and dress like sculpture, her white arms extended towards me in questioning surprise, I felt as if it would be no sin to fall at her feet, in adoration of what seemed more of Heaven than earth.

"Supper, Zell," said the old Jew, and darkness fell upon the scene. Zell had vanished.

The rest of that evening was a blank, with passing gleams of Paradise. Fatigue and inanition forced me to sleep, even while striving to eat. But, in those intervals of glory, I was conscious of sitting at a feast, between the Queen of the Fairies, and an exceedingly ragged old Hebrew whom she addressed as grandfather; sensible that the latter (speaking as though I had been absent) told the former a story about me and a sixpence, which seemed to be amusing; aware, finally, that Queen Titania remarked, in a pitying voice :

"The child! He ought to be in bed!" And, without further ceremony, put me there.

My couch was on the floor of that same apartment, and the last thing I remember was Titania's foot, so small, so purely white, so bluely veined, withal so near my lips, that I would have kissed it, if I dared—but went to sleep while thinking of it.

My rest was so profound, that, when I awoke to another day, Zell and her grandfather were finishing breakfast. Both were dressed as on the preceding day; the old man, with his squalid aspect, tattered garments, and rusty shoes, offering a strange contrast to the bewitching creature, fresh and sweet as a dewy moss-rose, who sat beside him. If her beauty had asserted itself in the semi-darkness overnight, the full light of day only confirmed it more. The countenance was unquestionably of the Jewish order, but of the richest tint, the most refined and delicate mould. I lay in a sort of joyful stupor, utterly unable to remove my eyes from the glorious object. If love were ever born at eleven years old, here was the nativity of a passion that could never die. O, angel!—Zell suddenly discovered that I was awake.

After bringing me some tea, she quitted the room, and the old man came and sat down beside me. Having questioned me about my home and friends—to which I candidly replied that I had, at present, none to speak of, being engaged in simply feeling my way—he went on :

"You have been frank with me, my boy. I'll be frank with *you*. Though a very poor, poor man—oh, a *very* poor man—I am not, as you supposed, a beggar. I have means of living, such as they are, but these compel me to be much from home. My granddaughter, my Zell (what fool gave her that name I know not; she is called Zeruiah), has neither relation nor friend. For reasons I cannot now explain, she never quits this house. My heart bleeds at the solitude to which I am forced to condemn her. Stay with us, child, for a while. You shall have board and lodging, it may be some trifle over, when times are good. You can go on messages for Zell, and help her in the house. What say you?"

If the old gentleman had intimated that the reversion of the crown of England awaited my acceptance, my heart would have throbbed with far less exultant joy! *Stay* with her! See her! Serve her! Be her blessed thrall!

What I replied, I know not. I only know that ten minutes later the old gentleman had shuffled forth, and I, washing teacups under the eye of my beautiful mistress, had broken one, and received a box on the ear, delivered without any ceremony whatever. Zell was evidently as impulsive as she was beautiful. Presuming on her immense seniority of four years, the young lady made no more account of me than if I had been a kitten.

The room we sat in, and a little nook above, where Zell slept, were, like herself, scrupulously clean : all the remainder of the mansion being apparently given fairly over to decay and dirt. Our slender meals were prepared in the sitting-room, and provided from a daily sum, of I should think about fourpence-halfpenny, doled out by the lord of the mansion before leaving. My lady would instruct me where and how to invest this capital to the greatest advantage, and, according to my success, reward me on my return with a radiant smile, or a sounding box on the ear.

Mistress Zell seldom making me the recipient of her thoughts and words, it was by slow degrees that I learned the following particulars : That my host, Mr. Moses Jeremiah Abrahams, was a gentleman of habits so penurious, that he might have rivalled, if not eclipsed, the most illustrious misers of the age, had he only possessed anything to hoard. That Zell was dressed as I beheld her, to preclude the possibility of her going forth—to incur expenses—in the public ways. (As, sitting on the ground, while she told me this, I looked up in my lady's glorious eyes, it struck me that the old man might have had a tenderer reason.) That Mr. Abrahams, absent, most days, till dark, was, on certain days, later still. Finally, that I must not be surprised if, on one or more of those days, I heard his signal on the window-sill, but not himself on the stairs. "And *woe* to you!" concluded my lady, threatening me with her little hand, "if you betray our secret!"

"Our!" My heart turned faint, I caught her meaning instantly, and experienced the first burning touch of jealousy. My mistress had a lover.

"What makes you colour so, you stupid foolish boy?" said my lady, half laughing, half angry. "Can we trust you, or can we *not*?"

I stammered some nonsense about being at her command, body and soul. And I have no doubt I meant it.

My devotion was soon tested. That very evening (one of Mr. Abrahams' late ones) a knock, like his, sounded on the window-sill. Zell, bidding me follow, flew down stairs, and, softly opening the window, was clasped in the embrace of an individual to all appearances as ragged and infirm of mien as her grandfather himself.

For a moment she suffered this, then drew back, leaving the visitor her hand, which that monster, whoever he was, seemed to devour with kisses. There ensued a whispered conversation, during which I observed that the speakers referred to me. Then, as if alarmed by a signal from without, the stranger vanished. We returned up-stairs.

Next morning my mistress gave me a note without address. I was to take it to a particular shop, and give it to a particular stranger who would accost me. No particular stranger was there. Afraid to return without fulfilling my mission, I was lingering over some trifling purchase, when a phaeton dashed up to the door, and a gentleman entered the shop. He was very handsome, wore thick black moustaches carefully curled, had long gilt spurs, and looked like an officer. He was well known to the shop-people, for he tossed about a number of articles, laughing and jesting with the mistress, but purchased nothing. Could *this* be my man? I managed, at all events, to let him see what I was carrying. We left the shop together.

"Toss it over! Quick, my lad!" said the gentleman, sharply.

"Take this, and *this*" (he gave me another note, and half-a-crown). "And meet me here to-morrow."

I told him I did not want his money, but would take his note. He looked at me, uttered a long low whistle—expressive, I take it, of astonishment—and drove away.

The joy in my sweet mistress's eyes, and a white hand stroking my curls, even while she read the letter, were a sufficient reward. Then she made me her confidant. Her suitor was Lord John Loveless, son of the proud Earl of St. Buryans, with whom, owing to some little financial misunderstanding, poor Lord John was, for the moment, on terms so far from satisfactory, as to render it improbable that the earl would yield anything like a cordial assent to his son's union with the granddaughter of an impoverished Jew. Hence the necessity for those clandestine interviews, which my mistress atoned for to her conscience, by sternly forbidding her lover ever to cross the threshold.

My lord was at the shop next morning as soon as I.

He took me familiarly by the arm.

"Come and take a pull on the river, boy. I want to have a talk with you."

It was not far to the river. We got a boat, and pulled off, my companion chatting pleasantly enough. At last he said :

"That old governor of yours keeps you pretty short, I take it? What does he do, now, with his money? Do you never hear him counting his guineas? Come !"

I positively denied it, and gave such candid reasons for my conviction that he was all but a pauper, that my companion seemed staggered. He became grave, not to say morose, and the row home seemed to bore him. I did not report to my lady all that had passed between us; I could not have left out his bad spirits when I described to him her poverty, and that might have pained her.

After this, my lord's visits became less frequent, and my mistress's smiles rarer. She moved about with a slower and a sadder step; and sometimes sat with her marble arms crossed on her lap, until I almost doubted if she lived. At which times, I would creep into the field of her eye, if but to change its fixed expression.

A terrible event came to rouse her. The old gentleman was brought home, one night, dying. He had been hustled, knocked down, and robbed, by some miscreants in the street. Though he had sustained no injury that should ordinarily prove mortal, the shock to his system, and, still more, the alleged robbery to which he perpetually referred, combined to give him to the grave. In spite of medical efforts he sank fast, and, at midnight, died.

My mistress, who had never left his side, bore all with a strange patience. I never saw her weep, but her white face and gleaming eyes struck me with awe.

A will, duly executed, was found, in which the old man, in general terms, bequeathed to his granddaughter, Zeruiah Abrahams, everything of which he should die possessed, appointing one Lemuel Samuelson guardian and executor. What money the old man had about him, when robbed, was never known. All the coin in the house amounted to no more than sufficed to pay the medical attendant, while the furniture was probably not worth more than twenty or thirty pounds. Part of this, with the assistance of a neighbour, we sold, to spare the old man a pauper's funeral; the rest, we thought, would provide clothes for Zell (since we must *both* now go out and feel our way), and support us both until we found our way. When this was done, the house looked desolate and wretched enough, and my poor mistress scarcely less so. Though she never spoke of it, the desertion of her lover—of whom in all that distressful time we never heard—cut her to the heart's core.

One day, before her clothes came, as I was moving restlessly about the room, thinking what I could say to comfort her, she suddenly lifted her head:

"Charley, will *you* desert me, too?"

"Zell! '*Desert* you!'" Like a young fool, as I was, I burst into a passion of tears.

"Don't—don't! My dear child—my good ch——!" And, infected by my tears, poor Zell laid her head on the table and wept aloud.

Almost at that moment my eye was caught by an urchin in the street, beckoning eagerly. Stammering some excuse, I ran out.

"Gem' giv' me a bob," said the boy, "fur to say as he's a waitin' at the corner."

At the corner; or, more correctly, *round* it, stood Lord John Loveless.

"Now, my boy," said his lordship, very hurriedly, "I am here at great risk to—to myself, and have only a moment to stay. About your mistress? Is she well? Is she cared for? Did the old fellow *really* die a beggar?"

I replied, that the old gentleman had neither lived nor died a beggar, but that we had no money, and intended to feel our way towards work, as soon as we could go out.

Lord John seemed struck at this, and made an irresolute movement in the direction of the house.

"Won't you come in?" I forced myself to say.

"N—no," was the reply. "I can't. Urgent business elsewhere. See, boy. Give her this. Say I have been absent with my regiment, or I'd have sent before."

And, if ever noble gentleman skulked away, I think Lord John did.

Kneeling at my sweet mistress's feet, I faithfully recounted the interview. Zell listened, without once removing her eyes from mine. Then she said : "Put his—his wretched alms—into a cover, and take it to the address I shall write." All which was duly done.

But, the events of the day were not over. As we sat towards evening, discussing projects for the morrow, a stranger somewhat peremptorily demanded admittance, and, in company with another individual who had apparently been lurking aloof, produced some papers, and declared himself in possession of the house. He was our landlord. Our rent was deeply in arrear. His applications and threats having been alike disregarded by the eccentric Mr. Abrahams, he had taken the necessary steps to resume possession, and now came, inspired with an intense hatred (as he openly declared) for all Jew tenants, to enforce his rights.

It was in vain to remonstrate. We had not one shilling in our possession, and, for furniture, only our beds, chairs, table, and cooking utensils : all which, united, would not have paid half the debt.

"At least, sir," said my mistress, "you will not turn us into the streets, *to-night*?"

"Well!" said the fellow, reluctantly, "hardly *that*. But I'm up to these dodges, *I* promise you. Let you stay, and here you *will* stay. We'll stop that game. Without beds and window-sashes, you'll soon be ready to go. Collect the traps, Bill Bloxam, and look alive."

"It will soon be night, sir," said Zell, pale as a ghost : "a night that promises to be both cold and wet; in charity, leave us the protection of windows."

"Pin up your petticoat," returned the landlord, coolly. "*Here* she goes!"

He roughly tore at the window-sash. Out it came, crashing. But the rotten woodwork at the side, deprived of its support, and yielding as it seemed to some pressure from within, came away also. There was a heavy rushing fall that shook the very house—a rolling, ringing, spinning, settling down! From end to end, the apartment was literally carpeted with *gold*!

"Phsh!" said the reeling landlord, as he wiped the dust from his eyes.

My mistress was the first to recover composure. A watchman, on his way to night-duty, attracted by the crash, stood opposite. She bade me call him in, and, dismissing the now subdued landlord, procured a trusty guardian for the night. My mistress also despatched a special messenger in quest of Mr. Lemuel Samuelson, who, arriving with the dawn, joined us in further investigations.

Two thousand seven hundred guineas had been scattered on the floor. In different parts of the house, generally crammed into chinks and chasms of the decaying woodwork, were bank-notes to the amount of thirty-two thousand pounds. But even *that* was a trifle compared to the crafty old miser's foreign securities, which, disinterred in one lump, represented the immense sum of two hundred and ninety thousand pounds.

"And now, my love," said Mr. Samuelson, when both search and calculation were exhausted, "you will give Mrs. S. and me the pleasure of your company, at my little box at Sydenham, until you decide what *next* to do."

My mistress at once assented. Since the discovery of the treasure, she had had intervals of the deepest melancholy. Was she thinking what *might* have been, had the old man been less reticent? She had hardly addressed a word to me, and, until Mr. Samuelson came obsequiously to hand her to the carriage, I knew not if she would even bid me farewell. At last it was her guardian himself who drew her attention to me, by asking if she had any directions to give the "lad."

"The lad," repeated Zell, abstractedly.

"Call at my office, boy!" said Mr. Samuelson, who seemed impatient to get away. "By-the-by, what's your name?"

I made no answer. I was looking at my mistress.

"Sulky, eh?" said Mr. Samuelson. "Worse for *you*. Come, my love."

"Charley! Charley!" said Zell.

Then I *could* not answer. She waved her hand towards me, but her guardian led her away.

All that day, I sat at the window, as though I had fully expected her to return; but, in reality, I had no such idea. I knew that my darling mistress was gone—for ever, ever, gone—and had taken with her all joy, all happiness, all desire of life. I was conscious of a sense of hunger, but had no heart to look for food; at the time when we used to prepare our supper on those happy evenings, I crept to my lady's little bed, and lay down *there*. A curious rushing sound was in my ears, and my pulse seemed rather to give a continuous shudder, than to beat. Dreams came, without introductory ceremony of the sleep. I heard myself shouting and struggling. Then, darkness. . . .

I awoke in my father's house. I had been there three weeks. Though very weak, I was in the path of recovery, and was soon in condition to return to school. But not to Glumper's. No

I learned that, in my delirium, I had given a clue to my name and residence. What after-communications I made, I cannot say: I only know that both my mother, and my saucy little Agnes, were as familiar with the name of Zell as my own daily thoughts were. She was my love, my queen, my darling only mistress. In that faith, and in the firm assurance that I should one blessed day see her again, I grew to manhood.

There was a grand ball at Dublin Castle, at which I, a young lieutenant of dragoons, chanced to be present and abetting. The reception was more than usually crowded and magnificent, it being the farewell of a popular lord-lieutenant.

As the latter moved about among his smiling guests, he halted at a group beside me.

"Well, young gentlemen," said his excellency, "who is the successful knight? Surely this prize is not to escape us all! Resplendent beauty—sweetness—accomplishments—twelve thousand a year. Shame to Ireland, if this Mexican belle quits us to-night, her last in the land (for I hear she returns to Mexico), a disengaged woman!"

"She will *not*, my lord," replied Colonel Walsingham.

"Hah! Who wins?" asked his excellency, hardly less interested than if he had himself been a candidate.

"That is doubtful, still," put in young Lord Goring. "Hawkins, Rushton, O'Rourke, Walsingham, St. Buryans, my humble self, have all been 'mentioned' in the race. St. Buryans for choice."

"Why so?" asked his lordship.

"The lady has been seated this whole evening beside St. Buryans' lady-mother," said Goring, in a low voice. "And she's the cleverest woman, at a finish, in Christendom—or Jewry either."

"You said it would be decided to-night?"

"Thus. The young lady will dance but once, the last dance. We have all solicited the honour. She reserves her choice. It has been agreed to accept the augury. Your lordship understands? The unsuccessful withdraw."

His excellency nodded, smiled, and passed on.

A few minutes later, a movement in the room drew my attention. All eyes seemed directed towards one object. Up the centre of the room, leaning on the arm of Lord John Loveless, now Earl St. Buryans, was passing my beautiful mistress! Taller—fuller, no whit lovelier, for that could not be. She looked full in my face. I thought she paused for a second. No, the superb brown eyes were languidly withdrawn, and, without recognition, she moved on.

The last dance was announced from the orchestra. As if under a spell, I placed myself opposite to my lady's chair, though remote from it. I saw the rival suitors, with well-bred self-possession, gather round, and each in turn prefer his claim. All were declined. St. Buryans—by whose haughty-looking mother my lady sat—alone remained. He approached her with confidence, his mother greeting him with a victorious smile. Before he could open his lips, Zell rose:

"Give me your arm. I wish to cross the room," she said to him haughtily.

She *did* cross. She came to *me*. Drawing her arm away from her conductor's, she held out both her little hands.

"Charley, Charley! Don't you know me? I come to ask you to—to dance with me—with your old friend, Zell."

We have more than one deer park—but it was from the Scotch one that, on Zell's reminder (she always pretends to be older and more thoughtful than I), I sent my friend Jack Rogers a haunch worthy of a king's acceptance.

V

The circumstances I am about to relate to you have truth to recommend them. They happened to myself, and my recollection of them is as vivid as if they had taken place only yesterday. Twenty years, however, have gone by since that night. During those twenty years I have told the story to but one other person. I tell it now with a reluctance which I find it difficult to overcome. All I entreat, meanwhile, is that you will abstain from forcing your own conclusions upon me. I want nothing explained away. I desire no arguments. My mind on this subject is quite made up, and, having the testimony of my own senses to rely upon, I prefer to abide by it.

Well! It was just twenty years ago, and within a day or two of the end of the grouse season. I had been out all day with my gun, and had had no sport to speak of. The wind was due east; the month, December; the place, a bleak wide moor in the far north of England. And I had lost my way. It was not a pleasant place in which to lose one's way, with the first feathery flakes of a coming snow-storm just fluttering down upon the heather, and the leaden evening closing in all around. I shaded my eyes with my hand, and stared anxiously into the gathering darkness, where the purple moorland melted into a range of low hills, some ten or twelve miles distant. Not the faintest smoke-wreath, not the tiniest cultivated patch, or fence, or sheep-track, met my eyes in any direction. There was nothing for it but to walk on, and take my chance of finding what shelter I could, by the way. So I shouldered my gun again, and pushed wearily forward; for I had been on foot since an hour after daybreak, and had eaten nothing since breakfast.

Meanwhile, the snow began to come down with ominous steadiness, and the wind fell. After this, the cold became more intense, and the night came rapidly up. As for me, my prospects darkened with the darkening sky, and my heart grew heavy as I thought how my young wife was already watching for me through the window of our little inn parlour, and thought of all the suffering in store for her throughout this weary night. We had been married four months, and, having spent our autumn in the Highlands, were now lodging in a remote little village situated just on the verge of the great English moorlands. We were very much in love, and, of course, very happy. This morning, when we parted, she had implored me to return before dusk, and I had promised her that I would. What would I not have given to have kept my word!

Even now, weary as I was, I felt that with a supper, an hour's rest, and a guide, I might still get back to her before midnight, if only guide and shelter could be found.

And all this time, the snow fell and the night thickened. I stopped and shouted every now and then, but my shouts seemed only to make the silence deeper. Then a vague sense of uneasiness came upon me, and I began to remember stories of travellers who had walked on and on in the falling snow until, wearied out, they were fain to lie down and sleep their lives away. Would it be possible, I asked myself, to keep on thus through all the long dark night? Would there not come a time when my limbs must fail, and my resolution give way? When I, too, must sleep the sleep of death. Death! I shuddered. How hard to die just now, when life lay all so bright before me! How hard for my darling, whose whole loving heart——but that thought was not to be borne! To banish it, I shouted again, louder and longer, and then listened eagerly. Was my shout answered, or did I only fancy that I heard a far-off cry? I hallooed again, and again the echo followed. Then a wavering speck of light came suddenly out of the dark, shifting, disappearing, growing momentarily nearer and brighter. Running towards it at full speed, I found myself, to my great joy, face to face with an old man and a lantern.

"Thank God!" was the exclamation that burst involuntarily from my lips.

Blinking and frowning, he lifted his lantern and peered into my face.

"What for?" growled he, sulkily.

"Well—for you. I began to fear I should be lost in the snow."

"Eh, then, folks do get cast away hereabouts fra' time to time, an' what's to hinder you from bein' cast away likewise, if the Lord's so minded?"

"If the Lord is so minded that you and I shall be lost together, friend, we must submit," I replied; "but I don't mean to be lost without you. How far am I now from Dwolding?"

z

"A gude twenty mile, more or less."

"And the nearest village?"

"The nearest village is Wyke, an' that's twelve mile t'other side."

"Where do you live, then?"

"Out yonder," said he, with a vague jerk of the lantern.

"You're going home, I presume?"

"Maybe I am."

"Then I'm going with you."

The old man shook his head, and rubbed his nose reflectively with the handle of the lantern.

"It ain't o' no use," growled he. "He 'ont let you in—not he."

"We'll see about that," I replied, briskly. "Who is He?"

"The master."

"Who is the master?"

"That's nowt to you," was the unceremonious reply.

"Well, well; you lead the way, and I'll engage that the master shall give me shelter and a supper to-night."

"Eh, you can try him!" muttered my reluctant guide; and, still shaking his head, he hobbled, gnome-like, away through the falling snow. A large mass loomed up presently out of the darkness, and a huge dog rushed out, barking furiously.

"Is this the house?" I asked.

"Ay, it's the house. Down, Bey!" And he fumbled in his pocket for the key.

I drew up close behind him, prepared to lose no chance of entrance, and saw in the little circle of light shed by the lantern that the door was heavily studded with iron nails, like the door of a prison. In another minute he had turned the key and I had pushed past him into the house.

Once inside, I looked round with curiosity, and found myself in a great raftered hall, which served, apparently, a variety of uses. One end was piled to the roof with corn, like a barn. The other was stored with flour-sacks, agricultural implements, casks, and all kinds of miscellaneous lumber; while from the beams overhead hung rows of hams, flitches, and bundles of dried herbs for winter use. In the centre of the floor stood some huge object gauntly dressed in a dingy wrapping-cloth, and reaching half way to the rafters. Lifting a corner of this cloth, I saw, to my surprise, a telescope of very considerable size, mounted on a rude moveable platform with four small wheels. The tube was made of painted wood, bound round with bands of metal rudely fashioned; the speculum, so far as I could estimate its size in the dim light, measured at least fifteen inches in diameter. While I was yet examining the instrument, and asking myself whether it was not the work of some self-taught optician, a bell rang sharply.

"That's for you," said my guide, with a malicious grin. "Yonder's his room."

He pointed to a low black door at the opposite side of the hall. I crossed over, rapped somewhat loudly, and went in, without waiting for an invitation. A huge, white-haired old man rose from a table covered with books and papers, and confronted me sternly.

"Who are you?" said he. "How came you here? What do you want?"

"James Murray, barrister-at-law. On foot across the moor. Meat, drink, and sleep."

He bent his bushy brows into a portentous frown.

"Mine is not a house of entertainment," he said, haughtily. "Jacob, how dared you admit this stranger?"

"I didn't admit him," grumbled the old man. "He followed me over the muir, and shouldered his way in before me. I'm no match for six foot two."

"And pray, sir, by what right have you forced an entrance into my house?"

"The same by which I should have clung to your boat, if I were drowning. The right of self-preservation."

"Self-preservation?"

"There's an inch of snow on the ground already," I replied, briefly; "and it would be deep enough to cover my body before daybreak."

He strode to the window, pulled aside a heavy black curtain, and looked out.

"It is true," he said. "You can stay, if you choose, till morning. Jacob, serve the supper."

With this he waved me to a seat, resumed his own, and became at once absorbed in the studies from which I had disturbed him.

I placed my gun in a corner, drew a chair to the hearth, and examined my quarters at leisure. Smaller and less incongruous in its arrangements than the hall, this room contained, nevertheless, much to awaken my curiosity. The floor was carpetless. The whitewashed walls were in parts scrawled over with strange diagrams, and in others covered with shelves crowded with philo-sophical instruments, the uses of many of which were unknown to me. On one side of the fire-place, stood a bookcase filled with dingy folios; on the other, a small organ, fantastically decorated with painted carvings of mediæval saints and devils. Through the half-opened door of a cupboard at the further end of the room, I saw a long array of geological specimens, surgical pre-parations, crucibles, retorts, and jars of chemicals; while on the mantelshelf beside me, amid a number of small objects, stood a model of the solar system, a small galvanic battery, and a micro-scope. Every chair had its burden. Every corner was heaped high with books. The very floor was littered over with maps, casts, papers, tracings, and learned lumber of all conceivable kinds.

I stared about me with an amazement increased by every fresh object upon which my eyes chanced to rest. So strange a room I had never seen; yet seemed it stranger still, to find such a room in a lone farm-house amid those wild and solitary moors! Over and over again, I looked from my host to his surroundings, and from his surroundings back to my host, asking myself who and what he could be? His head was singularly fine; but it was more the head of a poet than of a philosopher. Broad in the temples, prominent over the eyes, and clothed with a rough profusion of perfectly white hair, it had all the ideality and much of the ruggedness that characterises the head of Louis von Beethoven. There were the same deep lines about the mouth, and the same stern furrows in the brow. There was the same concentration of expression. While I was yet observing him, the door opened, and Jacob brought in the supper. His master then closed his book, rose, and with more courtesy of manner than he had yet shown, invited me to the table.

A dish of ham and eggs, a loaf of brown bread, and a bottle of admirable sherry, were placed before me.

"I have but the homeliest farm-house fare to offer you, sir," said my entertainer. "Your appetite, I trust, will make up for the deficiencies of our larder."

I had already fallen upon the viands, and now protested, with the enthusiasm of a starving sportsman, that I had never eaten anything so delicious.

He bowed stiffly, and sat down to his own supper, which consisted, primitively, of a jug of milk and a basin of porridge. We ate in silence, and, when we had done, Jacob removed the

tray. I then drew my chair back to the fireside. My host, somewhat to my surprise, did the same, and turning abruptly towards
me, said :

"Sir, I have lived here in strict retirement for three-and-twenty
years. During that time, I have not seen as many strange faces,
and I have not read a single newspaper. You are the first stranger
who has crossed my threshold for more than four years. Will
you favour me with a few words of information respecting that
outer world from which I have parted company so long?"

"Pray interrogate me," I replied. "I am heartily at your
service."

He bent his head in acknowledgment; leaned forward, with
his elbows resting on his knees and his chin supported in the palms
of his hands; stared fixedly into the fire; and proceeded to question me.

His inquiries related chiefly to scientific matters, with the later
progress of which, as applied to the practical purposes of life,
he was almost wholly unacquainted. No student of science myself, I replied as well as my slight information permitted; but the
task was far from easy, and I was much relieved when, passing
from interrogation to discussion, he began pouring forth his own
conclusions upon the facts which I had been attempting to place
before him. He talked, and I listened spell-bound. He talked
till I believe he almost forgot my presence, and only thought
aloud. I had never heard anything like it then; I have never
heard anything like it since. Familiar with all systems of all
philosophies, subtle in analysis, bold in generalisation, he poured
forth his thoughts in an uninterrupted stream, and, still leaning
forward in the same moody attitude with his eyes fixed upon the
fire, wandered from topic to topic, from speculation to speculation, like an inspired dreamer. From practical science to mental
philosophy; from electricity in the wire to electricity in the nerve;
from Watts to Mesmer, from Mesmer to Reichenbach, from
Reichenbach to Swedenborg, Spinoza, Condillac, Descartes,
Berkeley, Aristotle, Plato, and the Magi and mystics of the East,
were transitions which, however bewildering in their variety and
scope, seemed easy and harmonious upon his lips as sequences in
music. By-and-by—I forget now by what link of conjecture or
illustration—he passed on to that field which lies beyond the
boundary line of even conjectural philosophy, and reaches no
man knows whither. He spoke of the soul and its aspirations; of

the spirit and its powers; of second sight; of prophecy; of those phenomena which, under the names of ghosts, spectres, and supernatural appearances, have been denied by the sceptics and attested by the credulous, of all ages.

"The world," he said, "grows hourly more and more sceptical of all that lies beyond its own narrow radius; and our men of science foster the fatal tendency. They condemn as fable all that resists experiment. They reject as false all that cannot be brought to the test of the laboratory or the dissecting-room. Against what superstition have they waged so long and obstinate a war, as against the belief in apparitions? And yet what superstition has maintained its hold upon the minds of men so long and so firmly? Show me any fact in physics, in history, in archæology, which is supported by testimony so wide and so various. Attested by all races of men, in all ages, and in all climates, by the soberest sages of antiquity, by the rudest savage of to-day, by the Christian, the Pagan, the Pantheist, the Materialist, this phenomenon is treated as a nursery tale by the philosophers of our century. Circumstantial evidence weighs with them as a feather in the balance. The comparison of causes with effects, however valuable in physical science, is put aside as worthless and unreliable. The evidence of competent witnesses, however conclusive in a court of justice, counts for nothing. He who pauses before he pronounces, is condemned as a trifler. He who believes, is a dreamer or a fool."

He spoke with bitterness, and, having said thus, relapsed for some minutes into silence. Presently he raised his head from his hands, and added, with an altered voice and manner,

"I, sir, paused, investigated, believed, and was not ashamed to state my convictions to the world. I, too, was branded as a visionary, held up to ridicule by my contemporaries, and hooted from that field of science in which I had laboured with honour during all the best years of my life. These things happened just three-and-twenty years ago. Since then, I have lived as you see me living now, and the world has forgotten me, as I have forgotten the world. You have my history."

"It is a very sad one," I murmured, scarcely knowing what to answer.

"It is a very common one," he replied. "I have only suffered for the truth, as many a better and wiser man has suffered before me."

He rose, as if desirous of ending the conversation, and went over to the window.

"It has ceased snowing," he observed, as he dropped the curtain, and came back to the fireside.

"Ceased!" I exclaimed, starting eagerly to my feet. "Oh, if it were only possible—but no! it is hopeless. Even if I could find my way across the moor, I could not walk twenty miles to-night."

"Walk twenty miles to-night!" repeated my host. "What are you thinking of?"

"Of my wife," I replied, impatiently. "Of my young wife, who does not know that I have lost my way, and who is at this moment breaking her heart with suspense and terror."

"Where is she?"

"At Dwolding, twenty miles away."

"At Dwolding," he echoed, thoughtfully. "Yes, the distance, it is true, is twenty miles; but—are you so very anxious to save the next six or eight hours?"

"So very, very anxious, that I would give ten guineas at this moment for a guide and a horse."

"Your wish can be gratified at a less costly rate," said he, smiling. "The night mail from the north, which changes horses at Dwolding, passes within five miles of this spot, and will be due at a certain cross-road in about an hour and a quarter. If Jacob were to go with you across the moor, and put you into the old coach-road, you could find your way, I suppose, to where it joins the new one?"

"Easily—gladly."

He smiled again, rang the bell, gave the old servant his directions, and, taking a bottle of whisky and a wine-glass from the cupboard in which he kept his chemicals, said:

"The snow lies deep, and it will be difficult walking to-night on the moor. A glass of usquebaugh before you start?"

I would have declined the spirit, but he pressed it on me, and I drank it. It went down my throat like liquid flame, and almost took my breath away.

"It is strong," he said; "but it will help to keep out the cold. And now you have no moments to spare. Good night!"

I thanked him for his hospitality, and would have shaken hands, but that he had turned away before I could finish my sentence. In another minute I had traversed the hall, Jacob had locked the outer door behind me, and we were out on the wide white moor.

Although the wind had fallen, it was still bitterly cold. Not a star glimmered in the black vault overhead. Not a sound, save the rapid crunching of the snow beneath our feet, disturbed the heavy stillness of the night. Jacob, not too well pleased with his mission, shambled on before in sullen silence, his lantern in his hand, and his shadow at his feet. I followed, with my gun over my shoulder, as little inclined for conversation as himself. My thoughts were full of my late host. His voice yet rang in my ears. His eloquence yet held my imagination captive. I remember to this day, with surprise, how my over-excited brain retained whole sentences and parts of sentences, troops of brilliant images, and fragments of splendid reasoning, in the very words in which he had uttered them. Musing thus over what I had heard, and striving to recal a lost link here and there, I strode on at the heels of my guide, absorbed and unobservant. Presently—at the end, as it seemed to me, of only a few minutes—he came to a sudden halt, and said:

"Yon's your road. Keep the stone fence to your right hand, and you can't fail of the way."

"This, then, is the old coach-road?"

"Ay, 'tis the old coach-road."

"And how far do I go, before I reach the cross-roads?"

"Nigh upon three mile."

I pulled out my purse, and he became more communicative.

"The road's a fair road enough," said he, "for foot passengers; but 'twas over steep and narrow for the northern traffic. You'll mind where the parapet's broken away, close again the sign-post. It's never been mended since the accident."

"What accident?"

"Eh, the night mail pitched right over into the valley below— a gude fifty feet an' more—just at the worst bit o' road in the whole county."

"Horrible! Were many lives lost?"

"All. Four were found dead, and t'other two died next morning."

"How long is it since this happened?"

"Just nine year."

"Near the sign-post, you say? I will bear it in mind. Good night."

"Gude night, sir, and thankee." Jacob pocketed his half-crown, made a faint pretence of touching his hat, and trudged back by the way he had come.

I watched the light of his lantern till it quite disappeared, and then turned to pursue my way alone. This was no longer matter of the slightest difficulty, for, despite the dead darkness overhead, the line of stone fence showed distinctly enough against the pale gleam of the snow. How silent it seemed now, with only my footsteps to listen to; how silent and how solitary! A strange disagreeable sense of loneliness stole over me. I walked faster. I hummed a fragment of a tune. I cast up enormous sums in my head, and accumulated them at compound interest. I did my best, in short, to forget the startling speculations to which I had but just been listening, and, to some extent, I succeeded.

Meanwhile the night air seemed to become colder and colder, and though I walked fast I found it impossible to keep myself warm. My feet were like ice. I lost sensation in my hands, and grasped my gun mechanically. I even breathed with difficulty, as though, instead of traversing a quiet north country highway, I were scaling the uppermost heights of some gigantic Alp. This last symptom became presently so distressing, that I was forced to stop for a few minutes, and lean against the stone fence. As I did so, I chanced to look back up the road, and there, to my infinite relief, I saw a distant point of light, like the gleam of an approaching lantern. I at first concluded that Jacob had retraced his steps and followed me; but even as the conjecture presented itself, a second light flashed into sight—a light evidently parallel with the first, and approaching at the same rate of motion. It needed no second thought to show me that these must be the carriage-lamps of some private vehicle, though it seemed strange that any private vehicle should take a road professedly disused and dangerous.

There could be no doubt, however, of the fact, for the lamps grew larger and brighter every moment, and I even fancied I could already see the dark outline of the carriage between them. It was coming up very fast, and quite noiselessly, the snow being nearly a foot deep under the wheels.

And now the body of the vehicle became distinctly visible behind the lamps. It looked strangely lofty. A sudden suspicion flashed upon me. Was it possible that I had passed the cross-roads in the dark without observing the sign-post, and could this be the very coach which I had come to meet?

No need to ask myself that question a second time, for here it came round the bend of the road, guard and driver, one outside passenger, and four steaming greys, all wrapped in a soft haze of light, through which the lamps blazed out, like a pair of fiery meteors.

I jumped forward, waved my hat, and shouted. The mail came down at full speed, and passed me. For a moment I feared that I had not been seen or heard, but it was only for a moment. The coachman pulled up; the guard, muffled to the eyes in capes and comforters, and apparently sound asleep in the rumble, neither answered my hail nor made the slightest effort to dismount; the outside passenger did not even turn his head. I opened the door for myself, and looked in. There were but three travellers inside, so I stepped in, shut the door, slipped into the vacant corner, and congratulated myself on my good fortune.

The atmosphere of the coach seemed, if possible, colder than that of the outer air, and was pervaded by a singularly damp and disagreeable smell. I looked round at my fellow-passengers. They were all three, men, and all silent. They did not seem to be asleep, but each leaned back in his corner of the vehicle, as if absorbed in his own reflections. I attempted to open a conversation.

"How intensely cold it is to-night," I said, addressing my opposite neighbour.

He lifted his head, looked at me, but made no reply.

"The winter," I added, "seems to have begun in earnest."

Although the corner in which he sat was so dim that I could distinguish none of his features very clearly, I saw that his eyes were still turned full upon me. And yet he answered never a word.

At any other time I should have felt, and perhaps expressed, some annoyance, but at the moment I felt too ill to do either. The icy coldness of the night air had struck a chill to my very marrow, and the strange smell inside the coach was affecting me with an intolerable nausea. I shivered from head to foot, and, turning to my left-hand neighbour, asked if he had any objection to an open window?

He neither spoke nor stirred.

I repeated the question somewhat more loudly, but with the same result. Then I lost patience, and let the sash down. As I did so, the leather strap broke in my hand, and I observed that the glass was covered with a thick coat of mildew, the accumulation, apparently, of years. My attention being thus drawn to the condition of the coach, I examined it more narrowly, and saw by the uncertain light of the outer lamps that it was in the last state of dilapidation. Every part of it was not only out of repair, but in a condition of decay. The sashes splintered at a touch. The leather fittings were crusted over with mould, and literally rotting from the woodwork. The floor was almost breaking away beneath my feet. The whole machine, in short, was foul with damp, and had evidently been dragged from some outhouse in which it had been mouldering away for years, to do another day or two of duty on the road.

I turned to the third passenger, whom I had not yet addressed, and hazarded one more remark.

"This coach," I said, "is in a deplorable condition. The regular mail, I suppose, is under repair?"

He moved his head slowly, and looked me in the face, without speaking a word. I shall never forget that look while I live. I turned cold at heart under it. I turn cold at heart even now when I recal it. His eyes glowed with a fiery unnatural lustre. His face was livid as the face of a corpse. His bloodless lips were drawn back as if in the agony of death, and showed the gleaming teeth between.

The words that I was about to utter died upon my lips, and a strange horror—a dreadful horror—came upon me. My sight had by this time become used to the gloom of the coach, and I could see with tolerable distinctness. I turned to my opposite neighbour. He, too, was looking at me, with the same startling pallor in his face, and the same stony glitter in his eyes. I passed my hand across my brow. I turned to the passenger on the seat beside my own, and saw—oh Heaven! how shall I describe what I saw? I saw that he was no living man—that none of them were living men, like myself! A pale phosphorescent light—the light of putrefaction—played upon their awful faces; upon their hair, dank with the dews of the grave; upon their clothes, earth-stained and dropping to pieces; upon their hands, which were as the hands of corpses long buried. Only their eyes, their terrible eyes, were living; and those eyes were all turned menacingly upon me!

A shriek of terror, a wild unintelligible cry for help and mercy, burst from my lips as I flung myself against the door, and strove in vain to open it.

In that single instant, brief and vivid as a landscape beheld in the flash of summer lightning, I saw the moon shining down through a rift of stormy cloud—the ghastly sign-post rearing its warning finger by the wayside—the broken parapet—the plunging horses—the black gulf below. Then, the coach reeled like a ship at sea. Then, came a mighty crash—a sense of crushing pain—and then, darkness.

It seemed as if years had gone by when I awoke one morning from a deep sleep, and found my wife watching by my bedside. I will pass over the scene that ensued, and give you, in half a dozen words, the tale she told me with tears of thanksgiving. I had fallen over a precipice, close against the junction of the old coach-road and the new, and had only been saved from certain death by lighting upon a deep snowdrift that had accumulated at the foot of the rock beneath. In this snowdrift I was discovered at daybreak, by a couple of shepherds, who carried me to the nearest shelter, and brought a surgeon to my aid. The surgeon found me in a state of raving delirium, with a broken arm and a compound fracture of the skull. The letters in my pocket-book showed my name and address; my wife was summoned to nurse me; and, thanks to youth and a fine constitution, I came out of danger at last. The place of my fall, I need scarcely say, was precisely that at which a frightful accident had happened to the north mail nine years before.

I never told my wife the fearful events which I have just related to you. I told the surgeon who attended me; but he treated the whole adventure as a mere dream born of the fever in my brain. We discussed the question over and over again, until we found that we could discuss it with temper no longer, and then we dropped it. Others may form what conclusions they please—I *know* that twenty years ago I was the fourth inside passenger in that Phantom Coach.

VI

ANOTHER PAST LODGER RELATES CERTAIN PASSAGES
TO HER HUSBAND

[INTRODUCTORY NOTE BY MAJOR JACKMAN. The country clergyman and his quiet and better than pretty wife, who occupied my respected friend's second floor for two spring months of four successive years, were objects of great interest, both with my respected friend and with me. One evening we took tea with them, and happened to speak of a pretty wilful-looking young creature and her husband—friends of theirs—who had dined with them on the previous day. "Ah!" said the clergyman, taking his wife's hand very tenderly in his; "thereby hangs a tale. Tell it to our good friends, my dear." "I can address it, Owen," said his wife, hesitating, "to nobody but you." "Address it, then, to me, my darling," said he, "and Mrs. Lirriper and the Major will be none the worse listeners." So she went on as follows, with her hand resting in his all the time. Signed, J. JACKMAN.]

The first time I saw you again, after the years long and many which had passed over us since our childhood, I was watching for you on the peak of the hill, from whence I could see furthest down the steep and shady lane along which you were coming up to our hamlet from the plain below me. All day I had been anxious that when you arrived, our hills, which you must have forgotten, should put on their most gorgeous beauty; but now the sunset was come which would leave us the bare and grey outlines of the rocks only, and, from the kindling sky there fell bars of golden sunshine, with darker rays underlying them, slanting down the slopes of the mountain, and touching every rounded knoll and little dimpling dell with such a glory, that even the crimson and purple tints of the budding bilberry wires far away towards the level table-land where the summits blended, glowed, and burned under the farewell light. Just then there came a shout of welcome, like the shout of harvest-home, ringing up through the quiet air, and, straining my shaded eyes to catch the first glimpse, I saw you walking in the midst of a band of our sturdy, sunburnt villagers, with the same slight and delicate-looking frame, and pale, grave pleasant face, and shy and timid manner that were yours when we were boy and girl together.

Our little hamlet had gathered itself from time to time, without any special plan or purpose, upon one of the lower terraces of our cluster of mountains, separated from the nearest villages by a wide tract of land, only to be crossed by steep, stony, deep-rutted lanes, overhung with wild hedgerows, and almost impassable in the winter. During the summer, when the faint tones of the bells of our parish church were borne up to us on the calm air, a little procession of us, the girls and children riding on rough hill-ponies, were wont to wind down the lanes to the Sunday morning service; but in winter no one thought of the pilgrimage, unless some of the young men had sweethearts in the village whom they hoped to meet at church. Mr. Vernon, the rector, being an archdeacon, hardly less than a bishop in dignity and importance, was deeply distressed at the heathenish darkness of his mountain district; and he and my father, who owned the great hill-farm, which gave employment to the people of our hamlet, at last built the little red-brick church, with no tower, and smaller than our barn, which stands upon the point of the mountain terrace, overlooking the great plain that stretches away from our feet up to the very far horizon.

There might have been a difficulty in finding a curate who would live up at Ratlinghope, with no other social intercourse than could be obtained by a long march into the peopled plain below us; but I knew afterwards that the church, so far as my father's share in it was concerned, had been built for you. You were just taking orders, and you had a pleasant remembrance of the large old rambling half-timber house where you had spent some months of your childhood; so when we wrote to you that your dwelling would be in our own house, your study being the blue parlour which looked down the green sheltered dell where the young lambs were folded, you answered that you would gladly take the charge, and live with us again on the sweet, free heathery uplands, where you had breathed in health and strength in your early boyhood.

You were grave and studious, and withal so simple-hearted, that the seclusion and the primitive manners of our hamlet made it a very Eden to you. You had never forgotten our old haunts, and we revisited them together, for in the first moment of our greeting you had fallen into your habit of dependence upon me, and of demanding my companionship, as when you were a delicate boy of six years, and I a strong, healthy, mountain girl three years older. To me only, could you utter your thoughts freely, for your natural shyness closed your lips to strangers; and all were strangers to you, even those who had known you for a lifetime, if they did not possess the touch of sympathy which your spirit needed before it would open its treasures. Up on the hill-side, when the steady noontide seemed as unchangeable as the everlasting rocks about us, or when the tremulous dusk stole with silent shadows over the fading headlands, you and I sat together, while I listened to the unreserved outpourings of your thoughts and fancies, boyish sometimes, for you were young still, but in my heart there was an ever-growing tenderness and care for you, which could find no flaw, and feel no weariness. You were apt to be unmindful of the hours, and it was I who made it my duty to watch their flight for you, and see to it that the prayer-bell, the single bell that hung under a little pent-roof against the church, should be tolled at the due time; for Mr. Vernon, in consideration of our heathenish condition, made it a point that the evening service should be read three times a week. And as it was needful that our household should set a pattern to the rest of the villagers, and it interfered with my father's evening pipe, and my mother could not be troubled to change her afternoon cap for her church bonnet, it always fell to my lot to walk with you—do you remember?—only a few hundred yards or so along the brow of the hill, to the little church.

I was about to say that it was the happiest time of my life; but all true life is gain; and the sorrows that befal us are none other than solemn massive foundation-stones laid low in unfathomable gloom, that a measureless content may be built upon them. You remember the first burial-service you had to read, when you besought me to stand beside you at the open grave, because never before had the mournful words been uttered by your lips. It was only the funeral of a little child, and the tiny grave, when the clods were heaped upon it, was no larger than a molehill in the meadows; yet your voice faltered, and your hands trembled as you cast this first small seed into that God's Acre of ours. The autumn night set in while we lingered in silence beside the nameless coffin, long after the mother and her companion who had brought it to its solitary grave, had turned away homeward. It was the flapping of wings close beside us that caused us to lift up our eyes, and from the fir-trees above us four rooks flew home across the darkening sky to their nests in the plain below. You know how of old the flight of birds would fill me with vague superstitions, and just then the heavy fluttering of their dusky wings overhead, as they beat the air for their start, caused a sudden tremor and shudder to thrill through me.

"What ails you, Jane?" you asked.

"Nothing ails me, Mr. Scott," I said.

"Call me Owen," you answered, laying your hand upon my

arm, and looking straight into my eyes, for we were of the same height, and stood level with one another : "I do not like to hear you call me anything but Owen. Have you forgotten how we used to play together? Do you remember how I fell into the sheep-pool when we were alone in the valley, and you wasted no time in fruitless cries, but waded in at once, and dragged me out of the water? You would carry me home in your strong arms, though the path was along the hill-side, and you had to rest every few minutes; while I looked up into your rosy face with a very peaceful feeling. Your face is not rosy now, Jane."

How could it be, while your words brought such a dull heavy pain to my heart? I seemed suddenly to be so many, many years older than you! Sometimes of late I had detected myself reckoning your age and mine by the month, and the day of the month, and always finding, with a pang faint and slight, that you were indeed so many years younger than I. Yet the heart takes little heed of age. And I, for the quiet life I had led among the mountains, just one regular single round of summer and winter, coming stealthily and uncounted in their turn from season to season, might have been little more than some yearling creature, that has seen but one spring-time and felt the frosts of but one Christmas. While you, with your great acquirements of learning, and the weighty thoughts that had already wrinkled your broad forehead, and the burden of study that had bowed down your young shoulders, seemed to have borne the full yoke of the years which had laid so gentle a touch upon me.

"I remember very well, Owen," I said; "I was proud of having you to take charge of. But you must go in now; the fog is rising, and you are not over strong."

I spoke with the old tone of authority, and you left me, standing alone beside the little grave. The churchyard extended to the very edge of the steep hill, which looked far and wide over the great plain. It was hidden now by a white lake of mist floating beneath me, upon which the hunting-moon, rising slowly behind the eastern hills, shone down with cold pale beams; for the harvest was over, and the heavy October fogs gathered in the valleys, and hung in light clouds about the fading coppices in the hollows of the mountains. I turned heart-sick to the little open grave, the first in the new graveyard, which was waiting until the sheep were herded for the sexton to fill it up for ever with the clods; the baby hands and feet folded there in eternal rest, had never been stained with selfishness, and the baby lips, sealed in eternal silence, had uttered never a word of bitterness. So, I said, looking down sadly into the narrow tiny grave, so shall it be with my love; I bury it here while it is yet pure and unselfish, like a seed sown in God's Acre; and from it shall spring a plentiful harvest of happiness for Owen, and of great peace for myself.

It may be that the autumn fog was more harmful than usual, for I was ill after that night with my first serious illness; not merely ailing, but hanging doubtfully between life and death. I grew to think of our summer months together as of a time long since passed, and almost enwrapped in forgetfulness. My mother laughed when I stroked her grey hair with my feeble fingers, and told her I felt older than she was.

"Nay," she said, "we must have you younger and bonnier than ever, Jane. We must see what we can do for you before you come down stairs, and meet Owen. Poor Owen! Who would have dreamt that he could be more heartbroken and disconsolate than Jane's own mother? Poor Owen!"

My mother was smiling significantly, and looking keenly at me over her glasses, but I said nothing; only turned away my face from her scrutiny to the frosted window, where winter had traced its delicate patterns upon the lattice panes.

"Jane," she went on, clasping my fingers in hers, "don't you know that we all wish it, Owen's father, and yours, and me? We thought of it before he came here. Owen is poor, but we have enough for both of you, and I love him like my own son. You need never leave the old home. Jane, don't you love Owen?"

"But I am older than he is," I whispered.

"A marvellous difference," she said, with another laugh; "so am I older than father, but who could tell it was so now? And what does it matter if Owen loves you?"

I wish to cast no blame on you, but there was much in your conduct to feed the sweet delusion which brought fresh health and strength to me. You called my mother, "Mother." You sent fond messages by her, which lost nothing in tone or glance by her delighted repetition of them. You considered no walk too far to get flowers for me from the gardens in the plain below. When I grew well enough to come down stairs you received me with a rapture of congratulation. You urged that the blue parlour, with its southern aspect and closely-fitting wainscot, was the

warmest room in the house, and you would not be satisfied until
the great chintz-covered sofa with its soft cushions was lifted out
of its corner, and planted upon the hearth, for me to lie there,
watching you while you were busy among your books; and many
times a day you read some sentence aloud, or brought a volume
to my side that I might look over the same page, while you
waited patiently as my slower eyes and brain were longer than
yours in taking in the sense. Even when you were away at the
rectory—for during my illness you had begun to spend your
evenings there, when you had no church duty—I sat in your
study, with your books about me, in which there were passages
marked out for me to read. I lingered over getting well.

I was lying on the sofa one evening, wrapped in my mother's
white shawl, and just passing into a dreamy slumber, when I
heard you entering from one of your visits to the rectory. I cannot tell why I did not rouse myself, unless it seemed to me only
as part of a dream, but you crossed the floor noiselessly, and
stood beside me for a minute or two, looking down—I felt it—
upon my changed face, and closed eyelids. Had I been asleep
I should never have felt the light, timid, fluttering touch of your
lips upon mine. But my eyes opened at once, and you fell back.

"What is it, Owen?" I asked you calmly, for I felt as if by
instinct that the caress was not for me. "Why did you kiss me,
Owen?"

"I wonder I never did it before," you said, "you are so like a
sister to me. I have no other sister, Jane, and my mother died
when I was very young."

You stood opposite to me in the bright firelight with a face
changing and flushing like a girl's, and a happy youthful buoyant
gladness in it very different to your usually quiet aspect. As I
looked at you the old pain returned like a forgotten burden upon
my heart.

"I am so happy," you said, crossing over the hearth again,
and kneeling down beside me.

"Is it anything you can tell me, dear Owen?" I said, laying
my hand upon your hair, and wondering even then at the white-
ness and thinness of my poor fingers. The door behind you was
opened quietly, but you did not hear it, and my mother stood
for an instant in the doorway smiling on us both; I felt keenly
how she would misunderstand.

Then you spoke to me, shyly at first, but gathering confidence, of Adelaide Vernon. I knew her well: a little lovely graceful creature, with coquettish school-girl ways, which displayed themselves even at church, though her black browed and swarthy aunt sat beside her in the rector's pew. While you spoke, growing eloquent with a lover's rhapsodies, the fair young face, with its pink and white tints, and soft dainty beauty, rose up before me; and your praises seemed to flood my aching heart like a wide breaking in of water, which rolled desolately against me.

I need not remind you of the opposition your love met. Mr. Vernon was averse to marrying his portionless niece to his poor curate of Ratlinghope; but his disapproval was nothing to the vehement rage with which Mrs. Vernon, who had other views for Adelaide, set her face against it. The rector came up to our house, and told us—you remember?—with tears wrung from him, proud and reticent man as he was, that he dreaded nothing less than a return of that fearful malady of madness, which had kept his wife a prisoner for years under his own roof. There was as bitter, but a more concealed resentment in our own household, which you only felt indirectly and vaguely. I learned now with what a long premeditated plan your father and mine had schemed for our marriage. Your poor foolish love seemed to every one but yourself and me a rash selfishness. Even I thought at times that half Adelaide's love for you sprang from pure contrariness and childish romance, just feeding upon the opposition it met with. How I smoothed your path for you; how, without suffering the coldness of disappointment to creep over me, I sought your happiness in your own way as if it had been mine also; you partly know. So we prevailed at last.

In spite of all my smothered pain, it was pleasant to see you watch the building of your little parsonage, the square red brick house beside the church, with the doors and windows pricked out with blue tesselated tile-work. It was not a stone's throw from our home, and the blue parlour saw little of your presence, and the dust gathered on the books you had been wont to read. But you would have me to share your exultation. Whenever the large beams were being fitted into your roof, or the cope-stones built into your walls, or the blue tiles set round your windows, I must look on with you, and hearken to your fears lest the home should be unworthy of Adelaide. All my sad thoughts—for day after day you were setting your foot upon my heart—I worked away in busy labour at your house, and in wistful contrivances to make the little nest look elegant and pretty in the sight of Adelaide Vernon.

Your marriage was to be on the Tuesday, and on the Monday I went down with you to the rectory. The place had become familiar to you, all but the long low southern wing, with its blank walls ivy-grown, and with its windows opening upon the other side over a wide shallow mere, fed with the waters of a hundred mountain brooks. They were Mrs. Vernon's apartments, built for her during her protracted and seemingly hopeless malady, for her husband had promised her that she should never be removed from under his roof. She kept them under her own charge, rarely suffering any foot to enter them, and Mr. Vernon drew me aside when we reached the house, and implored me to venture upon making my way, if possible, to his wife, who had shut herself up in them since the previous evening, and had refused to admit even him. I crossed the long narrow passage which separated them from the rest of the dwelling, and rapped gently at the door, and after a minute's silence I heard Mrs. Vernon's voice asking, "Who is there?"

"Only Jane Meadows," I answered.

I was a favourite with her, and after a slight hesitation, the door was opened, and Mrs. Vernon stood before me : her tall and powerful figure wrapped in a dressing-gown, which left the sinewy arms bare to the elbow, while the thick locks of her black hair, just streaked with grey, fell dishevelled about her swarthy face. The room behind her was littered from end to end, and the fire at which she had been sitting was choked up with cinders, while the window, tarnished with dust, gave no glimpse of the mountain landscape beyond. She returned to her chair before the fire, and surveyed me with a sullen frown from under her reddened eyelids. The trembling of her limbs, muscular as they were, and the glistening of her face, told me not more surely than the faint and sickly odour pervading the room, that she had been taking opium.

"Jane," she cried, with a burst of maudlin tears, which she did not attempt to conceal, "come here, and sit down beside me. I am so miserable, Jane. Your mother was here on Saturday, telling me that you love Owen Scott, and everybody wanted him to marry you. Adelaide, the poor little painted doll, is not fit to be his wife, and she will make him wretched. And you will be miserable, like all of us."

My heart sank at the thought of your wretchedness. "I am not miserable," I replied, throwing my own arms round her, and looking up into her wrathful eyes. "You don't know how strong and peaceful we grow when we seek the happiness of those we love. We cannot decide who shall love whom, and it was not God's will that Owen should choose me. Let us make them as happy as we can."

She let me lead her to her seat, and talk to her about you and Adelaide in a way that tranquillised her, until she consented to dress herself with my aid, and return with me to the company assembled in the other part of the house.

But there was something in Adelaide's whole conduct which tended to irritate Mrs. Vernon. She was playing silly pranks upon us all, but especially upon her gloomy aunt, about whom she hovered with a fretting waywardness mingled with an unquiet tenderness, which displayed itself in numberless childish ways; but with such grace and prettiness, that none of us could find it in our hearts to chide her, except Mrs. Vernon herself. I was glad when the time came for us to leave; though you loitered across the lawn, looking back every minute at Adelaide, who stood in the portico : her white dress gleaming amid the shadows, and she kissing her little hand to you with a laugh whose faint musical ringing just reached our ears.

You slept that night, as we often sleep, unwitting that those who are dear to us as our own souls are passing through great perils. You slept, and it was I who watched all night, and called you early in the morning, with the news that the sun was rising over the hills into a cloudless sky, and that your marriage-day was come.

We were at the rectory betimes, yet the villagers had reared an arch of flowers over the gates. Mrs. Vernon, dressed with unusual richness and care, was watching for us at the portico, and received us both with a grave but kindly greeting. All the house was astir with the hurrying of many feet, and the sharp click of doors slamming to and fro; but though you waited restlessly, no one else came near us in the little room where we three sat together, until the door was slowly opened—you turning to it with rapturous impatience—and Mr. Vernon entered and told us that Adelaide was nowhere to be found.

"Don't alarm yourself," said Mr. Vernon to his wife, "but Adelaide has been missing since daybreak; she was gone when her companions went to call her. You remember she used to walk in her sleep if she were much excited; and this morning the hall door was open, and her bonnet was found on the way to Ratling-hope. The agitation of yesterday must have caused this."

"She was coming to me!" you said, with a vivid smile and a glow, which faded as you began to realise the fact of Adelaide's disappearance.

The hills stretched away for many a mile, with shelving rocks here and there, which hung over deep still tarns, black with shadows, and hedged in by reedy thickets. And there were narrow rifts, cleaving far down into the living stone of the mountain range, and overgrown with brambles, where the shepherds some-times heard their lambs bleating piteously, out of sight or reach of help, until the dreary moan died away from the careless echoes. "Children have been lost there," cried Mrs. Vernon, wringing her hands distractedly; and if Adelaide had wandered away in the darkness, she might be lying now dead in the depths of the black tarns, or imprisoned alive in one of the clefts of the rocks.

I never left your side that day; and as hour after hour passed by, I saw a grey ghastly change creep over your young face, as your heart died within you. Mrs. Vernon kept close beside us, though we soon distanced every other seeker, and her wonderful strength continued unabated, even when your despairing energy was exhausted. I knew the mountains as well as the shepherds did; and from one black unruffled tarn, to another like itself, gloomy and secret-looking. I led you without speaking; save that into every gorge, whose depth our straining eyes could not pene-trate, we called aloud, until the dark dank walls of the gulf muttered back the name of Adelaide. There was no foot-weariness for us as long as the daylight lasted; and it seemed as if the sun *could* not go down until we had found her. Now and then we tarried upon the brow of some headland, with our hands lifted to our ears that we might catch the most distant whisper of the signal-bells; the faintest tone that ever reached the uplands, if there were any to be borne to us upon the breeze, from the church belfry in the plain far away.

The search was continued for many days; but no trace of Adelaide was found, except a lace cap which lay soiled and wet with dew near to one of the tarns which we three had visited; but without discovering it then. Mrs. Vernon rallied our hopes and energies long after all reasonable ground for either was lost, and then she fell into a depression of spirits which almost threatened a renewal of her early malady. She collected all Adelaide's little possessions, and spent many hours of each day among them in her own apartments; but she was always ready to leave them, when you, in your sore grief, wandered to the old home of the lost girl; and then she strove to console you with a patient tenderness strange to see in a woman so rigid and haughty. But you refused to be comforted; and putting on one side all the duties of your office, you roamed ceaselessly about the hills; dragging yourself back again almost lifeless to our house—for your own you would never enter—and asking me night after night, as the sunset and darkness spread upon the mountains, if there were no place left unexplored. As though it were possible to call back again the dead past, and find her yet alive among the desolate hills!

In the midst of it all another trouble befel us. Before the new year came in, my mother fell ill of the sickness in which she died. I think that first roused you from the solitude of your despair. Though you could not yet front the kindly familiar faces of your old congregation, there seemed to be some little break in the cloud of hopelessness which hung about you, in the care you began to feel for her. It was but a few days before she died, and after you had been reading to her, as she lay very feeble, and often dozing away with weakness, that she suddenly roused herself, and looked at you with eager eyes.

"You'll always be fond of Jane, Owen?"

"Always. She has been the truest of sisters to me."

"Ah!" sighed my mother, "you little think how she has loved you. Not one woman in a thousand could have done as our Jane has. Boy, it's not possible you'll ever be loved so again on earth."

You had never thought of it before, and your face grew paler than my mother's. I sat behind the curtains, where you could see me though she could not; and you looked across at me fixedly, still keeping your station by her side. I smiled with the tears standing in my eyes, but with no foolish burning in my cheeks, for if it would comfort you in any degree, I was neither afraid nor ashamed that you should know it.

"Ever since you came," my mother murmured, "smoothing every stone out of your path, and only fretting because she could not bear every trouble for you! If you ever marry, Owen, she

will live only for you, and your wife and children. You will
always care for her, Owen?"

"I will never marry any other woman," you said, laying your
lips upon my mother's wrinkled hand.

I know it was a comfort to you. Perhaps in the suddenness and
mystery of your loss, you felt as if everything was wrecked, and
nothing remained to life but a bleak, black dreariness. But from
that hour, there was a light, very feeble and dim and lustreless—
a mere glow-worm in the waste wilderness—which shone upon
your path. You began to return to your old duties, though it
was as if you were leaning upon me, and trusting to my guiding.
There was no talk of love between us; it was enough that we
understood one another.

We might have gone on quietly thus, year after year, until
the memory of Adelaide had faded away, but that it was not
many months before my father, who had been younger than my
mother, and was a fine man yet, announced to me that he was
about to marry again. The news had reached you elsewhere; for,
on the same evening, while I was sitting alone with my troubled
thoughts, you called me into the blue parlour, and made me
take my old seat in the corner of the chintz-covered sofa, while
you knelt down beside me.

"Jane," you said, very gently, "I want to offer my poor home
to you."

"No, no, Owen," I cried, looking down upon your face, so
grey and unsmiling, with dark circles under your sunken eyes,
"you are young yet, and will meet with some other woman—a
dear sister she shall ever be to me—younger and brighter, and
more fitted for you than I am. You shall not sacrifice yourself
to me."

"But, Jane," you urged, and a pleasant light dawned in your
eyes, "I cannot do without you. You know I could not go alone
into yonder little house, which stands empty by the church; and
how could I go away from Ratlinghope, leaving you behind me?
I have no home but where you are; and I love you more than I
ever thought to love any woman again."

Maybe you remember what more you said; every word is in
my heart to this day.

I thought it over in the quiet night. You were poor, and I,
inheriting my mother's fortune, could surround you with comforts; secretly in my judgment, there had grown the conviction

that you would never be what the world calls a prosperous man. The time was come when we must be separated or united for ever; and if you parted from me, I could never more stand between you and any sorrow. So I became your wife nearly twelve months after your great loss and misery.

Those first weeks of our marriage had more sunshine than I had ever dared to hope for. You seemed to shake off a great burden, now that it was irrevocably settled that our lives were to be passed together. Not a single lurking dread remained in my heart that you were otherwise than happy.

We came back to England some days earlier than we intended, for a letter reached me after many delays, with the news that Mrs. Vernon was ill, and implored us to hasten our return. We stayed on our way homeward at the rectory, where I soon left you with Mr. Vernon, while I was conducted to the entrance of the long passage which led to Mrs. Vernon's apartments. Her lady, the servant said in a whisper, was ailing more in mind than in body, and she dared not disobey her strict orders not to venture further. I went on, for I knew her caprices; and once again I was admitted, when she heard me say, calling myself by your name, that it was Jane Scott who sought entrance. There was no new gleam of madness in her dark eyes. She grasped my hands nervously, and held them fast, while she questioned me about our journey, and what your manner had been. Were you happy? Had you altogether ceased to grieve for Adelaide? Was your whole love mine? Was there perfect unalloyed content in our mutual affection?

"Jane," she said, with her lips close to my ear, though she spoke in a loud shrill tone, "I had sworn that Adelaide should never marry Owen Scott. Partly for your sake, for your mother said it was killing you. Partly because it was better for her to marry my rich nephew. Jane, I must have what I set my mind upon, or I should die. What was Adelaide, that I should lose my life, or worse, ten times worse, lose my reason again for her sake? I did it for the best, Jane. I never thought how it was to end. It only seemed to me, if I could hide her from one day till the next, something would happen. But it was a long long time, a dreadful time, till Owen came to tell us he was going to marry you. You understand, Jane?"

"No, no!" I cried.

"It seemed so easy a thing to do, and best for all of us. I carried her here in the night, like the baby she is. I have never been cruel to her, never, Jane. But the time seemed long, long, and she was wild and cunning at first. I only thought of a little while, and afterwards I grew afraid. But she will not come out now, though I try to rouse her. Go in, Jane, and make her come out!"

Mrs. Vernon drew me across the inner apartment to the door of a small chamber, padded throughout, and with no opening except into the ante-room. It had been constructed for herself in the seasons of her most dangerous paroxysms, and was so carefully planned that no sound of her wild ravings could be heard, and no glimpse of her face could be seen, through the window which overlooked the mere. And here lay your Adelaide asleep, wan and emaciated, with a dimness on her golden curls, and all the rosy tints of her beauty faded.

"She has been taking laudanum," said Mrs. Vernon. "I gave it to her at first, when I was compelled to be away for a long time, and now she has a craving for it. I have never been cruel to her, Jane. She has had everything she wanted."

You know how I came down to the library, where you and Mr. Vernon were sitting, and told you and Mr. Vernon all. You know how, while Mr. Vernon bowed his grey head upon his hands, you stretched out your arms to me, and cried, with an exceeding bitter cry as if I could find a remedy for you, "Help me, Jane!"

Dear, my heart fluttered towards you for a moment, longing to be clasped in your outstretched arms, and pour out all my love to you, which had ever been tongue-tied, lest you should weary of it; but I hardened myself against the yearning. In the great mirror on the staircase I scarcely knew the white-faced despairing woman, who was sweeping by, erect and stern, and the two men with downcast heads and lingering footsteps who were following her. You spoke no word, either of you, but passed through the outer apartment, with its tarnished window and sullied disorder, where Mrs. Vernon sat cowering in the furthest corner, and entered the room within, where Adelaide lay asleep, but breathing fitfully, as on the verge of waking. I dragged myself (for I was faint) to the casement, which I pushed open, and looked out upon the purple hills, purple with heather-bells, where we had thought her unknown tomb was. Up yonder stood our home, the home we had built for Adelaide, and which we had never yet entered; and turning away my aching eyes from it, I looked back again upon you, who were standing beside her, with a depth of tender and horror-stricken pity on your bending face.

Whether it was the fresh air from the hills, or some mysterious influence of your presence penetrating her sleeping senses, we cannot tell; but while I looked, unable to turn away my eyes from you both, her mouth quivered, and her long eyelashes trembled, half opening and closing again, as if too languid to bear the light, until you touched her hands softly and timidly, and breathed "Adelaide!" And she awoke fully, with a sharp shrill cry, as if you were at last come for her deliverance, and springing into your arms, she clung to you, with her little hands clasped round you as though they would never unlock again; while you laid your cheek down upon her dim dishevelled curls, and I heard you murmur, "My darling!" Yet yonder was our home, yours and mine, Owen; and the ring that was on my finger—the only one I wore, I cared so much for it—was our marriage-ring.

You turned to me, Owen, with that full, searching gaze, eye to eye, and soul to soul, which we could bear from one another. Adelaide was come back from the dead to bring to us greater sorrow than her death had brought. We saw it all, you and I, while she was still clinging to you with sobs and childish caresses, and I stood aloof at the window. I knew how much you had to say to her which no other ear might listen to. I knew what it would be wisest and best to do. I took Mr. Vernon's arm, and I drew him away from the room, and I left you and Adelaide together.

I know now that it was not long before you came to me—only ten minutes—such a trifle of time as one gives ungrudgingly to the dreariest beggar on the roadside who has a piteous tale to tell. But all the past, and all the dreaded future being present with me, the moments seemed endless in their immortal bitterness, until you entered the room where I had shut myself in alone, and coming swiftly up to me where I stood upon the hearth, hid your face upon my shoulder with strong sobs and tears.

"I will go away, Jane," you said at last, "by myself for a few days, till she is gone from here. You will take care of her for me. She knows all now."

"I will do anything for you," I answered, still chary of my words, as it was my wont to be, lest my love should weary you.

You left me, as it was best you should do, alone, with the

charge of that perplexed household upon me; Adelaide broken in
health and spirits; Mrs. Vernon plunged into the frenzy of her
old malady; the story running far and wide throughout the
country. Every day I found my comfort and strength in the letter
that came from you, wherein you had the generosity to lay bare
your heart to me as frankly as ever. So the hard task began to
grow lighter; the tangled coil to unravel itself. Mr. Vernon procured a nurse to take care of his wife, and I accompanied
Adelaide to the distant dwelling of some friends, where we hoped
she might sooner recover her health; nor did I leave her until
I saw her resuming her playful girlish ways, and coquettish
graces. At last I was free to go home; to go to the home you and
I had built on the rock, watching together its beams laid, and
its roof raised. But I was alone there. If Adelaide had been your
young and beautiful wife, you would have crossed the threshold
hand in hand, uttering such words of welcome as would never
have died out of her memory, if it had been like mine.

The jealous misgiving was unworthy of you and myself, dear.
I paced the little rooms, taking up the trinkets which you had
bought anxiously and lavishly for Adelaide, and always laying
them down again with a sharper pang. Did you wish me to die,
Owen? Was your heart aching to take her back again? I rested
at last in your little study, where your books lay in scattered heaps
before the empty shelves. The days were gone for ever when we
had read them together on the hillside, in the first careless freedom
of your sojourn with us. I sat down among them, covering my
face with my hands, and I heard and I saw nothing.

Nothing, my love, my dear, until your hand rested on my
head, and your voice, in hearty cheery tones, fell on my delighted
ear.

"Jane," you said, "my darling, my wife! We are come home
at last. I meant to be here first, but it is ever you who welcome
me. The trouble is past. I love you better, love you more, than
ever I loved Adelaide."

You lifted up my head, and made me look into your face. It
was at once peaceful and exultant, as the face of a man who has
gone through a great conflict, and come out of it more than
conqueror. You laid your lips to mine with one long kiss, which
told me infinitely better than words could tell, that never more
need shadow of doubt or distrust of your love fall upon my
spirit. Such as I was, you gathered me into your inmost heart,

barring it against any memory or any fancy that might betray me. The deep foundations had been laid, and any storm that beat against our confidence and content would beat against them all in vain.

Love, we have learned to speak of the past calmly, and Adelaide has been to see us with her husband.

VII

MRS. LIRRIPER RELATES HOW JEMMY TOPPED UP

WELL my dear and so the evening readings of these jottings of the Major's brought us round at last to the evening when we were all packed and going away next day, and I do assure you that by that time though it was deliciously comfortable to look forward to the dear old house in Norfolk-street again, I had formed quite a high opinion of the French nation and had noticed them to be much more homely and domestic in their families and far more simple and amiable in their lives than I had ever been led to expect, and it did strike me between ourselves that in one particular they might be imitated to advantage by another nation which I will not mention, and that is in the courage with which they take their little enjoyments on little means and with little things and don't let solemn big-wigs stare them out of countenance or speechify them dull, of which said solemn big-wigs I have ever had the one opinion that I wish they were all made comfortable separately in coppers with the lids on and never let out any more.

"Now young man," I says to Jemmy when we brought our chairs into the balcony that last evening, "you please to remember who was to 'top up'."

"All right Gran" says Jemmy. "I am the illustrious personage."

But he looked so serious after he had made me that light answer, that the Major raised his eyebrows at me and I raised mine at the Major.

"Gran and Godfather," says Jemmy, "you can hardly think how much my mind has run on Mr. Edson's death."

It gave me a little check. "Ah! It was a sad scene my love" I says, "and sad remembrances come back stronger than merry.

But this" I says after a little silence, to rouse myself and the Major and Jemmy all together, "is not topping up. Tell us your story my dear."

"I will" says Jemmy.

"What is the date sir?" says I. "Once upon a time when pigs drank wine?"

"No Gran," says Jemmy, still serious; "once upon a time when the French drank wine."

Again I glanced at the Major, and the Major glanced at me.

"In short, Gran and Godfather," says Jemmy, looking up, "the date is this time, and I'm going to tell you Mr. Edson's story."

The flutter that it threw me into. The change of colour on the part of the Major!

"That is to say, you understand," our bright-eyed boy says, "I am going to give you my version of it. I shall not ask whether it's right or not, firstly because you said you knew very little about it, Gran, and secondly because what little you did know was a secret."

I folded my hands in my lap and I never took my eyes off Jemmy as he went running on.

"The unfortunate gentleman" Jemmy commences, "who is the subject of our present narrative was the son of Somebody, and was born Somewhere, and chose a profession Somehow. It is not with those parts of his career that we have to deal; but with his early attachment to a young and beautiful lady."

I thought I should have dropped. I durstn't look at the Major; but I knew what his state was, without looking at him.

"The father of our ill-starred hero" says Jemmy, copying as it seemed to me the style of some of his story-books, "was a worldly man who entertained ambitious views for his only son and who firmly set his face against the contemplated alliance with a virtuous but penniless orphan. Indeed he went so far as roundly to assure our hero that unless he weaned his thoughts from the object of his devoted affection, he would disinherit him. At the same time, he proposed as a suitable match, the daughter of a neighbouring gentleman of a good estate, who was neither ill favoured nor unamiable, and whose eligibility in a pecuniary point of view could not be disputed. But young Mr. Edson, true to the first and only love that had inflamed his breast, rejected all considerations of self-advancement, and, deprecating his father's anger in a respectful letter, ran away with her."

My dear I had begun to take a turn for the better, but when it come to running away I began to take another turn for the worse.

"The lovers" says Jemmy "fled to London and were united at the altar of Saint Clement's Danes. And it is at this period of their simple but touching story, that we find them inmates of the dwelling of a highly respected and beloved lady of the name of Gran, residing within a hundred miles of Norfolk-street."

I felt that we were almost safe now, I felt that the dear boy had no suspicion of the bitter truth, and I looked at the Major for the first time and drew a long breath. The Major gave me a nod.

"Our hero's father" Jemmy goes on "proving implacable and carrying his threat into unrelenting execution, the struggles of the young couple in London were severe, and would have been far more so, but for their good angel's having conducted them to the abode of Mrs. Gran: who, divining their poverty (in spite of their endeavours to conceal it from her), by a thousand delicate arts smoothed their rough way, and alleviated the sharpness of their first distress."

Here Jemmy took one of my hands in one of his, and began a marking the turns of his story by making me give a beat from time to time upon his other hand.

"After a while, they left the house of Mrs. Gran, and pursued their fortunes through a variety of successes and failures elsewhere. But in all reverses, whether for good or evil, the words of Mr. Edson to the fair young partner of his life, were: 'Unchanging Love and Truth will carry us through all!' "

My hand trembled in the dear boy's those words were so wofully unlike the fact.

"Unchanging Love and Truth" says Jemmy over again, as if he had a proud kind of a noble pleasure in it, "will carry us through all! Those were his words. And so they fought their way, poor but gallant and happy, until Mrs. Edson gave birth to a child."

"A daughter," I says.

"No" says Jemmy, "a son. And the father was so proud of it that he could hardly bear it out of his sight. But a dark cloud overspread the scene. Mrs. Edson sickened, drooped, and died."

"Ah! Sickened, drooped, and died!" I says.

"And so Mr. Edson's only comfort, only hope on earth, and only stimulus to action, was his darling boy. As the child grew older, he grew so like his mother that he was her living picture. It used to make him wonder why his father cried when he kissed him. But unhappily he was like his mother in constitution as well as in face, and he died too before he had grown out of childhood. Then Mr. Edson, who had good abilities, in his forlornness and despair threw them all to the winds. He became apathetic, reckless, lost. Little by little he sank down, down, down, down, until at last he almost lived (I think) by gaming. And so sickness overtook him in the town of Sens in France, and he lay down to die. But now that he laid him down when all was done, and looked back upon the green Past beyond the time when he had covered it with ashes, he thought gratefully of the good Mrs. Gran long lost sight of, who had been so kind to him and his young wife in the early days of their marriage, and he left the little that he had as a last Legacy to her. And she, being brought to see him, at first no more knew him than she would know from seeing the ruin of a Greek or Roman Temple, what it used to be before it fell; but at length she remembered him. And then he told her with tears, of his regret for the misspent part of his life, and besought her to think as mildly of it as she could, because it was the poor fallen Angel of his unchanging Love and Constancy after all. And because she had her grandson with her, and he fancied that his own boy, if he had lived, might have grown to be something like him, he asked her to let him touch his forehead with his cheek and say certain parting words."

Jemmy's voice sank low when it got to that, and tears filled my eyes, and filled the Major's.

"You little Conjuror" I says, "how did you ever make it all out? Go in and write it every word down, for it's a wonder."

Which Jemmy did, and I have repeated it to you my dear from his writing.

Then the Major took my hand and kissed it, and said "Dearest madam all has prospered with us."

"Ah Major" I says drying my eyes, "we needn't have been afraid. We might have known it. Treachery don't come natural to beaming youth; but trust and pity, love and constancy—they do, thank God!"